Praise for

BETTER CATCH UP, *Krishna Kumar*

"A sparkling, heartfelt rom-com that swept me off my feet from the very first page."
—**ANANYA DEVARAJAN,** author of *Kismat Connection* and *Sanskari Sweetheart*

"This vibrant, atmospheric rom-com will make you feel like you're flying down the expressway to Goa with the windows down."
—**CLARE OSONGCO,** author of *Midnights with You*

"An absolute must-read with all the cinematic charm of a Bollywood movie."
—**STEFANY VALENTINE,** author of *First Love Language* and *Love Makes Mochi*

"A laugh-out-loud (and sometimes snort-out-loud) story full of tender moments that will have you yelling 'Kiss, kiss, kiss!' at the pages."
—**TALIA TUCKER,** author of *Rules for Rule Breaking*

BETTER CATCH UP, KRISHNA KUMAR

ANAHITA KARTHIK

HARPER
An Imprint of HarperCollins*Publishers*

HarperCollins Children's Books,
a division of HarperCollins Publishers, 195 Broadway, New York, NY 10007

HarperCollins Publishers,
Macken House, 39/40 Mayor Street Upper, Dublin 1, D01 C9W8, Ireland

Better Catch Up, Krishna Kumar

harpercollins.com

Library of Congress Control Number: 2025939018
ISBN 978-0-06-334114-2

Typography by Chris Kwon
25 26 27 28 29 LBC 5 4 3 2 1
First Edition

To Pratyush,

whose love inspires every romance I write,

because you form the blueprint for every love interest I create

1

LIQUID COURAGE? MORE LIKE LIQUID EMBARRASSMENT

Mumbai, Thursday

"I'm about to throw up" is the last thing I expect to say inches from Amrit Acharya's glorious lips.

And yet, there's a searing burn in the back of my throat as the chole bhature from lunch rises up from my stomach. Panicked, I lurch to my feet and stumble away from the couch—where mere seconds ago I was about to have my first kiss with my ridiculously hot Ishaan Khatter look-alike crush, mind you.

My hand springs to my mouth as I stagger through the crowded living room of Rajeev bhaiya's house.

There're people everywhere—the air around me heavy with the scent of cigarette smoke, vape fumes, and alcohol. I wonder if I'm dreaming them all up, because when did our small end-of-the-summer cousins' get-together turn into a full-blown house party? I don't even recognize half the people I'm shoving out of the way to get to the bathroom.

Through the blaring music, I can faintly hear Amrit calling after me, but I don't register what he's saying, because that's when I catch sight of the long line of people waiting to use the bathroom. I can't possibly push through to the front without causing a scene, despite my leaving tomorrow being the reason this party's happening in the first place.

So it's either hurl right here and be forever brought up in anecdotes as "the girl who confettied Rajeev's floor with the inner lining of her stomach" and have Amrit chime in with "Oh, Krishna Kumar? She nearly threw up in my mouth, bro," or . . .

Get somewhere, *anywhere*, secluded. Fewer people equals less chance of being immortalized as "the vomit girl." Mind addled with alcohol, I slide open the nearest door and stumble through, and it's only when the hot summer air hits me in the face that I realize I'm on the balcony.

In the corner, through my blurring vision, I spot an embracing couple spring apart. It's not complete privacy, but it's still better than a room full of people—and blessedly far away from Amrit. Without another thought, I keel forward onto my knees and projectile vomit on the floor.

I should've known downing those four shots of vodka was a bad idea. At the time, I was feeling bold, relying on liquid courage to help me finally get my tongue into Amrit's mouth, but look where I ended up.

A hand finds my back moments later, rubbing soothing circles on my spine, while another twists my hair into a knot and gathers it at the nape of my neck. Sweat breaks out all over my body, and I don't know if it's the puking or Mumbai's heat that's doing it to me, but the cotton of my kurti is soaked through. Amrit appears in the periphery of my vision.

It's *his* warm hands on my back and curling into my hair.

Stomach emptied, I collapse against the railing, Amrit slowing my descent. The cool touch of the metal seeps into my bones, not unlike the oxidized jhumkas scraping the soft skin underneath my ears. It doesn't take long for the mortification to sink in after that, the acknowledgment of what just happened—or rather, what *didn't.* How, instead of him being all up in my guts, as I originally planned, they're on the fucking floor.

"Are you feeling okay?" Amrit asks gently, clasping my hand tight. I can't even get myself to be happy about the fact that he's holding my hand, because my mind's already thinking up ways to eject myself from this humiliating situation. If only Juhu Beach weren't so far away from Mulund, I'd have flung myself into the sea and swum halfway to Oman by now, ready to start a brand-new life in a brand-new country. "Do you want me to get you some water?"

"No," I manage, wishing I could turn into a puddle of Krishna goo.

"I warned you," a voice quips from the side after I finally have the chance to catch my breath. I look up to find my cousin and archnemesis, Priti, staring down at me, a scowl plastered across her striking face. Her best friend, Rudra, stands next to her, infuriatingly stoic, as always. "I told you not to have that many shots."

"I'll be right back," Rudra declares suddenly—before I can utter a single word—and marches inside.

I'm pretty sure he just wants to escape what he assumes is an ensuing fight between Priti and me. I wouldn't be surprised; I've lost count of the number of times the two of us have fought over the years.

But instead of reacting to Priti's comment or continuing to reel from the embarrassment of throwing up in front of Amrit, I scan her face. There are black streaks on her cheeks, her usually artfully drawn, inches-thick eyeliner and kajal having leaked down her face . . . as if she's been *crying.*

It hits me then that Priti and Rudra were the couple who jumped apart when I barreled out onto the balcony. Rudra might've been consoling her, but I don't, for the life of me, know why. I didn't think Priti was capable of tears.

She seems to register my bewilderment, because she wipes at her cheeks with the heel of her palm then, ducking her head so the ends of her short, wavy hair cover her face.

"That was literally your first time drinking, and there's something called *capacity*," she snipes, and I know she's just trying to bat the attention off herself, but it works. It doesn't take much for her to piss me off—at least, it hasn't these past eight years.

"I don't need *you* to tell me what to do," I retort, and it's such a silly, childish thing to say, but I'm equal parts mortified and irritated right now. Trust Priti to put me down when I'm literally on the ground.

Just then, Rudra comes back with a disposable cup of water and holds it out to me. I stare up at him in shock, not having expected Priti's quiet best friend—who's never bothered with me much despite having known me for nearly a decade—to willingly return to help.

Amrit takes the cup from Rudra before I can reach for it and raises the rim to my mouth, urging me to sip.

"Whatever," Priti says, her closing remark as her gaze swings between us. With a huff that makes her bangs twitch, she walks off. Rudra wordlessly follows her, leaving Amrit, me, and my pool of vomit alone.

The door shuts behind them, dulling the noise, and Amrit settles beside me, leaning his back against the railing. I gulp down the rest of the water and set the empty cup aside, trying hard to ignore the awkward silence that's settled between us and the heat creeping up my face at the reminder of what was about to happen before I ruined everything.

We were *so* close on that couch together earlier, flirting and touching all along our sides. I don't know if it was the alcohol or the general heady atmosphere of the house party, but it was as if all my dithering through the summer came to a sharp halt, and I found myself leaning toward him, his arm that was previously draped over the couch behind me sliding around my waist, making flutters erupt in my stomach . . .

Screw my luck.

A crackle beside me breaks me out of my thoughts, and I turn to Amrit, finding him unwrapping a strip of mint. "Want?" he asks.

"Yes, please," I beg, and take it from him, popping it into my mouth, needing to get rid of my bad breath before Amrit passes out from the stench.

He guffaws suddenly, and I stare at him, mid-chew, eyes wide, as he doubles over with laughter.

"What?" I say, afraid he's laughing at me.

"Their faces," he says, giggling uncontrollably. "When you rushed out and threw up in front of them. Absolutely priceless."

His laughter is so contagious that before I know it, the hysteria is catching up to me, and I'm cracking a grin. *Despite* everything.

It doesn't help that he looks gorgeous as always, his head thrown back against the railing, adorably crooked teeth shining in the moonlight. Wind-blown, deep-brown hair and eyes a shade that's just a touch lighter than his hair.

Damn it.

This is all Bollywood's fault, and Shah Rukh Khan's too, for injecting those *DDLJ*-esque fantasies into my head. They're the reason my idiot self ended up here in the first place, believing Amrit and I would have a whirlwind summer romance like Raj and Simran.

From the moment I first saw him two months ago, the signs have all been there. My cousins had invited him, along with a few other neighborhood friends, over to Nani's house for dinner. After being introduced, we spent the rest of the party talking, huddled in a cozy corner of the living room while sipping Nani's special masala chaas. I remember thinking I had never met someone like him: confident, driven, and charming.

And yet, all this time later—despite the obvious undercurrents of chemistry between us, the long late-night text conversations, and copious amounts of flirting—we haven't even confessed to liking each other. Can you really blame me for hoping that tonight might be *the night*?

Until a few disastrous minutes ago, he was supposed to be my solution to salvaging what's been the most unadventurous vacation ever. Sure, he was always strictly meant to be a fling, but over time, I've grown to like him more than I'd care to admit.

A sudden wave of melancholy hits me at the thought. I'm headed back home tomorrow night, and Amrit to a family wedding early in the morning. I've visited India every summer these past eight years, following the year after Mummy, Papa, and I emigrated to the US. But in a few months, I'm going to be at Johns Hopkins, away from home, and my vacations will be spent visiting my parents up north in Portland. Not Nani or my cousins, who all live in India. This might be the last time I'll see Mumbai for a while. This might be my last chance with Amrit *ever*.

As if reading my mind, Amrit turns to me, smiling. "I'm going to miss you, Krishna."

"I'll miss you too," I say dolefully, throat clogged with regret. "I can't believe I'm going back tomorrow. The summer's just flown by."

And you've spent your entire vacation not taking a single risk, like always, a voice in my head chines mercilessly. *Coward.*

Wrong, another voice pops up in support. *You had alcohol for the first time in your life!*

And you couldn't even do that right comes as a quick and easy rebuttal from—

"Don't worry," Amrit says, interrupting the argument flaring between the two Krishnas in my brain. He pinches my cheek, making warmth prickle under his touch. "If I ever come to the US, the first thing I'm going to do is hit you up."

"I'll hold you to that."

He bumps his shoulder with mine. "It's a date."

Before I have the chance to make any use of that signal to salvage the night, the balcony door slides open once more, and Srishti pokes her head out. "Krishna, I've been looking for you everywhere! Chakna is here, and I—Are you sitting next to someone's *barf*?" Her nose scrunches up with disgust.

Srishti's my favorite cousin—a title previously held by Priti, before . . . well, before she decided to become a Grade A bitch instead. Srishti's a year younger than me, but we're a pair of inseparable nerdy queers, only out to each other in our extended family. She's also probably the only person I know who's read even more than I have. We're barely halfway through the year, and she's already met her reading goal of thirty books. Mine's withering at ten, unfortunately.

"That's *my* barf," I say, ears pricking at the mention of chakna. I'm perennially hungry and have the appetite of a teenage boy, so it's a wonder my metabolism keeps up with me. It works overtime, and I don't give it nearly as much credit as it deserves.

"चलो, फिर,"[1] Amrit says. "I'm sure you're famished."

He knows me entirely too well.

---

1 *Language*: Hindi; *Translation*: Let's go, then.

He gets to his feet, and I try, but I can barely keep my head up, let alone my five-foot-three frame of flesh, bone, and blood that's more chai than water. Thankfully, Amrit grins down at me and sticks his hand out, pulling me up, and I stumble against him.

Inside, everyone's huddling around the kitchen island, which is piled with chakna—Lay's, Kurkure, Bikaner aloo bhujia, Doritos, and dips to go along with it. Divija didi, angel that she is, is paying the Swiggy delivery guy at the front door.

Not needing any more motivation, I grab a disposable cup and pile it with snacks. I'm starving and severely hangry, and the loud chatter and music are *not* helping.

Srishti drags me to the corner once I've filled the cup to the brim with all the chakna I can probably jam in, her eyebrows raised. Her short, straight hair is pinned back with orange butterfly clips, matching the rims of her glasses and oversize T-shirt. She looks like a middle grader—severely out of place here.

"*So?*" she demands.

I don't respond; my mouth is stuffed with aloo bhujia.

"Krishna!" she hisses. "After all that talk last night about grabbing his face and kissing his perfect lips—as unappealing as that sounds to my asexual ass—I've been dying to know. How did it go? And *why* was there barf?"

"I nearly threw up all over him."

"You *what*?"

I painfully chew and swallow the mouthful of bhujia, the salt coating the snack only furthering my dehydration. "I think it was the chole bhature."

"Or the four shots of vodka you chugged earlier."

"Not you too, please," I say, grimacing. "Priti already gave me shit about it. Jumped at the chance to say *I told you so* the minute she could. Speaking of, the two of them—Rudra and Priti—were on the balcony when I ran out. And Priti, she was crying. Or at least I think she was, because her eye makeup was running down her face."

"Priti?" Srishti looks just as baffled as I feel. "*Ice Queen* Priti?"

"Cross my heart and hope to die."

"That's so weird." Srishti frowns at Priti, who's standing to the side with Rudra, both drinking beers straight from the bottles. "Although, she *has* been off this whole summer. I know she's always avoided you, but usually she's at least cordial with the rest of us. I've barely spoken a word to her this time. Who knows what's going on with her?"

I certainly don't know, but my curiosity is piqued. Not that I'll ever find out, because Priti hates me. I'm the last person in the world she'd ever deign to confide in.

Believe it or not, we used to be best friends once. Sharing Barbie dolls and playing with them for hours, watching cartoons while devouring Nani's buttery pav bhaji, and attending Mulund's summer camps together. But that was before Papa got a job in the US and we moved abroad when I was ten.

Somewhere along the line, the 7,509 miles between Priti and me made us drift apart. Because when I came back the first summer after we emigrated, I found I'd completely lost Priti. She had a *new* best friend now: Rudra.

Ever since, my trips to India have been ruined by her constantly making faces in response to everything I do and say. Sure, my acquired accent, slang, and mannerisms have everyone here believing me to be cooler than I am, and Srishti often jokingly (and proudly) introduces me as her One and Only American Cousin, but Priti's more sardonic about it.

While Desis brought up in India are unnecessarily enamored with the US, which isn't all that great, they're also quick to judge, like my cousins automatically assuming I wouldn't sleep in the room without the AC because I'm too delicate. Or, if you're Priti, mocking me at the dinner table in front of everyone for pronouncing words and sentences wrong in Hindi.

Just because I've spent almost half my life in the US doesn't make me any less Indian. I've been brought up by the woman who's also Priti's aunt. Growing up, we might've been worlds apart, but our values are the same, and Priti forgets that. Or maybe she knows it and she just doesn't want to miss out on the chance to provoke me, to prick me where it hurts most.

"Off topic," Srishti says, dragging me back to the present. "But he's looking at you."

"Who? Amrit?"

"No, Rudra."

I start turning my head in his direction, the one she's not-so-discreetly glancing in, but she smacks me. Hard.

"*Ow!*" I protest, rubbing my arm.

"Don't you know the rules?" Srishti whisper-scolds me. "When someone says a hot guy's looking at you, the *last* thing you do is turn to look at them."

"Did you just say *hot* and *Rudra* in the same sentence?"

"Why, you don't think he's hot?" Srishti leans toward me. "Okay, you can look now. He's talking to Priti again."

I turn back to look at them, threading my eyebrows together. Priti's whispering something to Rudra. "I . . . guess? He has a nice ponytail."

"Fits his whole mysterious-guy-in-a-hoodie vibe."

"Did you know that ninety-five percent of mysterious guys in hoodies are stalkers?" my cousin and Srishti's younger brother,

Manas, says, walking up to us. "Don't tell me you guys are crushing on *Rudra*."

Srishti glowers. "Were you seriously eavesdropping?"

"You're loud."

"Get out of my face."

My attention is still on Rudra, who, by the way, *does* have a nice alignment of features. Dark eyebrows, deep-set eyes, square jaw, sharp nose. And, of course, there's the ponytail in question: dark, wavy hair that usually falls just short of his shoulders, now in a messy bundle, stray strands framing his face.

Huh.

But he isn't someone I'd crush on, even in my dreams. My type *talks*. I'm into sunshine boys, like Amrit. And I used to have a huge crush on this cute sunshine girl in my sophomore year. She was the whole reason I figured out I was bi.

As if sensing I'm staring at him, Rudra suddenly looks in my direction. There's a sort of coldness to his features, much like Priti's, a jarring contrast to the momentary tenderness I spotted when he handed me the water earlier.

I jerk my head away immediately, embarrassed to have been caught staring at *Rudra*, of all people, even though he technically got caught looking at me first. Priti was probably griping about me to him.

God, to think those initial summers in India I used to be jealous of Rudra because I hated that he took my place as Priti's best friend, even though none of it was his fault. It was Priti who let me down.

They're perfect for each other, in every way, I think bitterly, even though I've long put that envy behind me.

I find that Srishti and Manas are still arguing, so I head to the island to stock up on more chakna, when Amrit approaches, looking painfully sad. My hopes crumble to dust, and he doesn't have to say it for me to know. But he does.

"Hey," he says, his throat bobbing. "I have to go."

"Right *now*?" Amrit's house is five minutes away, and I haven't had the chance to say a proper goodbye. This horrible night is coming to a close a lot quicker than I anticipated.

"Mom's already called twice, and we have to leave for the airport in a few hours." Amrit cracks a lopsided smile. "You know how it is with dads."

I know exactly how it is. I know that even though Amrit's flight isn't until seven in the morning, they're going to end up at the airport three hours early because Desi dads are super paranoid about that sort of thing.

"So this is really it, huh?" I say, swallowing thickly.

I feel shittier about this than I thought I would, than I was prepared for.

"I guess it is."

"Have you booked an auto yet?"

"Yes, it's waiting for me downstairs."

"I'll drop you," I say, setting my cup aside. But I don't even make it two wobbly steps before Amrit takes my arm.

"Krishna," Amrit says firmly but kindly. "You're probably still out of it. Sober up and hydrate yourself. I'll manage." And for one wild moment, when he leans in toward me, I think he's about to finally kiss me.

But his arms go around me, and he hugs me instead.

Surprisingly enough, I find myself feeling grateful, because despite everything, I don't think I'm mentally or physically prepared for a kiss. Not right now. Not with a boy who's leaving, who I'm never going to get to see again.

I shut my eyes, my chin resting in the crook of his shoulder, savoring his warmth, before he pulls back, his eyes glittering.

"I'll see you around, Krish."

"Have fun at the wedding" is all I can get myself to say before he steps away, putting space between us again. I don't know what to feel, what to think right now. All I know is I'm going to miss this human version of a golden retriever.

As he wades through the crowd and to the door, pausing briefly to thank Rajeev bhaiya for hosting the party, I know I'm going to regret this tomorrow. But my feet don't move, rooted to the floor, as I watch him leave.

I can feel Priti's and Rudra's gazes on me, burning into the side of my cheek, but I don't turn to them, too tired, too dehydrated, and more than a little crushed.

The petrifying feeling of knowing I'm headed to college with zero romantic skill or experience begins to settle in. Maybe it's time I accept the truth.

This is who I'm always meant to be—studious, high-strung, high-achieving, risk-averse, inexperienced Krishna Kumar, who's yet again found herself at the end of a house party without having closed the deal.

A split second before Amrit walks out the front door, he turns around and mouths *See you soon* at me. I mouth *It's a date* back at him, making him smile again.

Srishti comes over and loops her arm through mine, and her citrusy scent replaces the aroma of Amrit's lavender-and-mint soap. "It's okay, boo," she says. "You can cry on my shoulder if you want. My tee is waterproof."

"No thanks." I laugh and lay my head on Srishti's shoulder as the door shuts behind Amrit, watching my Raj walk away from me.

Too dramatic, Krishna.

Guess I *am* going to end up being the only college freshman who's never been kissed, after all.

2

MORNINGS ARE THE BANE OF MY EXISTENCE

Mumbai, Friday

I'm *not* a morning person. It usually takes me a week at most to adapt to India's time zone, yet I'm still drowsy and irritable even after two whole months of being here. Mumbai's been having a god-awful heat wave this month, and it's fucked with my biorhythm—and my mood—severely.

But Mummy's stern voice lives rent-free in my head, always managing to pull me (apologies, yank me) out of my near-dead state. *In that house, everyone, especially Nani, wakes up early, so make sure you're not snoring until ten. Set an alarm, get up, take a bath, and help Nani make breakfast. You're going to college; you'll have to wake up early every day if you want to get your studying done and clear each semester.*

And it's this that gets me up somehow, even before my cousins have the chance to shake me awake—which has become quite the ritual for them. My alarm rings mere seconds later, loudly playing a

Zindagi Na Milegi Dobara song.

Srishti, who usually is the one to drag me out of bed, mumbles, "Shut it off."

"I can't." My eyelids are so heavy I can barely open them.

The living room's dark because no one's up yet to pull open the curtains. Everyone's fast asleep on the mattresses spread around the hall. Srishti, curled up on the futon next to me. Then there's Divija didi and Varija, sprawled on the inflatable bed. And finally, Manas, snoring on the pull-out couch. Priti—who lives here with Nani—is in her room, double bed all to herself.

I rub my eyes, and mascara smears on my knuckles. "Fuuuck."

We all got home at three a.m., and I was so sleepy I didn't even brush my teeth or remove my makeup. I just took off my sweaty clothes, put on a pair of Varija's pajamas, and collapsed onto the mattress.

Which explains why my mouth tastes like bird crap. I say that with conviction because a pigeon shit on my face once, and a drop of it accidentally rolled into my mouth. I'm squeamish at the mere reminder of it. Of course, the cause of the nausea could be from the excessive drinking last night, but the memory doesn't help.

"Seriously, Krishna," Srishti says, pulling her blanket over her head. "If you don't shut that damn alarm off right now, I'm going to murder you."

I sit up with a struggle. "*This* is what you get for dragging me out of bed every morning." Blood pulses behind my eyelids. My head throbs, a migraine setting in behind my temples. It's my first time being hungover, and I hate it already.

I feel my way along the side table for my phone, which died on the way back from Rajeev bhaiya's house. Luckily, the first thing I did when we got home was plug it in.

I find it and swipe the screen, turning off the alarm. Then I push my hair away from my face, running sticky fingers through the strands to get the knots out. I need to freshen up before I tip over. I have a shit ton of packing left to do, because, as always, I procrastinated until the very last day, with less than twenty-four hours left before my flight.

But first: water.

I grab the bottle propped on the side table, filled three-quarters of the way, and tip the entire thing down my throat. It goes down like honey, sweet and viscous, and when I've emptied the bottle, I wipe at the rivulets running down the sides of my mouth, wetting the front of my tee.

Burning with envy of my cousins, who can sleep until whenever they want because they'll all be traveling back to their homes here in Mumbai—not to another *country*—I head into the guest bedroom with its big oak cupboards. There's designated shelf space here for all of us.

I reach for a comfortable yellow chikankari kurti, torn jeans, a towel, and a toothbrush and drag myself to the bathroom. A hot shower is the only thing that'll wake me the fuck up right now.

Fifteen minutes later, I step out, a towel wound around my hair. Nani's the only one up—I hear her softly singing "Kuhu Kuhu Bole Koyaliya" by Lata Mangeshkar in the kitchen—so I shut the guest room door to get ready and pack in peace.

I blow-dry my straight, wet hair and run a fine-toothed comb through it, making it cascade down to my shoulders. Hair maintenance has been effortless since I got a keratin treatment this summer; the procedure is so much cheaper here. I do my skin-care routine, clip on a pair of artificial-gold jhumkas, and lean back to check myself in the mirror.

I look good. *Confident.* I look like a senior who was valedictorian in high school and got into one of the best undergraduate universities in the world. Both were a result of all the hard work I put into studying. All the weekends I spent attending science camps. All the hours I slogged volunteering at hospitals and health care centers.

But perseverance is a cage of sorts. My only respites have been my annual vacations to India, which is why I insisted on coming here one last time before moving to Baltimore, to live out my dreams of the summer before college everyone talks about. I promised myself I'd let go this time, because *I* wanted to be the one with exciting stories to tell my friends back in Maine for once.

Alas.

I guess I *could* still tell them about my first hangover and the almost-kiss moment and fill in the gaps with generous helpings of drama and sexual tension. Drama I have plenty of, but there won't be much sexual tension to cram into zeroth base.

Over the next thirty minutes, I get a head start on my packing. My flight isn't until eleven p.m., but I'll have to leave for the airport at least four hours early to tackle intra-Mumbai traffic *and* have enough time left to deal with the immigration counter. Even so, I tell myself I can afford a quick coffee break.

In the kitchen, Nani's talking to someone on the phone while steadily stirring the daal in the kadhai. She's wearing a simple green cotton saree, and her hair is wrapped in a thin white towel, the end of which drapes down her back. I gently pry the metal spoon from her to take over stirring the daal, and Nani gives me a quick, grateful kiss on the forehead in return before heading into the prayer room adjoining the kitchen to finish her conversation.

Truthfully, much as I thought I'd hate cooking when Mummy suggested I learn from Nani, I've had fun preparing Indian dishes over the summer. And Nani's such a good teacher. Way better than Mummy, who isn't nearly as patient.

Nani's already prepared the rest of breakfast—warm rotis in the casserole dish covered by a cloth to prevent the steam from furling out, a delicious-smelling malai kofta sabji, and a container of steamed, soft rice. She's even kept the curd out, and its surface is so irresistibly jiggly I long to break through it with a spoon.

Once the daal is done, I turn the gas off. Seeing that there's no more cooking to do, I make myself the coffee I came here for. As usual, I add two teaspoons of sugar and half a cup of milk to the concoction, making Nani cluck her tongue as she walks back into the kitchen, having hung up the phone.

"You want diabetes or what, baba?" she says, giving me a light smack on the shoulder.

I grin, slurping the hot drink, relishing the instant kick of caffeine. "Coffee is nothing without sugar."

"Please don't tell Divija that."

"Not unless I want *another* lecture on the harmful long-term effects of sucrose on the body."

Nani chuckles. "Also, I was just on the phone with your mummy, and I have some wonderful news." A beautiful smile appears on her wrinkly face. "Your flight got canceled because of staffing shortages since this election has kicked off a strike, so your papa got your flight rebooked. You get to stay four more days!"

"*Four* more days?" Holy crap. Does that mean I don't have to finish packing today? I nearly let out a whoop before I remember how expensive the flight was. "They didn't have to cover the cost, did they?"

"Don't worry, it was either a full refund or alternative flight options with no extra charge." Nani gives my shoulders a squeeze, and she looks so happy, I can't help but smile. "I asked your papa to reschedule the flight for Wednesday morning just so I would get to spend more time with my babu."

I pull Nani into a hug, inhaling her old-people-and-turmeric-soap smell. "That sounds wonderful, Nani."

"Why don't you see if you can get tickets for a *Dilwale Dulhania Le Jayenge* screening at Maratha Mandir tomorrow? I know you've been wanting to do a rewatch."

"Gosh, yes, I'd love that!" I exclaim, pecking Nani on her cheek.

I leave the kitchen, relief wringing my shoulders loose. But I can't help but feel a little disappointed as I pause in the living room, lips pursed, watching my sleeping cousins. It's great that I'm getting to stay a few more days and will have time to unwind and relax, but it isn't going to be as fun without them around.

Yes, there's the *DDLJ* rewatch to look forward to, and I do love spending time with Nani, but I've been pumped with adrenaline these past few days building up to my flight, and this feels like a damp squib of sorts.

Amrit's already in Goa for the wedding, and my cousins are leaving later today, because everyone's schedule was planned around *mine.* Which means I'm going to be stuck with Priti, who moved in with Nani when she joined V. G. Vaze college to complete her eleventh and twelfth grades (in Maharashtra, as opposed to the other states, the junior and senior years are coupled together and called junior college). Mausi and Mausaji live in Colaba, which is too far for Priti to commute from every day.

Local trains in Mumbai do make it easier to go from one district to another, but Priti wanted to stay away from home for a bit, and closer to Rudra, I assumed when I first found out she was moving. It works for her, because Nani's super chill—her only strict rule being that Priti return home by midnight unless she absolutely *must* be in college for design club–related work.

I collapse onto the futon next to Srishti, further vexed because I'm not even sleepy anymore. At least my phone's fully charged; I haven't had a chance to check it since I woke up. I scan my notifications, finding missed calls from Papa, who probably wanted to tell me about the flight cancellation, and loads of messages from my friends wishing me a safe trip. I vacantly scroll through them until my eye catches on one particular notification.

A text from Amrit.

The million Krishnas in my brain start screeching again: *Holy shit holy shit holy shit!*

I sit up, my body shaking with excitement, fingers trembling as I click on our chat. There are two new messages, typed in reply to the one I sent right before my phone ran out of charge last night.

@notkrishnakumar

Going to miss you, idiot ♡

@amrit_ka_achar

Dw, I'll see you on your next trip.

Still owe you a kiss 😉

3

THE PRICE OF A KISS THESE DAYS IS MY EGO, APPARENTLY

Mumbai, Friday

For a whole minute, I just sit there staring at the message, mouth hanging open. I read it once, twice, thrice, barely registering the contents. The fourth time, it finally hits me.

Still owe you a kiss.

Amrit Acharya, the boy I've been obsessing over all summer, just sent me a text saying he owes me a kiss, *with* a winky emoji. My fingers go slack and my phone drops onto my lap, bouncing off my thigh and landing on the futon with a soft thud.

I can't breathe. I can't think. I want to scream so loud I'll probably wake the entire house if I do.

I reach over and shake Srishti, hard. She sits right up, her hair comically sticking out like straws around her head and her face scrunched in irritation.

"Krishna, I swear to god I'm going to—"

I grab her hand, pull her to her feet, and drag her out of the living room and into the guest room, shutting the door behind us. Srishti stares at me in bewilderment, and I know she's seconds from cussing me out. I'm shaking and jumping on the balls of my feet as I shove my phone in her face. My body just feels so animated.

Srishti is only further aggravated as she takes the phone from me and skims through the contents. The first time, she doesn't register any of it, barely out of her sleepy state. But the second time, her brows knit together as she zooms in on the screen and rereads the last part.

"Krishna. Bro." She looks up at me, eyes as wide as saucers. "Is this what I think it is?"

"Yes!" I affirm, disbelieving of it myself, if I'm being honest.

My crush just sent me a text saying he wants to *kiss me*. That has *never* happened to me. I keep playing our moments together this summer over and over in my head until I can't take it anymore. The mere thought of kissing Amrit sends a rush of exhilaration to the pit of my stomach.

"Holy shit," Srishti says, matching my energy as she joins me in my prancing, and then we're just two idiots skipping around together.

"This doesn't feel real."

"Well, believe it, Krish, because it's *right here*," she says, waving my phone at me.

I flop onto the bed when I tire of all the jumping. "I wish he'd stayed just *one* more day."

Srishti frowns, pausing with one leg in the air. "What do you mean?"

"My flight got canceled. I'm flying out on Wednesday morning. Not tonight."

"No way! That's amazing, hello?"

"But you're leaving. *All* of you are leaving. Manas and Varija have school, you have that trip with your friends, Didi and Bhaiya have work, Priti . . . well, I don't know." I absent-mindedly draw circles on the Solapur blanket with my pointer finger. Every Indian household has one of these—it's a given. "What am I even going to do until Wednesday? Hang out with Priti?"

"Oops. I forgot about that." Srishti clucks her tongue. "Okay, that *is* a little sad." She sighs as she flops onto the bed beside me. "If only you could go to Goa and make out with Amrit, like, right now."

I snort at her statement, spread-eagling on the bed. The ceiling fan spins lazily above my head, squeaking just slightly.

That's when a sudden, wild thought pops into my brain.

"Hey, pass me my phone?"

She hands it to me, rolling over onto her side and propping up on one elbow. "What's up? You have that look on your face."

"What look?" I open my phone and type *how long from Mulund to Calangute* into the search bar. I remember Amrit telling me the wedding was happening in the Calangute district in North Goa, at Baga Beach Resort.

"That look you get when you're plotting your next winning move."

"Wait." The search results pop up: eleven hours and nineteen minutes by car. About half a day. I turn to Srishti, grinning from ear to ear. "I think I might have the wildest idea. And I think—I *think* it might just work."

"Should I be worried?" Srishti narrows her eyes. "What is it?"

"Road trip. To Goa. It's an eleven-hour journey from here. If I leave today, I'll be in Goa just in time for the mehndi ceremony. I could surprise Amrit, stick around for a few hours . . ." Feeling brave, I add, "Hell, maybe I could even stay a couple nights and get back before Tuesday."

Srishti stares at me for a whole minute, looking absolutely flabbergasted. I expect her to laugh in my face or just dismiss the idea altogether, but all she says is, "I'm going to regret admitting this, but that might actually work."

I grab her hands, my body vibrating with the sudden thrum of thrill and anticipation that races through me. "You're serious?"

"Goa's right next door, so it's doable, but only if you're up for twenty-two hours total of road travel, plus a long, long flight back to the US."

"I also have a layover at London Heathrow."

"And *that*. Mind you, motion sickness and jet lag won't be sold separately. They come as a package."

"I'll manage. At minimum, I'll have all of Tuesday to recuperate." I grip my phone tightly in my hand. "I'm just . . . so sick of holding back all the time, you know? Like, for once, I just want to do something unhinged." And if it all goes to crap, that's okay, because I'll at least not regret never having *tried*.

"It's going to be epic!" Srishti says proudly.

Ever since I can remember, I've brushed off my desires to be stupid and fun because I felt this need to prove to myself that I can be *more*. But now that I've been accepted to my dream college, I know I'll have the rest of my life to innovate and heal and change the world and be Dr. Krishna Kumar.

And only one summer to be the eighteen-year-old main character of a cheesy rom-com.

The next couple of hours, before Srishti has to leave for Kandivali, we occupy the guest room, curled up on the bed, laptop propped open on my knees. We dissect potential travel and stay options thoroughly, because a badly planned road trip is just a disaster in the making.

If we're being honest, it might not even end up being a road trip, because my permit doesn't let me drive in India, much less rent cars. Regardless, I wouldn't feel comfortable driving on the left side of the road.

But none of the alternate travel options seem viable either. Although the cabs would pick me up and drop me off where needed, they're way too expensive, and traveling alone with a driver for eleven hours just feels severely unsafe. Buses are cheap, but I'd have to figure out the pickup and drop-off points, and the duration is much longer—I don't exactly have all the time in the world. And while taking a train would be a fantastic option, there's nothing available until later in the night, and again, I wouldn't feel great about taking one alone.

The more we look into it, the more doubtful I get, the initial enthusiasm wearing off. But I can't bow out now, because there is *always* something that could go wrong. I've backed out of too many things in the past because of that bothersome seed of doubt that plants itself in my mind at the mention of anything remotely fun.

Like the time I didn't go to a house party sophomore year because one of my friends mentioned there would be alcohol. I told myself I didn't need to get caught with a Solo cup in my hand and be arrested for underaged drinking. While the party did get busted, no one actually got in trouble, and *I* ended up spending the night scrolling through my friends' stories, assuring myself I'd done the right thing but still feeling like shit about it.

I can't allow myself to do that this time. Not again.

"You know . . ." Srishti says uncertainly once we've narrowed my issue down to two linked pitfalls—traveling unchaperoned and the fact that we aren't even sure Nani will let me go on my own to begin with—"I'd suggest something, but I know you'd rather eat sand than do it, so I'm going to set it aside."

“Seriously? You can’t just say that and leave me hanging.” I poke her shoulder repeatedly in the way I know bugs her and will get her to speak up. “Tell me, tell me, tell—”

“Okay, *okay*.” Srishti swats my finger away. “You could . . . ask Priti for help.”

I stare at Srishti. “You can’t be serious.”

“Priti’s been living with Nani for two years now. She’s your age, and she’s stayed out all night lots of times because she has a ready excuse—college fests. I’m, like, a hundred percent sure she doesn’t go to college fests every time, but Nani wouldn’t know, right?”

“Are you saying I should ask her to cover for me with Nani because she’s done it before?”

“No, I’m saying you should ask her to *come along* with you. That way you’ll be safe *and* she’ll know how to get Nani’s permission.”

I stand, needing to get the jittery itch off my body. “I can’t take Priti with me. I don’t want to be cooped up in a vehicle with her for so long. Forget that—there’s no way she’s going to agree to it. She hates me. And if anything, she’ll rat me out to Nani, who will tell Mummy and Papa. I’ll be *screwed*.”

“Yeah, you’re right,” Srishti says, whistling through her teeth. “Forget I suggested it. Also, I should really take a bath right now. I have to leave in a bit.”

While Srishti heads to the bathroom, I go over my notes again until I’m sick of looking at them.

A couple of hours later, my cousins slowly start leaving, and when it’s Srishti’s and Manas’s turn to go, I pull Srishti into a tight hug.

She hugs me back with equal ferocity, pecks my cheek, and says, “I’ll miss you so much.”

“I’ll miss you too. Please start applying to US universities soon so you can come be with me!”

"Hundred and one percent." Srishti lowers her voice, whispering in my ear, "Keep me updated on your plans."

"I will."

Afterward, the house is suddenly quiet. It's just Nani, Priti, and me.

Nani gives me a kiss on my forehead and heads to her bedroom for her afternoon nap—which I know is just Nani code for bingeing episodes of *Mahabharat*. I sigh, standing alone in the middle of the living room, which, just a few hours ago, was packed with people.

If *I* feel this void in my heart, then how must Nani feel when we come over, only to leave all at once?

Having Priti at home doesn't make much of a difference, because she's either not here or penned in her room. It's like not having her home at all.

To add to it, the road trip idea seems more impossible than ever, and the day is already doomed to crawl by with no one to spend time with.

I think I know just what I need to do.

I head to the kitchen, open the cabinet, and pull out a big packet of Parle-G biscuits, which has multiple smaller packets within. I quickly whip up enough cake batter for two mugs using crushed biscuits, baking powder, milk, and vanilla essence. I put them in the microwave to bake as a plan solidifies in my brain.

There's whipped cream left over in the refrigerator from when we had a bake-a-thon the day before yesterday. I pipe it onto the mug cakes, grate some compound chocolate on top so it decorates the cream in tiny flakes, and dig two dessert spoons into the crusts.

Then, armed with my bribe, I make my way to Priti's bedroom. It's in the corner of the house, tucked away conveniently, making it easy for the rest of us to forget her sometimes. I hesitate for a few seconds outside her door, knowing now's the time to back out if I want to.

But what have I got to lose, truly?

My ego, yes, but it's worth it.

Making up my mind, I rap my knuckles on the wood, then wait. My feet nervously tap the floor, and I consider sprinting away every few seconds before assuring myself I need to stay put.

It takes a whole minute until I hear Priti push her rolling chair back and stand up on the other side.

The door creaks open a few moments later. Priti pokes her head out and stares down at me, as if I'm an alien creature that has dropped from the moon. Her eyes fall to the mug cakes clutched in my hands, filling with suspicion, like she thinks I'm here to poison her or something.

I paste on a smile that I hope says *I come in peace*, and it works.

The door swings open fully, and she stands there in her loose black death metal tee and boxers, hair tousled. "What?" she demands, blocking the door with her tall frame, preventing all means of unsolicited entry.

I glance inside her room, ask myself again if I'm a fucking idiot for doing this, and blurt, "Can I talk to you?"

Priti cocks one perfectly threaded dark eyebrow. It's fascinating to me how people do that. I've tried, but I can never seem to raise a single eyebrow. Both, yes, but I resemble a surprised goose when I do that.

"Talk," she says.

"I meant—inside your room." I raise the mugs to her, and for a second, I see her falter, because who wouldn't? The cakes look delicious. I made sure they would.

Her nostrils flare like a bull's, and with a grunt of irritation, she moves aside, motioning me in. I breathe a sigh of relief but very quickly discard the feeling. I'm walking into a lion's den, after all. The real challenge lies ahead.

Her room's an extension of her mien, always has been. Deep-purple fairy lights and black pennants—each with one of the twelve zodiac signs painted on it in silvery white—decorate the walls. The bedding is black, and the cushions are purple. At the moment, the black velvet curtains are pulled open to let the light in, but at night, this place looks like a sanctum where one might perform séances to summon demons and ghosts. And given how shady and secretive Priti is, I wouldn't be surprised if she were secretly a witch and conducting sacrificial killings here every night.

I can only hope I haven't walked right into the next one.

Obviously, she doesn't offer me a seat, so I start walking toward her study table. But then she snaps, "Don't sit there! You'll get cream on my sketches!" and I decide to go with the edge of the bed instead.

Priti's an aspiring National Institute of Fashion Technology student. Her artwork is gorgeous, and I've seen the way she moves her pencil across her paper, as if her mind's been possessed until she manages to breathe life into whatever pops into her imagination. She's good at what she does. *Really* good.

But I won't tell her that.

I catch a glimpse of what she's working on: charcoal sketches of svelte women (much like her) in clothes she's designed herself. But before I have a chance to properly look, she haphazardly stuffs the papers into a folder and slams it shut. She sits by the headboard, arms crossed over her chest, staring at me.

It suddenly hits me that I'm supposed to talk.

But before that, a treat for the lion.

I hold out a mug to her. She pauses for a second, then leans over and snatches the other one from me. Damn, she really must think I might've poisoned her or something, because she doesn't take a bite until I do.

I gulp the bit of cake down, the Parle-G taste melting on my tongue, and veer straight to the point. "So you know Amrit Acharya, right?"

Priti sneers. "Of course I know Amrit. You've been making eyes at him all summer and won't shut up about how much he reminds you of Ishaan Khatter."

I have half a mind to snap at her, but I'm here to ask (correction: beg) her for a favor, and snapping wouldn't be the best note to start on. I swallow the irritation and speak again. "He's in Goa for his cousin's wedding right now. And he just sent me a text saying he wants to . . . kiss me."

Priti fixes me with a stare, a momentary flash of dubiety passing over her face, gone as quickly as it comes. I'm filled with so much embarrassment, my face turns hot. Her voice is low, a monotone, when she speaks. "And . . . why should I care?"

"Because I want to go to Goa. To kiss him. Back." I take another bite of my cake and speak through the mouthful. "And I was hoping you'd come along with me. Nani won't let me go off on my own, and I haven't exactly told my parents I'm going, because obviously they wouldn't give me the permission to kiss a guy, let alone travel across cities to kiss said guy. But because you have your college fests as an excuse to stay out, I thought it might help in tamping down any suspicions."

Priti doesn't respond but continues taking bites of cake out of the mug, staring at me with that same dark gaze, barely even blinking. I take that as my cue to continue speaking.

"Anyway, um"—I fumble for my phone and open my Notes app for her, where Srishti and I wrote down the travel options and fares—"I was thinking we could take a train together, as it's the cheapest, safest option right now, and we'd be back before Tuesday.

The travel fare will be on me, of course."

I don't want to have to pay for Priti, but I need to spread all my cards on the table before her and give her zero reasons to reject my proposal. The only potential spoke in the wheel is her swollen ego, but there's nothing I can do about that. That's a fundamental problem with her. Unless I become a doctor and revolutionize research in the field of medicine so genetic correction becomes possible, there's no way *that* can be rectified.

But to my absolute shock and stupefaction, Priti finally breaks the scary stare, sets aside her empty mug, and says, "Fine."

"Hold up." I can't believe what I'm hearing. I think my ears might be buzzing. "Are you serious?"

"Yeah, whatever. I'm bored anyway. And Goa's a nice getaway."

Okay, I'm definitely hallucinating. Because there's no way Priti Gaikwad, my cousin-turned-enemy-who-hates-my-guts, just agreed to accompany me on a road trip that has nothing to do with her. Priti doesn't do things like that. Maybe the self-imposed isolation is finally getting to her.

"But we don't have to go by train," she adds. "We can ask Rudra. He can take us in his car."

"Rudra?" I ask, baffled. "As in Rudra Desai?"

"How many Rudras do you know?" Priti says, scowling.

I gulp. "Just the one."

Priti shrugs. "That will cut the cost entirely. And we won't have to rush back and forth in a day. The shaadi isn't until Monday, so we can stop at Pune आराम से[1] for the night and still reach Goa tomorrow. You can meet Acharya the day after."

"Wait, how do you know the shaadi is on—"

"I'll get changed." Priti cuts me off abruptly, getting to her feet.

---

1 *Language*: Hindi; *Translation*: Comfortably.

"Then we can go to Rudra's house and ask him if he's in."

I'm thrown by how fast things are moving. This is not how I expected this to turn out. *Priti*, so easy to convince? What the hell is happening?

"Can't we just borrow his car?"

Priti guffaws. "His car is his *baby*. He won't let his parents drive it, let alone me."

"Why don't you just ask him on the phone? Isn't he, like, your best friend?"

"If you want to make sure you crack a deal with the Desais, you've got to go to their doorstep. They're Gujjus, remember?"

Most Gujaratis are excellent entrepreneurs and businesspeople—every Indian knows that. The best in the business, pun intended.

Still, having to go all the way to Rudra's house doesn't make much sense to me. I watch Priti in amazement anyway as she goes over to her cupboard, pulls it open, and starts rummaging through her almost all-black wardrobe.

"What are you still doing here?" Priti turns to me when she's picked an outfit: a meshed, see-through top, a tank, jean shorts, and fishnet stockings. All black. She's going to bake in the heat.

"I—uh, yeah, I'll let you change." I get to my feet, grabbing Priti's empty mug from her bedside table. It's scraped clean, as expected. My Parle-G mug cake really does work wonders.

"Go talk to Nani about our plans," Priti says. "Tell her there's a camping trip V. G. Vaze is organizing that I'm taking you along for. If she hesitates, call me. I'll get ready."

The camping trip excuse makes perfect sense because Mummy and Mausi both studied in V. G. Vaze during their junior and senior years, and Nani will know field trips are common during this time of summer.

I pause halfway out Priti's door. I can't believe I'm doing this, but I say, "I'd rather we talk to Nani together. It'll be more convincing that way."

Priti glares at me, her right eye twitching.

"Or not," I add hurriedly, knowing it's a miracle she agreed to this in the first place and the smallest possible thing might make her change her mind. It's *us*—we are experts at getting on each other's nerves. "I'll do it. It's not your headache. You get ready."

Priti comes up and holds the door as I step out. To my surprise, she nods. "It will be easier to convince Nani as a team. Wait for me."

With that, she slams the door in my face.

4

KEEP CALM AND GIVE YOUR ENEMIES A CHUMTI

Mumbai, Friday

We find Nani in her bedroom adjacent to the kitchen, watching an episode of the 2013 remake of *Mahabharat* on her TV at full volume. Ever since Priti taught her how to use streaming apps, Nani's been spending all her free time bingeing the show. There's, like, twenty-plus seasons.

I'm relieved Nani's awake. I didn't want to wake her up just to convince her to let Priti and me go off on a silly road trip so I can kiss a boy. The fact that I'm lying to her only makes the guilt worse, especially since she was so thrilled at the prospect of having me all to herself for a few days.

Priti walks into the room first, taking the lead, and I automatically fall into step behind her. Nani looks up at us over the rim of her spectacles and presses the pause button on the remote. Her eyes widen with surprise as her gaze flicks between the two of us. Our rocky relationship is no secret—especially not to Nani, who has heard both Mausi's and Mummy's rants and sides of the story.

"मेरी बच्चियां,"[1] she says fondly as we sit, Priti next to Nani and I on the rocking chair by the bed. "क्या हुआ?"[2]

"Why do you think something's happened?" Priti asks, snorting. "Maybe we're just here to spend time with our darling Nani." She puts on her best puppy face, and I stick out my lower lip, both of us feigning innocence.

Nani narrows her eyes, skeptical. "That naughty glint in your eyes doesn't fool me one bit. It is the same look both your mothers used to give me when they had something up their sleeves."

I guffaw. We should've known Nani would smell the rat instantly. Priti and I exchange a glance, which honestly feels weird as hell, because it's been *ages* since we were in on anything together; a united front.

"Spit it out," Nani says, sighing. She strokes tender circles along Priti's back.

"You wanna ask, or should I?" Priti says, a smile curling her lips. I raise my eyebrows. Her entire face changes when she smiles. On top of her usual sullenness, she's been so withdrawn and miserable lately, I can't remember the last time I saw her smile.

The image of her tear-streaked face on the balcony flashes in my mind momentarily.

"Go ahead," I say, knowing she's done this tons of times before—asked Nani for permission to spend the night out. Even though it seemed a terrible idea at the time, Srishti was right in suggesting I approach Priti for help. I don't want to jinx this by blabbering—something I'm famous for.

---

1 *Language*: Hindi; *Translation*: My girls.

2 *Language*: Hindi; *Translation*: What happened?

"There's a camping trip thing happening in Lonavala," Priti says. "A bunch of my friends are going. I didn't want to go because Rudra had his internship work and wasn't able to make time when I first asked him. But he just called up to let me know he's turned it in early and changed his mind, and, well, Krishna's here until Wednesday, so I was thinking we could both go."

Nani doesn't look convinced.

"I know it seems weird or whatever because Krishna and I aren't chummy. But she overheard me talking to Rudra and she's always wanted to go to Lonavala, so she whipped up a mug cake and bribed me." Priti throws me a glare. Everything else she just said is a fib, but *that* bit is real. "Not that I'm too chuffed about it, but they assign tents in threes, and it makes sense. We'll be back by Tuesday morning."

I'm a bit stunned by Priti's ability to fabricate a story and make it so convincing. She's got all the bases covered: why our plan's so last-moment, why she's suddenly decided to go, and why she's taking me along. I mentally store all the information away so I can stick to the story later.

"There are spots available?" Nani asks.

"Yeah, I just spoke to Neeraja. She's on the volunteer team, so she'll be able to get me tickets."

Nani scans our faces for ten whole seconds, hunting for a lie. We keep our features schooled, but my palms are sweating. God, I need this to work out so, so bad.

"Fine." Nani relents, shaking her head as if to say *These kids*.

Our faces break into wide grins and we exchange a look of utter delight, which again throws me off, because I'm not used to this. Who knew having Priti on my side would make all this so effortless?

"But I want a WhatsApp every three hours so I can ensure you girls are okay," Nani says. I adore how she says she wants *a WhatsApp* instead of *a text*. "And if I don't get one, I will WhatsApp Rudra. You know I have his number."

"Of course, Nani Ji," Priti says, pecking Nani on the cheek.

Nani picks up her remote to resume watching *Mahabharat*, and Priti and I shuffle toward the door. Just as we're about to leave—

"Wait."

We stop short.

"Have you informed your mothers yet?"

Priti and I exchange guilty looks.

"Actually, we were hoping you could do that for us—" I start, before Priti whacks me in the stomach, making the air whoosh right out of my body. I clamp my mouth shut to stop myself from yelping in pain, fixing Priti with a murderous glare instead.

"You girls," Nani says, sighing. "ठीक है,[3] I'll do it. But I can't promise they won't be annoyed."

Hold up. That *worked*?

"Obviously, Nani," I say, smiling.

"Now go. Shoo."

Once outside in the living room, I give Priti a chumti. At the small but painful pinch, she whirls to face me.

"A return gift for that whack," I say, smiling innocently.

"Grow up."

"Never." We approach the front door. "Are we taking an auto to Rudra's house?"

"No." Priti grabs a set of keys from a hook behind the door. "We'll take my Activa."

My face lights up. Priti's *never* let me ride pillion on her scooter,

---

3 *Language*: Hindi; *Translation*: All right.

despite my having set aside my ego on multiple occasions and begging her to let me tag along.

I practically skip out the door after her.

I'm convinced Priti is trying to scar me forever.

Twice we nearly rammed into a cow on the street, and once we were almost flattened against the footpath as Priti attempted to overtake a truck from the left. I have an *American* driver's license, and even I know that in India you're supposed to overtake from the right.

I'm clinging to her for dear life by the time we reach the apartment complex the Desais live in—there is no shame in prioritizing self-preservation. When Priti finally brings the Activa to a stop in a vacant space in the parking lot, I secretly thank Lord Yamraj for delaying his collection of my soul.

She's parked right behind a sleek midnight-blue BMW. There's not much I claim to know about Rudra Desai, but I'd recognize his car anywhere, since I've seen it nearly every day these past two months.

It's symbolic to Priti and Rudra's morning ritual, which would begin with Rudra parking his car in front of Nani's apartment building and honking twice to signal his arrival. Mere seconds later, Priti's closed bedroom door would open, and she'd sashay out and roll her eyes (when she caught my gaze, though, that delightful scowl of hers would appear), yell "मैं जा रही हूं!"[4] at no one in particular, and leave the house for the day.

And cousins being cousins, the rest of us would rush to the first-floor window. I followed the others curiously that first time, climbing on the sofa and hoisting myself onto the windowsill next to Srishti.

One floor down, Rudra's car was parked right in front of the entrance. Through the windshield, I spotted him sitting in the driver's

4 *Language*: Hindi; *Translation*: I'm leaving!

seat, wearing a black compression T-shirt and aviator glasses. No one bothered him as he waited, not even the chowkidar. Nani lives in a quaint old-people colony, and the watchman is like a hundred years old himself. They have little entertainment.

My eyes widened as I spotted a familiar logo on the bumper. "Is that a BMW?"

"Yep, it's Rudra's," Srishti told me. Back then, I didn't know he was from a rich family, which might've explained why an eighteen-year-old boy already owned a luxury car.

"And he's *really* not her boyfriend?" I asked as we watched Priti get into the passenger seat. I was certain they both knew the six of us were watching, but neither of them threw us a glance as Rudra drove away.

"Definitely just her best friend," Manas responded. "I'm sure Rudra likes her, though. Why else would he chauffeur her around and drop her back home every day?"

"Maybe he's chivalrous," Varija offered.

"Poor kid's been friend zoned for years now," Rajeev bhaiya said.

We all burst into laughter, but the conversation did nothing to quell my curiosity. It's uncanny to me how Rudra's always (sort of) been around but I don't know anything about his life. I have vague memories of him collected across summers, always invited to the parties Nani used to throw for us but never really *there*.

He'd be sitting in the corner, legs swinging above the ground, watching the rest of us playing statue dance, pass the parcel, or limbo. That was, of course, until Priti would rush up to him, grinning from ear to ear, her bangs sticking to her sweaty forehead. He'd reluctantly take her hand and jump off his chair.

Ever since she was little, Priti has been the leader in any situation. Even now, she's already taking off her helmet and expectantly waiting for me to get off the scooter, while I'm still gawking at the other cars in the parking lot.

"Are you sure we're allowed to park here?" I croak, still a little winded from the death-defying ride.

"Chill, Rudra's parents own this parking space. And three others." Priti points to the burnished cars flanking the BMW. "All theirs."

Holy shit. I knew the Desais were rich, but not *this* rich.

I get off the scooter and run after Priti, who's already started off toward one of the doors leading into the building. I follow her through and up a small flight of stairs that opens into the foyer. My mouth drops open.

There's a waterfall next to a posh seating area, with soothing music accompanying the sound of the water splashing (very Thai spa–esque). Pockets of golden light reflect off the surface of the water, making it shimmer like strings against the glass as it plunges into the pool. I walk past it with my jaw unhinged, peeking at the chandelier poised above an exquisite centerpiece opposite the reception desk.

"Close your mouth," Priti mutters. "You look like you've never seen an indoor waterfall."

"I haven't. Not in someone's home." The floor below me is covered with an embroidered rug, and the air smells like roses.

"I thought you Americans all lived in big houses."

"Say that to the current American housing crisis," I scoff. "Plus, you don't even know—"

"I didn't ask for a lecture, smartass," Priti interrupts.

I'm usually immune to Priti's cutting remarks, but this one stings because I've been called "smartass," "oily plaits," and variations thereof all my life. The only difference is, back in Portland, it stemmed from the whole "smart Indian kid" stereotype.

Even when you work your ass off to achieve your dreams, some people will say it was because of your genes, not how much you studied or slogged, so you're not even allowed to appear proud of your success, because *hard work had nothing to do with it, right*?

The worst part is, they will never know how when you opened your acceptance letter, your shoulders slumped in relief because you could finally *breathe.*

Shoving down the sudden lump in my throat, I hasten to follow Priti as she approaches the manager's desk at the end of the foyer, her face breaking into a smile. That's the second time I've seen her smile today. The sight of it will never cease to amaze me.

"Priti Ji," the manager says. "तू कशी आहेस?"[5]

"छान आहे!"[6]

Marathi sounds enough like Hindi for me to be able to understand their exchange. Mummy's side is a mix of UPites and Maharashtrians, and Nani and Nana (before he passed away a few years ago) have always lived in Mumbai. So have Mausi and Mausaji, which basically makes Priti a Mumbaikar.

It's like Srishti says: *In Mumbai, you aren't Kannadiga, or Gujarati, or even Maharashtrian, although Mumbai's technically a city in Maharashtra. You're Mumbaikar. Through and through.*

Me, I'm somewhere in the middle. I'm not your usual American-Born Confused Desi, because I wasn't born in America. But I don't exactly qualify as Mumbaikar either, despite having been born here, because I don't *live* here.

I'm both. Or either. Or neither.

Like quantum mechanics.

"Earth to Krishna." I blink in surprise as Priti clicks her fingers in front of my face, her scowl back, reserved solely for me. It's like a

---

5 *Language*: Marathi; *Translation*: How are you?

6 *Language*: Marathi; *Translation*: I'm good!

zombie—keeps resurrecting itself. "Let's go."

I hurry after Priti as she struts toward the lift.

Then it's up twenty-four floors, the lift moving fast enough to make my ears pop.

We step out into a carpeted corridor illuminated by bright lights, with abstract paintings in glass frames separating the space between the doors to each apartment. Rudra's apartment is diagonal to the lift, barricaded by two doors, the outer one with an ornate grille and the inner with a keyhole at the center. The name plate next to it says *Desai* in English and Gujarati.

Priti rings the touchscreen doorbell and shoves her face in front of the camera lens. "Open up, asshole!"

"Priti!" I gasp. "What if his parents are in there?"

"They're not. It's before five, so they're at work. Besides, they've known me forever."

I glance at her sideways, pushing my hair behind my ears. I suddenly feel self-conscious, because this is probably the first time Rudra and I will have a proper conversation. Face-to-face. In his fancy house.

"Open up," Priti mutters, ringing the doorbell again. She is unusually impatient for someone who is *not* prepping to crash a wedding *DDLJ*-style and slay her first kiss.

Speaking of . . .

"Hey, Priti, can I ask you something?" I say hesitantly. Now that I'm going to have to spend the next couple of days cramped in a car with her and Rudra, I should probably get some things cleared so I don't . . . ahem, walk in on something. What if I, like, went for a pee break and came back to find them making out in the car? It doesn't even have tinted windows!

"Just because we're both here doesn't mean we have to force

a conversation, you know?" Priti says, narrowing her eyes at me. I start to regret saying anything at all, because what else could I have expected from her other than an icy shutdown?

But my curiosity gets the better of me. "It's about you. And, erm, Rudra."

"Not you too." Priti groans.

I raise my hands in defense. "Don't *Et tu, Brute?* me. It certainly looks like it."

"Looks like *what*?"

"Like you're screwing."

The inner door opens with a beep, and Rudra appears on the other side. Priti guffaws as he looks at us both through the grille, eyes widening briefly. Something clicks, and the second door opens outward, revealing him in a half-sleeved blue T-shirt and shorts. His hair is loose and looks surprisingly silky, tips waving by his chin and along his temples.

"Why're you laughing?" Rudra says, and flicks his gaze to me as if to say *And what the hell is* she *doing here?*

"Krishna thinks we're screwing." Priti shoves past him and into the house. She takes off her black boots on her way in. There's a shoe shelf right next to the door, as is the case in most Asian households.

"You came all the way here to tell me that?" Rudra walks in after her.

Realizing there's a high possibility they've left me stranded outside, I dart in, pulling the outer door shut behind me and slipping off my shoes. The inner door shuts on its own, and there's another beep and a click, the lock activated.

"No, I came here to have sex with you," Priti says, blowing Rudra a kiss before flopping onto one of the recliners angled toward the massive home-theater system.

"Okay . . ." Rudra seats himself on the long sofa.

His apartment isn't an apartment; it's a *penthouse*. It's massive, with floor-to-ceiling glass windows and sliding doors offering a panoramic view of Mumbai. The wallpaper has a sandpaper texture—which I'm assuming is just an illusion because of the contouring—and a burgundy backdrop with detailed Warli art painted on it in off-white. Everything from the furniture to the carpeting, partitions, and flooring has been designed in a palette of browns and beiges, complementing the murals well. It's classy, exquisite, and clearly expensive.

"Don't be shy, Krishna." Priti tilts her head to look at me. "Rudra's my sugar daddy. Come sit."

I make a beeline for the recliner next to Priti's, dodging the cream living room rug because Mummy would kill me for getting my dirty feet on it (she's not here, but her indoctrination is deep). The recliner dips below me as if it's about to swallow me whole, and I very nearly moan as I sink into it.

"What took you so long to open the door?" Priti directs the question at Rudra, pressing a button on the side of the recliner to push it back farther so she's at a one-hundred-and-twenty-degree angle.

"I had my headphones on." Rudra glances at me again. When Priti doesn't lead the conversation forward, I decide I better start breaking the ice with the two of them or I'm going to have a very, very awkward couple of days.

"So—" I bite my lip. "Are you?"

"Screwing?" Priti says, putting her hand to her head dramatically. *"Obviously."*

I can't tell if she's being serious or sarcastic, but there's no point in prodding further if she doesn't want to disclose the status of their relationship. Rudra isn't being particularly helpful either, because he doesn't say anything to rebuke or affirm what Priti's saying. Instead, he clears his throat and asks, "So, uh, why are you both here, exactly?"

Priti grins. "We're going on a road trip, so we need your car. And you, but only because you won't let me drive."

"Road trip? To where?"

"Goa."

"Taking the bus or train might be easier."

"But we'd be saving money if you drove us there. Plus, it'd be safer if you came along."

Rudra leans forward with his elbows resting on his lap. "Why exactly do you want to go to Goa?"

It's a fair question and one that Priti doesn't have an answer for, not really. It's weird enough that she was surprisingly easy to convince in the first place, but the way I don't have even an inkling of what her ulterior motive might be is altogether super sus. Before I can dig into that thought, though, Priti turns to look at me. "Are you going to say something?"

Rudra turns his gaze toward me, and I find myself tongue-tied. The old apprehension and embarrassment at revealing *why* comes back. Earlier, I almost backed out because I didn't want to give Priti another reason to mock me. It seems silly trying to make such a big deal out of a first kiss. But it's important . . . to *me*, at least.

"I have to go to a wedding," I say, straightening up. "The one Amrit Acharya's attending."

I school my features to look secure in my decision, because unless I'm one hundred percent convinced about chasing this wild fantasy, I can't convince Rudra.

"It's Friday today. The mehndi's tomorrow, sangeet day after, and the shaadi and reception are on Monday. I have to reach Goa before then."

"Tell him why you want to go," Priti prods.

I take a deep breath, look Rudra square in the eyes, and blurt it out. "I want to kiss him."

Rudra blinks. "What?"

"You heard her," Priti says. "She wants to kiss the Acharya dude. He apparently sent her a text this morning—"

"Not apparently," I interject. "Actually."

"Whatever. He promised her a smooch and Krishna wants to go do that."

"Wait a second." Rudra holds a hand up. "You want to go all the way to Goa for a kiss? Why not just wait for him to come back and *then* kiss him? Not exactly the fastest, but it's less tedious."

"You literally attended my going-away party last night," I say, scoffing. "You know I was supposed to leave today."

"But you didn't because . . . you want to kiss Amrit?"

"No." Ohmy*god*. Rudra Desai sure asks a lot of questions for someone who's hardly spoken to me before. "My flight got canceled because of some staffing shortages. My parents rescheduled it to Wednesday, which is why I'm in a hurry. And Amrit doesn't come back until next weekend, so I can't wait around for him."

Priti already has the map—where we saved the route details earlier—open on her phone. "The plan's to leave this evening, stay over in Pune tonight, leave early morning tomorrow, drive to Goa nonstop, stay overnight there, and intercept the sangeet on Sunday. Krishna fucks Amrit; we leave Monday and get back that night or Tuesday morning, tops."

"I'm not going to fuck Amrit," I say hotly.

"You're certainly not going to be *just* kissing him and hopping back into the car right after."

"And you both just expect me to drive you there and back?" Rudra cocks his eyebrows.

"Yes," Priti and I say in unison.

"No."

Priti jams her thumb into the button at the recliner's side and it pops upright, straightening her with it. "Why not, asshole?"

"I have work to do. You know I have to complete my final internship module before leaving for Juilliard."

"It's just a few days, Ruds!"

"Wait a second," I say, frowning. "Juilliard? As in, *the* Juilliard?"

"Yeah," Rudra says, almost shy.

"I didn't know you were going to New York," I say dumbly, because I make it sound like I should've known that when I know nothing about Rudra at all. "I mean, Priti didn't tell me. But you have an acceptance already?"

"Yeah." Rudra shrugs. "I've had it for months. I'm moving in August."

"Wow. Juilliard. You must be really good."

"He is, but that's not the point," Priti says. "Ruds, you can do your work on the way. In fact, you could work the whole time if you'd just let me drive."

"That's not happening," Rudra says.

Priti glares at him, and I mentally give up. I couldn't have expected it to go any other way. Because besides this being the Wildest Idea™, it also involves Rudra, who doesn't owe me anything. No one would be willing to drive someone they hardly know to another city just so they can fulfill some silly fantasy.

Then why am I so disappointed?

"You know we're going to split the petrol prices, stay, tolls, et cetera." Priti is still arguing. "I don't expect you to pay for everything just because you can afford it. I can—"

"Priti," I interrupt. "Leave it. It's not that big of a deal." I sigh, turning to Rudra. "I'm sorry we looped you into this stupid plan."

Rudra looks at me for three whole seconds before letting out a breath. "Fine, look. Maybe—if you do something for me, I'll drive you there and back."

"Oh-kay?" What the hell can *I* do for *him*?

"There are some care packages I was going to take for my family in the States, along with my luggage. But if you could take them for me when you get on that flight this Wednesday, that would leave me more space for my actual belongings."

"You mean some of the recording equipment you were planning to leave behind?" Priti asks.

"Yeah. The problem's not really the extra charge. I just don't want to lug around too much on my first trip there."

I debate the proposition in my head. "That's doable, I guess. How much do they weigh?"

"Five kilos."

I do the math, converting from metric to imperial system. "Um, that would be around eleven pounds?" Eleven pounds would mean *precious* luggage space removed from the fifty-pound weight limit for my flight. Ugh.

Can I afford to leave some stuff behind?

Do I really want this that much?

Is it worth the effort?

I shut my eyes tight, the questions swirling through my brain. It's honestly the least I can do for Rudra, considering he's going to be sacrificing internship time to drive us. If I were in his place, I probably wouldn't be so willing to help out.

I can afford to leave some stuff behind.

I do want it that much.

And yes, it is worth the effort, especially when so little is being asked in return.

"Okay," I say. "I'll take your care packages for you."

Priti whoops, which is something I haven't seen her do before. Not in a decade, at least.

I guess we're going, then.

5

I HAVE THE MOST BASIC INDIAN BITCH NAME EVER

Mumbai, Friday

The three of us decided to meet up at R Galleria since it has a bunch of eateries alongside the salons and shops. Surprisingly, it doesn't take much time for Priti and me to pick a place to eat while we wait for Rudra: Chaayos, a popular chai café chain with cozy interiors and passable tea.

We *need* caffeine because we intend to stay up even though Rudra's going to be driving. I read somewhere that the likelihood of an accident reduces when all the passengers in the car are awake.

Rudra's a good driver—he drove us to Juhu Beach once—so I'm not really worried about that. It's more of the whole driving-after-sundown thing. Plus, Priti said the Mumbai–Pune expressway is smooth, winding, and monotonous, all of which only exacerbate the possibility of an accident.

And I intend to die *after* I've appended a *Dr.* to my name. I'm not leaving a measly Krishna Kumar; do you know how many Krishna Kumars you'll find if you search my name on Google? Hundreds.

(Okay, *fine*, I did a search once and there are lots of Dr. Krishna Kumars as well, but that's not the point.)

We find ourselves a table by the entrance, under a poster that says *Stories Are Best Served with Chai*. I wait with our luggage while Priti heads to the counter to place our order: pav bhaji and adrak chai for me, and an anda bun and filter coffee for her.

Once we have our food in front of us, Priti doesn't bother to make conversation and instead scrolls through her Instagram feed, so I occupy myself with my chai.

I sigh as the taste of the ginger and masala immediately kicks awake my tired senses. The pav bhaji is spicy, so that helps as well. I barely got any sleep last night, and I've been busy packing and then unpacking to separate some stuff for the road trip all afternoon.

Without looking up from her phone, Priti asks, "Have you texted Amrit again, by the way?"

I turn to her. She's looking at me with her eyes narrowed. "No, why?"

"Just checking."

"I don't want to distract him from the wedding. Besides, how am I supposed to tell him I'm headed there to meet him? It's meant to be a surprise."

Until now, I was convinced that putting off messaging Amrit was the right thing to do, but I can't help the frisson of anxiety that erupts in my gut. *Should* I be texting him? Should I have texted him *already*? Will my unresponsiveness make him think I'm not interested in him anymore? Or will texting him make me appear too eager? Oh god, is this going to ruin—

The glass doors at the entrance swing open, breaking me out of my thoughts, and Rudra walks in. Unlike usual, he's pulled his hair into a half ponytail, a few strands drifting down the sides of his face as the AC blasts down on him. He's wearing a cream button-down shirt and baggy olive-green chinos and is carrying a guitar case and laptop bag.

Rudra pulls up a chair from the table next to ours and sits between Priti and me. The table's small and our knees touch briefly, and I shift backward self-consciously. His eyes lock with mine, just for a second, and although he looks away just as quickly as I do, my heart races.

I'm always awkward around new people. I know Rudra's far from new, but I've never been this close to him before. The fact that he looks kinda-sorta good (okay, *very* good) right now doesn't help in the least.

Knees at an appropriate distance, Rudra frowns at the luggage on the floor beside me. "How many bags have you both got?"

"Laptop bag, duffel bag, handbag," Priti says.

"Laptop bag, suitcase, fanny pack," I say.

"We're going for, like, three days," Rudra says. "Why do you need so much stuff?"

Priti sighs. "You do know that your enormous guitar bag is going to occupy more space than my and Krishna's luggage combined, though, right?"

I peek at the label inscribed on the bag. "Wait, is that a Taylor acoustic?"

Rudra's eyes go wide. "Uh, yeah."

"Do you know how *expensive*—" I pause. "Of course you do."

"You're familiar with guitars?"

"My dad plays, and I used to play keyboard. I've always liked to sing, so it's nice to learn an accompaniment instrument. I'm just okay, though. Not an expert or anything."

"You're pretty decent," Priti says.

I turn to her in surprise. "You've heard me sing?"

"I watched your covers on Instagram." Priti flaps her hand, looking embarrassed. "Don't look so surprised—we follow each other."

"Do you have any guitar covers up online?" I ask Rudra.

"A couple," Rudra says, his eyes falling to the table.

Priti blows a raspberry. "A *couple*? Quit acting modest. You got into Juilliard, for fuck's sake." She starts typing into her phone. "He has loads of covers up. Plenty of originals, instrumentals with his guitar, ukulele, keyboard, cajon, some new instrument he picked up a few months ago—"

"Kalimba."

"—yeah, that, and then he has his beats up for sale on BeatStars and some stuff on SoundCloud. Not to mention"—Priti turns her phone toward me—"one hundred and forty thousand followers on Instagram."

I take the phone from her, my eyes nearly popping out of their sockets as I scroll through his page. *A couple* was an understatement. And all his reels have six-figure views. Some have even crossed a million.

"You could do with a new handle, though," Priti says to Rudra. "@rudradesaimusic is bleh."

"It's easy to find," Rudra protests.

"There's a *million* Rudra Desais on Instagram. Your name is the John Smith of brown dudes."

"My name is *not* that common."

"I can prove it to you right now. Watch." Priti twists to the side, cupping her mouth in an O with her palms, and yells, "ANY RUDRA DESAIS IN HERE?"

"Jesus." Rudra cringes.

"I don't know you," I say, ducking.

Everyone in the café turns in Priti's direction, shooting her surprised glances. Priti, being Priti, yells *again*, "I ASKED, ANY RUDRA DESAIS IN HERE?"

Pin-drop silence.

Priti drops her hands. "Fine." She sticks her tongue out at Rudra. "You win."

"I wasn't competing."

I go back to scrolling through his page. I notice he hasn't shown his face in a single post. He either has his camera angled below the neck or he's turned away from it, hood up. He probably doesn't like being perceived. But he makes sure to use aesthetic setups—like blue fairy lights, cloudy Mumbai skies, and clear mugs of black coffee—and high-end production equipment.

"You have a nice mysterious-guy-in-a-hoodie mood to your page," I say, handing Priti back her phone.

Priti snorts. "That's one way to put it. If only he'd show his face so he doesn't look like Joe Goldberg the guitarist."

"I don't like to draw attention away from the music," Rudra says, shrugging.

"A little attention to your dashing face might get you even more followers." Priti pulls at his cheek as she gets to her feet. "I'm going to pee. Be right back."

As Priti heads to the bathroom, Rudra watches her go with an unreadable expression on his face. And it hits me then that I . . . know that look. Very well.

That's the look *I* gave Amrit all summer. The trying-really-hard-to-suppress-my-yearning-but-failing-miserably look.

Oh god.

Rudra definitely likes Priti.

I mean, all of us cousins suspected they were screwing because they're so attached at the hip all the time. So even if they aren't screwing *now*, who's to say they don't want to? Neither of them denied my assumptions earlier either. Priti's flirting is playful, but she's probably using it to mask her real feelings. And by the looks of it, Rudra's in deep. And hard.

Very dirty, Krishna.

I take the last bite of my pav bhaji as an awkward silence settles between us. Rudra clears his throat and stands. "I'm going to get myself some coffee."

I nod as he pushes his chair back and walks to the counter.

Priti is still not back by the time Rudra returns with a cup of black coffee. How pretentious. If you ask me, black coffee drinkers don't actually like the taste of the concoction. I had a sip *once* and spit it right out.

As Rudra sits, I get a trace of his cologne—sharp enough that I know it's not his soap, subtle enough that I know it's not his deodorant. The heavenly apricot scent suddenly stands out because it's just him and . . . Gross, why am I thinking of Rudra's cologne?

I text Srishti, cringing at myself.

@notkrishnakumar

I despise you

Her reply comes instantly.

@srishti_without_an_h

omg whaddid I do

@notkrishnakumar

I'm supposed to be setting off to kiss Amrit

But bc of you I'm thinking
of how Rudra smells instead

@srishti_without_an_h

i am losing it sksksk

how DOES he smell tho?

@notkrishnakumar

Really good like apricots or
some shit but now I feel GUILTY

@srishti_without_an_h

why?? it's not like you're dating amrit.

you are single and not hooked to any ONE person

you can kiss whoever you want
and you can smell whoever you want

@notkrishnakumar

But it's *Rudra*

@srishti_without_an_h

so . . . ?

he's hot and he smells good

@notkrishnakumar

Ewww and no . . . he likes Priti,
bro. He's like down *bad.*

@srishti_without_an_h

ok fine im changing the topic

did you text amrit back?

@notkrishnakumar

No I didn't want him to be sus

Should I??? Priti asked
me the same thing.

@srishti_without_an_h

ngl it's going to be weirder

if you show up after ghosting him

but text him or don't, you always have Rudra 😉

@notkrishnakumar

You're right (except for the Rudra bit)

Okay I'll text him.

@srishti_without_an_h

lmk what he says

I lock my phone and set it aside, sighing, and spot Priti walking back to our table from the corner of my eye.

"Let's get going, kids," she says. She's so weirdly cheerful and chatty around Rudra—it's going to take getting used to. "We're already late."

After we gather our things, we head out of the café and down the stairs to where Rudra's car is parked by the side of the road. He opens the trunk and loads our things in. Priti mock swoons at me as we stand behind him, and I roll my eyes.

A few hours more of this and I'm going to barf.

"All right." Rudra shuts the trunk. "Who's navigating?" Earlier, we decided Priti and I would take turns navigating even though Rudra's car has GPS because it would make sure at least one of us stayed awake with him if the caffeine didn't work its wonders.

"Krishna, you go first," Priti says. "I'm shit at directions anyway."

"Okay," I say. If I navigate, I can also control the music, so it's a win-win.

"You can sit in the passenger seat, up front with me, then," Rudra says.

"Cool."

We get into the car, and Priti stretches like a cat in the back, splaying herself out across the length of the seat. I open the map on my phone. "Straight to Pune, right?"

"Yep, I've booked us an OYO there," Priti says, her shoes off and bare feet resting on the ledge of the window.

"What's the address?"

"Give me that."

As Priti types, Rudra starts the car. He turns to me, gesturing with his eyes to the seat belt. "You should put on your seat belt."

"Oh, right." I pull the strap down. "Where's the buckle?"

"One sec," Rudra says, unbuckling himself. He leans toward me, and I get another whiff of his cologne. His fingers are long and slim, I notice as he tucks them under the seat cover to retrieve the missing buckle. He has a true pianist's hands, the way my tutor used to say—unlike my tiny ones with their nail-bitten fingers.

I become hyperaware of our proximity as he gets the buckle out and reaches around me for the strap. We both fumble with it for a few seconds before getting it into the buckle. I get a close-up view of his face: clean-shaven, smelling like a hint of aftershave, and dotted with a light sprinkling of acne scars. His eyebrows are really thick, and I'm filled with the sudden desire to—

"Here," Priti says, and thrusts my phone between us.

I blink and stutter my thanks as I take the phone from her.

Rudra moves away, his face taking on a distant expression again, and while I'm struggling to tamp down these wildly ill-timed urges, he's already grabbed the stick and switched to first gear.

"Road trip, baby!" Priti cheers.

Rudra may be pining for his best friend, and I may be spinning over a boy who *isn't* destined to be my first kiss, but at least Priti seems happy.

6

WHY WOULD ANYONE NAME THEIR BLUETOOTH *JIMI HENDRIX'S GROUPIE*?

Mumbai, Friday

The route is pretty straightforward. We experience the worst traffic on Mulund–Airoli road, but it's smooth from there on, all the way to Mumbai–Pune expressway. It takes more than an hour to commute within the city itself, but that's just how it's always been navigating traffic in Mumbai—a real pain in the ass. We picked a time when it would take us a minimum of four hours to get to Pune, so this is better than usual.

Rudra drives like he knows the roads like the back of his hand—which he probably does since he's lived in the city all his life. I don't even have to navigate the route to the expressway half the time. He's cool and silent, as usual, and I almost forget that, until a while ago, he was actually making conversation with me.

As for Priti, she looks like she's having a grand old time in the back seat. She's lying down, a car bolster placed under her head, her long legs resting on the window ledge. She barks out a laugh, and I turn, squinting at her reflection in the window, to find her watching a scene from the K-drama Srishti and I asked her to binge with us last month. Back then, she gave us a dirty look.

Now look at her, snickering away there.

At least Rudra's playlist is nice. He's got a decent collection of songs, mostly English, a far cry from my curated Bollywood road trip playlist, which would suit the current vibe better. But I'm not comfortable enough asking him to share his Bluetooth with me.

I turn back to my phone, glancing at the map, and frown. "Hold up, why are you getting off the highway?"

"Tank's almost empty," Rudra says. He turns the car into the petrol pump station, doing that hot rotating-the-steering-wheel thing. Because he's wearing a half-sleeved shirt, his right bicep pops up when he does it, and it takes me a whole five seconds to realize I'm staring.

I swiftly turn back to my phone, dousing the heat creeping up my face.

Priti sits up as Rudra stops the car in front of the pump. He presses the button to open the tank and steps out of the car.

"Where are we?" Priti asks me, slipping on her shoes.

"Navi Mumbai," I say, and jump out of the car.

"Already?"

I almost say, *If you'd look away from your phone for a second, you'd know*, but I just nod instead.

We wait as Rudra tells the attendant to "टाकी पूर्ण full करा."[1] I stretch my limbs, taking a deep breath. I've always loved the smell of petrol. It's so satisfying.

Priti heads to a nearby tuck shop, leaving Rudra and me alone. *Again.* It goes from zero to awkward in less than two seconds. And

---

1 *Language*: Marathi; *Translation*: Fill up the tank fully.

like the idiot I am, I left my phone in the car, so it's not like I can avoid him, much less contact anyone if I get kidnapped here, like Alia Bhatt in *Highway*.

Rudra just stands there, hands in his pockets, watching Priti as she buys some gum from the shopkeeper. He has the smallest smile on his face, and my suspicions about him having feelings for Priti are only further confirmed.

He turns to find me looking at him, the hint of a smile gone. Oops. I need to initiate escape mode, which means only one thing: say the first thing that comes to my mind.

"So does Priti make you watch K-dramas with her?" I blurt, regretting it a second later. Rudra does not look like the kind of guy who is itching to have K-drama discourse. Worst conversation starter *ever*.

"Yeah," Rudra replies shortly, and then adds, "But she watches anime with me in exchange."

Wait, seriously? "Any chance you're into manhwa? One of my favorites got adapted into a K-drama."

"Tried it. Same with manga. But I'm better with purely visual stuff. I have dyslexia."

"Oh. Filling out applications must have been tough for you, then. For Juilliard, I mean. The portals aren't exactly accessible."

"Yeah, Priti helped me out," Rudra says, feet fidgeting. Am I making him nervous? Fuck me. "We filled out our applications together."

"What applications?"

"For US colleges?"

What.

The.

Actual.

Fuck.

I am so shocked by this piece of information that I go stock-still for a moment, just staring at Rudra. Rudra frowns down at me, noting the change in my body language and expression.

Just when I thought Priti and I could start being cordial to each other . . . I discover she's been lying to me. This whole time.

My mind flips through every moment we discussed our post-summer plans, when my cousins would ask me to show them pictures of Johns Hopkins and I would eagerly tell them how stoked I was for college, and Priti would not say a single word. She said she had been giving entrances to go to NIFT.

But the whole time, she was applying to American universities?

Rudra's starting to look suspicious, so I swallow my shock and crack a smile. "Yeah, she said something about that. Which colleges was she applying to, again?" If Rudra and she were applying together, the chances are at least one college in New York made her list. I make a quick guess. "I know of FIT."

The suspicious look on Rudra's face vanishes. My guess was correct. She *did* apply to FIT—Fashion Institute of Technology.

New York City is just *three* hours away from Baltimore.

This is too much to take in, even for me, and I usually have a high tolerance for anything Priti related. Worse, it *hurts*. It hurts so bad tears spring to my eyes. I'm trying hard not to let them roll out because it would be super embarrassing to start crying in front of Rudra.

His attention is off me, though, and back on Priti, who's walking our way. I quickly swipe at my eyes as Priti approaches, holding out a palm piled with blueberry-flavored Big Babol strips.

"Gum, anyone?"

Rudra takes one. I shake my head stiffly.

I rarely lose my wits, but I want to smash something hard right now. Only, I have to be smart about this. I can't tell Priti I know. Not yet. I'll just use this piece of information as a trump card instead and fling it at her when she's least expecting it. Maybe then I'll be able to get her to be honest. For once.

The attendant signals that he's done, and Rudra moves past me to pay him, whispering, "Excuse me."

I stay quiet, but Priti's hawk eyes note the sour twist to my features. "Why are you sulking?"

"I saw you," I grit out.

Priti looks slightly taken aback by the intensity of my tone, but she doesn't sway. "Saw what?"

"I saw what you were watching. In the car."

"So?"

Rudra gets back, and that's a sign we need to leave, but the challenging arch of her eyebrows sends me over the edge, and I can't help it. "What do you mean, *so*? Priti, Srishti and I asked you if you wanted to watch the show with us and you said you weren't interested. You could've just said you didn't want to spend time with us."

Rudra looks comically confused at having waltzed right into the middle of our silly fight, but we both ignore him.

"I had work to do," Priti says, her nostrils flaring. "And that was the *only* time you asked. Otherwise, you usually don't bother. You're always giggling away in the corner, sharing jokes. Completely ignoring your other cousin—*me*!"

"*Ignoring?*" I say, and it comes out in a high-pitched squeak of disbelief. "I try to bond with you every time, for fuck's sake! Every summer I'm here. And everyone—not just me—ends up getting snubbed."

"Hey," Rudra says, glancing over at the few people in the petrol pump, who are all beginning to look in our direction. "I think we should leave—"

I step toward Priti. "You know, even though you've been so nasty to me this whole summer, I still hoped we might be able to have a decent trip. But you make it impossible."

"*I* make it impossible?" Priti takes a counter step, and we're practically fuming in each other's faces. "I know what you call me, you know. *Ice Queen.* You think I don't notice you rolling your eyes every time I'm in the room, but I do."

"If you weren't so horrible to me, maybe I wouldn't. Mocking my accent, my Hindi—"

"I wouldn't do any of that if you didn't try so fucking hard all the time."

"Try what?"

"To be Indian."

"I don't try to be Indian. I *am* Indian."

Priti's eyes turn dark. "Wearing a saree for prom or posting about your Desi identity for brownie points doesn't make you one of us. It just makes you a wannabe."

I shrink back like I've been struck across my face. Those tears teetering at the edge of my eyelids finally slip out and roll down my cheeks. I'm stunned more than hurt. The headlamps of passing vehicles become muddy puddles of light. I don't know why I'm crying. All I know is Priti is standing in front of me, Rudra too, and both are looking at me while I'm crying, and that is humiliating.

"That's enough," Rudra says, suddenly and sharply. He shakes his head at Priti. "Too far, Priti."

"Why me? *She* is the one who started making a big deal of nothing."

"That wasn't cool," Rudra says, sounding firmer than I'd ever imagined him being. "Get in the car. Front seat. You're navigating."

"No."

"I didn't ask you. Don't forget it's *my* car, and *I'm* driving, and I can drop both of you back in Mulund right now."

Priti stares at him in disbelief for three whole seconds before turning on her heel and stomping to the car. At first, I think she's going to slam the door after she sits inside, but she doesn't.

Rudra starts walking toward the tuck shop, and after a moment's hesitation, I follow him, my head swirling with a torrent of emotions.

I am furious with Priti, but more so with myself for crying in front of the two of them, because the only thing that managed to do was satiate Priti's malice. Her words keep echoing in my head no matter how hard I try to drown them out as I look through all the snacks on the shelves.

Priti pricked a sore point for me. The rational part of me knows she was wrong and just being nasty to hurt me, but it still stings.

Wearing a saree for prom or posting about your Desi identity for brownie points doesn't make you one of us. It just makes you a wannabe.

I did both of those things. And the way she said it . . . it makes me feel so small.

When I first moved to America, I faced my share of bullying for being too brown, too modest, too Indian. But then, in high school, it became *cool* to be Indian. It became cool to wear sarees for prom, wear jhumkas in place of hoops, throw Holi parties instead of Halloween parties, and bring lunch boxes full of homemade Indian snacks and delicacies to school.

I can't remember the exact moment the switch happened, but suddenly, my classmates were fawning over the intricate embroidery of the kurtas I wore over jeans, voicing how wearing a bindi brought out the brown of my eyes, and in general swooning at the "exoticism" of it all. And perhaps I was finally beginning to realize that embracing the culture I'd been trying so hard to leave behind in India was the *in thing* now.

Is it wrong that I started to appreciate my Desiness only when it was convenient, instead of having embraced it all along? Would it be better to never have embraced it at all?

"Here," Rudra says, handing me a packet of wet wipes. I blink, staring down at it. I was so lost in my thoughts I didn't realize he asked the shopkeeper for it.

"Th-thank you," I stutter. He stares at my hand as I rip the plastic off the package. When he notices me looking, his gaze darts away,

"Do you want anything else?" he asks gently.

I look around at the shop. "I'll have a Frooti, I think." The shopkeeper hands me a small bottle of cold Frooti. After I pay, we walk back to his car. "I appreciate you stepping in for me. I didn't expect you to," I say.

Rudra shrugs. "She didn't mean it, though, you know? She doesn't think any of that."

"I know. She's not dense. The opposite, in fact, which is why she knew if she said that, it would hurt me most." I turn to him as we reach the car, letting the cold of the bottle soak into my palms. "I don't blame her. I'm pretty sure everyone feels the same way about diaspora folk. Even you."

Rudra pauses with his hand on the door handle. He appears to hesitate for a moment. "I don't want to lie. I *did* think of you as a spoiled American kid. But you're not. Not that my opinion matters."

I smile. "It doesn't, but thanks nonetheless."

"And for the record," he adds, "I don't think you try hard to be Indian or any of that." That almost shyness I saw earlier skates across his face, coloring his cheeks. "Your Indo-western style's pretty dope."

"Thank you," I say, and bite my lip. Did Rudra Desai just . . . compliment me? "Your style's *pretty dope* too." A small laugh escapes me.

Now, why *would you say that?!*

Rudra grins. "Thanks. That's the first time someone's said that to me."

Wanting to brush away the fact that I just *complimented* Rudra Desai's style, I quickly shift the topic, "Oh, before I forget—I have a playlist. For the road. It's all Bollywood songs, though—not sure if that's your taste. Could I play it?"

"Yeah, of course." He shrugs. "You could've asked before."

"I didn't want to impose. You are driving us all the way there, after all."

As we both get into the car, I mentally let out a sigh of relief, surprised at the turn of events. Rudra is so much nicer than I thought he would be. I just assumed he'd been brainwashed by Priti into always taking her side, but I won't forget the way he stood up for me. My mind takes me back to the moment at the party yesterday when he handed me the water, genuine concern creasing his face.

I'm touched by his kindness, even if I don't say it.

"I've turned off my Bluetooth," he says, starting the car. "You can connect yours. It's, uh . . . Jimi Hendrix's Groupie."

I guffaw so loud Priti takes out an earbud, staring at us. "What's going on?"

"Ignore the name," Rudra says, rolling his eyes. He starts pulling out of the petrol pump station and turns the knob of the AC. Thank god, because I'm already starting to sweat. Mumbai is excruciatingly sultry this time of the year. "It used to be just Jimi Hendrix, but Priti decided to change it. *For funsies*, in her words."

"Never say *funsies* ever again," Priti says. "You sound like an ass."

"You can't gatekeep *funsies* from me."

"Watch me." Priti points her finger at him accusatorily. "And can you blame me? You used to be *obsessed* with Jimi Hendrix when you started playing the guitar. Like, you would *not* shut up about how he was the most legendary guitarist of all time."

For a brief moment, the image of a tween Rudra Desai yapping his head off about his favorite guitarist pops into my mind, and I have to admit, it's kind of adorable.

"So if I have this right, *you* are the aforementioned groupie?" I laugh.

"He *is* the most legendary guitarist of all time," Rudra says, resolutely ignoring my question. He drives us back onto the main road. "Besides, if we were to start unpacking the shit you used to obsess over, Priti, this conservation would never end."

"Oh, shut up." Priti turns to me. "Is this your playlist?" Her face changes suddenly, as if she's just realized who she's speaking to. "Oh, wait, I'm not talking to you."

I ignore her statement and finally click play. At first, I'm annoyed Priti's still acting like *I'm* the one that did something wrong, but then Rudra forces her to start navigating, "Dil Dhadakne Do" plays through his terrific speakers, and a calm sets in.

This road trip isn't off to a great start, but at least I get the sweet relief of AC and have the whole back seat to myself now.

7
THE INTERNET HAS SERIOUSLY CORRUPTED OUR GENERATION

Mumbai, Friday

We get on the Mumbai–Pune expressway, and from there it's a straightforward route to Baner. We plan to stop once at the food mall that falls on the expressway, about fifty minutes before we hit Lonavala, to grab some coffee and use the toilet.

Since I have some relative privacy in the back seat, I *finally* text Amrit.

@notkrishnakumar

Hey, I'm sorry I didn't text before.
It's been a long day.

The three dots and *seen just now* appear on the footer of the chat so quickly I get whiplash. My heart starts beating really hard behind my rib cage, and Priti shoots me a death glare right at the moment Amrit's text pops in.

@amrit_ka_achar

No that's okay! I knew you were traveling today

Oh, right. I'd forgotten he thought I was on my way back and not on my way to *him*. A nervous "ha ha" squeaks out of me at that, making both Rudra and Priti glance back at me.

"Sorry," I mumble.

Priti gives me a look that has *What the fuck is wrong with you?* written all over it, but I ignore her, reading the next few texts Amrit's sent me.

@amrit_ka_achar

I should've thought about that before hitting send on my previous text

I've been a nervous wreck the entire day

The entire day? Over silly old *me*? I nearly squeal as I type out my reply, shaky fingers goofing up a few spellings. But it doesn't matter, because Amrit Acharya has been a nervous wreck. For me!

@notkrishnakumar

Don't be! My phone's been on flight mde all day. I omly saw the text just now

I wonder if I sound too eager and should be playing more hard to get. It's what my friends would tell me, but I'm so sick of doing that. I've been tiptoeing around Amrit all summer, dropping hints but never really making it obvious (not that I was particularly good at any of that). If I hadn't, if I'd trusted my gut about Amrit's feelings for me, I probably would've had my tongue in his mouth last night.

Instead, I'm here, still a unicorn and stuck in a car (a very comfortable car, granted) with Priti and Rudra. I need a new plan of action. I need to be genuine about what I want and not fling this last shred of a chance out the window.

@notkrishnakumar

Look, Amrit. I really wanted to kiss you last night.

This is the first time I've ever been this direct with *anyone*. It feels unreal but freeing. Like I'm finally catching up in a race I've been falling behind in for so long.

I set my phone aside, facedown, and open the window, letting the cool night air whoosh into the car. It's beautiful outside, with the dark silhouettes of trees and hills against a navy-blue canvas sprinkled with stars. I close my eyes and inhale deeply, clasping my hands tightly in my lap as my heart turns into a hot-air balloon.

When my heart is the size of my fist again, I pick up my phone and gingerly open the chat.

@amrit_ka_achar

I'm such an idiot.

I should've kissed you before I left. I wanted to.

@notkrishnakumar

This doesn't feel real to me

Like wow . . . you like me back.
Kick me.

@amrit_ka_achar

Never. But yeah . . .

I clutch my phone to my chest. The wind pushes my hair onto my face as a car with bright headlights zooms past us. Through the gaps between my strands, I spot a sign saying *Food Mall*, and Rudra swerves onto a road that forks off the highway.

We find a free spot in the huge parking lot, and I'm surprised that although it's just past nine p.m., the mall is brightly lit up and packed with people.

"We'll take twenty minutes, max," Priti says, undoing her seat belt. Rudra and I nod, and the three of us get out of the car.

I practically hop up the small set of steps to the food mall. It's a rectangular, open plaza of sorts, with a bunch of eateries crowded along the perimeter and seating arranged at the center. I desperately need a coffee if I have to stay up until we get to Baner. *With* milk and sugar, not the tasteless, bitter brew Rudra had earlier.

I pass a street corn thelawala and the heavenly scent of buttered corn peppered with masala wafts to my nose, briefly interrupting my quest for coffee. Before I know it, I'm asking the vendor for a large serving of masala corn (with extra butter, please) and digging into it with an ice-cream spoon.

Then I stop by the café, get a mocha, and start walking, checking the place out.

To my utter delight, there's a book stall on the opposite side of the plaza. Under a big banner with *Sai Book Fair* printed along it in bold letters, there are tables piled with paperbacks, and a staircase winds behind them, piled with even more books. I excitedly rush toward it, coffee cup in one hand and masala corn in the other.

I scan the stacks on the tables first and then shuffle up the stairs, finding the collection slowly becoming better the more I dig in. It looks like there's another floor up there, which means more books.

"Where are you going?"

I turn to find Rudra standing at the foot of the stairs, a CocoCart cup in his hand.

"Upstairs," I say, frowning. It's not like our twenty minutes are up—I have fifteen to spare. "To check out the books."

"It doesn't look safe," Rudra says. "There's barely any light up there."

"It's just books." I turn back to the towers of books. "I'll be fine. I have my phone."

I resume walking up the stairs, eyes widening as I spot the collection on the floor above. Gosh, how many books are up here? That's when I hear a scuffle, and when I look back, Rudra's standing right behind me.

I nearly jump out of my skin. My foot catches on one of the book piles, and I trip, barely avoiding falling flat on my face. But Rudra grabs my arm just in time, very *Ishqbaaaz* style (don't judge me, I watched the show only because of my mom) and pulls me up.

Fortunately, I manage to save the books from being splashed by my coffee. Unfortunately, I drop my cup of masala corn in the process. I watch in horror as the corn spills all over the stairs, rivulets of red-stained, masala-filled juice running toward the stacks.

"Shit, shit, shit!" I gasp, setting my coffee on the ground, pulling the packet of wet wipes out of my pocket.

Rudra crouches down and helps me out. Luckily, we get the

staircase clean and the corn picked up before the shopkeeper catches us.

"You startled me," I say, looking down at my cup of corn forlornly.

"I'm sorry," Rudra says, and he genuinely sounds apologetic as he rubs the back of his neck. "I thought it'd be better if I just went with you."

"Why aren't you with Priti?" I ask before I can stop myself.

Rudra narrows his gaze. "We're not attached at the hip."

"No, I mean, is she okay on her own?"

"She's in a brightly lit food court with dozens of other people loitering about."

I choose to not say anything to that; instead, I pick up my coffee cup and climb the last few stairs. Rudra follows me closely, and I quickly forget my disappointment from having dropped my corn when I reach the second floor.

"Holy shit."

My jaw is practically sweeping the ground. Rudra's hands fall out of his pockets as we step into what looks like the biggest book warehouse I've ever seen, piled with thousands of paperbacks and hardbacks. Flickering white lights hum above us, filling the silence of the space. It's like a thrift bookstore, but ten times the scale. I rush to the first table and grab a title I recognize, bringing it to my nose and sniffing deeply.

I *love* it. It's so musty and new yet old at the same time.

I never imagined this being up here. It's like a whole other world. A book dimension with its portal at the base of the staircase. That I have only ten minutes left, probably less, is a crime!

I zigzag between the tables, running my fingers along covers and embossing. My fingertips are collecting dust, but I don't care. I glance behind me once to find Rudra walking at a much slower pace, stroking the spines with such tenderness it's as if he's afraid they'll crumble underneath his touch.

The lights at the far end of the warehouse are turned off, so it gets darker as we move, and I find myself being grateful he came along, because I do feel safer. I turn on my phone's flashlight and dodge through the tables to the walls lined with bookshelves.

"I hope the bookstores in Baltimore are this big," I say as Rudra comes up to stand next to me. I tend to ramble about books without caring who I'm rambling to, but it's his fault he followed me up here. He walked right into it. "I didn't get to see much of the city when I was visiting the college campus."

"You'll find out soon enough," Rudra says, plucking a volume off the shelves and combing through it. "Though I'm sure becoming a doctor is going to keep you more than a little busy."

"How do you know that?" My eyes widen in surprise. "The doctor thing, I mean."

"You've mentioned wanting to be on the premed track before." Rudra says, ducking his head back down to the book. He follows the words with his fingers as he reads them—one of my friends who's dyslexic does the same thing. They say it makes it easier for them to focus on the letters on the page.

He flips a page before turning the book over to read the back. He's not that tall, I notice now that he's standing right next to me. I'm about five foot three, and he looks like he could be five foot seven or five foot eight, max. Priti's probably just an inch or so shorter than him.

As I watch him, my mind goes back to what he said. I can't remember having mentioned my plans to him, so I'm assuming he overheard me speaking to my cousins. Not, like, eavesdropping, but during a group hangout, like the house party last night, when everyone was together. Was it something I said during one of those conversations—not knowing he was listening—that had given him such a poor impression of me?

"So I have a question," I say, sipping on my coffee, "about what you said earlier. It's kind of been nagging at me."

"You're going to need to be more specific," Rudra says as he puts the book back on the shelf.

"You said you thought I was spoiled—what did you mean by that?"

"Does it really matter?" Rudra leans against the bookshelf. Another thing people do that I find sickeningly attractive (fuck you, internet, you've corrupted our generation).

"I'm curious."

"It just felt to me like you were used to getting things your way."

"Like?"

"The whole Amrit thing." His eyes flash when he says that, though I don't know why. "As it turned out, *Priti* was the one who was more insistent."

So it wasn't just me who noticed Priti's own interests in getting to Goa. I really couldn't care less, though. She didn't bother to tell me she was applying to American universities; far be it from her to let me know her *real* intentions behind accompanying me to Goa.

"But isn't that good?" I ask haughtily. "Going after what you want? Amrit likes me, this is my last summer before college, and I want to be able to say I did something. At least I know what I want and I'm going after it."

"Knowing what you want is great, and I get that you're kind of a hopeless romantic, but it's the delusion behind it that seems, I don't know, over-the-top."

"*Delusion*?"

"The whole thing with the big romance of it all. You've built this fairy tale in your head. Having the perfect kiss with the perfect golden boy."

"Oh, I'm *sorry* if I don't want to feel regretful about what's supposed to be a special moment—my first kiss—for the rest of my life," I huff.

"Wait . . . your *first* kiss?" Rudra says, quietly shocked even as his eyes soften. "I—I didn't know."

It takes me a moment to figure out what he's so surprised about until I realize he had no clue about my . . . romantic inexperience.

But I have too little time to feel embarrassed before Rudra regroups to add, "That just proves my point even more. It can be a special moment without having to be perfect. It can be with someone who doesn't end up being 'the one' for you. Under spur-of-the-moment circumstances. You might like to meticulously organize every aspect of your life, but unplanned things are best sometimes."

"First off, you know you're totally mansplaining me right now, right?"

"I told you my opinion doesn't really matter. You're the one who asked for it."

"Second, what part of this heading-off-on-a-road-trip-to-crash-a-wedding-and-kiss-a-boy thing seems meticulously *planned* to you?"

"You're setting yourself up for disappointment. What if it doesn't turn out the way you want it to? What if he's not 'the one' for you?"

"FYI, I don't expect a fairy-tale kiss. And who said *anything* about Amrit being 'the one'?"

Rudra seems to pause at that, his face open and questioning. "You don't think he's 'the one' for you?"

"How could I? Our paths are heading in entirely separate directions. We're not even in a relationship!"

"So what does he mean to you, then?" he asks, and I might assume he was nervous if I didn't know any better.

"He's a crush. I like him—I've liked him all summer—and more importantly, he likes me back. As far as my expectations go, wanting to kiss a nice boy who's interested and knows what he's doing doesn't seem particularly *delusional*, Rudra."

"Experience doesn't really decide how good a kiss is going to be." Rudra's eyes fix fast on me when he says that, and I fight the urge to shake off the sudden, fluttery feeling that crawls up my body at his words. "It's all about confidence."

"Confidence comes with experience, genius."

"That *kind* of experience isn't everything. Look at you—you're smart," Rudra says. "You've done all those internships. Won those awards and medals. Headed all those clubs. You were valedictorian. If anything, *you* are the catch in this scenario."

I have to force myself to keep my mouth closed because it nearly falls open when I hear those words come from Rudra. I really must've stepped into an alternate dimension.

"How do you know all that?" I ask, flinging my now-empty coffee cup into a bin nearby. Him knowing about my dreams of being a doctor, I understand—I know how often I talk about it—but everything else?

"You followed me earlier today. On Instagram? I checked out your page."

Wait.

I forgot about that. I—being the idiot I am—didn't remember that in addition to my academic successes, I also have very juvenile song covers uploaded on my page. Given the number of followers he has, I assumed he wouldn't notice @notkrishnakumar with her measly seven hundred followers. Much less scroll through my page.

I want to bonk my head into the shelf right about now.

"Why are you making that face?" Rudra asks, and I register that my face is all scrunched up like I'm constipated or something.

"Just pretend you didn't ever look at my account."

"Uh. Okay," Rudra says. "Can I ask why, though?"

"I mean, it's embarrassing that you saw my page. With my mediocre singing reels. You have one hundred and forty thousand followers who love your music—you're *talented*."

"Thank you," he says bashfully. "You're a good singer. Definitely *not* mediocre—another thing to add to the list of why Amrit is the lucky one. Not that you have much to worry about to begin with. I've seen the way he looks at you—he knows it too."

For a moment, I'm taken aback Rudra noticed that at all. He's always been so quiet and distant, lurking in the background, that I forgot he was there during most of our parties and hangouts. Were Amrit and I so obvious about crushing on each other that even he noticed?

I raise my chin, tamping down the surprise and going back to the pressing matter at hand. "You know what I think?"

"What?"

"I think it's rich calling someone spoiled when you're loaded yourself," I say, thinking back to what started this whole argument.

"True." Rudra straightens, dusting the sleeve of his shirt. He discards his CocoCart cup.

I look at him in disbelief. "You're not going to counter that?"

"No."

"Why not?" I sound absurd, but Rudra has pushed all my buttons—and call it an achievement kink if you want, but now, I need to win this argument.

"Because you're . . . right?" he says, a smile playing along his lips. "Anyway, we should head back. Priti will probably be wondering where we are." He starts walking away, and I follow him, rolling my eyes, because *obviously* he's gone right back to thinking about Priti. Not that it concerns me, because my Raj is waiting for me in Goa.

And you bet I don't need anyone to tell me "जा कृष्णा जा, जी ले अपनी जिंदगी"[1] for me to go claim him.

Rudra takes a left, slipping out of the alley of bookshelves, and I start to turn, when there's a sudden jerk on the strap of my fanny pack. I look back, frowning, and find the denim material stuck on the hook of one of the racks.

"Wait up!" I call after Rudra, and yank at the strap.

Rudra halts, and I stumble, finally free. But to my utter horror, the rack, constructed out of rickety metal, wobbles dangerously for a moment. Before I can find my balance and rush to stabilize it, it teeters, piles of books falling to the floor.

And then the entire thing topples like a house of cards.

There is a loud, resounding crash as metal hits cement. Books skid across the floor, and a cloud of dust whirls upward, whooshing right up my nostrils. Rudra and I are both frozen, watching the mess I've just created. My nose tickles, and I shut my eyes, hoping to let the sneeze out, but nothing comes.

Great.

Just fucking great.

Trust me and my clumsy ass to pull over an *entire rack of books* when we're already running late.

There is a shout from the other end of the warehouse, and it takes me a second, mid-sneeze, to realize we're going to get caught. But Rudra is quick to react, and he's grabbing my arm and pulling me to the right, into a narrow corridor between bookshelves set so close together I can barely move without almost shoving more racks to the floor.

---

1 *Language*: Hindi; *Translation*: Go, Krishna, go, live your life.

Rudra stops at the end of the corridor, where a rack is stacked up against the wall, creating a dead end. I skid to a stop, breathing heavily.

"Where—"

"Shh," Rudra says, pressing his fingers to my lips, and that successfully manages to shut me up.

He's squinting through the gaps in the metal frame, distracted. I watch him, not daring to even breathe. I can't think beyond the facts that his fingers are *on my lips* and that he's closer than he's ever been.

It's dark here, but I spot a flash of movement from the corner of my eye, and the grumbling of a man in Marathi. I don't understand what he's saying, but he sounds very annoyed. Annoyed enough that if we get caught here, we're royally screwed.

Rudra turns toward me, and retracts his hand, as if just realizing he was touching my lips. He suddenly looks all flustered and sheepish. It hardly compares to how I'm feeling, enveloped in this dark, tiny space with him and that inviting apricot scent of his.

My neck is turning hot, whether from the lack of air here or Rudra standing inches away from me, I don't know. The last time I was this close to a guy was when I was with Amrit last night, sitting on the couch.

It feels like that happened weeks ago.

The man mutters something, sighs, and starts walking away, back in the direction he came from. Thankfully, he seems to have decided to sort the clutter out later. Because I don't think I could spend one moment more here with Rudra Desai without feeling like my legs will turn to jelly.

"Let's leave before he gets back," Rudra whispers, and I jerk my head to the side so fast I get a face full of book dust in my nose.

Unfortunately, that triggers the sneeze I was about to let out minutes ago. I clamp my palm over my nose, fighting the ticklish, uncomfortable sensation, but before I know it, the sneeze rips free. And it's not muted or dainty, as I hope it will be.

The sound is deafening in the quiet of the space.

And it doesn't happen just once. I sneeze again, and then *again*.

Rudra looks stunned. I don't know whether to be horrified or laugh.

When I finally come up for air, my hair falling into my face, I hear footsteps again, this time more hurried. Yells and curses in Marathi follow, and my mind goes, *Oops*.

But Rudra and I are already running. We dash out of the corridor and twist toward the staircase before the man has a chance to get a glimpse of us. Then it's down the flight of stairs, a sharp turn, and into the chaos of the food mall again.

There's no one behind the book tables, thankfully, so once we mingle into the crowd, there's little chance the man is going to find us. Rudra and I stop to take a breath by a juice shop, hands on our knees and adrenaline buzzing in our ears.

Then our eyes meet, through my mess of hair, and I can't help it. I burst into laughter. Rudra watches me, and although he doesn't laugh, he's grinning.

I've never seen him grin like that before. The shock on our faces when the rack initially fell, and then the astonishment on Rudra's when I sneezed, both play in my head, and at this point, I'm wheezing between chortles.

"Your face!" I say, wiping tears from my eyes. I know I'll look back on this moment in the future and cringe with embarrassment for my past self, but at this moment, I don't care. This day is turning out to be comically shitty.

"You sneeze like my dad" is all Rudra says in return.

8

IS A ROAD TRIP EVEN COMPLETE WITHOUT TWO PEOPLE FIGHTING FOR THE GOOD SEAT?

Mumbai, Friday

Rudra and I find Priti seated at a table near a chaat shop, an empty paper plate and half-full (or half-empty, if you're a pessimist) cup of lemon tea in front of her.

We join her, and she eyes us with a dirty look on her face that is drifting between annoyance—which isn't new—and curiosity. There are a few bhel morsels scattered across the plate, so I gather she probably had a chaat. Maharashtra's chaats are truly unbeatable.

"Where the hell were you guys?" Priti demands.

"The book fair," Rudra says, reaching for her cup of tea and taking a sip.

"The book fair?" Priti looks even more suspicious now. *"You?"*

"He came with me," I say. "It was dark upstairs, so he thought it'd be better if we went together."

She snatches her cup back from Rudra. If I'm not mistaken, she looks slightly . . . jealous. "You two were supposed to be here five minutes ago."

"Actually, we're just on time," Rudra says, glancing at his Titan watch. It beeps on cue, and he turns it off. "See?"

"What are we waiting around here for, then?" Priti gets to her feet. "Let's go."

As Priti marches away, Rudra's and my eyes meet, and we exchange a knowing glance, which is so new to me, because Rudra's not someone I would look at like we're sharing a secret. But since he doesn't know why Priti's so eager to get to Goa either, that's one thing we have in common.

The sight of Priti opening the door to the back seat of the car breaks me right out of my thoughts. Before I know it, I'm racing across the food mall to her, past Rudra, who jumps out of my way in surprise.

"You're supposed to be navigating!" I grab the door and slam it shut before Priti can get in.

Priti snatches her hand away just in time. "What the fuck, Krishna? You nearly broke my fingers!"

"The back seat's mine."

"Says who?"

"Says the owner of this car." I point to Rudra, who walks up, sighing.

Priti tries to wrench the door handle out of my grip, but I stay put, matching her glare with my own. I'm acting like a ten-year-old, but I'm not giving up the back seat privileges without a fight. Especially not after how she spoke to me at the petrol pump.

"Get out of my way, Krishna," Priti says, fisting her hands by her sides. "Before I hit you."

"No."

"Ruds!"

Rudra pauses on his way into the driver's seat. "What?" He thought he was being real smooth sneaking into the car. It's laughable.

"Tell her it's *her* turn to navigate."

"I'm not getting into this."

"Then why did you get involved earlier, bitch?"

"Because *you* were the one being a bitch."

Priti uses her shoulder to try to butt me out of the way, but I stay put, tightening my grip on the handle. She stamps her foot in frustration. "This isn't fair! I already did my turn."

"Fine," I say. "You want the back seat?"

"Yes," she says through her teeth.

I lift my chin. "Then apologize to me."

"Apologize to you for *what*?"

"For what you said earlier."

Priti crosses her arms over her chest. "I'm not apologizing for that."

"Great. The back seat's mine, then."

Priti glares at me for a whole minute before Rudra sighs, speaking up, "Just apologize to her, Priti."

"I thought you weren't getting into this?"

Rudra raises his hands defensively. "I just want to be on my way again."

I expect Priti to take the front seat just so she can avoid apologizing to me, and I prepare myself for the mix of glee at retaining my back seat privileges and feeling terrible that Priti doesn't even know how much she hurt me, or maybe she *does* know but doesn't give a—

"I'm sorry."

"What?" I say, dumbfounded.

"I said I'm sorry." Priti drops her hands, resigned.

I'm so shocked I think I temporarily paralyze myself.

"I crossed a line earlier," she says, and I'm not dreaming it up—she sounds *genuine* about it. "That bit about the Desi identity thing especially. I'm sorry, okay?"

When I can finally get my feet to move, I mumble, "Okay," and step aside.

Priti doesn't mutter anything when she gets into the car, not like I expect her to.

I'm still reeling from her apology when we're back on the highway. I did demand it in exchange for something else, but I guess Priti has a heart after all.

Cruising along the expressway at this time of the night is a cinematic experience. I lean my head against the window, my warm breath fogging the glass, soaking up the view outside.

We're moving at a speed of over a hundred kilometers per hour, which might be fun for the passengers but can get quite monotonous for the driver, so I keep glancing at Rudra to make sure he isn't dozing off. But he remains alert, hands steady on the steering wheel, body relaxed in his seat.

When the first tunnel comes, I roll my window down and stick my head halfway out, relishing the bite of the cool night air. The lights lining either side of the tunnel flash by, blurring together into a single gold strip. The wind is so strong my hair nearly comes undone from my butterfly clip, and I crow, "*Woo-hoo!*" with joy. I grin as my voice boomerangs back to me.

We emerge on the other side and I close the window, pushing my hair out of my face. I glance in Rudra's direction, half expecting to find him annoyed by my rowdiness, but I'm beyond surprised to find him smiling instead. It's nothing like Amrit's full-on, toothy smile, but the corners of Rudra's mouth are hiked up in amusement. It's nice to see Rudra smile, because he looks ridiculously cute. He has these small dimples below his lips, and I wonder how I didn't notice them before . . .

Hold up.

Shit.

Am I so boy-deprived that I'm finding Rudra increasingly cute with every passing moment? It's not like it's been *days* since I last saw Amrit. It's been less than twenty-four hours.

I need to see a doctor. There has to be some sort of treatment for extreme horniness.

"There's a sunroof in this car, by the way," Rudra says, taking a long, winding turn. "You can use it. At the next tunnel."

"Seriously?"

"Of course. It's coming up in a bit."

Half an hour later, I unbuckle myself from the seat as Rudra presses the button to open the sunroof. There's a hissing noise and a low hum as the panel above slides open, fast-moving air gushing in. Priti sits up, startled, taking out her earbud as I wriggle between the seats to the back.

She frowns. "What are you doing?"

"Using the sunroof."

Priti shuffles to the side as I slip through the gap. My shoes are already off, and I unclip my hair, letting it flow loose. I climb onto the seat, gripping the edges of the panel, and hoist myself up.

"Careful," Priti says. "There's a tunnel coming. Don't let it lop your head off."

I'm surprised at her worry about my head remaining attached to my person—but I suppose decapitation is a fair concern even for your least favorite cousin.

The wind hits me sharply as I stick my head out, knocking the breath out of me for a moment. I push myself up until I'm standing at full height on the seat and waist-high out the sunroof.

"Holy mother—" I yell, voice cutting off abruptly as we enter the tunnel.

The people in the cars overtaking ours stare at me as they pass. I throw my hands up, my hair flying in a sheet behind me. My voice bounces off the curving walls of the tunnel, amplified as it ricochets back toward me. This feels *incredible*.

There's a tug on the hem of my kurti. I look down. I'm surprised to find Priti squatting on the seat and pushing herself up.

"Scoot," she says, shimmying her lithe body through the gap to stand beside me. Because she's taller, her torso's almost all the way out. I grin as her hair blows back, bangs parting and exposing her forehead.

Priti catches me looking and holds her bangs in place with her hand, covering the forehead she's been self-conscious about since she was six. "Don't look!" she has to yell for me to hear her over the soaring wind.

"Can you not? Everyone loves your face!" I yell back, and she rolls her eyes, but a hint of a smile pulls at her lips as she lets her hair fly back once more.

"This is amazing!" Priti howls, her hands cupping her mouth.

I join her, and we bay like twin wolves until the end of the tunnel, cramped close together in this small space. We leave the lights behind, rushing out the other side, and the expansive, open sky fills my vision again.

"The stars look so beautiful," I effuse, craning my neck upward. The trees and hills fringe my vision, scraping the horizon, and it feels like we're driving through a huge dome. It's in moments like these I wonder how people before Aristotle ever believed the Earth could be flat. How people *still* believe the Earth is flat.

There's one more tunnel on the expressway, and then Rudra has to inform us, "That was the last one," for us to finally settle down.

My eyes are so dry I have to keep them closed for long intervals. Priti's wavy hair stands up in a frizzy halo around her face, as if she's been cupping a Van de Graaff generator, and she looks ridiculous. I burst into laughter.

But there's no bitter clapback or heated glare. Not like usual. In fact, she laughs too, acting more like the Priti she used to be before I moved.

More like the Priti who used to be my best friend.

9

ASEXUAL PEOPLE ARE EXCELLENT AT DOLING OUT ROMANTIC ADVICE—OR SO THEY CLAIM

Pune, Saturday

When we reach Pune, it's midnight, but the city is as alive as it would be during the day.

"Take a left, just here," I say, glancing down at my phone.

Rudra takes the turn into a driveway leading to a massive food court occupying two floors of the five-story building. There's a sign saying *Pure Veg Restaurant* above the glass entrance, and golden lights illuminate the interior. The floors above house other restaurants, and at the very top, perched on the roof of the building, is a red neon sign reading *OYO Townhouse*.

"*This* is the OYO?" Rudra asks. "It looks fancy."

"What, you thought I'd book us a cheap-ass room?" Priti says. "Phoo. I might be broke now, but I have standards. Oh, and you both owe me a thousand rupees each." I'm already taking out my phone to send her the money. I *hate* owing people, especially Priti.

After Rudra finds a space to park, we get out of the car and I stretch my arms and legs, sighing in satisfaction as I hear four distinct pops.

"Grab your bags, bitches," Priti says, hauling out her three pieces of luggage. I tug mine out too—I packed lighter than usual, so they're easy to carry.

As Rudra loops his hand through the strap of his guitar case, hefting it onto his shoulder, a lock of hair unlooses from his ponytail. I stretch my hand out to push it away, then realize what the *hell* I'm doing and jerk it back so hard my suitcase topples and falls smack on my toes.

Owwww.

I wince and start doing a one-legged hop while clutching my foot, and Rudra watches me, his lips twitching as he tries to repress a smile. When the throbbing pain from my toes subsides, I set my leg down and sheepishly look up at Rudra, who witnessed the whole Krishna-being-a-clumsy-dork-for-the-millionth-time-in-her-life debacle.

"You good?" he asks, and purses his lips.

"Yeah, erm—I'm fine. Let's go."

Once inside the OYO, we walk into a huge lobby that is miles better than I thought it would be. Not that I have much experience with OYOs, but they're the same as Airbnbs—mid-quality, affordable, and unmarried-couple-friendly rooms, which helps when you have partner(s) to have sex with. Me? Zero partners, and definitely zero sex. I'm so *anything*-deprived I nearly brushed Rudra's hair away from his face.

Priti checks us in, and we're taken to the fifth floor, where we're handed keys to two rooms on opposite sides of the corridor. Rudra takes the room on the right, while Priti and I enter the one on the left.

There's an awkward moment as I pause, unsure whether I should say *good night* or *see you tomorrow* to Rudra. But Priti doesn't, and Rudra barely throws me a glance before he enters his room. I think the better of it, not wanting to embarrass myself any further (I've already hit max on the meter for the week), and lumber in after Priti.

"This is neat," I observe, scouring the room. Spotless sheets on the double bed, no weird marks on the wall (the last time I stayed in an OYO was during our cousins' trip to Daman, and there were these handprints on the wall; I didn't dare imagine where or whom they'd come from), and a clean-looking toilet.

Thank god. A road trip is the *worst* time to get a UTI.

Priti sprawls on the bed, her shoes discarded to the side and luggage tucked away into the wardrobe. "Could you turn on the AC? I'm drowning in sweat."

I grab the remote from the bedside table and turn it on, sighing in relief as the cool wind gusts through the room. I lie on the bed beside Priti, both of us watching the ceiling fan spin.

"Are you going to sleep?" I ask her.

"Yes. I'm dead tired."

I give my underarms a quick sniff and make a face. *Okay*, nope. I push myself off the bed, grab my suitcase from the wardrobe, and pull out my towel, bathrobe, and nightclothes. "I'm taking a bath."

"Hmm," Priti mumbles, her eyes shut and body splayed out like the Vitruvian Man.

I sigh. "Priti, you haven't even brushed your teeth."

"Hmm-mm."

"Priti."

"Just wake me up when you're done," she says, irritation coating her voice.

Anyone who ever says *Wake me up blah-blah* never actually

means it. When Priti gets up tomorrow with her mouth smelling like shit, the previous day's eye makeup running down her face, and a pimple poking out of her chin, she's going to regret having given in to slumber.

I hang my clothes on the hooks behind the bathroom door, strip, and drag my feet toward the shower, turning the knob all the way to the left. I've always preferred a hot bath to a cold one. I have lazy muscles and slow circulation, so the heat tends to get my blood flowing. Besides, it's cooler here in Pune, so it's not like Mumbai, where some days it gets so hot that you absolutely can't *not* take a cold shower.

I wrap my arms around my body, waiting for the water to get hot, intermittently dunking my toes in. But for some reason, the water stays ice-cold. I stand there, buck naked and shivering, for nearly five minutes before giving up.

A groan tears out of me. Should I hop into the shower for a moment? I can't risk ending up with a cold, though. How am I supposed to kiss Amrit with a runny nose?

That horrifying thought motivates me to put on my clothes again, and when I step out, I have an idea—I could use Rudra's bathroom.

I glance at Priti, snoring peacefully on the bed, and consider waking her up. But then I'm reminded of how she looked at Rudra and me weirdly back at the food mall. Priti is too shrewd, and I don't want to give her another reason to suspect I have a thing for Rudra. Because I *don't* have a thing for Rudra.

Besides, Rudra is in love with Priti. And given her twinge of jealousy earlier, I'm sure she's in love with him too.

I replace the room key in the key card holder with a visitor card I find in my fanny pack so the electricity in our room stays on, and shut the door closed behind me.

I knock on Rudra's door once, then again a minute later. When he doesn't open the door even after that, I press my ear to it, brow furrowed, straining my ears for the faintest sound within.

And *of course* he chooses to open the door that very second. I feel myself tip forward, balance lost, and grab the first thing I can to support myself.

Rudra's T-shirt.

Imagine (seriously, just imagine) you open your door, and you find a girl you barely know eavesdropping before she stumbles into your room, her forehead smacking your chin. Not just that. She grabs a *fistful of your clothing.*

Bad, isn't it?

It gets worse.

Because I don't move. I just stay there, frozen, face smushed into Rudra's collarbone, inhaling a new scent, a good scent, even better than before, his freshly showered hair wet and cold.

"Um," Rudra says, clearing his throat. "Could you—"

"Ohmygod," I say, leaping away from him. "I'm sorry . . . I didn't . . . I thought you . . ." *And she can't even string a coherent sentence together.*

"It's fine," he says, brushing me off. It's probably my bizarre imagination, but I think (I *think*) I see a blush redden his cheeks. "What's up?"

"I—There's no hot water in our bathroom, and I need a shower. I was wondering if there's hot water in your room?"

"Oh. Yeah, I bathed. The water's warm. Come on in." Rudra steps back, leaving the door ajar, and I shuffle in reluctantly.

"Great. Thank you so much."

I quickly step into the bathroom and shut the door behind me, eager to not look him in the eye and be reminded of that disastrous moment again.

I'm *such* an idiot. What was I thinking, putting my ear to his door like that and stumbling right into him? And staying there? God!

The bathroom floor is still a little wet, but most of the water has been wiped to the drain. I nod in approval. I despise it when people don't wipe the floors after they shower. It smells like lemon soap in here, and I spot the cologne he must've used perched on the windowsill. Of course Rudra owns a luxury scent. No wonder he smells so good. Maybe once I've taken a bath, I'll sneak a couple of sprays, just to experience what it's like trying on expensive perfume.

I repeat the ritual and stand before the shower, bracing myself for the cold again, but piping hot water greets me instead.

Ten minutes later, I'm feeling so much better and cleaner. It's a wonder what a shower can do to a person. I put on a loose pair of shorts and an oversize T-shirt, wipe the bathroom floor, and quickly spray Rudra's scent under my arms. Instantly worried he might detect it, I spritz on some of my own deodorant, and once I'm convinced I've rid the crime scene of evidence, I step out.

I clutch my dirty clothes and towel in one hand and comb my fingers through my hair with the other. The AC is on, and the steam from the bathroom clashes strongly with the cold. Goose bumps erupt all over my arms as I shut the door behind me.

Rudra is perched on the edge of the bed, playing the guitar. He hums softly under his breath, intermittently mouthing something indiscernible, his gaze fixed on his phone. Only the small golden lamps by the sides of the bed are turned on, so his face is mostly illuminated by the blue light of the screen. I wince, praying for his poor eyes because he clearly doesn't have night mode turned on.

"I'm done," I announce, shivering.

"Cool," he replies without looking up.

There's something annoyingly attractive about guitarists that I've never been able to put a finger on. And this is *especially* annoying because it's Rudra Desai, the *not*-sunshine boy, who, by the way, is in love with my cousin. In case we all forgot that teeny tiny detail there. Especially attractive because I can't help but notice how slender his fingers look as they move over the strings of his guitar, and how his Adam's apple bobs in his throat as he hums, his voice a low vibrato, and how his loose, damp hair falls in flowy waves around his face. It's only when he raises his hand to push his hair behind his left ear that I realize my nipples are hard from the cold.

Oh *god*, I forgot to wear a bra!

"What?" Rudra looks up, staring at me.

I wrap my arms around my chest and stare back at him, trying to look nonchalant. "What?"

"Do you need something else?"

Valid question, Krishna. What excuse do *you have for not having left already?*

"Oh, not really," I say, pursing my lips and desperately trying to think of something else to say. "I was just trying to figure out what song you're covering?"

There, perfect.

"Not covering." Rudra turns his attention back to his phone and guitar. "Composing."

"Composing? As in, an original?"

"Yep," he says, chewing on his lower lip, probably not having expected me to be interested in what he's doing. Or maybe he thinks I'm just trying to be polite because not asking at all and leaving might be rude.

A part of me wants to leave, given my current braless state, but the other is itching to listen to Rudra sing.

The latter wins.

"Can I listen?" I ask, arms still around my chest, hoping he sees that I'm being sincere.

Rudra hesitates. "It's not complete."

"That's okay."

"All right." He scoots back on the bed, and the sheet smooths out in front of him, leaving space for me to sit. I dump my dirty clothes and towel on the chair nearby. Then I perch on the edge of the bed, which creaks ever so slightly, and peek at his phone. His Notes app is open, with a bunch of lyrics and chords haphazardly written down.

"Ready whenever you are," I say, propping my bare legs on the bed. Rudra glances at them once before hastily looking away.

"Here goes." He inhales deeply, eyes shuttering closed, and begins to strum. He plays a soothing fingerstyle pattern, periodically tapping the wood of the guitar in a distinct rhythm. The tune reminds me of the songs one would play in open cars on road trips, like "Khaabon Ke Parindey." His fingers move smoothly over the frets and strings, and I watch them in fascination.

And then he starts singing.

His voice is soft yet deep, and his lyrics switch between English and Hindi with ease, much like in Prateek Kuhad's songs. His enunciation is clear, so the lyrics are easy to follow, and at one point, I shut my eyes to pay attention to them. It takes me a bit to figure out the meaning, but when I do, I find myself pleasantly surprised.

I open my eyes about halfway through the second verse, finding his still closed. I fixate on his Adam's apple again, his lips, and the fluid motion of his hands. He finishes the song with a beautiful, melodic outro. I gulp as his eyes finally open, a dazed look in them.

I'm *floored.*

And so on edge that when he directly meets my gaze, my insides turn to mush.

He sets aside his guitar. "So yeah. That was it."

I think I've forgotten how to speak, because I can't come up with a single adjective, let alone a sentence, to explain how I felt about his song. And how it shot an arrow so close to everything I've felt the past couple of years.

There's only a bare gap on the bed between us. The room is so quiet all I can hear is the sporadic dripping of water in the bathroom and the groan of the AC.

"The song was about . . . bisexuality, wasn't it?" I finally say, tentative. "About questioning if your identity is valid because you haven't been with a boy?"

Rudra's eyes widen in surprise. "H-how did you know?"

"I feel the same way. Always questioning if I'm bi enough."

"Oh." Rudra looks away, biting the inside of his cheek. "That's, um . . . me too."

I can't help the warmth that pours into me.

Rudra is *bi*, like me!

A goofy grin splits my face. I just love getting to know other queer Indians; it makes me feel a lot less alone. I rub my arms as a fresh wave of goose bumps pops up. "Also, that was beautiful. That fingerstyle was orgasmic, and so was your voice."

It's only when I've uttered the sentence out loud that I grasp how it sounds.

One corner of Rudra's mouth hikes up. "*Orgasmic*?" That maddeningly cute dimple appears again.

"You know what I mean," I say, flushed.

"No, please, enlighten me," Rudra teases, which is so unlike him.

After a moment, he adds, "Thanks, though."

I duck my head, vacantly drawing lines on the bedsheet with my finger. "I—I'm not out to everyone yet. So would it be okay if you said nothing of this to Priti?"

"Of course," Rudra says. "Though you might be surprised to find she's a lot more understanding of this than you think."

I shake my head. "Things are just too rough between us right now. *You* know."

"I understand."

"Does she know? Priti—does she know about you?"

"Yes, she does. But hey"—I lift my head, meeting his gaze—"whether or not she knows about me doesn't matter. I won't tell her about you."

We look at each other again for a moment too long, and I notice how soft his eyes are, his sclerae dotted by the deepest-brown irises. Were they always this . . . *warm*? There's a tug on the corners of his mouth, the hint of a smile, and my gaze drops to his lips—before my conscience is suddenly activated and gives me a swift roundhouse kick. I drop my legs to the floor, face poker-hot and body ice-cold.

"All right—I guess I'll get going."

Rudra nods quickly. Too quickly. "Yeah."

"Good night," I say. "Thanks for letting me use your washroom."

"No problem." Rudra ducks his head back down to his phone. "Good night."

I rush to the door, my face burning. I'm surprised I haven't turned into a beetroot already. It's only when I'm out in the corridor again and the door's shut behind me that I take a second to pause.

I haven't had many *moments* with people in my life, but the few that came close were with Amrit. The heat filling my cheeks, the butterflies flapping their wings in my stomach, the feeling of nervous anxiety that makes me want to throw up and give in to the skittishness at the same time. They're as familiar as a next-door neighbor.

Oh god.

Am I starting to *like* Rudra?

When I'm back in my bed, it's that thought that keeps me from falling asleep, so against my better judgment, I start scrolling through Rudra's Instagram, stalking his account thoroughly, scouring every video or post he's ever put up.

Talk about desperate.

The worst part? It makes my silly crush on Rudra just *grow*. Everything about him suddenly feels new, as if I'm discovering him for the first time instead of, you know, getting to know him better, having met him first seven years ago and all that. The fact that he's so talented doesn't help. Like, talent is *the* single most attractive thing in a person, right after intellect.

I hate this.

I'm on my way to kiss a boy who might be the nicest guy I've ever met, happens to be cute as shit, *and* likes me back. That has never happened to me! And here I am, having *moments* with Rudra Desai when Amrit Acharya is less than a day's journey from me. Amrit Acharya, the boy I've been obsessed with all summer.

The boy who wants to kiss me.

I want to throw up. I told him I liked him yesterday, and I do, I really do. So why is *this* happening?

Once I've hit the end of Rudra's page, his oldest posts going back six years, I text Srishti and tell her everything. As always, she's up and responds immediately—which, she *shouldn't* be, because she's leaving for her trip early tomorrow.

@srishti_without_an_h

wow krish i just checked out mr desai's page

dude he's too good. im mind blown.

he could do with a better handle tho

@notkrishnakumar

Bro I need advice on what I'm supposed to do.

I can't spend another day with Rudra bc I'm finding him more and more attractive by the second

@srishti_without_an_h

okay so like . . . team #krishudra all the way then?

@notkrishnakumar

THAT IS NOT WHAT I'M SAYING!!!

IM ON MY WAY TO KISS AMRIT, REMEMBER??

Besides, Priti likes him too. It isn't right.

@srishti_without_an_h

only if she had explicitly told you she likes him

but she hasn't

you have no idea about her really.

@notkrishnakumar

Weren't you team #krishrit until yesterday??

@srishti_without_an_h

#krishrit has a nicer ring to it, but imho amrit is so done

rudra has got that grumpy thing
going which is like perfect for you,
opposites attract and all that

@notkrishnakumar

You're not making this any better

Besides, he's not really . . . grumpy.
He's just quiet, and reserved, and
he broods.

You know he told me
I had delusional ideas
about romance?

@srishti_without_an_h

it's like y'all are made
for each other lol

@notkrishnakumar

SRISHTI!!!! THE CHOICE
SHOULD BE REALLY CLEAR!!!
It's Amrit

@srishti_without_an_h

look, if you were THAT into amrit,
it wouldn't HAVE to be a choice.
you wouldn't (and i say this respectfully)
be crushing on another guy within
24 hours of saying goodbye.

@notkrishnakumar

God, I'm a terrible person.
I should just change my handle to
@terribleperson

@terribleperson2491

There

@srishti_without_an_h

AHSJNDJWKNS NOT YOU ACTUALLY DOING IT!

CHANGE IT BACK BEFORE SOMEONE SEES IT IDIOT

and you are NOT a terrible person!!! you're a normal teenager, with hormones and feelings AND YOU ARE NOT AMRIT'S GIRLFRIEND

you just wanted a fling with him anyway ffs

there's only one thing that can help you atp tbh

@terribleperson2491

What???

@srishti_without_an_h

change ur handle first

@notkrishnakumar

Okay fine. Done. TELL ME.

@srishti_without_an_h

a pros & cons list

@notkrishnakumar

Omg I'm not going to make a pros and cons list to pick between two guys

@srishti_without_an_h

why not? it's a perfectly good way to land upon a decision

ace peeps give really good romantic advice, you know that, which is why you should trust me on this

now will it be #krishudra or #krishrit? tune in to the next episode!

also, I should get some sleep, I've got to be up early tmmrw

when I get back on tuesday, tell me E V E R Y T H I N G

@notkrishnakumar

Pakka promise

I lie in bed with my phone facedown on my chest, Priti blissfully snoring next to me, and *really* think about it for a few moments.

A pros and cons list might be a good idea.

I pop open the Notes app and start typing. Except . . . I don't type in anything besides their names. Because a second later I feel like the shittiest person in the world for making a pros and cons list about them.

Here I am, feeling awful, when I *know* I'm not here to claim "the one." I'm here to add some tadka to my unromantic life. Rudra is a distraction, and an unattainable one, at that.

The choice isn't between Rudra and Amrit. The choice is whether to claim my kiss. *Without* drama. And Rudra comes with drama.

Which is why I finally set aside my phone, settle into the blankets, and shut my eyes.

10

CALL 911—THIS JAIN BOY EATS MEAT!

Pune, Saturday

Somebody throws a sock in my face. It reeks *so* bad, I'm yanked through all the stages of sleep and into consciousness in a split second. Hell, the Big Bang took more time.

I gag, sit up, grab the disgusting thing by its hem, and fling it as far away as I humanly can.

I'm going to kill Priti.

"Thank god," she says, picking up the horrid thing and stuffing it in her backpack.

She's fully dressed in a pair of sage-green camo pants and a black tee that's knotted at the front, baring her abs. She's wearing a black choker to match and a pair of *Phantom of the Opera* mask earrings she designed herself. Her hair is blow-dried and adroitly messy, and her eyes are lined with deep-black kajal and graphic liner, as always.

When did she even get ready?

"What the *hell* is wrong with you?" I yell, punching the blankets. I absolutely *detest* being woken up early. I got so little sleep last night (yes, it's my fault, but it's not like I did something bad enough to warrant getting socked in the face! Literally!).

"We are leaving in five minutes. So get your ass up and out of bed."

Again, what is her problem? Why is she so desperate to be on schedule? *I'm* supposed to be the one eager to get to Goa on time.

"Fuck you! We are not leaving. It's, what . . ." I grab my phone and glare at the screen. "Ohmygod. You threw a *sock* in my face at seven thirty a.m.! I'm going to murder—"

I'm interrupted by a sudden snort.

I frown, turning to the side, and am mortified to find *Rudra* seated on the sofa, his legs propped up on the glass table. He's wearing a loose half-sleeved maroon T-shirt and a pair of jeans and has a huge grin on his face. He looks so hot—especially because his hair is in a man bun this time—I forget for a moment that he's been there this whole time.

Shit.

He's been there *this whole time*.

"What are you doing here?" I squeak at Rudra, blood rushing to my face and filling it with heat.

"Waiting for the two of you," Rudra says, still grinning.

"Does privacy mean nothing to you? I'm still in bed!"

"Chill, Krishna," Priti says. "He came in, like, a minute ago."

"And where's the trust?" Rudra says, putting his legs down, eyebrows raised. "You literally took a shower in my room last night."

I fight the urge to pull the blankets up over my face and cover myself. My cheeks are fever hot.

"Back up," Priti says, her eyebrows knitting. "You took a shower in Rudra's washroom? Why?"

"There was no hot water."

"I *just* took a shower. It was perfectly warm."

"It wasn't *last night.*"

I can feel Rudra staring at me from the corner of my vision and get the feeling he thinks I lied to him. Great. Priti has me pinned with a suspicious glare, tinged with possessiveness, and it's similar to the one yesterday, except this time she's not even being subtle about it.

"Whatever," I say, breaking the silence. I hate this. "I'm going to change."

"Thank you," Priti says, throwing her hands up in relief.

Rudra gets to his feet as I swing my legs to the side of the bed, muttering darkly under my breath.

"I'm going to my room," he says. "Give you your *privacy.*" The cheeky asshole pauses just outside the door, dropping the final bomb. "Also, you left your clothes in my room last night, so I brought them back for you."

I glare at him as he walks out, the truth hitting me much too late.

Oh no.

Oh fuck no.

In my hurry to leave his room last night, I left my dirty clothes, my dirty *underwear* in his room!

Why does this sort of thing only happen to me?

Priti's staring at me with her eyes narrowed again, and if I don't get up now, she's going to fling another sock at me. The bed and cozy blankets implore me to stay as I get to my feet, and I'm so sleepy I want to throw a tantrum again. But I remind myself I can sleep in the car (fuck the rules about all of us staying up, I don't care) and somehow muster the energy to get ready.

Because I took a shower last night, I just need to brush my teeth, wash my face, and change. I grab my short, white, sleeveless kurti, a pair of high-waisted shorts, white eyeliner, and silver jhumkas, hoping it'll all blend into a cute outfit.

But when I go stand in front of the mirror, I'm horrified to find a pimple poking out the side of my face. And it's one of those pus-filled monsters that get uglier and bigger as the day moves along. Plus, they hurt like hell.

Could this day get any worse?

It *does*. It gets worse. And not just your regular mishap. Things go to shit. Smelly, diarrhea-induced shit.

But I'm not surprised. It's been building up to this.

Rudra's car doesn't start.

When we get in, he tries. Presses the ignition button, shifts gears, does some other stuff I don't really understand but find hot (*wrong time and place, Krishna*), and even gets out to open the hood.

He jumps back in shock as white smoke starts curling out of the engine. For a moment, I think the car's going to blow up and I'm going to die a virgin, but he walks back to us and speaks through the rolled-down window.

"It's a gasket failure. The engine's overheating."

"What does that mean?" I squeak. "Is it going to explode?"

Rudra's lips twitch. "Um, no, but you both should get out of the car while I figure out what to do."

It's the way he says *I* that gets me, because Priti looks even more blank than I do, and that's saying something.

We hop out of the car and stand to the side as Rudra looks up the nearest mechanic. As always, a few creeps in the parking lot stare at us, especially at Priti's stomach and my legs, and Priti throws them a sharp glare.

"Fucking sons of bitches," she mutters.

It's a miracle how no matter where in the world we might be, there's no shortage of unemployed randos who happen to be up at eight in the morning to ogle us as if they've never seen girls before.

Rudra gets on a call, pacing the gravel in front of the car, and I stand there uncomfortably, watching Priti and the men have a staring contest. Priti looks like she's about to stomp up to them and give them a piece of her mind, but I prefer not to engage. Especially not this early in the day.

Rudra gets off the phone. "I called the mechanic. He's on his way." He notices the men staring and steps in front of the two of us protectively, his jaw locking. "Let's head in and get some breakfast until then."

"How long will it take him to get here?" Priti asks, arms crossed over her chest.

"Fifteen minutes. I told him the car's overheated, but we'll have to wait to find out."

"Back up. The car will need repairs?"

"It *might* need repairs. And a gasket failure leading to a coolant leak means it needs to be replaced, usually, so it should take a day. Less if we tell them it's urgent."

"A *day*?" Priti and I shout at the same time. She looks just as horrified as I feel.

"That is going to put us behind schedule!" she cries.

"We won't get there on time!" I exclaim.

"Aren't the shaadi and reception the day after tomorrow?" Rudra says, surprisingly calm. "We'll be a day late and you'll miss some of the shaadi, but you'll still get to see Amrit."

That's true. I bite my bottom lip. "Yeah, but we won't get back in time for my flight home."

The thought of having to back out *after* making it to Pune is stressing me out, but Rudra sounds confident when he says, "We will, don't worry." He's beginning to look antsy. I think the sight of those men leering at us put him off. "Can we head in?"

But Priti's too agitated to notice. "The shaadi is the day after tomorrow, guys!" she says, looking about ready to throw a fit. "What if—what if, um . . . Amrit leaves right after the shaadi and doesn't even attend the reception?"

I raise my brows. "Amrit is going to be there until the reception, Priti. He's leaving the weekend after."

"This is bad. This is really bad."

"Priti," Rudra says pointedly. "What is actually bothering you?"

"Yeah, *I'm* supposed to be the one panicking about not making it in time," I say. It's so strange Priti's acting like this, and only weirder that Rudra has no clue what's going on either.

"It's just—" Priti looks flushed, at a loss for words. "I'm sorry if *I* don't want this trip to be an absolute waste of my time. I have so much to get done back home and instead I'm here, stranded with you both."

"Balls," Rudra says. "I've known you since fifth grade. I know when you're lying through your teeth."

"We're not exactly stranded," I say. "And I think Rudra and I are great company."

"Okay, jeez, stop ganging up on me," Priti says, seeming to quickly realize we're cornering her to get her to cave. "Let's just go inside. *Please.* I'm hungry." She huffs and marches toward the restaurant, escaping our questions and leaving Rudra and me exchanging glances. Again.

"You really don't know what's going on with her, do you?" I ask.

"I don't," Rudra says, and his eyes are brimming with hurt as they follow Priti, despite how hard he tries to hide it. He's down so bad, it makes me feel sorry for him. I'm indifferent to Priti's intentions—as long as *her* desperation gets *me* to Goa, I couldn't care less. But I can see that it's bothering Rudra. "I have no clue what's gotten into her lately."

I'm reminded of something similar Srishti said to me during the house party after I told her I'd seen Priti crying: *I know she's always avoided you, but usually she's at least cordial with the rest of us. I've barely spoken a word to her this time. Who knows what's going on with her?*

"Can I ask you something?" I say, and purse my lips thoughtfully.

"Yeah?" he asks, and turns to find me staring (*fuck*).

"During the party, Priti was crying when I rushed out onto the balcony to throw up." Relating the incident to Rudra, despite him having been a witness, is still embarrassing. "You were comforting her. Did that have something to do with whatever's going on with her now?"

Rudra shakes his head. "I don't think so." He doesn't let on to anything more than that, but I can't make out if he's telling the truth or simply avoiding the question. It's not like he would be willing to reveal Priti's secrets. "We should head in," he adds, although he does look thoughtful, brows knitted, as if what I said connected two invisible wires in his brain.

I nod quickly. So quickly I almost crimp my neck in the process.

"And seriously, don't worry about making it back on time," he says as we hurry away from the men in the parking lot. "If we are late and the repairs take time, I'll drive us back without stopping."

I'm grateful for his reassurance, because with Priti and I both distraught, we need at least one person to be optimistic. And he's the only one who's not here for his own selfish reasons. He's here for his best friend—and her clown of a cousin. It's rare to find people like that nowadays, who take time out of their own schedules to do things for others.

"Thank you for doing this, Rudra," I say, voicing my thoughts. "This whole trip."

Rudra fidgets with his hands, resembling a human version of the two-shy-fingers-pointing-at-each-other emoji. "Oh, it's nothing."

We join Priti, who's already seated at a table in the corner, and scan the menu. The variety is fantastic. And so much of it sounds mouth-wateringly good. I'm *famished*.

Priti gets a paper masala dosa and filter coffee (she's obsessed with South Indian food), while Rudra makes a comment about how he wishes this wasn't a pure veg restaurant and reluctantly asks for a plate of aloo paratha and achaar. I get some rajma chawal. The service is swift, so I offer to wait at the counter while Priti and Rudra find a table, and carefully walk back with the trays of food.

"Tell me vegetarian food lacks variety again and I will cut you open," Priti is saying.

"You literally eat eggs," Rudra says. He thanks me as I set down the trays.

"It doesn't matter. My argument is about you nonvegetarians constantly reducing vegetarian food to paneer and aloo. Would you have this variety in a nonveg restaurant?"

"Yes," Rudra says, scooping up the aam achaar with a morsel of his paratha and popping it into his mouth. "Thrice as much."

"Even when the curries and accompaniments are all vegetarian?" I say. It's rare for me to find myself agreeing with Priti, but I'm on her team here.

"But the *taste*. That comes from good meat."

I roll my eyes. "Sorry, I stand firmly with Priti on this one. The argument is about vegetarian food apparently lacking variety, which it doesn't. Also, you're Jain." I recall Priti mentioning it once. "Aren't Jains strict vegetarians?"

"Oh yes," Priti says, brandishing her sambhar spoon at him. "He's been lying to his parents for years now."

I tut. "Not exactly a model son, then." I spoon rajma chawal into my mouth. It's steaming hot, spicy, and delicious. "You'll just eat anything that walks, swims, or crawls, won't you?"

"Yes," Rudra says, looking directly at me. "And I'm damn good at it too."

My mouth goes dry. The rajma chawal gets stuck in my throat, and I have to swallow thickly to get it to go down.

Did Rudra Desai just make a *specifically* bisexual dirty joke and look directly at me while saying it?

Priti grimaces, flinging a bit of dosa at him, "Ugh, shut up, you dirty bastard!"

Okay, I guess I'm not making things up. Rudra *did* make a dirty joke. While looking at me.

That is the single hottest thing anyone has ever done in my presence.

I cough as the rajma chawal finally goes down, beating my chest with my fist and gulping down some water, anything to look away from him.

Luckily, his phone rings, and he picks it up, raising a finger to excuse himself. As he walks away, Priti pins her stare on me. "Are you blushing?"

"What?"

"Your face is blotchy."

"No it's not." I bring my hands up and rub at my face, suddenly self-conscious. I didn't think I could visibly blush, given my brown skin tone. I'm not sure I like it.

"Wait a second." Priti bangs her fist on the table. "You *like* Rudra."

I'm at a complete loss for words. "What are you . . . I'm *not* . . .

I *don't* like Rudra." I think I'm mildly freaking out. There's no way Priti's caught on to it already!

"You totally do!" Priti doesn't look too chuffed about the fact. "I've never seen anyone look redder than you do right now."

"That's such bullshit, Priti! In case you forgot, I am on my way to kiss Amrit. *Amrit,* whom I spent my whole summer pining after, remember?"

"*Puh-lease,* it's not like you guys were a thing anyway."

"That doesn't—" I huff. "You're being ridiculous. It's literally Rudra. I barely know him."

"Look, I don't care if you like Rudra or not," she says, brandishing her spoon at me threateningly. "You're not allowed to date him."

"I don't even *want* to date him. I like Amrit!"

"Whatever. I'm not going to stand for *my* best friend dating *you.*" That last word is laced with so much possessiveness I feel like I've been barked at by a guard dog.

Before I can retort, Rudra walks back, running a hand through his hair. "They're here. I'm heading out."

Rudra leaves the restaurant, and I pointedly make sure not to look in his direction, instead staidly stare at my food, downing mouthfuls. Priti starts using her phone, ignoring me.

I'm furious with her. And not because she thinks I like Rudra, but because of the way she said *I'm not going to stand for* my *best friend dating* you, as if that were the worst possibility ever.

Not that I'm desperate to date Rudra—I barely know him *and* I've already decided against encouraging my silly crush—but he likes Priti. And given the way Priti just reacted to the idea of me liking him, I'm convinced she likes him too. We've all always suspected it.

A hot wave of irritation and anger surges inside me. It suddenly hits me that perhaps the reason why Rudra flirted with me in front of Priti was because he was trying to make Priti *jealous*. He knew whatever the fuck that comment was would rub her the wrong way.

Maybe this is all just his plan. Maybe I'm part of it. And maybe this is an elaborate game to elicit a reaction from Priti. He seems like a nice enough guy, but I don't know him well. Not the way Priti does. I'm just a कबाब में हड्डी.[1]

That shouldn't bother me, though, right?

I swallow my anger, realizing it's pointless, and finish my food. By the time we're done, Rudra's back. I finally look behind me, scanning the parking lot for the car.

It's not there. It's gone.

"I was right—the gasket needs replacing," Rudra says, sighing as he sits back down. "They towed the car to their shop."

"What the hell?" Priti exclaims. "How long is it going to take?"

"I don't know. They said the repair itself should take six hours once they have the part, but they need to place an order for a gasket suited to this particular model. I paid them extra, though, so they guaranteed they'd have it by tomorrow afternoon at the latest."

I groan. "That's more than a day's delay."

"I know, I'm sorry." He looks genuinely apologetic, and the cute furrow of his brow gets me. Ugh, why is he so nice? "It's the best I could do."

I'm shocked by how quickly my anger from moments before fizzles out. "It's not your fault your car decided to malfunction."

"We'll have to drive until midnight tomorrow to make it to Goa in time," Priti says. "You and I can alternate, Ruds."

"No thanks, I can stay up," Rudra says, finishing the last of his food.

---

1 *Language*: Hindi; *Translation*: Bone in the kebab.

Priti rolls her eyes. "Fine. I'll call the owners of the place I booked in Goa and defer the stay."

"What are we going to do for the rest of the day, though?" I say. "We've already checked out of our rooms."

"We could rebook the place," Rudra suggests.

"No," Priti says. "We're not spending two rooms' worth of money right now. The repairs are going to be expensive, and we can't overspend."

"It's *my* car, and I'm not letting you guys pay. It was overdue for a repair anyway."

"Thanks, but no thanks, Ambani."

"You're making this trip because of us, and we're splitting *all* expenses," I say. "How much does it cost?"

"Seven thousand rupees," Rudra says.

Okay, that's a *lot*. My parents have never denied me pocket money to spend on myself, but I don't think I want to spend seven thousand rupees on a *gasket*. I don't even know what that is!

Rudra sighs, clearly noting the horror on my face. "It's fine, honestly."

"So the OYO's off," Priti says, grabbing her phone from the table. "Let me look up alternate options of stay."

"In the meantime, we could do some street shopping at FC Road," I suggest. "Unless that's not something you're into." I direct this at Rudra because I know Priti's always down for clothes shopping. He just doesn't strike me as the sort of person who would roam around in the heat of the afternoon sun to look at cheap clothes. Have you seen the stuff he wears?

"Why would you think that?" Rudra asks, frowning. He doesn't exactly sound hurt by what I said, but there's a slight fall in volume to his voice.

"I don't know," I say, hesitating, then remember that he's always honest about his opinions of me. "You wear branded, expensive stuff. Stuff that's bought in three-floored luxury stores in air-conditioned malls. Not in roadside shops."

Rudra watches me for a moment before shrugging. "Sure, I wouldn't *buy* any of that stuff, but I don't mind going with you both. I've been to Linking Road with Priti."

I'm bemused by his honesty, but what surprises me is how *not* vain he manages to sound. "Like, once?" I tease.

A smile tugs at Rudra's lips (his very pink lips, I notice). "Twice."

"How very noble of you to have graced Linking Road with your presence."

"Oh well, it wasn't too much of a burden to bear," Rudra says, his eyes twinkling with mischief. "You never know if you'll find something worth keeping there. Like these jhumkas you like to wear." He reaches out and pokes my jhumka to emphasize his point, and it swings against my jaw, metal tinkling. I turn red, ducking my head.

My stomach is fluttering so hard I can't help but squirm in my seat. But before I can string together a clever enough response, Priti slaps the table. Rudra and I nearly jump.

"Wait!" Priti says excitedly. "How could I have forgotten? I have relatives here! From my dad's side. The Sinhas. We could go to their place."

"Where do they live?" I ask, not sure if I want to hang out with my cousin's cousins, much less stay over at their place. I've met them once before, at a shaadi, but I don't remember much; I was quite young.

"Hinjewadi. It's super close to here." Priti beams, looking between the two of us. The sight is unnerving. "What say?"

"I guess—" Rudra starts, and that's all the encouragement Priti needs.

"Perfect, I'll call them right now," she says, hurrying out of her seat so fast her chair nearly crashes to the floor. She moves to the side to make a phone call to her relatives. And I suppose that's the end of discussion.

Because once Priti is dead set on something, there's no stopping her.

11

I'M NOT ASHAMED TO ADMIT *KAL HO NAA HO* MAKES ME CRY LIKE A LITTLE BITCH

Pune, Saturday

"No more for me, thank you," I say when I'm offered samosas for the third time.

I lean back in the Sinhas' living room couch, clutching my stomach uncomfortably. I've already polished off my rasmalai, and the rajma chawal is dangerously close to being ejected out of my body like the chole bhature at the party Thursday night.

Charu, the youngest of Priti's three cousins, sets down the plate, ceramic clinking against glass. Aunty and Uncle are both at work, and Rudra's off with the other two—Varun and Jalaj—in their bedroom, gaming on their PlayStation.

"I'm done, man!" Jalaj groans.

"Wuss!" Varun exclaims. "You're just saying that because Rudra totally took you out."

"I'm tired."

"So get off the battlefield and quit holding us up."

I roll my eyes, sick of their ceaseless yelling in the background while we're trying to watch a forgettable Hollywood rom-com. Charu giggles, her usually wide light-brown eyes crinkling and plump cheeks resembling cotton candy.

If I'm being honest, this whole meeting wouldn't be that bad if I weren't sick of watching Priti whisper, giggle, and gossip away with Digha—Varun's girlfriend and the Sinhas' neighbor—in the corner.

Digha's pretty, with bangs like Priti's—except hers are straight—wisping around a small, sharply defined face. And now I'm discovering that she's *also* Priti's BFF. Because apparently, the moment she heard Priti was coming, she hurried over. The two have been all smiles and girly *tee-hee*s since we got here.

A part of me feels bitter and envious seeing Priti so engaged and happy with her paternal cousins. At Nani's, she's always so distant, locked up in her room and refusing to mingle unless she *has* to, especially this summer. The only time we cousins meet up is when I'm visiting, so the rest of them haven't interacted with Priti while I've been away either. And, well, Priti hates me, so it ends up affecting her rapport and relationship with the others.

I'm the reason Priti has a better relationship with her paternal cousins. I glance over to see her slapping Digha's shoulder as the two explode into raucous laughter over a shared joke. I'll never know what I did that pushed her away from me and made her resent me, but it's not worth mulling over. There's only so much a person can try, repeatedly, to heal a broken relationship before they tire of it.

I swallow the hurt to stop it from spilling over and make a promise to myself to take Priti at face value. We're on this journey because there's something awaiting both of us in Goa. While I'll never know what she's after, we share a common goal, and that's all we need from each other. Nothing more.

She made it clear she doesn't want anything to do with me after this summer when she hid getting into FIT from me. So if this road trip continues the way it's been going . . . the only option left might be to cut myself off from her completely.

Sensing the heat of my gaze (correction: glare) on her cheek, Priti turns to me, her eyes narrowing, but she doesn't say anything cutting like she normally would. Of *course* she'd care about the impression her paternal cousins have of her—with us, she barely hesitates before spoiling the mood.

"Let's watch *Kal Ho Naa Ho*," I quickly say, picking up the remote, not too keen on having Priti embarrass me before strangers either.

"I've never watched that movie," Charu says sheepishly as my mouth falls open in shock.

"You *haven't* watched the most heart-wrenching KJo movie ever?"

"Um, no?"

I press play. "Your life is about to be changed forever."

Kal Ho Naa Ho is a three-hour-long movie, so it's past noon by the time we're done. I don't expect Priti and Digha to watch with us, but they do.

Charu, Digha, and I are a sobbing mess. Priti—the stone-hearted Ice Queen that she is—rolls her eyes at us before walking into the bedroom to ask the boys what plans they have for lunch.

When they finally join us in the hall, Rudra looks in my direction, startled.

"अरे बाप रे,"[1] Varun exclaims, pulling Digha into a tight hug and squeezing her shoulder. He's about as tall as Rudra, lanky, and has a goofy smile. "Why are you crying?"

"They were watching *Kal Ho Naa Ho*," Priti says, snorting.

---

1 *Language*: Hindi; *Translation*: Oh my god.

"That explains it," Jalaj says. He's well-built (Charu mentioned he's sort of a gym buff), slightly taller, and more reserved than his fraternal twin, Varun. "That movie is the saddest thing I've seen." He turns to Charu, joking, "Are you sure you should've been watching it, kiddo?"

"I'm just two years younger than you, idiot," Charu says.

Rudra's smiling as he sits on the floor beside the couch I'm seated on. I frown at him. "Why are you smiling?"

He glances up at me, blinking innocently. "Who, me?"

I narrow my eyes. "Yes, you."

"I'm not smiling. Did you like *Kal Ho Naa Ho*?"

"Of course I did," I say slowly, still suspicious. "But I won't be distracted. You're literally smiling right now!"

Rudra props his elbow on the sofa, resting his chin on his palm and tilting his head to look up at me. He has a really nice forearm, I suddenly notice, taut and peppered with soft hair. "Nothing, I just think I was right before. You *are* a hopeless romantic, though I am starting to see the appeal."

"*What?*" I splutter.

"You heard me, Krishna."

I think something short-circuits in me when he says that, because my insides are most definitely malfunctioning. Priti flops down next to me, giving us both the stink eye, and I'm pretty sure she caught at least part of our exchange.

Charu speaks up just then, cutting off whatever remark Priti's about to make. "Where are we going for lunch? Mumma and Papa said we could order in or go out."

"Let's go out," Digha says. "I don't want you boys going back to gaming."

"We wouldn't have anyway," Varun chimes in. "Rudra totally took

Jalaj out. *Multiple* times. It was so fucking cool."

Varun gives Rudra a fist bump, and all us girls exchange looks like, *Boys*.

"If y'all are done bromancing," I say, "can we decide on a place?"

"Hey, what if we took them to the Mahishmati thali place?" Charu says, excitedly getting to her feet.

"Good idea, but it's like forty minutes away," Varun says. "We should take them somewhere closer. There are decent places nearby."

"But we have a big enough group to be able to finish the whole thing!" Charu insists.

Now, *that's* intriguing. "What exactly would we be trying to finish?" I ask.

"You'll see," she says mysteriously.

"It'll be fun," Varun adds, nudging his brother.

Jalaj looks doubtful. "I know, and I don't mind, but I need to be back in time to prepare for the trek."

"Trek?" Priti asks.

"Oh, Jallu leads these treks during the summer with his group," Varun says, grinning. "He's guided more than fifty treks around Lonavala already."

"He has a certificate and everything," Digha adds proudly. "Very legit."

Jalaj bats away the compliments. "Today I have a group of about six college kids booked, and we'll be taking a hired minibus at eight p.m."

"Isn't that a bit late for a trek?" Rudra asks.

"It's a midnight trek. It's jugnu season, so we take a lot of trekkers to the points where the fireflies gather and mate in swarms. We start at the base of Prabalmachi and get back to Pune by noon the following day."

He takes out his phone to show us a video. My breath hitches in my throat. It's the most *gorgeous* thing I've ever seen. Fireflies illuminate a tall, dark tree like strings of flickering Christmas lights.

"It's mostly the male fireflies that emit light, in order to impress the females," Jalaj explains.

"So they put on a whole light show for the females?" I say, clasping my hands. "That's so adorable."

"It rewired my brain that first time, for sure." Jalaj shuts his eyes, a small smile playing along his lips, and I can see just how much these treks mean to him. He speaks about fireflies the way I would about human anatomy.

"You said you'd be back in Pune by noon," I say. "Isn't that when you're expecting the car back, Rudra?"

"Yeah," Rudra replies.

"Please tell me you're not thinking what I think you're thinking," Priti says. "We can't go on the trek, Krishna."

"Why not?" I say. "It's not like we have anything to do but wait for Rudra's car, and we'll be back by noon tomorrow."

"Well, after noon, realistically speaking," Jalaj adds.

"We'll be dead tired after the trek," Priti says. "And we can't afford to be late. We've already been delayed enough. Don't you realize we'll be going backwards? We crossed Lonavala last night."

"Even if we leave later tomorrow, we'll get to Goa in time," I insist. "Chill out, Priti. This is literally the opportunity of a lifetime. How many chances do you get to see a view *that* stunning?"

"Not often," Rudra affirms.

"Varun and I have gone before," Charu says. "I almost didn't complete the second leg, but Prabalmachi is beautiful. Plus, you'll get to camp at night and wake up to the most glorious sunrise tomorrow."

Varun nods in agreement. "We'll all come along with you guys. If you go, that is."

But Priti's lips are still pursed in doubt.

That's when Rudra speaks up. "Let's do it. Krishna's right. We can't pass up an opportunity like this. That is, if you can accommodate us on such short notice, Jalaj."

"Absolutely," he says, raising a thumb. "I will need to charge you, though."

"That's no problem."

I stare at Priti hopefully, knowing Rudra is the only one who can convince her to do anything at all. And to my utter delight, she sighs, giving in.

"Let's do it."

12

THERE WILL NEVER BE A GOOD PLACE OR TIME TO BURP (OR BARF) IN FRONT OF YOUR CRUSH

Pune, Saturday

Varun drives us all in the Sinhas' Innova to JM Housefull Paratha, the place Charu referred to as the "Mahishmati thali place." Priti, Rudra, and I end up in the very back of the car, with me in the middle. I spend the whole drive jittery because of how close Rudra and I are sitting. I can't stop thinking about everything he's said to me.

Rudra Desai is definitely flirting with me, and with each passing minute, he is being less subtle about it. Even as Varun parks and we exit the car, I can't help the dreadful feeling that Rudra's doing it only because he wants to make Priti jealous. He made that last comment right before Priti sat next to us, and I'm, like, one hundred percent sure she heard it.

That he *intended* for her to hear it.

Now, that wouldn't be much of a problem if I weren't into the flirting. But the truth is, I *am*. I am so into it that it sickens me.

At the paratha place, a few tables have been arranged just outside the entrance, where hordes of people sit taking bites out of their ginormous thalis and sipping tumblers of chilled lassi. I'm already starving, and the sight of the food makes my mouth water. We take one of the larger tables inside the restaurant, right under a poster that flaunts actress Anushka Shetty from *Baahubali* with a large thali photoshopped in front of her.

Priti snorts as she flops into a chair against the wall, staring at the poster in amusement. Rudra sits beside her, which leaves one vacant spot, right next to him. Digha passes us a menu, and the pages are flipped open to the section with the thalis.

At the top right corner of the page, there's a picture of actor Prabhas from *Baahubali* hefting a thali onto his shoulder. I haven't watched the movie, but there's a famous scene in it where Prabhas carries a Shivalinga across a waterfall. In the poster, they've replaced the Shivalinga with the thali, and the hilarity of it makes me giggle. It's creative, I've got to give them that.

"Is there some sort of eating challenge for this?" Rudra asks, reading the menu closely.

"Yeah, but it's for an individual," Varun says. "If someone manages to finish the Baahubali thali by themselves, their money is refunded, and the restaurant will give them free meals for the rest of their life."

"Whoa, that's a hell of a deal. Have any of you ever tried?"

"Tried and failed, yes," Varun says, sighing. "It's impossible. No one's ever won."

"No one in the history of this place?" I ask, amazed. "It can't be all that hard."

Charu grins. "Once you see the size of the thali, you'll know."

We place an order for the Mahishmati thali, which is apparently even bigger than the Baahubali thali, and something the Sinhas have been wanting to try for a while. Priti, Rudra, and I watch in utter shock as not one, not two, but *three* waiters heave a humongous thali the diameter of a ceiling fan from the kitchen over to our table and set it at the very center. Charu bursts into laughter as the three of us stare at it with our jaws unhinged.

"Still doubtful, Krishna?" Digha asks, covering her mouth with her fist to control her laughter.

"No!" I exclaim. Any shred of doubt I had about the impossibility of the challenge flies right out the window. I don't think even the *seven* of us together can finish it; surely this needs an army of starving soldiers? There are a dozen different types of parathas, rotis, rice, sabjis, and sweets, accompanied by glasses of virgin mojitos and lassis, and other condiments like salads, raitas, pickles, and papads. The waiter tells us about each item in detail, and even just *looking* at the thali makes me feel bloated.

"I was thinking we could have a contest," Varun says enthusiastically. "Our *own* contest."

Digha groans. "Could we just eat? I'm starving."

"No, hear me out. Let's divide ourselves into groups of two, two, and three, and compete. Whichever team finishes first wins."

"Won't the team with three have an advantage?" I ask.

"Nope. We can have Digha be the third, and considering she barely eats, it won't matter."

"Hey!" Digha protests.

"It's true," Varun says, ruffling her hair. "You know it is." Jalaj and Charu nod in agreement.

Digha relents. "Fine."

"What would the winning team get?" Priti asks.

"A pass on having to chip in on the check?" Jalaj suggests.

"I think we can raise the stakes," I say, grinning. "How about that *and* covering the trek fees? The losing teams can split the cost among themselves."

"I like the sound of that," Priti says. "You're on."

I look around at the others, one by one, and they each nod in turn, all toothy smiles. I can already feel the thrill of the challenge burbling up within me. If there's one thing I *can't* resist, it's the pull of a good competition. It's like a high for me, watching the jealousy and disappointment roil over my opponents' faces while I ride the euphoria that comes with the win. And when it comes to food? I bet you there's no one at this table that can eat the way I can.

And it would help to save some money. I've been spending way too much.

"How do we divide the teams?" Rudra asks.

"Pugata," Priti says, stretching her hand out, palm facing downward. It's a simple way of dividing teams; I used to do it all the time when I played kabaddi or kho-kho with my friends in Mulund.

Once we've stacked our hands, one on top of the other, Priti calls out, "Pugata!" and we draw out, flipping our hands either palm upward or downward. Priti's and Charu's hands are palms up, while the rest of our hands remain palms down. So they form one team, exchanging high-fives.

We do another round. When we draw out this time, Digha, Varun, and Jalaj are palms up, while Rudra and I are palms down. The trio cheers, while Rudra and I exchange shy glances.

We call for the waiter to help divide the food into three parts, and Priti and I switch seats. That leaves Rudra and me on one side of the table; Digha, Varun, and Jalaj on the opposite side; and Priti and Charu adjacent to us.

As the waiter piles the portions of food onto three separate plates, I turn to Rudra, eyes gleaming with determination and voice lowered so only he can hear me. "I want to win this thing. So I hope you can eat."

"*I* can." Those dimples appear, drawing my attention. They're shaped like tiny hearts, etched on either side of his chin. *Not the time, Krishna.* "Though I have my doubts about you."

I narrow my eyes at him. "Excuse the fuck me?"

Rudra looks me up and down, eyes grazing my body so fluidly I can feel them on my skin. "You're . . . small."

"I'm five foot three, for your kind information," I huff, sizing him up in return. "Mr. Five Foot Seven?"

He looks so offended I nearly bark out a laugh. "Five foot *eight.*"

"Same difference."

Rudra shakes his head and turns away. I smile cheekily to myself. The waiter sets down the plate with our portion of food in front of us, and I drag my chair so close to Rudra's that our arms are brushing.

"Okay, remember, not a morsel of food should be left on the plate!" Charu says, cracking her knuckles.

"Someone count to three," I say, hands poised and ready.

"One . . ." Priti says. Adrenaline pulses through me. "Two . . ." Rudra and I exchange resolute nods. "Three!"

We practically attack the food.

Rudra and I start with the rotis and naans first. We tear into them, scooping up mouthfuls of a different sabji at each turn, stuffing our throats. I take gulps of the mojito and the lassi between bites, knowing I won't be able to drink them with a full stomach later. It's a strategy I've utilized plenty of times in the past at countless thali places.

We're barely halfway through the rotis and naans and I already feel like I'm going to be sick, but I power on, packing my mouth with so much food it gets difficult to swallow. At one point, I nearly choke on a bite of roti, and Rudra has to thump my back until the food goes down. But if there's anyone who can do this, who can *win* this, it's me.

It's close so far; the three teams are neck and neck (and neck). I'm amused by how right Varun was about Digha eating less, because even with three people on their team, they're falling behind.

Priti groans from where she's struggling with her last roti. "Look away, boys," she says, reaching for the waistband of her camo pants. "I'm unbuttoning my pants."

"Whoa, whoa, hey!"

Varun and Jalaj protest as Priti undoes the first button, and Rudra jerks his head to the side so fast it's a wonder he doesn't sprain his neck. There's color blotting his cheeks, and I hastily look away to avoid him catching me staring.

I don't know whether to laugh at how mortified he looks or feel jealous. The resulting feeling is a gut-churning mix of confusion, and I accidentally end up biting down on a green chili.

A sudden, sharp sting of spice explodes in my mouth. "Ohmygod!" I gasp, waving my hand frantically in front of my face, eyes already watering. "Chili!"

"Here, have the gulab jamun," Rudra says, sliding the cup toward me as he starts spooning up rice, chewing with impeccable speed.

I don't bother with a spoon and instead directly stuff a gulab jamun into my mouth, the sweet and sticky sugar syrup coating my fingers. Unfortunately, that doesn't do the job either, and I have to force down half the gajar ka halwa to douse the spice.

The heaviness of the food settles in the pit of my stomach, making me press the back of my hand to my mouth. Rudra looks over to me, eyebrows raised.

I open my mouth to assure him I'm okay and can keep going, but

I can't speak because I think I actually may be on the verge of puking up everything I just ate.

Oh no. Oh hell *no*.

There is no way this is happening right now.

Not in front of another boy.

Not *again*!

But no matter what I do, I can't hold it in, and when I open my mouth, it's not vomit that comes out—it's a full-blown, sickening belch.

Everyone looks up, staring at me in shock for a moment, as if unable to believe such a sound could come from me.

But no one is more shocked than I am.

Rudra is staring at me, his eyes wide, as if he's been rendered speechless by my sudden expulsion of gas. I thought throwing up in front of Amrit was the most embarrassing moment of my life, but can people have *two* most embarrassing moments of their lives? Because this is going to torment—

That's when, to my utter, unmatched amazement, he burps.

Rudra Desai burps. Even louder, even longer than I did.

That sets off a round of burps from Varun, Jalaj, and Charu. Priti tries her best, poking her neck out like an ostrich and even pressing her stomach to force the gas out, but all she manages is a gag.

Charu and I burst into giggles. Digha looks around at us with her face scrunched in disgust, but there's a smile playing at the corners of her lips, "Are you all done? Because we still have to eat, you know?"

We dive back into the food, and while I dig into the daal rice, I can't help but feel grateful again. I smile sheepishly at Rudra, whispering so only he can hear. "Thanks for that."

"I don't know what you're talking about." Rudra snorts, but there's a warmth in his words that tells me he does. "And I take it back. You can *eat*."

I smile, and although I'm seconds away from bursting, I'm filled with newfound determination to see this through. "Oh, I'm not done, but I don't see *you* eating, Mr. I'm Five Foot Seven. Oops, sorry, *eight.*"

"So that's how it's going to be, huh?" And if I had thought someone couldn't look hot taking a bite of paratha, I was mistaken, because it seems Rudra can.

I can't believe that Rudra is flirting with me. *Again.* It takes everything in me to not blush like a nineteenth-century housewife.

Oh, to be that paratha.

Ten minutes later, Rudra is cramming the last spoonful of gajar ka halwa into his mouth and I'm polishing off the nimbu achaar (we made it clear there would be nothing left on the plate). At this point, a few people from the surrounding tables have come over to watch, and even the waiters from earlier are standing by our table, cheering us on.

And then we're done.

Rudra leans back in his chair, clutching his stomach with both hands and groaning. I swallow the bile scraping the back of my throat, sweating from overeating. A cheer bursts out among the crowd, causing the others to look up.

Varun sighs when he sees our empty plate. "Ah, shit."

The crowd starts clapping, and even though I'm convinced I won't ever be able to eat again, let alone a thali, I'm *ecstatic.* Rudra turns to look at me, and he's smiling, and the moment takes me over, carrying me like a beach ball over a wave.

I scream, "*We won!*" and throw my arms around his neck, my hair tangling in the space between our cheeks.

Now, this would've been salvageable had it been a one-armed hug, or something short and quick, with maybe a few platonic pat-pats landed on his back. But I practically fling myself onto his lap, throwing the whole weight of my body on him, common sense whisked away by the sheer force of my enthusiasm.

And Rudra, not knowing how else to stop himself from toppling backward, hugs me back, his hands circling my waist. It's a surprise I haven't combusted from embarrassment. Thankfully, no one looks like they've made the action out to be anything but friendly—until I catch Priti's dumbfounded expression.

I hasten to sit back down, but Rudra isn't letting go. Instead, he looks dazed, and just when I'm starting to think about what that could mean, he suddenly lurches away from me and onto his feet.

"I'm sorry, I need to—" he starts to say, but his words cut off as he dashes out of the restaurant, nearly knocking over a table on his way out.

Is he . . . is he running away from me?

At first, I stay seated, mortified at having had a boy run from me just seconds after I threw myself on him (correction: *glomped* him), but then the concern takes over, and I'm running after him before anyone else has the chance to raise an alarm.

"Rudra!" I call out behind him, and as I round the corner, past the JM Housefull Paratha board, my shoes squeak against the footpath.

I run a corner by a dustbin and spy Rudra propping his hand against the (possibly paan-stained) wall, ducking and clutching his stomach as he retches on the ground.

"Rudra, ohmygod, are you okay?"

"I'll be fine—" Rudra groans, but he does *not* sound fine in the least.

I stare at him in shock, cursing softly under my breath. When I place my hand on his spine, I find his T-shirt damp from sweat. I hold his hair back for him, reminded of how Amrit did the same for me during the house party.

I always thought I was the sort of person who wouldn't be able to stand the sight of someone else throwing up in front of me, but at the moment, I'm only filled with worry for him.

When Rudra's done, he pushes himself away from the wall, stumbles over to a tree nearby, and leans against the trunk. I follow, planting myself next to him, and look up, concerned.

Rudra's hair is pasted to his cheek, sticky with sweat. At first, I fight the desire to push it away, but seeing he's in no state to do it himself, I reach out and do it for him. My fingers brush his sharp cheekbone as I pluck the strands away one by one, tucking them behind his ear. Rudra flinches at the first touch but quickly relaxes, eyes shutting. The pads of my fingers tingle with sensation even after I've dropped my hand back to my side.

Rudra grimaces, not looking at me. The stricken look on his face matches the one I felt on mine from the party. He's *embarrassed*, even though he has absolutely no reason to be.

What he says confirms it for me. "I'm sorry you had to see that."

"Stop." I can only smile at the thought that follows. "I guess we've sort of canceled each other out now, huh? Besides, I'm pretty sure the intimacy of literally spilling our guts in front of each other automatically bonds us for life."

Rudra cracks a smile at that. "I suppose. Thanks for helping me out."

"Hey, *you* stepped in to help me out first earlier," I say, giggling. "Peak chivalry, to save a girl with a truly epic burp."

"Very manly of me, I daresay," Rudra says, snorting.

"Oh, for sure. But I didn't come here to boost your ego. Are you *really* okay?"

"Better." He finally turns to look at me, and under the afternoon sunlight, there's a sheen on his face that makes him glow.

Our eyes latch for a staggering second, then another. I'm not breathing, and I don't think he is either, because his chest no longer rises and falls rapidly. Our shoulders are touching, and neither of us moves away, my bare skin grazing the soft fabric of his T-shirt . . .

"There you are!"

Priti rushes toward us, crossing the street and coming to a stop in front of us, bending over to catch her breath.

"I couldn't find you both. What happened?"

"The food didn't sit well with me," Rudra says, pushing off the tree, away from me. "But I'm fine now."

Priti pats his cheek, puckering her lips in concern. "See, this is why rich boys like you shouldn't eat at roadside restaurants."

Rudra scoffs, but he's grinning. "And yet you're the loser."

Priti smacks him before pulling at his cheek. "Cutie. Such a sensitive stomach."

It's never been more obvious to me how in love they are with each other.

I stand there, off to the side, watching their exchange, having been forgotten. I'm taken right back to that moment seven years ago, my first summer back in India after we moved, desperate to meet my Priti, my best friend again, after not having spoken to her for more than a year, only for her to break my heart and tell me she had Rudra now. That she didn't need me anymore. That I was no one to her.

I thought I'd left my jealousy of their friendship behind after years of having the wound punctured again and again. But the roiling in my gut tells me that I haven't. I still envy their bond, what they have; this irreplaceable connection that no one can match.

Especially not me.

13

NOT ARGUING WITH A BOY WHO HAS DARK-BROWN EYES AND LONG LASHES—WHATEVER YOU SAY, BABY GIRL

Pune, Saturday

For the trek, I borrow a pair of loose nylon shorts and a Mickey Mouse T-shirt from Digha. Jalaj said we'd get food and water at the trek site, so I leave the rest of my belongings behind and carry just my fanny pack with a few essentials.

While we're waiting for the minibus Jalaj's club booked for the group, I twist my hair into a knot and secure it with a butterfly clip. Frankly, I'm exhausted, but the excitement at the prospect of seeing fireflies and camping out tonight overshadows that.

We're all sitting in the boys' bedroom, soft songs playing through Jalaj's portable Bluetooth speaker in the background. They've turned on the cerulean fairy lights strung along the walls of the room.

Priti, Charu, Digha, and I are on the lower bunk; Varun is perched on the beanbag, Jalaj on the desk chair by the study table, and Rudra on the floor on the opposite side of the room, back resting against the wall, right under a gaming poster. He looks better since he threw up outside the paratha place, having claimed repeatedly afterward that it was worth it because we won.

The boys are all on their phones, Charu's head is bent over her Kindle, and Priti and Digha are whispering furiously to one another. *Again.* It's not that I'm curious or anything, and at first, I try my level best to focus on my audiobook. But they're literally sitting right next to me, and I can't help but overhear what they're saying. At some point, I press pause, but I keep my AirPods in so I don't look suspicious, eyes trained on my phone screen.

"You have to know what you're doing is really brave," Digha is saying, her voice soft.

"Brave?" Priti says, and I'm shocked to hear the vulnerability and . . . fear in her voice. It's so unlike her to let her guard down like that. "I feel like I'm about to shit my pants."

"What are you so afraid of? Rejection?" Digha shakes her head. "You're still following each other, and it wasn't even you who sent the re-follow request."

"I know, but a re-follow request doesn't prove someone's still in love, right? You do that when you've already moved on."

Oh my fucking god.

Priti had a *breakup*. And recently, by the sound of it.

It sort of explains why she's been so detached and bitter this entire vacation. This has to be why she was crying on the balcony during the house party.

I can't help but feel sorry for her when I'm reminded of the way she attempted to conceal her tears that day, even though it was so visible. I can't forgive her for everything she's said and done either, but if I had a breakup, I would take forever to recover from it. Or maybe it's just *me* who's made that way—I tend to get attached too easily.

Then again, despite how prickly she is, Priti would—literally—kill you if you hurt someone she loved. She's fiercely protective and feels everything on a magnified level. I know, because I have experienced firsthand what it's like to be hated by her. And people who can hate someone like that . . . can also love someone with an equal level of ferocity and measure.

"What about the likes on your posts, then?" Digha is saying, and my attention drifts back to their conversation.

"Likes are inconsequential."

"DMs?"

"I haven't gotten any. I told you that." Priti shoots a glance in my direction. "I think we're being too loud."

Oh shit, I've been looking.

I duck my head back down to my phone and pretend to scroll through something, being the opposite of subtle. I don't want Priti to think I'm eavesdropping, or that I care about what she shares with Digha. Because I don't.

But the bits and pieces of their conversation I overheard replay in my head, and wheels start turning, slowly at first, then faster. Puzzle pieces fall into place quicker than I anticipate.

When Priti excuses herself and goes to the bathroom to take a dump (damn, she really did need to shit her pants earlier), Digha joins Varun on the beanbag, lightly threading her fingers through his short, mossy hair. And in that moment, I wonder what it is about Digha that makes Priti connect to her in a way that she can't connect to *me.* It's not like they live in the same city. From what I've gathered, they rarely meet.

Yet Priti has managed to maintain a solid relationship with her.

"Isn't it a relief to see her like this again? Happy?" Jalaj says suddenly. Digha doesn't say anything; she shoots Jalaj a pointed look, which he doesn't seem to notice.

"Who?" Varun asks blankly.

"*Priti*, you idiot," Charu says.

"Oh." Realization crawls back over Varun's face. "Oh, yeah, she was depressed as hell, bro."

I frown, glancing at Rudra, wondering if he knows what they're talking about. He looks less befuddled than I do, but it's obvious he's paying close attention to what they're saying, like he's looking for clues.

"Depressed?" I ask.

"Yeah. I'm not sure, but I think she had a breakup or something," Varun says.

Bingo.

I glance at Rudra again, and this time, realization is blooming in his eyes. So he *does* know about this. And so do the rest of her cousins. Everyone knows, or at least has an inkling of what's happened, except me.

"And frankly, we couldn't ask because we were afraid she'd bite our heads off," Varun says, throwing his hands up defensively when Digha shoots him a glare. "What? She can be scary sometimes." He turns to Rudra. "Please don't tell her I said that. Unless you want me dead in a ditch."

"Don't worry about it," Rudra says matter-of-factly.

"We did think it was someone from Powai, though," Jalaj says thoughtfully. "Because Priti was doing an internship there last year."

"Okay, can we stop talking about Priti?" Digha says suddenly and firmly. "I don't feel comfortable doing this behind her back, and neither should you."

Jalaj, Varun, and Charu exchange guilty looks, changing the topic.

My eyes drift to Rudra.

His gaze is distant, focused on the artificial wall creepers swaying in the cool swish of the AC. He's wearing the same T-shirt from this morning and a borrowed pair of tracks. His hair is down again, gathered behind his ears, and he fiddles absently with a black tie wrapped around his wrist. His lips are pursed in thought, forming the shape of a small Cupid's bow, fascinatingly delicate.

I get off the bunk, walk over, and sit cross-legged against the wall next to him. He flicks his gaze to me, dark eyes reflecting the blue fairy lights, lashes enviably long. It's so unfair how boys can go around walking with lashes like that while I have make do with my mascara.

Up until this moment, I never thought blemishes, acne scars, or pimples could be pretty, but Rudra's features are so sharp they almost *fit.* Perhaps all those people who told me it's pointless being conscious of those bad-skin or random-zits-popping-up-in-the-worst-spots days were right. Because when I look at him, I don't notice them as separate, glaring entities that stand out and distort his face. Instead, they're just part of him, part of who he is, never taking away from how striking he is.

I'm so mesmerized by how he looks I nearly forget what I came here to talk to him about. But he blinks at me questioningly, and I snap out of my trance.

"Hey," I say, clearing my throat. "Are you feeling better?"

Rudra scratches the back of his neck. I don't know if he's blushing, because the lighting doesn't show it. "Yeah. But that's not why you came over, right?" he says, raising an eyebrow. "Let me guess. Priti's breakup?"

"Not exactly," I say, biting my lower lip. Rudra glances at it once, then back up at my eyes, and I lose my train of thought. "I mean—I—uh, not about her breakup specifically. But I'm wondering how come you don't know why she's headed to Goa." *Too harsh, Krishna?*

"What do you mean?" Rudra says, sounding a little . . . put off, as if I've said something wrong.

I try again. "I was wondering why you barely seem to know anything."

Jesus.

I can tell by the way his eyes fill with hurt that I've only made this worse.

"It's not like I don't know anything," Rudra says. Oh god, I feel like I've kicked a puppy.

One last time. *Please don't mess this up.*

"I'm sorry, I'm just—This is all coming out wrong," I say, twisting toward him fully. Facing him squarely might help. "I should've put it in a better way. I didn't mean to sound like you don't care or that Priti doesn't—"

"It's fine," Rudra says, cutting in. At least that hurt look in his eyes has dimmed. "I get it. I knew she was dating someone in Powai, and I knew she had a breakup, but I don't know who her ex is or why she wants to go to Goa so badly." He licks his lips, and they shimmer in the blue light. "That's what you wanted to know, right?"

"Yes," I say. He looks the complete opposite of the cold, unapproachable guy I've known him to be all these summers. "And I'm not going to ask you about Priti's relationship because it doesn't concern me. But I can tell you're bothered by her hiding these things from you."

"I'm not bothered," he insists, though his expression says otherwise.

"Fine, you're not," I say gently. "But I know it can be scary when someone keeps secrets and you have to hope they don't make you drift apart."

"That's because Priti . . ." Rudra says her name like it's a prayer. "She means everything to me."

Something cracks beneath my ribs right then, discomfort sprouting all along my body. I don't know why. It's not like I've been in love with Rudra for years and am having my heart broken because of the realization that I'll never match up to Priti in *his*.

It's a crush, barely a day old, nothing compared to the decade-long relationship Rudra and Priti share. But I can't help but feel envious of how he speaks about her, as if he'd make the earth rotate backward for her.

Part of me wants to believe I'm just jealous because I'm lacking that in my life. It makes me feel foolish for doing all this, putting in all this effort to reach Amrit even though I don't even like him in that all-consuming way you're supposed to, let alone love him the way Rudra loves Priti.

I don't think I've ever loved anyone like that.

The other part of me knows it's because it's *Rudra*—whom I somehow never noticed my entire life, all the years I've known him. Whom I'm discovering for the first time, even though he's been around this whole while. He was like a fossil in a quarry, right in front of my eyes, always there, existing, seemingly unimportant. And suddenly, in the exasperating way that life works, I dug him out, seeing him . . . no, *more* than seeing him, far too late. Because he and Priti are meant for each other.

There's a boy less than a day's journey away from me, a sweet, smart, beautiful boy who likes me back. Who isn't hopelessly in love with his best friend. Who will be the perfect person to ride pillion with into the summer romance of my dreams.

Yet, here I am, slowly falling for Rudra Desai.

14

LET'S SEE HOW MUCH I CAN GET AWAY WITH BY USING MY (MANY) ACHIEVEMENTS AS EXCUSES

Pune, Saturday

The minibus is a twenty-seater, excluding the driver's and conductor's seats. The moment I get on, I rush to the very back, snapping up a window seat. The others follow me, and as I slide open the window to let the night air in, I'm secretly hoping Rudra takes the empty seat next to me.

Unfortunately, Charu flops down there, and I fight the urge to groan out loud. But then she shoots me an adorable smile, her big brown eyes twinkling, and I melt. *Fuck me.* I'm the worst for not wanting this absolute sweetheart sitting next to me.

Priti and Rudra follow, Priti taking the other window seat and Rudra the one next to her. I get a whiff of his scent even with Charu seated between us and shut my eyes, cursing myself because I'm down so bad.

Absolutely ludicrous, Krishna, Mummy's voice echoes in my head.

That's what she always says when I'm being—well, me. If she knew the thoughts that were going on in her daughter's head, she'd disown me.

Varun and Digha take the double seat right in front of us, while Jalaj takes the single seat, the aisle partitioning them. As the bus rumbles to a start, my phone buzzes in my fanny pack. When I pull it out, I see it's Mummy calling me.

Talk of the devil.

"Oh shit," I say out loud. "Everyone, keep quiet for a minute. My mom's calling."

The noise inside the minibus levels off almost immediately, and the only sound that can be heard is the roar of the wind as it rushes in through the window. It's instinctual for all of us, because even brown girls with relatively cool parents, *American* parents, are always on the alert when there are boys involved. And Mummy, who I'm sure knows only what Nani must've told her, would skin me alive if she knew I was traveling across cities just to go kiss a boy.

"Hello?" I say as everyone watches me, dead silent.

"Krishna Kumar." Oops. It's never a good sign when your parents call you by your full name. I wince, while Varun mimes getting his throat slit. I quickly lower the volume of the call so they can't hear whatever Mummy's going to say next. "Do you not think it necessary to let your mother know you're alive?"

I'm not really the call-my-parents-every-day sort, but Mummy's reaction is justified because I haven't texted or called her since before the house party.

"Sorry, Mummy Ji," I say, biting my tongue. "I lost track of time."

"So much time that you couldn't even drop a text saying you're okay? Do you know how worried Papa and I have been?"

"I know, I'm sorry. I just—"

"And what is this Nani has been telling me about you going off to a camping trip with Priti?"

"It's this field-trip thingy organized by V. G. Vaze," I say, sticking to the story Priti and I told Nani. "When Priti found out my flight was postponed, she asked if I wanted to join her. Her friend's on the volunteer team, so she was able to get me a ticket."

"Why didn't you tell me about it earlier?" Mummy demands.

"It was very last-minute. I—erm—forgot?"

"Or you knew there was a chance I'd refuse to let you go and risk missing your flight, so you decided the best thing to do would be to let Nani know, go off on the trip, and get scolded by me later."

Damn it. I'm not even surprised she can read me so well. She's my mom, after all. That, and I'm a terrible liar.

I give in, realizing there's no point in lying further. Like I said, I sort of suck at it. "I'm sorry. Please don't kill me." Just to be safe, I add, "I got into JHU."

Mummy snorts. "बेवक़ूफ़ लड़की![1] How many times will you use that excuse?"

I smile cheekily, even though she can't see me. "As long as it continues to work."

"Well, this is the last pass you get. All right?"

"Noted."

"Also . . ." Mummy's voice is laced with curiosity. "How come Priti took you along? Have you two finally resolved your issues?"

I glance once at the others, who are either listening to music on their earphones or talking in low voices. "Not really, but since she was going, I guess she thought it'd be rude to leave me behind. Or maybe Mausi told her to take me along; I don't know."

---

1 *Language*: Hindi; *Translation*: Foolish girl!

"The latter seems more believable," Mummy grumbles. Even though she adores Mausi, she's never really liked Priti. I mean, most of my relatives don't, but their reasons are rooted in bigotry, unlike Mummy's.

They find Priti rebellious and arrogant—which are labels plastered on every Indian girl who isn't a vision of purity or obedient of every rule and restriction her family sets for her. Priti's septum piercing, outfits, nape tattoo, and dark complexion never really helped either.

I've heard the comments aunties have made about her being बोहोत सावली,[2] too garish, too bold, too shameless. Honestly, it's all part of the reason why I've always admired her so much, especially when she turned up at that one wedding in a glittery black lehenga choli that exposed way more of her dark torso than it covered, hair pinned up so her tattoo was visible for everyone to see, and makeup so bold it completed the most daring *FUCK YOU* fit I'd ever seen.

Mummy's not like them. She doesn't like Priti because of how she's treated *me*. She knows how much Priti's jibes and taunting have affected me over the years, how difficult it has been for me to set it all aside and still look forward to my vacations in India. She knows how much I cried that one time Priti told me I couldn't wear a nath because I was American now.

I know for a fact Priti isn't the problematic person she'd like me to believe. Someone who goes so out of their way to be a misfit in a society that's quick to judge yet continues to hold their head high isn't someone who'd harbor the belief that a diaspora kid like me isn't Indian enough.

Priti said all that not because she meant it but because she knows my weak spots, knows exactly what to say to hurt me the most.

---

2 *Language*: Hindi; *Translation*: Too dark.

That doesn't make any of what she said *right,* but the more I get to know Priti again and see how much she's been hiding from everyone, the more I'm beginning to understand.

"She's been better this time, Mummy," I say, unable to believe I'm defending her as the words leave my mouth. "I don't think we're going to go back to being best friends, but it's better than it has been."

"That's good to hear," Mummy says, her voice softening. "Don't let her get to you, okay, baccha? You know she doesn't mean whatever she says. She just wants to trigger you. Mausi told us long back, remember?

"When we moved, she thought you had become too cool for her, and she mocked you for the very thing she was insecure about. It was her defense mechanism. But she was just a child then. Now that she's growing up, things are bound to improve because she's maturing. Give your relationship time and space to breathe.

"Sometimes, just the passage of time is enough to heal a wound. People think addressing the issue helps solve any problem, but that can trigger the wound instead of putting a salve to it. If you let the wound breathe, it'll learn to heal on its own. It'll be slow, but nothing comes without patience, hmm?"

I smile, feeling a slight prickle in my eyes. I don't know why this conversation is making me so emotional, but Mummy always manages to make things better, or at least *seem* better. "Thank you, Mums."

"*Tch*, don't thank me. Now go. Priti must be waiting for you."

"Probably not, but yeah, I'll go."

"Take care. And please, at least text me an *I'm alive* message whenever you can. Is your passport with you?"

"Safe and sound," I say, patting my fanny pack, feeling the shape of the document through the material of the bag.

"Good. Love you, beta."

"Love you too, Mummy."

As we wait near Xion Mall in Hinjewadi, where the rest of the trekking group will be picked up, I text Amrit again because I need to get my feelings in check. That, and there's something that's been on my mind ever since we left the Sinhas' house.

@notkrishnakumar

Hey

It takes a few minutes for him to reply, and while I wait, my leg bobs up and down urgently.

@amrit_ka_achar

Hey, I was just thinking about you

I read the message once, then again, and a hot flush creeps up my face, making me duck my head down to the phone. Charu's busy talking with the others, so she's not looking, but I feel like I'm sexting Amrit; I'm so giddy and embarrassed.

This feeling can't match having an unrequited crush on Rudra. Like, it's not even comparable, right?

I glance over at Rudra, who's leaning back with his head tipped over the headrest of the seat. His face is turned up, and his eyes are closed, headphones propped against his ears. With his neck arched like that, his jawline is razor sharp and pronounced, and his Adam's apple sticks out in his throat. I have the sudden vision of pressing my lips to it, before I fling the thought away at lightning speed.

Okay, maybe not, Krishna.

I can't believe how quickly I've gone from resolving myself to crushing on one guy to thinking about *kissing* another! Something is severely wrong with me.

@notkrishnakumar

Stop. Also I wanted to ask you smth real quick.

Are u free tho? It's the mehndi right?

@amrit_ka_achar

No I'm sorry I'm getting my palms painted rn

I'll ttyl

I roll my eyes, a smile tickling the edges of my mouth.

@notkrishnakumar

LOL anyway . . . before Mulund you used to live in Powai right? And this cousin's wedding you're attending. Do they live in Powai too?

@amrit_ka_achar

Um yeah. Why do you ask tho?

@notkrishnakumar

Priti was mentioning this fashion internship she did in Powai last year so I was wondering if by any chance your family knew her.

@amrit_ka_achar

I mean could be possible
but only Soumyaroop bhaiya
still lives in Powai. He's the groom.
I've mentioned him to you before.
I could ask him if you want.

And the plot thickens!

I sit up straight in my seat, my hands shaking as they clutch the phone. I still have some digging to do before I can say anything for sure, but at least I know I'm headed in the right direction.

@notkrishnakumar

No omg no! It's not
that big a deal.

@amrit_ka_achar

Gotcha! I'll be back in a min, tho.
I'm needed. There are damsels
in distress here.

@notkrishnakumar

You mean ladies with mehndi
all over their hands who need
to be fed?

@amrit_ka_achar

Yep

@notkrishnakumar

Not sure if I like the idea of you
feeding other women.

I reread the text after I've hit send and cringe inwardly. Oh god, why do I sound so possessive? And *minutes* after I imagined kissing Rudra. The hypocrisy is staggering.

@amrit_ka_achar

Oh don't worry about it. These hands would be all for you if you were here.

This guy.

I smile stupidly at my phone, grinning from ear to ear.

But back to the pressing matter at hand: I need to do some stalking.

I head to Amrit's Instagram and type *Soumyaroop* into the search bar above his following list.

The first name that pops up is Soumyaroop Maheshwari, @soum_papdi. The handle is witty, because it's a spin on the wording for soan papdi, one of my favorite desi sweets. I click on his profile, frowning at the screen. His page is public, and the topmost picture on his feed is one where he has his arm around a pretty girl, underscored by a cheesy caption: Finding you was the best thing that happened to me this year, Mansi @_mxnsijoshi_

I tap on the bride's profile, check what's written underneath, and double back to Soumyaroop's page to find the same thing: Followed by amrit_ka_achar and pritigirlmantra.

Both the bride and the groom are followed by Amrit . . . and *Priti.*

Digha's words replay in my head, and the nerves in my brain nearly frazzle. It feels like I've made the next big discovery. Like I've found a cure for the common cold.

You're still following each other, and it wasn't even you who sent the re-follow request.

My heart speeds up in my chest as the realization washes over me, slowly at first, a gentle tide, before submerging me like a tsunami. The reason why Priti was so easy to convince and is so desperate to get to Goa on time is because she wants to stop the wedding.

Because the groom, Soumyaroop Maheshwari, is her ex-boyfriend.

15

DAMN, I'M NOT GIVING MAIN CHARACTER AFTER ALL—PRITI IS

Pune, Saturday

For a minute or so after, I just sit still, phone clutched in hand, staring at Soumyaroop's profile, a million thoughts flooding my mind at once.

Here I was, thinking *I* was the one on the whirlwind road trip of a lifetime to kiss my summer crush, but Priti has absolutely outdone me. She isn't just headed to Goa to infiltrate a wedding. She's there to *end* it. A Bollywood-level grand romantic gesture to get her ex-boyfriend back.

I let that thought sink in slowly before finally looking up from my phone. I'm reeling from the revelation as I look over at Priti, who has her head down and resting on the backpack in her lap. Her arms are crossed and concealing her face, so all I can see is a messy nest of a head. Rudra sits next to her, gazing out the window.

I reach for him behind Charu, trying to be as sneaky as possible. The tips of my fingers brush his shoulder. He looks over at me, brows knitting.

Look at your phone, I mouth while motioning at my own phone with my hands. My pitiful attempt at Dumb Charades is successful, because Rudra unlocks his phone. I head over to his profile and click on the message button.

A brand-new chat with him opens. It feels weird, chatting with him when he's right there, one seat away from me (never mind the fact that it's *Rudra*).

@notkrishnakumar

So I think I know who Priti's ex is

The *seen* text appears below my message, and I glance at Rudra, who starts typing. His expression is neutral, revealing nothing.

@rudradesaimusic

who is it?

@notkrishnakumar

You're not gonna ask me how I found out?

@rudradesaimusic

well, how did you find out?

@notkrishnakumar

I followed a hunch. You know how Priti's been desperate to get to the shaadi on time? And how you mentioned her ex lives in Powai?

@rudradesaimusic

yeah?

@notkrishnakumar

I figured chances are the ex

is one of Amrit's relatives,
but I found out from Amrit
that only the groom lives in Powai.

Her ex is Soumyaroop Maheshwari!

@rudradesaimusic

i doubt this is about him

@notkrishnakumar

Digha said smth about
Priti's ex refollowing her.

AND SOUMYAROOP IS FOLLOWING PRITI

SO IS HIS FIANCÉE MANSI

IT HAS TO BE HIM

@rudradesaimusic

hmm

I stare at the three-lettered reply for a second before scoffing out loud.

@notkrishnakumar

Hmm?!

I give you all this info and
all I get in return is a hmm?

@rudradesaimusic

what do you expect me to say?

@notkrishnakumar

Whatever.

I'm not surprised.

@rudradesaimusic

not surprised by what?

@notkrishnakumar

By the fact that you're such a dry texter

@rudradesaimusic

not everyone is as upbeat as you, sunflower

I peek at Rudra and find him smiling. My stomach literally swoops at the nickname, but now is not the time!

@notkrishnakumar

What do we do about it? Priti is going there to *stop* this wedding!

@rudradesaimusic

nothing, if you're right it's priti's call

we can't do anything to stop her

@notkrishnakumar

So we do nothing? And let Priti get away with attempting something so reckless? How is this not bothering you more?

@rudradesaimusic

how is this bothering *you* so much?

what priti does doesn't really affect your plans

I pause for a moment, recalling suddenly that Rudra would, in fact, *not* be keen on Priti getting back together with Soumyaroop. I think back to our conversation in the Sinhas' bedroom.

He doesn't strike me as the sort of person who would sabotage Priti's chance at love because he has feelings for her. Then again, how well do

I really know him? I can't be sure he isn't secretly vindictive like that.

@notkrishnakumar

It doesn't, I know, but can you blame me
if I want to see Priti happy again?
Her smiles barely reach her eyes anymore.
Soumyaroop looks like he might have feelings
for Priti too. If getting them back together
makes her happy, isn't that the right thing to do?
For not just Priti and him, but also Mansi,
who might be getting into a marriage
with someone hung up over their ex?

I almost wince when I read back through my messages because oh god, why do I sound so corny?

@rudradesaimusic

i didn't think you cared
about her that much

@notkrishnakumar

I didn't think I did either
but Priti has always meant
something to me.

I'm not sure I can forgive her after everything
but I understand her, I guess.

@rudradesaimusic

you don't owe anyone forgiveness,
but I do think you would
both be happier if you were able
to give that to each other

@notkrishnakumar

Maybe, but thanks for seeing my side of things too.

With Priti, I mean. You barely know me.
At least you barely *knew* me up until yesterday.

Rudra doesn't type anything for a long minute after that, so I assume he's done with our conversation. I move my index finger to the lock button to click my phone closed, but then the three dots appear below my message, and I hold my breath as his text comes through.

@rudradesaimusic

maybe we never really spoke
to each other until yesterday

but i've known you since we were kids

I stare down at the message for a long while after that, even when Rudra shuts his phone and rests his head back, not looking at me. Something warm cradles my heart, making me all fuzzy from within.

I inhale deeply, glancing out the window as I finally set my phone down, watching the remaining trekkers approach the bus. They get in, chatting among themselves, and their laughter fills the silence of the space.

Right now, I wish I could reverse time, back to when I was an eleven-year-old, when I met Rudra Desai for the very first time.

Only this time, instead of letting him stay a still figure in the background of the memories I have from my childhood, where I'm dancing at the very front with all my cousins while he remains quietly seated on the chairs by the wall, I would walk up to him . . .

And I would befriend him.

16

GUJJU BOYS WILL KILL YOU IF YOU INTERRUPT THEIR BHAI FEST—UNLESS YOU'RE PRETTY (OR *PRITI*. SEE WHAT I DID THERE?)

Pune, Saturday

I'm just about to doze off when Jalaj starts clapping his hands together. Charu nudges me gently, and I sit up in my seat, my eyelids so heavy it's a struggle to keep them open. We're on our way again, off to Prabalmachi.

"What's happening?" I mumble, glancing around through my lashes.

"Group bonding sessions," Charu says, grinning with excitement. "This is always my favorite part of the trip."

"I'm too sleepy." I yawn, leaning back against the seat. "Can I skip it?"

"No way, he'll flip out."

That makes me sit up again. "I didn't think he was the sort of person to flip out."

"Oh, he *does*. Rarely, but it's possible. And trust me, you don't want to see it." Charu pats my arm. "C'mon, it'll be fun. We're playing antakshari."

Normally, I wouldn't be one to turn down a good game of antakshari, but in case we forgot, I spent most of last night stalking Rudra on Instagram and making (or at least, attempting to make) a pros and cons list. And in case we *also* forgot, I get extremely crabby when I'm sleepy. Jalaj might be one to watch out for, but I'm no less, thank you very much.

"Since we're all going to be heading on an adventure together," Jalaj starts, "it's important for us to get to know one another."

"And you think antakshari is the way to do that?" Varun says, snorting.

"Yeah, you got a problem with that?" Jalaj says, cocking his eyebrows. His face is a terrifying mix of cool composure and challenge. All my thoughts of battling him for sleep go right out the window.

"No," Varun mutters, his grin faltering. "Sorry, boss."

Charu shrugs, whispering to me, "I told you."

"Anyway, I'm sure all of you know how antakshari works," Jalaj continues. "We'll divide the twelve of you into two teams, and one team will begin the game by singing a song starting with the letter assigned to them. Once the first team has stopped singing, the second team will make note of the last letter and start a song with that. I won't play, as I'll be the neutral entity and judge. That, and I'm a terrible singer."

"I can vouch for that," Varun says, his grin back up and splitting his face. "Trust me, you don't want to hear him sing."

"Did he already forget Jalaj checked him in front of everybody?" I whisper to Charu, thoroughly amused.

"Don't even start. He's like a Daruma doll. Bounces right back up."

"Can we sing in Gujarati?" one of the six college boys who joined our group asks.

"You can sing in any language," Jalaj says.

"Cool."

"You guys are Gujjus?" Rudra asks, and it's startling to hear him initiate a conversation with someone. But I guess when it comes to your ilk, you'll always find yourself feeling more comfortable.

"Three of us are," the boy says, pointing to himself and the two boys seated opposite him.

"I'm Gujju too," Rudra says, smirking. "કેમ છો?"[1]

"મજામાં!"[2] the boy replies enthusiastically.

"તારું નામ શું છે?"[3]

"પદમ પટેલ."[4]

I've heard enough Gujarati spoken in Bollywood movies to know what they're saying until *Padam Patel*, but whatever follows sounds like gibberish to me.

"Okay, boys, much as this little Gujju bhai gathering is endearing as hell, can we begin the game?" Priti says, clearing her throat.

Frowning, the three boys snap toward Priti, but the moment they see her, they all go quiet. One of them—not Padam—even gawks shamelessly at her, jaw hanging open.

Predictable. *The perks of pretty privilege*, I think, sighing. Priti really has no clue.

"No, that's fine," Jalaj says, shrugging. "I mean, it *is* bonding."

"Exclusive bonding, sure," Priti says.

Rudra sighs, but he doesn't say anything. The things people do for love . . .

---

1 *Language*: Gujarati; *Translation*: How are you?
2 *Language*: Gujarati; *Translation*: I'm good!
3 *Language*: Gujarati; *Translation*: What is your name?
4 *Language*: Gujarati; *Translation*: Padam Patel.

(Okay *fine*, I'm not exactly the best example here because I'm literally on a road trip to kiss Amrit and I'm not even in love with him, but still.)

"Let's divide the teams. Who here can sing?" Jalaj asks.

Digha raises her hand. So does Charu. Padam raises his hand as well. I glance at Rudra, waiting for him to do the same so I can follow suit, but when he doesn't, I think the better of it. What's the point of letting everyone know I sing, anyway? What if I say I do and end up sounding awful? I haven't sung in ages.

"हे भगवान!"[5] Priti says, grabbing Rudra's hand and raising it for him. "There's no need to be modest." Rudra groans, but Priti keeps his hand up in the air, pointing an accusatory finger at him. "*This* guy has a hundred and forty thousand followers and is going to Juilliard. So yeah, he can bloody well sing."

"Priti—" Rudra starts, turning red.

"Shut up." Priti turns to me, squinting. "Do you want me to come up there and make you put your hand up as well?"

"N-no," I say sheepishly, raising my hand.

"So that's five singers," Jalaj says. "Charu, Digha, and you"—he points to Padam—"can be on one team. Rudra and Krishna, you can be in the other. Seems only fair because Rudra's such a prodigy." He divides the rest of us, which leaves Priti, Rudra, me, and three of the college boys in our team. Charu, Digha, Varun, and the other three form the second team. "Shuffle around so you're sitting next to your team members."

Obviously, that means Charu and I have to swap seats. I'm trying to quell my delight at the thought of Rudra being on my team again, but I can't help it. It puts us at a huge advantage. And I'm not one to shy away from bagging another win, however small it may be.

---

5 *Language*: Hindi; *Translation*: Oh god!

My heart starts pounding faster in my chest as I sit next to Rudra, my thigh brushing his. My toes curl inside my shoes. Rudra throws me a glance, worrying at his lower lip with his teeth.

Jalaj does the antakshari anthem to assign the starting letter, "बैठे बैठे क्या करें, करना है कुछ काम। शुरू करो अंताक्षरी, लेकर प्रभु का नाम। बोलो राम राम राम, बोलो श्याम श्याम श्याम।"[6] The final word lands on Charu's team, kicking off the game with the letter *M*.

Antakshari is one of those overplayed games that somehow never gets boring. We quickly exhaust the usual Hindi songs, the ones that always crop up: "Barso Re," "Gulabi Aankhen Jo Teri Dekhi," "Aaja Aaja Main Hoon Pyar Tera," "Ek Do Teen Char," "Lakdi Ki Kathi," "Yeh Shaam Mastani," "Give Me Some Sunshine," "Sunny Sunny," and so on.

What's funny is no matter who's playing, we always end up singing older songs from our parents' generation. It's probably because our introduction to the game was during sangeets or family functions, where a majority of the crowd was much older.

There are a few Gujarati, Marathi, and Punjabi songs here and there, and even an Odia number, but we barely sing any English songs. With Rudra on our team, we're clearly leading in terms of melody, but our teams are neck and neck with song suggestions.

I'm smiling and laughing the whole time I sing, straining to hold my pitch while everyone around me strays. But it doesn't matter. All my sleep is forgotten, and I can't remember the last time I had so much fun.

What I love about games like antakshari and pugata is how none of us is really *taught* how to play these online or through some rulebook. Every single Indian kid will know these games because it's passed by

---

6 *Language*: Hindi; *Translation*: What do we do while sitting, some work must be done. So, in the name of God, let's play some antakshari. Say Ram Ram Ram, say Shyam Shyam Shyam.

word of mouth through generations. It just makes my heart so warm to know there's this small part of me that connects to everyone here, that connects me to *home*.

Because isn't home supposed to be the place you can come back to even if you leave it, as it's always going to be yours, no matter how much you change or how far away from it you move?

At some point, Varun pulls out his LED speaker and Jalaj turns off the lights of the bus entirely, breaking me out of my thoughts. The technicolor projection splashes over all our faces as we sing until our throats are hoarse. The windows are thrown wide open, and the wind whirlpools its way in, whipping at our hair. It's my team's turn, and I notice Rudra and Priti getting stuck on the syllable *Sh*.

The song choice for me is obvious, what with all the thoughts that have been running through my mind.

"Sham."

It's a campfire song by Amit Trivedi from the movie *Aisha*. It's popular, so everyone joins me when I sing the opening verse. I close my eyes, trying to lose myself in the song, imagining sitting by a warm, crackling fire under a night sky full to the brim with stars. Everyone else's voice is drowned out by the roaring of the wind.

Then, through it all, one voice breaks through. It's a male voice, in a gentle, lower register than mine, joining me in my singing. I keep my eyes closed, brow furrowing as I wonder what it could be about this voice that broke through into my little fireside reverie.

It takes me a moment to realize the voice belongs to Rudra. My eyes open slowly, lashes sticking to the bottom lid because I have them shut so tight, and I'm surprised to find that he and I are the only ones singing. Everyone's watching us, some humming along but not singing, others with their eyes shut as they listen, and Priti . . . staring.

Her expression reflects her realization of what us—*this*—looks like. I ignore it for once, not letting it faze me.

Instead, I turn toward Rudra, who turns to look right back at me, and the fervor with which our gazes hook together makes a tingle shoot through my body. We sing the last verse of the song while looking at each other, voices harmonizing in near perfection.

I inhale sharply when I finish singing the last word, and my heart is beating so hard my pulse is in my throat. My hands are clutching the fabric of my borrowed shorts, and my palms are sweaty. I finally tear my gaze away from Rudra's, turning to look at the others. Everyone starts clapping, and Digha says something about how Rudra and I shouldn't be put in a team together again for anything because we keep winning.

Priti's stare is burning a hole in my cheek, but I'm not going to look at her. Not after what—whatever *that* was—happened.

Luckily, the bus rolls to a stop just then, bouncing over gravel and lifting everyone's attention off us, including Priti's.

"Pit stop," Jalaj says, checking his watch. "You have fifteen minutes."

All of us file out. Priti and Digha rush to the bathroom while the others enter the dhaba we've parked in front of. I will need to pee eventually, but I'm not a huge fan of public toilets. I'd rather attend nature's call in the bushes during the trek.

Plastic chairs and tables have been arranged within the dhaba, and there are a few groups of truck drivers seated within. I feel self-conscious at first, because I'm in my shorts, but they don't really spare us a glance, which is new and, honestly, welcome. We sit down, and I settle back against the plastic chair.

Varun asks, "Chai, anyone?"

"Yes, please," I say immediately. I can feel the beginning of a deep sleep starting to creep into my eyes, but I have a whole night of trekking awaiting me. *Sleep* needs to be gotten rid of as soon as possible.

All the six college guys opt for chais. Charu and Rudra grab a Maaza and a Red Bull respectively from the refrigerator at the far end of the dhaba. A bright white light buzzes above us, and I'm grateful to have applied Odomos before we came here because there are mosquitoes under the table and flitting lazily over our heads.

Rudra and Charu take seats on either side of me, and I try my best to not look at Rudra as he pops open the can of Red Bull and starts gulping the thing down. Within seconds, he's emptied the can. His tongue sticks out cutely to take the last few drops, and I tamp down any thoughts of having his tongue in my mouth before they can sprout up.

Rudra yawns, covering his mouth with his hand. "God, I needed that."

"Clearly." For some absurd reason, I feel like ending our conversation on *clearly* would be unimaginative, so I blurt the first thing that comes to mind. "That duet back there."

Rudra glances at me. "What about it?"

Fuck me.

Seriously, fuck me.

I just had to say something, didn't I?

Got an awkward conversation or topic to tackle? Don't worry, Krishna Kumar will dive headlong into it!

"Our voices go well together," I say, the million Krishnas in my brain hurling curses at me left, right, and center.

Rudra sets the can on the table, dragging his finger in a circle along the rim. "You're a beautiful singer." He clears his throat, shifting in his seat. "Uh, I mean—you've got a beautiful voice."

I smile teasingly at him. "There's nothing wrong with accidentally calling me beautiful." Wait, *why* did I say that? What genetic mutation in the forty-six chromosomes that my parents passed onto me went *this* wrong?

Rudra fiddles with the hem of his sleeve. Wait, am I making him nervous? "I meant your voice, but if I had to call you . . . that, it wouldn't really be accidental."

I stare at him, my heart picking up pace. "What do you mean?"

Rudra scans my face, his pupils blowing. "I mean. It's the truth. You being—beautiful. Not accidental."

If I were a cyborg, all my parts would probably fritz at this very moment. But I'm not, and I have no wires (that I know of), so I manage to get out a mumbled "Thank you."

Rudra may be flirting with me—again!—but this is the first time Priti isn't even here. So if he isn't doing this to try to make her jealous, does that mean Rudra has meant everything he's said?

I've had my share of crushes, like what I had for Amrit—no, like what I *have* for Amrit—and they've all been accompanied by that squishy warmth within, as if torching my insides. And butterflies, so many of them, flapping a violent rhythm in my stomach. Nothing about these feelings is out of the ordinary, special, or new. What it is, what *this* is . . . is unexpected.

I've never found Rudra attractive in the sense that I ever gave him a second glance and went *damn*. The first time I realized he even remotely fell into the attractive category was when Srishti pointed it out to me during the house party. And I need that easy humor and charisma in people to be drawn to them—the sort of ease Shah Rukh Khan oozes in all his movies.

Rudra is the opposite. He's not like SRK from any of his movies. He's like Sidharth Malhotra's character, Abhimanyu, from *Student of the Year*, I think. My type is Shanaya. Not Rohan. And certainly not Abhimanyu.

Then why Rudra? And why *now*?

A waiter gets us our chais, pulling me out of my rant. I cradle the paper cup in my palms, letting the steam waft over my face. There's something about dhaba chai that remains unmatched when compared to the chai they sell at bigger, posher places. Every sip is full of flavor, and I can taste so many spices at once—elaichi, adrak, laung, dalchini, and even a hint of haldi.

"Uff," I sigh. "This has to be one of the best chais I've ever had."

"Really?" Rudra asks.

"Second it," Varun says, slurping loudly as he sips. Frankly, it's the only correct way to drink chai.

"Take a sip," I say, holding the cup out to Rudra. He takes it from me, and his fingers brush mine briefly. His touch is cool from clutching the Red Bull can. It contrasts sharply with the heat of my hands, and the sensation makes my pulse vault.

Rudra sips the chai from the exact same spot on the rim where my lips were a second ago. The action draws my attention to his mouth. He swallows, making that damn protruding Adam's apple bob again.

He passes the cup back to me, and I sip the rest of the chai, hyperaware of the fact that Rudra's lips were on my cup. I wouldn't be if it were anyone else, but it is *Rudra*, with his pretty lips and pretty lashes. And this time, without any guilt or regret, I wonder what it would be like to kiss him.

To kiss Rudra.

But before I have the chance to take my thoughts any further, Priti and Digha return, giggling as they take the two vacant seats left for them, one beside Rudra and the other beside Varun.

My muscles tense as Priti glances at me, dragging the plastic chair forward. It's silly to think someone might know what's going on in my mind, but with Priti it almost seems possible. Rudra pulls her attention away by sliding the menu toward her.

I've let this trip get extended beyond measure. We should be checking into that hotel in Goa right now, and I should be gearing up to meet Amrit tomorrow. Instead, I'm being put into these exasperating situations and warring with thoughts of kissing someone I barely spoke to until a couple of days ago. I long to talk it out with Srishti, but she's going to be incognito until Tuesday, and it's all on me to handle this, *without* her blessed advice.

It's just one more day; I'll be in Goa tomorrow, I tell myself, gulping down the jealousy that stings the back of my throat when I notice how Priti's and Rudra's knees accidentally touch under the table. This unexplainable dynamic, tension, and affection between them wasn't my problem to begin with. I'm just here to get to Goa and hopefully never have to see either of them again.

I take in a deep breath, convinced.

I can do this.

17

I CAN'T FUCKING DO THIS

Prabalmachi, Saturday

We're about fifteen minutes from Prabalmachi, and the bus has descended into a peaceful hush. Varun, Digha, Priti, and Charu are fast asleep, and so are a couple of the college boys. Jalaj is deep in conversation with Padam about something fitness-related.

I tried to sleep earlier, but the chai will probably keep me up for the next few hours, so I resign myself to staring out the window, listening to my audiobook, until I see something move in the corner of my vision.

I turn and find Rudra getting to his feet, lumbering to the front of the bus. I frown, wondering if he's going to ask the driver to stop the bus so he can attend nature's call or something, but he flops onto the metal steps that lower toward the entrance instead, disappearing from view.

For a few minutes, I stay put, but I can't help myself. I get to my feet, sneak past a snoring Charu, and tiptoe down the aisle between the seats.

Rudra is sitting on the second step from the top, staring at the view outside, his elbows resting on his thighs. His headphones curl around his neck instead of his ears, playing muffled music. I hesitate for a second, reminded of what I told myself back in the dhaba. I need to keep my feelings in check.

But what could the harm in just sitting beside him be? I need to talk to him about the Priti situation anyway. I doubt I'm going to get another moment alone with him without her shooting me wary stares.

Giving in, I clear my throat to alert him of my presence, making him turn back. As he looks up at me, the breath is snatched out of my body, because he looks so . . . *sad*. His eyes are brimming with emotion. He probably didn't expect me to come up here, and for a moment, everything about him is unguarded and vulnerable, walls down.

But then he blinks, and whatever I saw there momentarily is gone. Replacing it is that neutral expression again, the one he's clearly mastered. I wonder if it's because he now knows who Priti's ex is and why she's going to Goa. I wonder if the possibility of Priti getting back together with Soumyaroop is breaking his heart.

"Can I join you?" I ask softly.

"Sure," he says, shifting so I can sit next to him. I step down and instantly regret it, because the space is so narrow and the step so steep, I nearly trip. I reach a hand out to steady myself against the railing bar, but Rudra takes it. I carefully sit next to him, and he immediately withdraws. We're touching all along our sides, my right shoulder resting against his left.

Even though it's summer, a chilly draft blows in through the entrance, and I instinctively seek the warmth oozing from Rudra's body. Goose bumps sprout along my bare arms and legs, and I rub them absent-mindedly.

The ends of my loose hair tickle my cheeks. I pucker my lips, blowing them away, realizing I should've probably tied my hair into a ponytail.

Rudra is smiling at me when I finally look at him, making those dimples appear in his chin again, along the lower corners of his lips. I want to press my fingers to them, as if to smooth them out.

I raise my eyebrows, struggling to look at him through my hair. "What?"

He shakes his head, turning away. "Nothing."

"You're smiling again."

"I have a hair tie, if you want," he says, pointing to his (stupidly hot) man bun.

"Don't you need it?"

"I have a clip. I'll manage. My hair is wavy, unlike yours, so it'll stay."

I consider refusing it—but what could be so wrong in borrowing a hair tie from him? Nothing romantic about it.

"Thanks," I say.

Rudra grabs the band and tugs it off, making his silky waves tumble from the bun. He hands the black hair tie to me, running his fingers through his hair to get the knots out. The wind gives him an assist, and when he places his clip between his teeth so he can gather his hair in his hands again, it's impossible *not* to stare. I watch, fascinated, as he tugs the clip from his mouth, securing his hair expertly, not a strand brushing his face.

Most guys I've known have had short hair, so hair-related actions have been exclusively attractive in girls for me. Like that one time I watched my crush in high school amass her amber locs and pineapple them, exposing the nape of her neck. But there's something so relentlessly attractive about watching a guy do that to his hair too.

He glances down at his hair tie, still clutched in my hand, then back up at me. "Aren't you going to tie your hair?"

"Oh. Um—yeah. One sec." I fumble with my hair, which is flying all over the place at this point. I tie it up, hoping it stays, but the strands just keep breaking free. "Damn it," I say, pulling the hair tie out and thrusting it back into his palm. "My hair is too straight for this."

"Turn around. Let me do it for you."

"Do what?"

"Just turn."

I hesitantly turn, my back facing him, staring at the view rushing past outside. Rudra shifts closer to me, until I can feel his warm breath on my neck.

"Can I—?" he asks. I nod.

Rudra brings his hands up and collects the hair from the front of my scalp to the back, accumulating it at the base of my neck. His fingertips are feather soft as they brush against my temples, then the space between the tip of my eyebrows and hairline, and loop over my ears. I shut my eyes tight, the sensation of being touched so gingerly—in spots I never thought could elicit any reaction in me—nearly bowling me over.

It's warm and comforting, the way he gathers my hair, combing it with his fingers, grasping strands as they slip loose and tucking them back in place. I've only ever had a few people touch my hair like this before: Mummy whenever she used to comb it for school, Papa when he used to give me coconut oil massages every Sunday, Nani when she used to stroke my hair back so she could properly feed me dahi shakkar before my exams. And Priti . . . when we used to watch all those hairstyle tutorials together on YouTube and experiment on each other's hair.

The memories send a wave of nostalgia through me.

I shiver as Rudra's fingers accidentally touch the sensitive skin at the nape of my neck. He separates my hair into three partitions, then braids it expertly, tying the end of the plait with the hair tie.

"Done."

I am clutching my hands together so tight the blood has drained from my palms. I can still feel the ghost of his fingers in my hair, his tender touch on my ears. What would it be like . . . to be kissed there?

"Thanks," I croak, repositioning myself so we're side by side again.

"No problem. You should braid your hair when it gets into your face. Especially because it's straight now." His eyes are like cups of hot chocolate. "It used to be wavy before, right?"

"Yes, like yours. I got it done at the beginning of the summer. My hair was always too frizzy to manage."

"When the treatment wears off, you should try wavy hair creams. They work for me."

My next words are unexpected, but they spill out anyway, because there seems to be little connection between my brain and mouth these days. "Why? You don't like the straight hair?"

Rudra looks surprised by my question. "No. It looks good either way."

"Sorry," I say, kicking myself inwardly. "Didn't mean to put you on the spot. I was just curious; I'm not sure if I'm going to keep it this way."

Rudra's eyes scroll across my face, glazing over. "You have a heart-shaped face, and the wavy hair complemented that. Especially when you used to part it at the center. But the straight hair brings out the brown in your irises. It makes the crinkles in the corner of your eyes stand out and . . ." His voice suddenly trails off, as if he's just realized what he's saying. He coughs, breaking his gaze, flicking his eyes to the dark trees outside.

I stare at him, speechless. A million thoughts are careening through my mind all at once, and I can't seem to grasp a single one, can't seem to maintain a hold on my emotions.

"Rudra—" I start, but a ping cuts me off. I glance down at my phone on my lap, screen turned upward and lighting up our dark little corner in warm blue. It's a message from Amrit.

@amrit_ka_achar

Well, what do you know,
I'm still thinking about you.

Discomfort lodges in my throat. For the first time, I don't feel *anything* when I read the message from him. I lock the screen, looking up at Rudra, collecting my thoughts again—

When I see it.

The look on Rudra's face. His features have hardened, and the skin around his jaw tautens.

He saw it. He saw the message.

I open my mouth to offer an explanation, not knowing why, because we're all here only because of Amrit, aren't we? But the bus comes to a halt, and Jalaj calls out to let us know we've arrived.

Just like that, the moment's gone.

18

IF I CAN MAKE IT UP THIS MOUNTAIN WITH AN UNHOOKED BRA AND BUTCHERED CONFIDENCE, WHAT MAKES YOU THINK YOU CAN'T?

Prabalmachi, Saturday

It's so dark outside I can barely see my hand in front of my face. Flashlights are flicked on, and I have to squint to let my eyes adjust to the light.

"All right, everyone, gather around," Jalaj says. He points to a flickering dot of light in the distance, nestled among the dark mountains. "That's the base camp we're trekking to. We'll head there, eat our food, and get some sleep before the trek to the Prabalmachi peak point."

Digha gasps. "*That's* the base camp? But it's so far away."

"It seems far away, but it's just a one-and-a-half-hour trek."

"And you think that's short?" Digha says, her eyes wide. "There's no way I'm going to be able to do this."

"Don't worry about it," Varun says, wrapping his arm around her shoulder. "If it gets tough, I'll carry you."

And who's going to carry me if I *collapse?* I think, obviously not voicing it out loud but concerned nevertheless.

I've never been a fitness freak or even someone who exercises regularly. I spent most of my free time caught between studying and extracurriculars, and I was on zero sports teams. I did try track for a while but failed miserably at it. And by "failed miserably," I mean stumbled, rolled, skidded, and fell flat on my face during a relay race, nearly impaling myself on my baton, in front of what seemed like the entire school (actually it was just a bunch of freshmen, but that doesn't make it better). If I had any hidden talent for exercise, I'd know by now.

Priti gyms regularly; she's got those washboard Disha Patani abs, and she's flaunting them right now in her black tank top and spandex yoga pants, her jacket sleeves knotted around her waist. I'm sure *she's* going to have no problem trekking.

I don't know the college guys well enough, but they did mention earlier that they'd been trekking all summer, so I'm assuming they have some experience. Varun said he'd carry Digha if he had to, so I'm guessing he does as well. Charu said she's done this same trek before, and she looks pumped. Rudra's lean, but that's no indication of stamina.

That leaves Digha and me. We exchange an uneasy smile as the group shuffles forward, and I'm reassured because there's at least someone who's feeling the same way as me.

We follow the dark, tree-bordered path zigzagging up the mountain at a steady incline. At first, the route is easy to follow. The trees aren't thickly interknit around us, so the path is weakly lit by the creamy moon.

But it starts to get rocky about ten minutes in, and that's when I hear myself panting out loud. My T-shirt is already damp with sweat, cloth sticking to my spine and stomach, because places near Lonavala, while cold, are still humid. Perspiration forms droplets on my face, and I wipe at it hastily with the back of my hand, feeling icky.

See, this is one of the main reasons why I despise exercising and working out. I sweat a *lot*, and anything that gets me moving for more than five minutes has the tendency to make me look like a soaked rat. Now, I'm not sure if it's my tight sports bra that's making it harder to breathe, but I'm wheezing so loud that Rudra, who is walking a few feet ahead of me, pauses to look back.

"Hey," he says. "You need some help?"

"N-no," I say, but my voice comes out as shrill and airy as a half-assed whistle. I manage to trek for a minute more, the path getting trickier with each passing second, before my lungs feel like they've caught fire, and I can't walk another step, close to blacking out.

Luckily, Digha times out before me. She raises both her hands, palms perpendicular to each other, and barely manages a croak. I slump against the nearest rock, breathing deeply, in and out, in and out, until some of my lost consciousness pours back into me.

Once I feel reassured that nothing I swallow will go down the wrong pipe, I take long gulps of the water mixed with ORS from my bottle clipped to my fanny pack. I empty half the bottle down my throat.

Much better.

This is barely the start of the trek, not even the highlight, which is the journey to the Prabalmachi peak and watching the fireflies. Jalaj said the base camp is an hour and a half from the starting point; it's been, like, thirty minutes, and I'm done. Screw my enthusiasm from earlier; I should've known I wasn't built for this.

Around me, the wind lightly rustles the leaves and branches of trees, darting between gaps in the wilderness and wrapping me in cool comfort. We're paused at a slanting, rocky climb, gravel and loose stones sliding and crunching under our feet. Although it's dark, my eyes have adjusted better to the little light the moon provides, and I can make out the others' silhouettes. Because of my embarrassing slowness, I've somehow drifted to the very back of the group.

Great, now I'll be the *first* to get eaten by a bear if it decides to target our group from the back.

I tilt my head up and look at the sky, gaze flicking from one star to another, then another, then another, my vision swimming, until it's time to resume walking.

"Single file, everybody," Jalaj says as Varun begins scaling the rocky incline, one hand holding Digha's and the other stretched out to balance his frame. "If you're sure-footed, you can climb with just your feet; think of it as ascending steep, tall stairs. If not, don't hesitate to go down on all fours. The more limbs you have steadying you on the rocks, the more your body will feel grounded."

The others follow. Three of the college boys, then Priti, who doesn't need to use her hands at all. She uses her long legs to propel herself up from one rock to another. The remaining college boys follow, then Charu, who gingerly goes down on all fours, using her hands to help with the climbing.

Rudra looks back at me, at the (possibly) empty space behind me (unless there's a bear waiting in the shadows of bushes for the right moment to pounce), and motions me forward, saying, "After you."

I hesitantly survey the climb. It looks easy enough. Now, if I crouch right, like Charu did, I might just be able to do it. I grab a rock sticking out about a tenth of the way up the incline, using the support to pull myself up. I repeat the motion a few more times and, with a steady hold on the rocks, scale diagonally upward. There's a crunch of gravelly mud behind me as Rudra starts climbing.

At the very top, I clutch a rock and hoist myself up . . . but it comes loose and tumbles out of the way, narrowly missing hitting Rudra in the face. The sudden loss of grip makes me lose my footing, and my foot scrapes the slope, sliding into empty air.

I let out a squeak, knowing, in those disastrous few moments, that I'm going to fall hard and injure myself and bleed out and possibly die—

A hand snakes around my waist from my left, holding me in place. I wince as my bare knee scrapes against the sharp ridges of a stone. Heat blooms, blood trickling out in ugly dots.

My foot flails for a second or two before finding a hold again.

"Just reach for that rock there," Rudra says beside me, taking my left hand, which lost its grip on that dratted two-faced bitch of a rock. He guides it up, releasing it only when I've gripped one much more stable than the last.

The pain in my knee is sharp and piercing. But Rudra's hand is on my waist again, diverting my attention, his fingers touching my bare skin where my T-shirt has ridden up underneath the strap of my fanny pack.

His hand is warm and steady, holding me with the assurance of a guitarist holding his instrument. I turn to look at him, and our eyes lock in the semidarkness.

"You steady?" Rudra asks, his voice soft. "You lost your balance there."

"Yes," I squeak, the near-death experience making me ramble. "Yep. Super. All cool. Never been better." *Stop talking. For the love of god, please stop.*

"I'm going to need you to get to the top," he says, motioning to the break in the rocky wall on his left, which reveals nothing but dark-green blades of grass and damp, monsoon-soaked mud. "I can't climb until you do."

I nod, trying my best to ignore the feeling of his hand cupping my bare hip and failing miserably. He grips my calf as I shimmy up the last bit, giving me a boost. The pads of his fingers elicit a tingly, tickly feeling as they touch the soft, thin skin right behind my knees, and it's all I can do to not let it faze me.

I get to my feet, dusting dirt and tiny stones from my body, watching as Rudra edges himself to the middle, climbs, and joins me. He's covered in dust and grime, and there are dark patches of sweat where his T-shirt sticks to his body, his hair coming undone from his bun, and yet, he smells *so* good it's unfair.

We both sit in the dirt for a few seconds, staring at each other in the flashlight of my phone. My mind goes back to the moment on the bus, his hands roving through my hair, his breath skittering over my neck and ear. I break eye contact first, getting to my feet, ignoring the sharp pain in my knee.

"Will you be able to walk?" Rudra asks, standing and pointing to the scrape on my knee.

"Yeah, it's just a scratch," I say. "I'll clean and bandage it at the camp."

"Guys, what the hell." Priti materializes from the darkness between the trees, her hair wildly framing her face, flashlight bouncing around. Jalaj and Charu are right behind her. "Could you be any slower?" Priti glances down at my knee, noticing the scrape. "Wait, what happened? Are you okay?"

At first, I'm so startled that those words came from Priti's mouth, I have no clue how to respond. But Rudra speaks up, saving me from the embarrassment of not being able to say a simple *Thanks, I'm fine.*

"She slipped. Didn't fall, though." He doesn't say anything about how his hand grabbed me at the right moment, how it felt on my bare waist, how close we stood on those rocks together . . .

"We have first aid at the camp," Jalaj says. "Don't worry."

"Okay," Priti says, looking between Rudra and me. "So can we go now?"

"Yes," I say, ignoring the twist in my chest, fighting the temptation to attempt to gauge Rudra's expression.

The rest of the trek to the camp goes much better. I narrow the problem of my breathlessness down to my bra and swiftly unhook it when no one's looking. I can breathe much better after that, so I'm not panting like a dog as much.

The night air gets cooler, and the sweat ices on my body, making me shiver as we ascend. There are multiple stops along the way, small hutlike constructions that Jalaj says are juice stands and chaat stalls run by the locals during the day. A wave of shame deluges me. The locals make this ascent *every day* to tend these stands. And they do it while carrying heavy stuff, like water cans, fruit and vegetable baskets, and jars of sugar and salt.

And here I am, struggling to make it up with an unhooked bra and a fanny pack.

"Ohmygod, look!" Digha calls out suddenly, making us stop in our tracks. My heart stutters, and I think that the bear has finally caught up to us and is going to rip me open on the forest floor—

Fireflies.

Above us, glowing against the dark shadows of interlocking branches, are *hundreds* of fireflies, flashing in perfect synchrony.

"Switch off your torches," Charu says. "Bright lights interrupt their mating process."

All the lights go off, one after the other, and we're veiled in darkness again. I gape at the fireflies in awe. They're like tiny drops of lemon-yellow light, bobbing and twinkling all around us. I'm so mesmerized by the sight that I don't even get my phone out to capture the view, but the others do.

"Fuck Android, man," Varun says, groaning. "Can't see shit."

"Perks of having an iPhone," Priti says, grinning as her shutter goes on and off, capturing pictures.

Varun grumbles, muttering something about how he *would* buy an iPhone if he weren't broke, then shoves his Android back into his pocket.

"You'll see more up ahead, especially during the second leg of the trek," Jalaj says.

Priti accidentally turns on the flash on her phone as she takes another picture, and all of us protest in unison, horrified yelps cutting through the silence of the forest.

"*Jeez*, I'm sorry," Priti says, nearly flinging her phone to the ground in shock as we all attack her. "What's the problem, though?"

"The fireflies take it as a threat," Charu says. "They're all competing for the females' attention, and any light *that* bright is an alpha to them. It discourages them."

The funny image of a dejected firefly packing its things into a potli and giving up on mating pops into my head, and I giggle. The others glance at me, and I cover my mouth with my fist, the humor only furthered by their expressions.

"What?" Priti asks, lips pursed.

"Nothing."

"Hey, look, there's one!" Digha says, pointing to a spot about a foot above our heads. The firefly floats above us, secluded from the swarm. "Why's it not with the others?"

"You demoralized it, Priti," I say, snorting.

"Ha ha, very funny," Priti says, rolling her eyes so hard, I'm convinced she can see inside her head.

"Fireflies have cliques," Charu says, grinning. "If you're not cool enough to flash like them, you're kicked out of the group."

“Look what you did, Priti,” I say, my lips turned downward but mirth making my shoulders shake. “You’ve bullied the poor thing out of getting laid.”

Priti smacks my arm, annoyance written all over her features, but I don’t miss the slight twitch of her lips before she turns away from me and hides her smile.

19

SOMETIMES A GIRLIE JUST WANTS SOMEONE TO PROFESS THEIR LOVE FOR HER THE WAY SRK DID IN *RAB NE BANA DI JODI*

Prabalmachi, Sunday

We reach the campsite after what feels like a decade. It's a bunch of connected one-story buildings laid out over the rocky, uneven landscape. There's a bathroom that's so dirty I don't dare use it, a kitchen, a few bedrooms, and multiple tables and chairs arranged along the breadth of the main building.

All of it looks like it might've been part of a village school complex, with open corridors and thatched roofs. There are a few men here who come to help us the moment we arrive, probably Prabalmachi locals, handing us parcels of food. In each parcel, there's one samosa, two theplas, kaccha mango pickle, a Britannia cake, a Frooti, and a packet of chips.

"The tents are set up out back," Jalaj says. "There's a water cooler to your right. Take a ten-minute break—eat, drink, freshen up—and we'll assign you your tents."

We sit in a row on the raised floor of the main building, a step higher than the ground. After borrowing a first aid kit from the helpers and bandaging my wound, I set my food on my lap and scarf it down, only now realizing how hungry I am. Rudra gets up to go fill his bottle and offers to fill mine and Priti's. I smile gratefully at him, unclipping my bottle and handing it to him.

After I'm done eating, I dump the parcel into the garbage bin and walk over to the wooden railing looking out over the valley. The view from here is breathtaking.

The stars are bright, and it's like a few of them broke off from the sky and decorated the town, lighting it up from within. Because of the hilly topography, there are points where there's no illumination, only the darkness of forests and shadows of mountains, while at others, there are clumps of civilization.

It reminds me of the scene from *Rab Ne Bana Di Jodi* when Shah Rukh Khan spelled out the words *I love you* for Anushka Sharma using the lights of the city of Amritsar. The first time I watched the movie, with my laptop on my lap and a tub of popcorn in my hand, I was filled with longing to have someone love *me* that much one day.

God save me. Bollywood has shaped the hopeless romantic in me, and no amount of indoctrination or hypnosis will ever be able to change that. Not that I want it to, but I wish it didn't unnecessarily raise my expectations for romance and make me do impulsive things like go on a whole road trip for one kiss.

"Hey."

I break out of my flurry of thoughts, turning to look back at Rudra, who walks over. He comes to stand beside me, leaning his arms on the railing. His hair is down again, which is how I like it most, one side hooked behind his ear while the other flows in swelling waves.

"Hi," I say, realizing I'm not as surprised he joined me as I once would have been. We've been having all these *moments* together, but he probably doesn't see them the same way I do. For him, they're just moments, not *moments*. Because he's head over heels in love with Priti and I'm, well, a stranger to him.

But does that even matter anymore? When both of us know Priti's been wanting to get back together with her ex this whole time? Or is Rudra still an option to her, in her head? A backup, if she gets her heart broken?

"I've been thinking about what you said," he says, turning his body toward mine, making me aware of how close he's standing.

My heartbeat snags for a second as a million possibilities of what I might've said to him whirl around in my head.

"About how it's been a while since Priti genuinely looked happy," he says, a pained emotion flitting across his face.

"It's true," I say, glancing over at Priti, who is playing with a few stray dogs by the water cooler. "It sounds like her breakup with Soumyaroop really shattered her."

Rudra gazes in Priti's direction, his eyes conveying his conflicting emotions, his inner battle with ethics.

"That's why I think we should do it," he says.

"Do what?"

"Reunite Priti with her ex."

I stare at him, letting the words sink in. He looks at me again, his eyes latching onto mine with such ardor I nearly lower my gaze. "You mean—you want to actually *stop* the wedding? Like, sabotage it? *End* it?"

"Yes, Krishna," Rudra says, his lips curving upward. "Stopping, sabotaging, ending. All of it. We need to make sure her ex doesn't go through with the wedding, or at least delay it until Priti has had a chance to confess her feelings."

My body quivers with excitement and terror at the prospect of doing such an outrageous thing. I've never intentionally screwed up a major event for someone before (emphasis on the word *intentionally*, because I might've *accidentally* done it, like that one time I knocked over a drinks table during someone's wedding reception).

"You'd do that?" I ask.

"Of course I would. Why wouldn't I? It's for Priti."

"Because you're, like . . ." *In love with her.* "Because I didn't think you were the sort of person to ruin someone's wedding."

Rudra bursts into laughter. I watch him, amazed and mesmerized at once, because this is the first time he's *laughed* in front of me, with his full chest, eyes sparkling. A smile breaks out on my own face because his laughter is so infectious.

It makes me want to find every chance to make him laugh like that, again and again, until I'm sick of it.

In that moment, I fall for him twofold—no, *tenfold*—in a manner there's no coming back from. And it's not just because he's so freakin' cute, those dots in his chin popping in and out of view, eyes crinkled and lashes sticking out, hair escaping the trap of the curve of his ear. It's also because I'm awestruck by how he's able to set aside his own feelings and think about Priti's happiness instead of his own. I don't think I'd ever be able to do something like that—get over that crass bite of jealousy and think about what the other person wants.

Krishna Kumar, you're fucking screwed.

"Well, I guess there's a first time for everything," he says, smiling down at me. "Not everyone's as chaotic as you."

A blush creeps up my neck and pours into my cheeks. "Well, you'll learn. I'll teach you."

"I'd love that," Rudra says, running his fingers through his hair. "We should go—it looks like they're leaving."

The campsite is a half-minute walk from the compound where we ate, tents arranged on a grassy patch of land overlooking the gorgeous view. When we get there, Jalaj asks us to split up into pairs because the tents are twin sharing. I turn to Charu expectantly, ready to crawl into a tent and get the sleep I've been lacking.

But then the most bizarre thing happens.

Priti turns to me—*me!*—and says, "We'll share."

I gawk at her. But I'm not the only one. Everyone—Digha, Charu, Varun, Jalaj, and Rudra—looks even more surprised than I feel at her sudden declaration.

But I should have been anticipating this, what with all the *looks* Priti's been giving Rudra and me this whole time. I'm more surprised she hasn't confronted me already.

Okay, she did, in Pune, when Rudra flirted with me right in front of her, but I denied her assumptions. A lot has gone down since then.

Guess I'm not getting that sleep tonight after all.

When I merely nod, the others quickly recover and pair up. The tents are small, just enough to fit two people, with a Solapur blanket laid out at the bottom and lending warmth to the space. I'm a bundle of nerves when Priti and I crawl into the tent, because she looks deadly calm.

The moment we're inside, though, she doesn't waste a breath.

"Okay," she says, folding her arms over her chest. Her features are hard, set in stone. "What the actual fuck?"

I avoid her gaze, taking off my fanny pack and placing it at the edge of the tent because I need *something to do*. "What?" I try my best to keep my expression blank, but I know it's probably in vain.

"Look," Priti says, her voice low but lacking any anger, which is surprising. Instead, she just sounds exhausted. "I don't know what's going on between Rudra and you, but I'm not stupid."

"I know that."

"Which means you also know that all your whispering and secret conversations haven't gone unnoticed."

I know that too. But a wishful part of me hoped Priti either wouldn't care or would ignore it. Now that part of me just feels silly, having wished for the impossible.

"Did you hear us?" The question is out before I can stop it, and I regret letting it slip like that. Even if Priti's right about her suspicions of whatever's been brewing between Rudra and me, she *can't* know of our plans. She'll lose her shit if she finds out we're trying to help her. She doesn't appreciate unsolicited help, ever. I would know better than anyone.

Four years ago, during one of my summer vacations in India, I finished her eighth-grade holiday homework for her when she fell asleep at the table the night before her submission. I'd been an idiot to hope she'd wake up all teary and happy to find her work complete, like the shoemaker from the story about the elves that magically finished his work overnight, and that she'd finally stop being mean to me.

Instead, she started panicking, even though I'd tried my best to emulate Priti's handwriting and had used the same color pens she had. When she found out I'd done it, she started yelling at me so loud there were tears pouring down my cheeks by the time she finished.

That was the day I learned my lesson—*don't help Priti*. Not unless she asks you for help personally. Which she never will. That's why what Rudra and I are doing isn't just risky because it involves a very messy plan to secretly help her sabotage a wedding involving two individuals we don't even know—it's also because we're doing it for Priti, who hates to be at anyone's mercy or owe anyone anything. Including her best friend.

"No, I didn't hear you," Priti says, scoffing. "I don't pry, although

I did wonder for the longest moment what on earth you two might have in common to talk about. And when you both started getting all lovey-dovey with each other, it genuinely made me want to throw up inside my mouth."

The pent-up anger and frustration from all the years of being snubbed and taunted and talked down to by Priti well up inside me like a volcano minutes from erupting.

"Why, Priti?" I seethe. "Why is the idea of us together so bad?"

"Together?" Priti's face tightens. *"Together?"* Her voice is high-pitched, cracking. "How long has this been going on?"

"Just since the road trip started, for god's sake! Not long."

Priti looks almost . . . heartbroken. "Then how the *fuck* are you two together already?"

"We aren't! I didn't mean *together* together. We've just been, I don't know, flirting! I don't even feel that way about Rudra." The last part comes out in a stream, but it's a total lie. I just don't have the mental bandwidth to think about that right now.

Priti leans toward me, her voice dropping to a whisper and a scowl spreading over her face. "Oh, so you're just messing around with him, then? Like the way you messed with Amrit before getting bored of him?"

I erupt.

All the rage inside me just bursts out like the lid popping right off a pressure cooker. "How dare you!"

"How dare *I*? How dare *you*! You've been crushing on that Acharya dude all summer, and now suddenly I find out that you're using Rudra? This is out of nowhere!" Her voice breaks unnaturally. "You stay the fuck away from him, Krishna. Or else I'll—"

"Or else you'll what?" I get to my knees and jab her in the shoulder. "Or else you'll what? Try to get with him yourself, the way you've been wanting to all these years?"

How can she be so possessive, so jealous, so *judgmental*, when she's doing something so much worse than I am? She's ready to ruin someone's wedding because she is still in love with her ex, but it's never been clearer that some part of her loves Rudra.

Priti blinks. "What?"

"Admit you're in love with each other, already!" I say, chest heaving. "And keep me *out of it*!"

I can't help the dreadful thought I had yesterday in the restaurant creeping back in. About Rudra doing all this just to get a reaction out of Priti. Because if this was all part of his master plan, it's *working*. A hundred thoughts sprint through my mind, sending me into a tizzy.

It seems too unreal for him to have caught the same kind of feelings for me that I've caught for him in this short span of time, especially when he's been pining after Priti for *years*.

No.

It doesn't seem believable.

And perhaps all that sincerity I saw in him is just a facade. Priti is right. All of this is so out of pocket, so out of nowhere. Guys like Rudra don't fall for girls like me. And when guys like Amrit do, I drop them.

I am so stunned by my own jarring thoughts I can't speak, can't move. I feel embarrassed, more than anything, because I should've known this was coming. Admittedly, finding out that Priti was still in love with her ex made me think I might have a chance with Rudra, when I should've trusted my gut all along and not let his flirting get to me. A guy says a few nice things to me and I tumble ass over kettle for him.

"Why aren't you saying anything?" I cry, frustrated, when Priti just keeps staring at me.

"You're such an idiot" is all she says.

"I am," I say, sick of how malleable and easily puppeteered I am. "I'm stupid because I knew you guys liked each other this whole while, and yet—"

"Krishna, can you shut up for a moment?"

I'm surprised to find my mouth clamping shut.

Priti rubs a hand over her face, then turns her gaze to the top of the tent. "I can't believe *this* is how I'm going to come out to you."

I stare at her. "What?"

Priti exhales heavily. "I am not in love with Rudra. And neither is he with me. Because I'm into *girls*, you idiot. I'm a lesbian."

20

THAT RAINBOW SHIRT AT TARGET IS DEFINITELY TURNING YOUR KIDS GAY—AND YOU DIDN'T HEAR IT FROM ME

Prabalmachi, Sunday

Why am I not as surprised as I should be?

"It's obvious why you thought Rudra and I were unrequitedly in love with each other or something," Priti says, "but aside from the fact that Rudra isn't my type because of his broodiness, I'm *not* straight."

I'm *such* an idiot. All the hints have been staring me right in the face, but clearly, my gaydar has been way off. How could I have not seen it?

When I don't respond, Priti shrugs.

"I haven't come out to anyone in the family yet. Digha and Rudra, yes, but they're both technically friends. And now you." Her eyes flash, the sudden frisson of anxiety in them as familiar to me as a second skin. It mirrors the feeling I had when I came out to Rudra. "So please, don't tell anyone, okay?"

I finally find my voice. "Oh no! No, god, no. I would never out you. Not just because that would make me the shittiest person ever, but because *I get it.* I'm bi, and the only people who know in our family are Srishti and my parents. And, well, now Rudra. We came out to each other last night."

Priti's features soften at that. "Damn."

"Yeah, no shit."

It just hits me that we've come out to each other.

And just like that, the ice is broken.

I crack a laugh. "You know what's funny? When I came back to India the year after we moved, I was so jealous of Rudra. You and I hadn't talked in months, and I was hoping we'd be fine when we met face-to-face and that you'd be the same. But when we got to Nani's house, I found you sitting there, with *Rudra*. You didn't get up and rush to greet me, the way you used to, even though back then we used to see each other nearly every day. I went up to you—I was so excited to see you—and the first thing you said to me was that Rudra was your best friend now."

Priti stares at me, speechless.

"You're so angry at the idea that, what, I'll take Rudra away from you? Is that it?" I scoff, like that could ever happen. "What about the fact that you replaced me with him? You guys have managed to stick by one another all these years; meanwhile, I'm over here resentful that we didn't last *one* year apart!"

Not to mention that she applied to American colleges and didn't tell me about it. She applied with Rudra, to be closer to *him*, not me. I suppose it is selfish to think that way, because I'm sure Priti had a hundred other reasons why she was applying, and I'm sure being close to Rudra was only one of them.

It bruises my heart, regardless.

I consider bringing it up now, not as a one-up to her as I initially thought, but as an attempt to lay it all out, but this is the first time Priti's hearing me out. She might not take my knowing about her secret well, and the last thing I want to do is ruin the moment.

If things are better with us after tonight, she might one day tell me about it herself.

"Sometimes I wish we could just turn back time and go back to how we used to be," I find myself saying. I have Srishti now, but *Priti* used to be my best friend once. The kind of best friend you could talk about your queerness with. "I wish I hadn't moved at all, because at least then I wouldn't have lost you."

Priti sucks in a breath, weighing my words. This is the first time in years that I've confessed to her how much she meant to me, how I would've undone my move in a heartbeat if it meant she would've still been *my* Priti.

"It's not your fault, I know," I continue. "It was unreasonable of me to think you wouldn't move on and make new friends after I left. I changed too, but I didn't think that would mean you wouldn't accept me back."

Priti's quiet for a long time, shaken up, marinating in what I've said. When she finally speaks, all she says is this: "But you had so many new friends."

"Are you saying that because of the pictures Mummy sent to Mausi?"

Priti doesn't respond directly to that, but what she says confirms it. "You were surrounded by people. You were so popular."

"They were pictures of me with my after-school club. Doesn't mean any of them were my *friends*. I had no friends for the longest time. I ate alone at lunch. No one would talk to me. Even the other Indian Americans at school—I was too Indian for them to stomach. And here, I was too firangi for you. I wasn't welcome anywhere, incapable of being liked by and befriending other people."

Priti shuts her eyes, grimacing. "And I thought—I thought you didn't care about me anymore because you'd made American friends who had cool accents and wore outside clothes to school, whose parents would probably be okay with them being queer . . ."

"Is that why you stopped calling me?"

"I didn't want to bother you." When Priti's eyes open, they're glistening with tears. "I thought you had no time for me anymore. And when you didn't call me either, I started believing it."

We stare at each other, and I feel like I've been gutted open, the roots of our emotions and separation spilling out all at once. I can't believe the real reason we strayed apart was because of a misunderstanding. And lack of communication.

I want to say so much. I want to tell her how we could've had the best friendship, and *more*, if she hadn't distanced herself from me. How she's the reason we missed out on the most amazing relationship. How every summer wouldn't have been ruined if not for her.

But that would be wrong. Because it wasn't just her fault. Sure, she started it, but I shouldn't have let her drift away from me that first time. I shouldn't have made myself resent her for her comments. I shouldn't have bitched about her to Srishti or any of the other cousins behind her back.

I should've heard her out, resolved things while I could've. She'd been the one to start the fire, but I'd been fanning the flames as well. Relationships are always two-sided. They can't be built on one-sided effort. It must be equal, collective, and worked on, *constantly*.

The reason why Priti and I drifted apart wasn't just because of her. It was because of both of us.

But now's not the time for regrets. We *did* end up talking about it, albeit eight years late and admittedly not under the best circumstances.

"That doesn't change what I think," Priti says, but her voice isn't harsh. She looks almost as relieved as I feel at the weight of secrets being lifted off our shoulders. "And it's not because of jealousy. Rudra's my best friend, and I care about him. A lot."

"I know."

"He's got a big heart, and he's not the sort of person to hook up or mess around. That's not him." Priti's voice breaks. "I *know* him."

I swallow the lump in my throat. "I know you do."

"So . . . ?" She looks at me expectantly.

I see it then. I see how badly she wants me to say I'll back out, that I'll stop trying to hope for something with Rudra. If I'm being honest with myself, I know exactly what she means. I get why she's being protective of Rudra.

At the start of this road trip, I had one goal in mind: to have my first kiss. The perfect person for that would've been Amrit, but maybe I've been building this all up to what I think it *should* be like rather than letting it play out organically.

And now, with all this tension bubbling up between Rudra and me, maybe I've been doing the same thing to him, if only subconsciously. I don't know if he likes me in any serious way, or what any of this could become, but I can't keep stringing guys along to satisfy my definition of *fun*. I can't make this a pattern I inadvertently keep falling into.

Because if I do, I won't just rope another genuinely good guy into my whole mess—I'll also ruin things further with Priti.

"I understand," I say. And I do. I really do. I understand exactly why the possibility of Rudra and me would be wrong.

But then what's driving me? What's going to keep me on this trip? What's going to help me see this through?

Rudra's voice echoes in my head.

I've been thinking about what you said. About how it's been a while since Priti genuinely looked happy.

My mind goes back to my discovery of finding Priti following both the groom *and* the bride. It didn't strike me as anything out of the ordinary, but it's just one of the hundred in-my-face clues that's been dangling in front of me, just out of reach. Like how Rudra never said Soumyaroop's name or "the groom" but still went along with the plan. It was always "Priti's ex." Because Rudra must have known all along that Priti couldn't have been in love with the groom.

The discovery is just as wild as before: *Priti is after the bride!*

And just when I thought the plot couldn't thicken more than this. This is straight out of a Karan Johar movie, with the fruit-o-meter turned up.

This is what will drive me to see this through: getting Priti back together with the bride, Mansi. My summer fling might've abruptly flamed out, but Priti is still the main character here. Her story hasn't ended.

I don't want her to spiral back to her old self and resent me if I snatch away her chances at love by abandoning this trip. Things with Rudra and Amrit might be doomed, but Priti's my cousin. She used to be my best friend, my everything.

I want that back. And it doesn't matter if I just want to go back home and forget any of this ever happened. Because I need to make sure Priti at least has a chance at being happy again. If getting her back together with Mansi is the answer, then that's what I need to do.

And that has to start with me setting aside what I want.

But I can't tell Priti that I know about Mansi. I can't predict how she'll react. She might chicken out, and our plan to help her will be ruined before it has the chance to come to fruition. I can't have her worrying over Rudra and me either, so I have to make her believe I'm still in this for Amrit, though that's way off from the actual truth.

The truth that I'm not going to admit to even myself anymore . . . because it doesn't matter.

"I'm going to the wedding," I say, obstinately tightening my shoulders. "I'll meet Amrit and resolve things with him. Nothing happened between Rudra and me, and I intend to keep it that way. I promise you that. And once that's done, we'll leave."

Priti nods. Her shoulders slump with visible relief, and I comprehend just now how much this trip truly means to her. I was always supposed to be the beacon guiding her on, but she's the one making the journey.

I might've lied to her about why I'm going to the wedding, but it's still true that things with Rudra or Amrit were never meant to be. And that's okay, because I'm not risking ruining my second chance with Priti.

I won't regret it. I won't let myself regret a single moment. Not if it's Priti.

She's indescribably brave for going after and professing her love even though she knows there's a good chance she might return with her heart broken further, and it might never mend. But she's still willing to take that chance. I admire her for it. If she can be this stubborn, driven, and resolute for love, then I can do the same for her.

Tomorrow, the chapter closes on *both* Amrit and Rudra.

And a new chapter begins with Priti, who is all that matters.

21

IN TODAY'S THERAPY SESSION, LET'S EVALUATE WHY YOU LOVE HYPOTHESIZING ABOUT OTHER PEOPLE'S LIVES, KRISHNA. SHALL WE?

Prabalmachi, Sunday

After that difficult conversation, I thought I might doze off from exhaustion, but I'm unable to sleep a wink. Priti's fast asleep already, snoring loudly, but I lie with my face resting on crossed arms, looking out at the view, AirPods playing soft songs in my ears.

A few college-aged trekkers from other groups have lit a bonfire about ten feet from the tents. I long to go outside and warm my hands over the fire, but I don't want to interrupt what looks like an intimate gathering of friends. They're laughing and whispering to each other, seated in a circle, bundled in Solapur blankets clearly stolen from their tents.

It looks like they're playing truth or dare, because at one point, one of the girls crawls over to another girl seated opposite her, and they kiss, giggling as they pull away. The second girl, the one who breaks the kiss first, looks dazed, a taut set to her shoulders.

I smile to myself, recognizing that look of utter sapphic longing on her face. If I'm speculating correctly, those two girls are good friends. The bolder one, who crawled over to the other girl, is taking the kiss as just that—a *dare*. The shy one's either closeted or hasn't confessed she's in love with her yet.

Perhaps I'm wrong about the whole situation and making up stories in my head, but a part of me hopes these two girls get together one day. There's nothing that fills me with more buttery warmth than the thought of queer people being happy and experiencing their own love stories.

I've always been like this. Gauging absolute strangers from a distance and making up stories about them in my head. They have no idea there's a girl with an overactive imagination looking at them, hypothesizing about their probably wildly different lives.

The image of the two girls kissing plays in my head again, the lingering touch of their lips, and I shut my eyes, wondering, not for the first time, what it would be like to kiss someone. I've overhyped the thought of it in my head, deluded myself into thinking the experience of that first kiss needs to be picture-perfect, with the perfect person.

It can be a special moment without having to be perfect. It can be with someone who doesn't end up being "the one" for you. Under spur-of-the-moment circumstances. You might like to meticulously organize every aspect of your life, but unplanned things are best sometimes.

I turn my head, resting my cheek against the back of my hands, eyes closed. Rudra's right. I'm giving it too much importance, building it up to a fairy tale in my head. It doesn't and shouldn't matter so much. Just because it hasn't happened to me yet doesn't make me any less worthy or undeserving of love and romance. It will happen in its own time, take its own course. I know it. I can feel it.

In the meantime, I can try to continue to heal my existing relationship with Priti.

And for that, I need Rudra.

I open my phone and shoot off a *You up?* text to him, and after a quick back-and-forth, we agree to meet near the edge of the row of tents.

I'm the first to arrive. My feet tap the ground nervously as I wait.

I don't know what I was thinking shooting off a *You up?* text like that to him. Everyone knows it's *the* pick-up line, *the* booty call. Luckily, when Rudra emerges from the tent he's sharing with Varun, he doesn't look like he thinks much of it.

I hate how good he looks.

"Did I disturb you?" I ask, arms wrapped around my chest to trap some of the warmth and protect my torso against the chill.

"No, I was up."

For a second, we stare at each other, not knowing what to say, and I turn red, lowering my eyes to the ground. "You want to go somewhere else? I thought we could talk about Priti and the wedding." I tip my shoulder in the direction of the trekkers around the campfire. "Somewhere more . . . private?"

Rudra funnels out a breath from between his lips. He looks nervous. But he nods anyway. "Yeah."

We start walking away from the campsite, in the direction opposite to the one we came from, where I saw a few of the campers going. There's a dirt path that leads into the thick awning of trees.

We pass small, closely set-together houses made of mud and clay, with thatched roofs and tiny glassless windows. This is where

I assume the locals—whose businesses profit off the trekking and camping tourists—live. I can peek through the windows into the dark interiors, the path lit by the dull yellow bulbs swinging in the wind.

After a few minutes, we leave the village behind, and the dirt path ebbs into the forest again.

"We could sit there," I say, slowing my steps as I spot a couple of rocks up ahead. Rudra nods, and we sit. The trees rustle around us, leaves dipping and rising in the wind, branches reaching for the sky, wreathed by fireflies.

"So what's the plan?" he asks, leaning toward me with his elbows resting on his thighs. I appreciate it when people sit like that when we're conversing; it makes me feel like they actually care about what I'm saying.

"Before we get into that, I just thought I'd let you know," I say softly. "Priti came out to me."

Rudra's eyes widen. "Oh."

"I know that she's after the bride, not the groom. Don't worry, I didn't tell her about our plan. That's still a secret."

I scan his face, thinking about how I misread his emotions for Priti and interpreted them so wrong all this time. The love and care were there, of course, but they were platonic and familial rather than romantic. I let my cousins' gossip lead me astray.

"I'm sorry for not telling you sooner," Rudra says. "I couldn't out her until she was ready for you to know."

"That's okay. You know I understand."

Rudra smiles. "Of course."

"It's the same reason why I asked you not to tell her about me—because I wanted to be the one to do it."

"I hope it goes without saying that even if you hadn't, I wouldn't have broken your trust."

"Did you always know Mansi was Priti's ex?" I ask, hoping I'm not prodding too much.

"No. Everything else I told you about Priti was true." Rudra sighs. "I knew she was dating this girl from Powai, that they broke up, and she's been heartbroken for a while. Her cousins were right about her being secretive, but I knew she would've told me when she felt ready. Only then, her relationship ended, and I didn't see a point in asking her about it when it seemed like the last thing she wanted to talk about. I didn't realize until today that Digha knows."

"You overheard them too, I guess?"

"Yeah, and it kind of stings, but I'll reconcile with it, because at least Priti is talking to Digha. Sometimes we need different things from different people, and she deserves to have someone to share this with."

"You have, like, grad school–level emotional intelligence," I joke, even as my throat is choked with emotion. Priti was right. She was so right. Rudra is an amazing guy, with such a large heart.

He's making me miss something I've never had—and now, never will—with him.

Rudra shakes his head. "It's just decency, honestly." We sit quietly for a while, letting our conversation steep in our minds, before he asks, "So what's the plan now?"

"Amrit told me the shaadi is at sunset on Monday, in a beachside resort in Calangute." Which is tomorrow, because it's just past midnight.

"So it's in North Goa. I've been there before."

With whom? Priti? Other friends? An ex? I want to ask, but it doesn't make sense to pry in the context of our current conversation. The thought of Rudra having an ex makes me squirm, but there's nothing I can do about his past. He's single *now*, or I think he is.

Wait.

What if he's *not* single?

You're being paranoid, I assure myself. He is very single, and it shouldn't matter to me even if he weren't, because I'm not hoping for anything with him. Or at the very least I'm trying not to.

"I think we should get Mansi and Priti alone sometime during noon, so we can give both of them the time to gather their emotions and make a decision in the right headspace," I say. "This isn't going to be easy for either of them, and there's no guarantee Mansi doesn't actually *want* this wedding. She might've moved on, unlike Priti."

"I doubt it," Rudra says. "They didn't break up that long ago. There's a good chance that whoever this Mansi is marrying is a rebound. It's not even been a year since she and Priti ended things."

"We still can't tell Priti about our plans," I say. "She doesn't want us interfering in any of this, or she would've told us—at least you—the real reason why she's been so desperate to get to Goa on time. But we've got to help her out."

"See, Priti might bow out at the last moment and decide to not go to the wedding at all. So we will need a contingency plan."

"What do you mean?"

"If she tries to back out, we'll need to let her in on our plan to sabotage this wedding so we can convince her to take the plunge." Rudra's jaw sets. "You should also probably get in touch with Amrit and learn more details so we don't screw anything up. If we're going to help Priti, let's do it right."

I chew at my lower lip, my mind going back to the message Amrit left me. I can't text him asking for details about the wedding and completely ignore the *still thinking about you* message he sent me last. Do I reply with a simple *me too* and make up an excuse even though it would be a blatant lie at this point? It's not right to raise someone's hopes and lead them on like that, is it?

"I'm going to bonk my head into a wall," I mutter, not knowing I've said it out loud until I find Rudra looking at me, a confused expression lining his face. "Sorry," I add hastily, "I'm just stressed."

"Because you're meeting Amrit soon?" Rudra asks, his eyes darkening.

"No . . . maybe . . I don't know," I say, a little struck by the intensity of his gaze. "It's just all a mess. And I hate to admit it, but you were right."

"Right about what?"

"About me building it up to a fairy tale in my head. About me being delulu about the whole *romance* of it." I'm saying way more than I intended to, but the words just keep pouring out.

"For the record—I don't think you're delulu."

I snort. "Please don't say *delulu*. It doesn't suit you. Like, at all."

"My point stands," he says, and leans toward me, scanning my face in a manner that makes me hyperaware of every single cell in my body, before adding, "and to be honest, any guy who wouldn't trip over his own foot wondering what he did to deserve someone like you traveling across cities to kiss him would be an idiot."

"That's . . ." I pause, struggling to maintain a hold on my wits. "I hope that's true." At this point, what Amrit thinks of me doesn't really matter, because everything's changed, but I can't tell Rudra or Priti that. They both need to believe I'm still headed to Goa to kiss Amrit.

They can't know my emotions have taken a one-eighty.

"Guys don't admit it, because of toxic masculinity or whatever, but we appreciate grand gestures more than you might think, especially because they hardly ever happen to us. They would be lying if they said they don't like to be spoiled sometimes." A flicker of emotion passes through Rudra's eyes so quickly I almost miss it. "I hope Amrit realizes how lucky he is."

I open my mouth to respond when his eyes suddenly dart to a spot behind me. For a moment I think it's a wild animal and completely freeze, not wanting to move in case there's a chance any movement might get me eaten up. But Rudra smiles. "Hey, look."

I turn back, craning my neck. Up a twisting, rocky path that splits into two, there's a flash of light. The path to the right is shaded by overhanging branches and thick trees, and fireflies festoon the bridge like fairy lights coiling around an arch.

A gasp slips through my parted lips, and Rudra gets to his feet, motioning for me to follow him. Sticking close, we walk to the fork in the path, take the right, and find ourselves on an ascent, right under the arch.

I can't form coherent words to express how beautiful it is, so I just stare, rotating on the spot, looking at the fireflies. There's so many of them here, even more than we saw on the trek up to the campsite, shimmering in patterns so mathematical it's like they're all following a precise atomic clock of their own.

"There's one sitting in your hair," Rudra says, smiling up at me. He's standing on a rock lower than mine, so I'm an inch or so taller than him now. I twist around, trying and failing to locate the stray firefly that has found a second home in my hair.

"I can't see it!" I say, frustrated.

"Wait." Rudra rummages through his pocket for his phone, takes it out, and holds it in front of him. His tongue pokes out the corner of his mouth as he focuses the lens, and it's so cute I can't help but smile. The shutter snaps before I'm even ready, and Rudra flips the phone around to show me the picture.

For a moment, I'm so shocked, I don't say anything, just stare at the picture.

It's the best photo anyone has ever taken of me.

If anyone were to glance at it for more than a second, they'd realize I'm not actually looking at the camera but at something behind it. *Rudra.* I'm smiling dreamily, and some of my hair is in my face. And while I'm wearing a Mickey Mouse T-shirt and look grimy and sweaty, the picture is natural, *real*, beautiful, the kind you could make your display picture. The kind you'll keep coming back to look at because you like it so much. I'm lit up by the fireflies circling the branches around me and the stray one sitting in my hair.

And because it's a live photo, it's dynamic, showing the exact moment when my face breaks into a smile, the passing wind blowing strands of my hair onto my eyes, the firefly's wings quivering.

I shouldn't be surprised by how good the picture is, though, because Rudra's Instagram posts are aesthetic and well shot—they could be professional. He's excellent at what he does, and within seconds, he's photographed possibly my favorite moment of me for weeks to come.

"I look like a Disney princess," I gush without meaning to, because it sounds so conceited. That's the sort of thing you say in your head, or out loud when you're by yourself, preening in front of a mirror, pretending you're filming a "Get Ready with Me" video.

But Rudra gazes directly up at me and says, "Yes, you do."

"This is the prettiest picture anyone has ever taken of me." My blood rushes to my head, making me feel dizzy.

"It's not the picture, Krishna," Rudra says, his voice soft yet distinct in the silence of the forest surrounding us. I follow the movement of his hand as he reaches up, knuckles brushing the shell of my ear, where the firefly hovers inches above it. "It's you." That last part is so hoarse it's like his throat has been rubbed with sand-paper.

My eyes shut as the gentle stroke of his knuckles sends a ripple of shivers through my body, originating from the point where his skin and my skin meet and spreading like a shock wave. Before I know it, my entire body shudders, caught in an earthquake of its own.

Rudra's knuckles skim the curve of my ear, my earlobe, then touch the sensitive spot right behind my ear, tracing the dip in the skin. His touch there nearly makes my body change states and turn to fluid. At every point of contact, tiny seismic waves of pleasure whip outward, swathing me whole.

I don't know what's happening, or why it's happening, but if he keeps doing *this*, whatever it is, I will lose it. I will lose every ounce of control that's keeping me upright and stopping me from crumpling into him. I have never felt this way in my entire life, never had anyone touch me the way he's touching me right now.

My eyes are closed as I wholly give in to the sensation, so I can't read his expression. Part of me is afraid to, because what if I open my eyes, spot a confused look on his face, and realize he was just reaching for the firefly in my hair?

I would simply combust and die from mortification. I would never be able to look him in the eye again, never escape the constant feeling of regret that would fold over me every time I thought back to this moment.

But I can't stay like this forever. Especially because his hand has paused just above the curve of my neck, halting. I need to look at him.

I open my eyes, bracing myself for the worst. Our gazes link almost immediately, and what I see floods me with both relief and nervousness.

That is not the look of someone who was reaching for the firefly in my hair. It's the look of someone who knew exactly what they were doing. Whose every movement was intentional.

My breath is trapped in my throat, and we're so close that half of me screams to move away and the other half yearns to close the distance between us. At some point, Rudra must've stepped forward, because he wasn't this close before. He pulls his hand back, dropping it to his side, fingers flexing.

I wordlessly look down at him, noticing more the longer my gaze lingers. And I see it.

The apprehension.

It mirrors mine. So much doubt, yearning, and embarrassment, as if he's been following my every movement to see what I'm thinking, as if everything I'm feeling isn't written in bold letters across my face.

"Rudra," I say as his gaze falls to my lips, desire hanging in those beautiful irises like dewdrops from a leaf. "You look like you're about to kiss me right now."

Rudra's expression doesn't falter. "Do you want me to?"

"I . . ." *I want you to. I want to kiss you so bad it physically aches.* "I can't."

"That's not an answer."

If I were in his place, I'd have taken my response as an instant rejection, fled from the spot, and never looked back. But the fact that he's questioning me again is probably because I've never been able to keep what I'm feeling or thinking off my face.

"I want you to," I whisper, unable to believe this is happening to me. This entire moment feels like it's part of a dream montage. All my life, I've been so attuned to everything panning out exactly the way I've planned it, and I was only prepared to kiss Amrit because it was all part of *a plan*. Plan Bs and backups—those have always been inconsequential because I've never failed at a plan A in the first place.

I was *not* prepared for this detour.

"But I can't," I say.

I promised Priti I didn't feel anything for Rudra, that I wouldn't let anything happen between us. She came out to me, she *trusted* me, after so many years, and this is all she's asking for in return. And she's not even wrong. Rudra . . . he's too good for me. I might be worthy and deserving of love and romance, but I'm not worthy or deserving of *him*.

And no matter how much I want this, I don't want to treat Rudra like he's a plan B. I'd rather not let anything happen between us at all.

"Because of Amrit?" he says, and his face is such a hardened mask that any shred of feeling I saw there is gone, evaporated.

It pains every inch of me to say it because I know I'm lying through my teeth, but I say it anyway: "Isn't that why we're here?"

Something cracks in his eyes. But he doesn't respond. He just nods brusquely, stepping away from me, making me instantly miss the closeness of his form.

Regret storms down on me, but what's done is done. What's said is said. There's no going back, and lord knows I can't just press the reset button on how I am and how I need to be.

Rudra starts to turn, but I can't help myself from asking, "Did you, though? Did you want to kiss me?"

He scoffs, but I know he's not mocking me. He's mocking himself. "Does it matter, Krishna?"

I stand there, pondering the question, knowing it's not a response, and knowing he doesn't owe me one but wishing for it all the same. By the time I can think of an answer, though, he's already walking back down the path, leaving my unsaid words dangling in the air.

22

MY EGO IS LITERALLY GOING TO GET ME KILLED ONE DAY (AND THAT DAY MIGHT BE TODAY)

Prabalmachi, Sunday

After I get back to my tent, I'm prepared to lie awake, physically unable to sleep a wink and replaying each millisecond with Rudra over and over in my head until I'm sick to the core.

But when I collapse next to Priti, heart beating a mile a minute, I fall asleep almost instantly.

It doesn't last long, though.

A couple of hours later, Priti shakes me awake, grumbling about how we need to leave for the second half of the trek *right now*, and how if I don't wake the fuck up, she's going to make me smell her sock again.

At the sock threat, I sit up so fast the speed disorients me momentarily. My head is throbbing, as if someone is slowly hammering away at my skull. But this time, I don't protest at Priti's utter lack of humanity because the moment I register where I am, what I'm doing, and why I'm here, it all comes crashing back to me.

Everything.

Rudra, standing achingly close to me, looking up at me, deep-brown eyes illuminated in the light of a hundred fireflies, his hand braced on the slope of my neck, a million tender emotions swimming across his face. I shut my eyes, brows knitting, and every moment with him plays in my head like a movie, captured in high definition.

Everything I feel when I recall those moments with him—it's all too real and raw. It's funny how when it was all happening to me, I felt like I was wading through a dream, but now that it's part of my memory, branded into my brain, it feels realer than ever.

Rudra and I almost kissed last night, and the thought of it makes every square inch of my skull ache. I don't think I can look at him ever again after what happened. After I *rejected* him.

I wrap my arms around my chest, ducking my head so my temples touch my knees. I think I'm having a migraine. My eyes are burning, and my eyelids are stitched together so tight that trying to open them feels like trying to pry the lid off a can. My whole body is shaking because it's chilly. I didn't realize how cold it was until now.

Rudra was so warm yesterday is the first thought that comes to my mind. He exuded heat, standing so close I would've only needed to take a step forward to fall into his arms. Steal some of that warmth.

"Krishna?" Charu says, poking her head in through the tent's flap.

"If you don't move your ass this instant, we're leaving you behind," Priti says from somewhere outside the tent, her voice dripping with annoyance. I'm a little surprised at the harshness of her tone. Didn't we reach an equilibrium last night? Why is she speaking to me like that?

I wish I could just shut my eyes again and slump back, crumple into a ball, and never get up again.

That's when Rudra speaks up, making my heart nearly stop. "It's okay if she can't go for the second half of the trek. Maybe she's just tired. I can stay back with her if that would be better."

Priti lets out a sound that's halfway between a scoff and a shocked burble. "Dude. Don't encourage her."

"No, no," I hear myself say before my body shimmies out of the tent of its own accord. My hand grabs my bag, slinging it on as I sluggishly get to my feet. I feel hungover—no, *worse* than hungover. It's even colder outside, and my teeth chatter as I get to my feet. "I'm coming. I'm ready."

Priti mutters something under her breath before stomping away to the group that's gathered by the extinguished bonfire from last night. Ohmygod, what's her deal? I groan, too exhausted to think about what might've made her sour again.

My eyes take a second to adjust to the barely dawning sky. My hair is still in the braid from last night, so I just have to push a couple of strands away from my face and behind my ear. The thought takes me back to the feeling of Rudra's fingers deftly braiding my hair, movements gentle and smooth.

I shift my glance to Priti, who has the most rotten look on her face and refuses to glance in my direction or even acknowledge me. Great. Just when I thought things were finally getting better between us, Priti's officially giving me the cold shoulder again.

"You're shivering," a voice says from a few feet away, and I turn, heartbeat ratcheting. It's Rudra. He looks just as tired as I do, purple bags hanging beneath his eyes, hair pulled into a messy ponytail. It looks like he woke up a minute before I did, because the sleep hasn't left his eyes and most of his hair has spilled from his ponytail. A few blades of grass stick out of his hair in a haphazard manner. Despite myself, I nearly melt at how adorable he looks.

"I'm okay," I say, barely able to look at him. My chest twists painfully, and I'm just so tired. I can't stop picturing the hurt expression on his face, his pitiful scoff when I asked him if he wanted to kiss me and he responded with *Does it matter, Krishna?*

Of course it matters! When it shouldn't. It shouldn't matter because I made my choice yesterday, and he knows it. Which is why I don't get why he's still being so nice to me. It's a complete contrast to Priti's behavior right now, when he has every reason to be angry with me and she has no reason to.

I literally turned down Rudra *for* her.

"Here," he says suddenly, taking off his dark-green hoodie. He holds it out to me, and I stare at it, touched by the action. Then back up at him, his eyes, his hair, his lips. The urge to kiss him is so strong I have to pinch my palm to stop myself.

"Thank you." I take the hoodie from him and slip it on. He's about my size, so it fits me perfectly. It's soft, and really warm from having hugged him. It smells like him. The scent is faint, but it overpowers me with the memories it brings back from last night.

He starts walking away to join the others, and once I've (sort of) forced myself to forget everything that's happened with him, I follow.

We take the same path through the trees that Rudra and I took last night, then trail along the fork to the left this time and pass the archway, now dark, with only a few stray fireflies. Nothing like the sight we saw last night.

The sky slowly lightens, a rich blue mixed with a palette of orange and yellow oozing out of the horizon. The dawn light seeps through the trees, and the forest doesn't seem nearly as intimidating and spooky as it did last night. In fact, it looks harmless, really. Just trees, rocks, and grassy inclines. Not the sort of place you'd find a bear. The difference is jarring.

The chill is gone, and I'm sweating again by the time we take our next pit stop. I remove Rudra's hoodie, tying the sleeves around my hips.

There's a small wooden stall to our right, where a wrinkled man with snowy-white hair sits in front of a wooden plank, an array of items strewn before him. A pyramid of fresh green cucumbers; piles of bright yellow lemons; a couple of knives; jars of red chili powder, salt, and sugar; and a stack each of paper plates and newspapers.

Behind him, the view is glorious. A wooden railing looks out over a wide green valley radiant in the morning sun, surrounded by misty mountain peaks and rocky slopes. I walk to the railing and peer over the edge, heart beating rapidly against my chest. It's a solid drop from here, and if I fall, I'm sure I'll be skewered by the rocks before landing in the thick pockets of trees, body never to be found. The sunlight prisms out from behind the mountains, enveloping everything in a warm glow. The view steals my breath with its beauty, yet terrifies me all the same.

To our left, there's a steady rocky incline, all smooth stone. A rope snakes down it, but there's no harness or support otherwise.

"Is this the end of the trek?" I ask hopefully, staring at that single rope with mixed horror and apprehension.

Varun laughs. "Oh, no."

"This is where the actual climb starts," Jalaj says, pointing to the rope. "We go up that rope to a set of stone stairs, then climb a vertical wall, and finally, we'll reach the peak, where there's a Chhatrapati Shivaji Maharaj Mandir."

Varun guffaws at my horrified expression. "ये तो बस इंटरवल था। पिक्चर अभी बाकी हैं मेरे दोस्त।"[1] That's Shah Rukh's dialogue from the movie *Om Shanti Om*, and it does nothing to calm the nerves that have spiked in me at Jalaj's words.

I swallow thickly. "Do we—do we all have to go?"

"No," Jalaj says. "Since this part of the trek is the most challenging, do it only if you think you can and truly want to."

This is *not* what I signed up for. I thought we were going to see some fireflies, sleep in tents, and light a bonfire, that's all. This is getting too खतरों के खिलाड़ी[2] for me to digest.

My hesitation is painted across my face in bright crimson, and the others immediately notice it. Priti shrugs. "You don't have to come if you don't want to, Krishna. There's no pressure."

Why is *she* speaking to me all of a sudden? Her words instantly make my ego swell, and the pungent taste of competitiveness presses the back of my throat. And I know that like I always do, I'll regret it and curse myself later if I stay behind. Or, more likely, when I tumble to my death down those rocks. "No. I'll come."

After a few minutes of taking photos posed against the gorgeous view, we order a round of nimbu panis. I also ask for a plate of spiced kheera chaat and watch with fascination as the old man bisects the cucumber lengthwise, then rubs the insides with red chili powder and salt. He places it on a paper plate and hands it to me.

I take it from him, mouth watering at the sight of the spicy kheera slices on my plate. It's funny how I never imagined something as simple as sliced cucumbers seasoned with chili powder and salt could look so delicious.

---

1 *Language*: Hindi; *Translation*: This is just the interval. The picture is still left, my friend.

2 *Language*: Hindi; *Translation*: Players of danger.

I sit on one of the wooden planks next to Charu, closing my eyes as I bite into the fresh cucumber, the flesh cracking satisfyingly between my teeth. Maybe it's the much-needed electrolytes in the salt and water from the vegetable, or just the simplicity of the chaat, but I love it so much I'm craving another plate when I'm done. I shouldn't overeat, though, as has been my lifelong tendency. I can always have a plate on my way back.

We guzzle down our nimbu panis—again, incomparably delicious—and I watch as the college guys begin the ascent. The first one, Padam Patel, is hoisted up by his friend behind him, and time drags as he stretches his hand out toward the rope and grips it tight, knuckles poking out. My breath is trapped in my throat, and I set my empty glass aside, reconsidering my decision to continue.

But I know myself. I will end up having the worst FOMO if I don't do this. And that will be much worse than potential death. It always is. At least when you're dead you can't feel anything.

One by one, the rest of the college guys scale upward toward the stone staircase, disappearing around the rock face. The rising sun makes the jagged surface of the mountain shimmer as if there are shards of jewels embedded in the rocks.

And then it's our turn.

Jalaj stayed behind for us because the college boys seemed confident enough to manage the rest of the climb on their own, with another local accompanying them. What's shocking to me is that these locals hardly use the rope, barely skimming it with their fingers, cruising up the mountain in their chappals without a care in the world.

Varun and Digha go first, followed by Charu. Digha slips once, her hand scraping the rope, and I gasp, eyes scrunched closed to avoid looking. But luckily, Varun catches her in time.

Jalaj turns to us when the three of them have reached the staircase and stand perched on the rocks there, clutching the grooves tightly. "Who's going next?"

Priti turns to Rudra and me, and when neither of us responds, she sighs. "I'll go."

My heart is in my throat as Rudra hoists her up, her long leg nimbly propelling itself off his interlocked fingers. She finds the rope, steadies herself, and starts scaling.

"Krishna?" Jalaj says, waving a hand forward. Rudra won't go first, just like he didn't last night. Which is good, because I don't want to be the last one left standing down here, and I'd rather Rudra hoist me up than Jalaj.

I nod, gulping, walking toward the cliff face. I survey the height. It doesn't look like much, to be honest, but I'll need to make use of what little arm strength I have to get onto the slope and begin climbing. Rudra meets my eyes, a flicker of emotion passing through his and then gone.

He gets down on one knee, forming a tiny hammock with his crossed fingers. There's something so intimate about how he's kneeling before me, looking up at me with those endless brown eyes. For a wild fraction of a second, it looks like he's proposing. I send the thought flying out my head with a swift kick, my face burning.

"Go on," Jalaj says.

I eye the nest of Rudra's hands uncertainly. He did hoist Priti up quite effortlessly, and although she's slimmer, she's much taller as well, so she probably weighs the same as me, maybe a little less. But . . .

"I don't know if I should do this," I blurt, looking down at Rudra.

"The trek?"

"No. The stepping-onto-your-hand bit. What if your fingers break or something?"

Rudra's previously worried face splits into a smile, and my heart nearly skips a beat. "They won't, Krishna. I'll be pushing upwards too." I just love how he says *upwards* instead of *upward* and the way he pronounces my name. He enunciates the *na* correctly, unlike my American counterparts, who make it sound like *nuh*. "The momentum will prevent my fingers from breaking."

I love the way he smiles, the way he looks at me. I love everything about him—

"Okay," I say, snuffing out my internal monologue and the dangerous direction it was headed in. I gingerly lift my foot and place it on his palms, hesitating when they dip with the weight.

"Trust me," Rudra says. I can feel Jalaj looking at the both of us, and when I dare a glance at him, he immediately looks away, a small, embarrassed smile playing along his lips, as if I've caught him eavesdropping on our private conversation. *Even* though there's absolutely nothing private about this.

I give in and put my full weight onto Rudra's palms and feel a pressure propelling me up. I grab hold of the edge, leap, and flail unsteadily for a few moments, hanging on just using my arm strength.

But Rudra's hands grab my legs, pushing me up, and, using his help, I get onto the slope, breaths heavy as the rope slips into my hands, instantly steadying me. It's not as much the rope as it's the feeling of its coarse threads brushing my palms, assuring me that even if I slip, it's there. I can just wrap my fingers tight around it and it'll break my fall.

Just like Rudra will.

Some of the comfort leaves me as he lets go, stepping away and brushing his hands on his track pants. I bite my lip and start moving. It takes a minute for me to gain the confidence to push my body up to standing, but after that, it's much quicker. I avoid the loose gravel, toes curling into the grooves on the rocks instead.

Priti helps me onto the first step, hands gripping my arm tight until I'm stable on my feet. The rope shudders when I let go, undulating as Rudra and Jalaj make their way up.

I catch my breath, crouched on the step. My legs are shaking, and I need a moment to regain my balance, but I still snatch my hand from Priti's.

"What's wrong?" she asks, noting my change in expression.

"I don't get why you're being mean to me again," I say before I can help it.

Priti doesn't look directly at me when she says, "I'm not . . . being mean to you."

"And here I was," I say, my voice cracking, "thinking that things could be all right between us again."

"Krishna . . ."

Her voice trails off when Rudra joins us on our perch, flopping down in the empty space next to me. There are rivulets of sweat trickling down the sides of his face, and he gathers his astray hair into a high ponytail at the top of his head, exposing way more of his face than I've ever actually seen clearly.

I never noticed how sharp, almost pixielike, his ears are, and how there's this delicate angle formed by his hairline just behind his ears. And how small his forehead is and how *I shouldn't care anymore*.

Rudra opens his mouth to ask what's up. Priti continues staring at me helplessly, but I stand, dust off my shorts, and resume climbing on my own.

23

THIS COULD VERY WELL TURN INTO A LIVE MANIFESTATION OF *MANJUMMEL BOYS*

Prabalmachi, Sunday

I avoid Priti and Rudra for the rest of the ascent. I don't give either of them a chance to talk to me because I have my AirPods in and am blasting music at a volume that's probably going to induce irreversible damage to my ears.

It helps that the ascent is so petrifying. While there are stairs, which I wrongly presumed would be better than unstable rocks, they're way worse because they are so narrow. I have to stick to the rocky wall, back vertical and pressed entirely to it, inching up every step.

There are a few sharp turns, and my heart leaps to my mouth when my shoes slide on the ground, making gravel tumble off the edge. One fall and I'll crash-land straight onto rocks that will not just spike me like barbecue but break every single bone in my body into tiny, tiny pieces.

I don't want to *die* here. I'd become an example for parents to quote to warn their children not to lie to them, ever; not to run after boys, ever; and not to go on night treks, ever. I can almost imagine the headline:

Indian American Teen from Maine Goes on Prabalmachi Trek Without Telling Her Parents and Falls to Her Death

While the others pause intermittently to take photos and selfies, making quirky faces and poses, I don't dare include myself in any of them until I'm assured I have a tight hold on something so I won't fall. I stay at least a foot away from everyone else because I can't tell you the number of times I've seen those posts where a bunch of people went to some waterfall or something and one of them accidentally tripped, taking everyone down with them.

Surprisingly, I'm the one who is at the very front of the group this time, so I'm able to avoid looking at both Priti and Rudra.

The morning sun is beating down on us when we reach the top, and I pause at the ledge, looking out over the whole view. It's so, so beautiful. And quite literally breathtaking, because it took a draining hike to get here.

This isn't the end of it, though, as Jalaj warned us. There's still a vertical wall—and when I say vertical, I mean it is perpendicular to the ground. The last of the college boys is completing his climb, helped up by three locals who lounge at various places along the wall in their chappals. A few boys who don't look a year over ten scurry around us, giggling at the weary looks on our faces.

I hide my face, hoping it'll take some of the burn away from the embarrassment. Jalaj gathers us around, pointing to the wall. "That wall is very tricky. There's no harness, but there's one rope, and you'll need a lot of muscle strength to pull yourself up using just your arms and legs. Those three men will help you at all points, so you won't fall, but I'd strongly recommend backing out if you don't feel a hundred percent confident."

"Is this trek ever going to end?" Digha wails, flopping to the ground. She's got the kind of pretty face that make her sunburned cheeks look like they've been patted with rouge. "I'm not going."

"Me neither," Charu says, sitting next to her. "I did it last time, so I've been to the mandir before." She takes her huge thermos out and guzzles water from it.

"You've been carrying that this whole time?" Varun says. "No wonder you're tired, Chubbs. You could knock someone out with that bottle."

Priti uses her hanky to wipe the sweat from the back of her neck. The sun has made her even more brown. I glance down at my own arm, which looks browner than ever, but I don't mind it. When I was a kid, for the longest time, I avoided staying out in the sun for too long even after applying sunscreen because I got so conscious of tanning, but now I don't care. The sun feels surprisingly good, warming the chill from the wind drying the sweat on my skin.

Jalaj looks around at us again. "Anyone else?"

I wait for the Krishnas in my brain to tell me to raise my hand and back out now—but I'm surprised to be met with radio silence instead. And I find that I *want* to do this. I came this far, and I want to see it through to the very end.

I shake my head, soaking up the sunlight, nerves riding a cresting wave. It's true, what all those fitness freaks keep going on about. The toughest part of exercise is *starting*. But once you do, once you push above and beyond your limit—that's when it starts feeling good.

"Who's going first, then?" Jalaj asks.

Varun sits next to Digha, wrapping an arm around her shoulder and pulling her cheek. They're so disgustingly cute. I want what they have. "I'm going to stay with Digha for a bit," he announces.

Rudra raises his hand. "I'll go."

"I'll go after him," I say. Priti snaps her head toward me in surprise, but I ignore her, amping up the volume of the music again.

Rudra walks to the wall and rolls the sleeves of his T-shirt up even farther until they're bunched around his biceps. He stretches his arms out in front of him, his bones popping. Then he grasps the rope with both hands and begins climbing.

He's like a monkey, quick and sure-footed. The three guides direct him in Hindi on where to keep his hands and feet, boosting him whenever he needs it. The wall is about thirty feet tall, and he's at the top in minutes, pulled up at the end by Padam.

I walk to the wall, surveying its height, finding my frame tiny in comparison to its intimidating span. I take off my AirPods, shoving them into the case and jamming it into my pocket.

I can do this, I convince myself, feeling everyone watching me, and take the rope. Priti, who filmed Rudra climbing, starts recording for me as well, and I am determined to not fuck up on camera. The first few feet are easy because I keep my grip on the rope tight, not letting go unless I have to reach for grooves above me. The men guide me patiently.

But then there's a point where the rock I need to grip feels too far out of reach, and I'm afraid I'm going to fall. A mind-numbing panic takes me over, and one of the men notices it.

He says, "नीचे मत देखो।"[1] and being the idiot I am, I do exactly that. I look down. My head spins. We're dizzyingly high.

---

1 *Language*: Hindi; *Translation*: Don't look down.

"मैं नहीं कर सकती!"[2] I gasp, gripping the rope so tight my skin stretches over my knuckles and the blood drains from them, turning them white.

"होजाएगा, tension मत लो।"[3]

I shake my head firmly, all resolve to complete this thing gone. I'm determined to stay here, to go neither up nor down unless a chopper comes to fetch me and deposits me on solid ground. I can't do this, I can't—

"Krishna!"

I inch my eyes open, looking up at the source of the voice. It's Rudra. His head pokes over the edge of the cliff and he stretches his hand out toward me.

"You can do this!"

"I can't!"

"You can! Just look at me. Don't look away."

I scan his face, knowing I'll be damned if I do, but he looks so earnest, *genuinely* concerned for me and my safety . . . and those eyes. God. They anchor me.

I suck in a deep breath, wait for the panic to subside just a little, and let go of the rope with one hand. It's a mighty stretch, grabbing the rock way above me, trusting that my hands will take my weight when I lift my leg and rest it on the groove the men point to, calling out encouraging words to me.

"बस, ज़रा और!"[4]

I grunt, straining to hold on, barely swinging on the rope for a few moments.

And then my feet find stability.

---

2 *Language*: Hindi; *Translation*: I can't do it!

3 *Language*: Hindi; *Translation*: It'll happen; don't take tension.

4 *Language*: Hindi; *Translation*: That's it, a little bit farther!

"बस . . . बस . . . देखो! होगया।!"[5]

The rest of the climb is quicker, and while I don't hold Rudra's gaze the whole time—because, well, I need to focus on where I'm keeping my hands and feet—every time I glance up, his hand is outstretched, and he's always looking at me. It pumps confidence into me, and when I'm near the top, I grab his hand, relieved to find it firm. And strong.

The man below pushes me up, and I scrabble away at the ground, my face scrunched in concentration. There is a sudden, painful pull on my right arm, pressure rushing to my bicep, and I gasp as I'm hauled up and over the ledge. My torso finds the ground, then my legs, and Rudra yanks me harder than needed. My body practically sails over the edge, and lands—

Right on top of him.

He falls back with the momentum, our bodies tumbling together. I instinctively grab his T-shirt as we roll on the ground. My hand accidentally slides it up, and my fingers touch his spine, nails digging into his flesh.

As we finally stop a foot away from the edge, clutching each other as if we're holding on for dear life (which, frankly, we are), I find myself lying astride him, our faces so close my braid brushes his cheek.

I'm suddenly aware of his hands squeezing my hips, tight, as if he's afraid of letting go. Or as if he doesn't *want* to let go.

He pushes my braid off his face and tucks it under the hem of my T-shirt at the nape of my neck, the tips of his fingers hardened from skimming the frets of his guitar and playing bar chords. They rest on the curve of my neck now, the spot he didn't touch last night, and a visible shiver racks my skin.

I know he sees it, the effect he has on me with the barest of touches.

---

5 *Language*: Hindi; *Translation*: That's it . . . that's it . . . see! You're done!

I need to pull away, but I don't want to. He looks so hot lying under me like this, my legs on either side of him, his hand gripping my hip with the sort of ferocity that floods my mind with the wildest of thoughts.

Thoughts I should definitely *not* be having right now, at the edge of a cliff with all the college boys and locals staring at us. I can feel their eyes boring into me, but I can't seem to get a single part of my body to move, can't seem to get myself to look away from Rudra.

His thumb skims the pulse fluttering in my neck, coming to a stop so it's resting on the dip in my throat. It takes me a second to realize the rest of his fingers are behind my neck, while his thumb applies the slightest amount of pressure to the front.

His lips hike upward, and his eyes fall from mine to the spot where he's clutching my neck, making a million sensations come alive inside me. "You look like you're about to kiss me right now."

Ohmyfuckinggod.

I immediately push away from him, scrambling to my feet and smoothing my fingers over my clothes and hair. I can't help it, even when Rudra sits up and looks right at me, challenge swimming in his eyes—I touch my neck, the spot where he gripped me.

This is getting out of hand.

Rudra stays seated there, one leg bent and on the ground, the other folded up, and the hand that was on my neck just moments ago rests on his knee. His smirk has stretched into a full, shit-eating grin, because he basically just said the same thing to me that *I* told him last night: *You look like you're about to kiss me right now.*

The worst part is, I did. I *do*. The urge and the want are stronger than ever, and every time I start to feel like I catch a grip on my self-control, I lose it just as quickly.

I turn away from him, my face bursting into flames. I'm glad the sun's up, because my face feels redder than ever, and I'm hoping the others will think it's just a sunburn.

I pass them, trying but failing to ignore their stares, and climb a boulder to the highest stretch of ground, where the Chhatrapati Shivaji Maharaj shrine is. I make sure to take off my shoes and socks and tuck them behind another boulder where the others have left theirs. Shivaji Maharaj was a man, but he's worshiped like a god in Maharashtra because he was the founder of the Maratha empire. To keep our shoes on would be blasphemy.

I walk up to the shrine. Embedded in a huge stone is a small brick-red idol of Shivaji Maharaj on his horse. I sit on a boulder next to it, soaking up the calm and trying to soothe my fritzing nerves. It's windy here, and air rushes into my clothes, cooling all my sweaty crevices.

It takes me a moment to catch my breath, push all thoughts of Rudra out of my head, and focus on the up-and-down movement of my chest as I stare at the rolling hills and sharp trees, the blues and greens and yellows.

I can't believe it. I did it.

I managed to complete this trek that at one point felt like it was never going to end. I'm here, legs swinging from a ledge that looks out over a swathe of green stretching out toward the horizon, the sky literally the color of cornflowers.

Priti's voice sounds behind me a little while later, startling me out of my thoughts. "Can I join you?"

I don't look back at her as I say, "When have you ever been the type to ask?"

Priti snorts, climbing onto the ledge beside me. For a moment, we just sit there in silence, listening to the others talk and click photos on their phone. I'm calmer than I was just minutes ago, with the wind drying the sweat on my skin and the stunning view laid out before me.

Priti's voice is quiet when she finally speaks up. "I wasn't trying to be mean."

I don't say anything. I keep my gaze straight ahead, waiting for her to keep going.

"I just—" she says, a tinge of frustration in her voice. "Things have been so horrid between us for so long, it's almost become a habit to be this way with you, if you get what I mean? But I appreciate you hearing me out about Rudra last night. And I'll make it up to you. I'll be better—*we'll* be better. I just need time. Okay?"

Normally, I would just roll my eyes at that, but she's being honest, and genuine, and that is all that matters to me. I haven't been entirely loyal to my promise to her either, what with everything that's been happening with Rudra. But I'm intent on doing better by her from now on.

Because I'm Krishna Kumar, the girl who sees things through. Even when the going gets tough, I don't back out. And if I was able to make it here, to the top of this peak, I can keep my feelings in check. If not for me, then for Priti.

I finally turn and look at her. Then I nod, exhaling heavily.

"Okay."

24

CLASS, TODAY WE'RE COVERING FLIRTING 101—AND POINT ONE JUST SO HAPPENS TO BE "DON'T FUCKING ACT LIKE KRISHNA KUMAR"

Pune, Sunday

We hike back down to the tents, and that takes *forever*, but I go through the motions mechanically, stuck in limbo between a dream and a nightmare.

About an hour or so past noon, we're on the bus again. This time I don't share a seat with anyone because I feel so icky and dirty. I'm both irritated and teary, but that's just the sultry afternoon heat and the extreme fatigue.

So it's no surprise when I *actually* shed a tear after reaching the Sinhas' place.

After the best shower I've ever had in my life, I feel like I've just washed off years of grime packed into the layers of my skin. Under the water, the dirt just kept pouring out, mixing with the water and spiraling into the drain. It was like the earth had seeped into my bloodstream through the pores of my skin. Only when I was convinced I was completely clean did I turn the shower off.

Now I put on a loose, flowy churidar that flares around my ankles, allowing my skin to breathe while protecting it in its current sun-sensitive state. On top, I shrug on an olive-green angarkha kurta—one of my favorites, with delicate mandala cream designs—that's like a jacket with one flap tied over the other under my left arm. The dori used to tie the flaps together have tiny cream tassels at the ends, and they shimmer in the bathroom light.

My brown skin doesn't really let me get sunburned, just tanned from melanin accumulation, but because today's exposure was severe, I'll need my skin to heal before I can parade around outside in shorts and tank tops again.

Priti is out with Varun collecting Rudra's car from the mechanic. Digha and Charu went to her house down the hallway to freshen up, Rudra and Jalaj are taking turns bathing in Jalaj and Varun's bathroom, and I'm in Charu's bedroom. For once, Rudra gave in to Priti's begging and let her drive his car back here, too exhausted to argue.

Drying my hair with a towel, I walk over to the tall mirrors stuck to Charu's wardrobe, surveying my reflection. I have dark bags under my eyes, but at least that pimple from yesterday is gone, reduced to a red bump. I grab my makeup bag from the side table and quickly put on some black liquid liner, draw a small black bindi between my eyebrows, and don a pair of oxidized silver earrings with olive-green beads hanging from them.

There's a knock on the door as I run my fingers through my hair, easing the knots out. Rudra walks in, freshly changed into a pair of loose black tracks and a half-sleeved gray T-shirt. His hair is wet again—in its current state, it's barely combed and damp, sticking to his chin. He leans against the doorframe, watching me watch him.

"I don't think I've seen you in an angarkha kurta this trip," he says without a beat of hesitation. “You look pretty.” I turn back to the mirror to avoid looking at him, untangling the last of the knots from my hair.

“Thank you,” I respond, pushing my hair behind my shoulders. It falls in a sheet, draping down my neck. I don’t let it show, but I’m giddy from his compliment. “You look good too.” A pause. “You always do.”

“I doubt that, but okay.”

I turn to him, surprised. I’m not used to hearing that sort of a response from a guy as good-looking as him. Does he not see it?

“Why?”

“Why what?”

“Why do you doubt it?”

“Because . . .” Rudra looks awkward all of a sudden, hands shoved into his pockets. “I don’t know. I’ve just never had anyone say that to me before.”

I raise my eyebrows at him. “Priti has.”

Rudra snorts. “Priti keeps saying it. Doesn’t count.”

“Well, you do.” I drop my eyes to the ground. “You’re nice to look at.”

“Not as nice as Amrit, I’m sure.”

I snap my head up. “Why would you say that? There’s no comparison.”

“Oh.” Rudra seems surprised. He steps toward me but then hesitates.

“It’s fine. You can come inside.” I point behind him. “But shut the door.” Rudra’s eyes widen, and I hastily add, “The AC’s on.”

He closes the door, and then it’s just us in here. The space between us doesn’t feel as large anymore. Memories float back into my mind: his thumb resting on the hollow in my throat, his hand gripping my hip. The way he looked right up at me and said *You look like you're about to kiss me right now.*

I turn on my heel, pressing my palms to my cheeks to cool the heat spilling in. I sit on Charu's bed, leaving enough space before me so Rudra's not as close when he joins me.

For a moment, I think he's about to broach the topic of whatever happened between us last night and today, so I decide to speak up before he has the chance to. "Are you sure you're not too tired to drive straight to Goa?"

"I just need coffee. I'll be okay."

"We don't have to leave today, you know." I grab Charu's beige satiny pillow and place it in my lap, fiddling with the hem. "If you're too tired. We can leave early in the morning tomorrow."

"It's a nine-hour journey," Rudra says, sighing. "We'd be cutting it too close. Especially since we planned on having Mansi and Priti meet around noon so Mansi can have *some* time before probably making the most important decision of her life."

"And Priti will flip if we suggest leaving tomorrow," I add. "She practically ran out to pick up the car in her eagerness to leave for Goa. What beats me is how she thinks she's being slick and secretive with all this. It's so obvious."

"She's always been like that," Rudra says, smiling fondly. "And trust me, I'm fine to leave. That way, we won't have to rush tomorrow. We might even have a chance to actually take Goa in, between everything."

"You mentioned having been to North Goa before," I say.

"Yeah, loads of times. It's a good getaway."

"With your friends?"

"Yeah?" He says it like a question.

"I just—" I'm blushing again, shamelessly, and I'm hoping my sunburn helps cover for it. "I just wondered if you went with an ex."

Rudra ducks his head, and I'm shocked to find he's even redder than I am. We're pathetic, both of us. When he looks at me, his face is lit up, the apprehension from before gone. "If you were curious about my past relationships, you could've just asked."

I'm pretty sure I'm starting to resemble a tomato at this point. "Relationships? Plural?"

Rudra chuckles. "No. Just one."

"Who was it?"

He's looking at me so bashfully I want to fling a pillow at him. "You wouldn't know her."

I do fling the pillow at him then. "Just tell me, damn it! I'm curious!"

Rudra catches it deftly, laughing. "Okay, okay, fine! It was this girl from my class, back in eleventh. We dated for three months before breaking up."

"Why?"

He leans back, head against the wall and eyes on the ceiling. "This is going to sound really cliché, but we didn't want the same things."

I smile. "That *is* very cliché."

"Yeah."

"So no one besides her?"

"Nope. Just her."

"Why haven't you dated anyone seriously since?" I ask, grabbing another pillow to smooth out about a hundred times.

"The same reason you haven't."

"And what is that?"

"Because we were pursuing our dreams." I love the way he says *our*; it makes me feel like he's as invested in this conversation as I am. "You wanted to go to JHU, so you shut yourself off from the outside world and focused on just that. I wanted Juilliard, have always wanted Juilliard, and want to sign with a record label for my music one day—I did the same thing."

"How do you know me so well?" I ask, voice soft, almost a whisper.

"Because we're the same . . . because I told you this before, Krishna," he says, an incomprehensible emotion eddying in his eyes. "I've known you since we were kids. I was always there."

Even if it was just in the background.

He doesn't say those words, but they echo in my mind anyway.

"To be honest . . ." I say, ready to admit out loud what I've been keeping in my head all summer long. There's something about Rudra that makes me *want* to tell him, even if the truth is embarrassing to share. "That's what this whole trip has been about for me, you know? I missed out on so much by doing all that.

"All I remember about high school is waking up in a panicked frenzy every day, ticking things off my to-do list because there was always something left and absolutely no time. And once it was all over, I realized I'd done everything I was *supposed* to do—and yet, I felt like I'd done nothing. I know my friends"—the few I have—"think I'm boring because I have nothing to gossip about. Not anything *fun*, at least. No parties, no sneaking out of the house, no kissing—all I have are grades and my spotless track record of following the rules to the tee. The first time I even drank, I did that wrong too."

"Rarely is anyone's first time drinking a good experience," Rudra says. "The first time I drank, I ended up passed out next to the toilet. Woke up with god knows whose piss on my clothes."

I can't help but chuckle at that.

"And why are you talking like it's all over? You're eighteen, Krishna. You haven't missed out on anything yet. In fact, you have so much to look forward to."

"That's easy for you to say," I say, not harshly. "You did it all and also got into your dream college."

"I didn't do it all," Rudra says. "I didn't . . . you know." He trails off suggestively, all toothy and shy and pretty.

I blush. "You're still a virgin, Rudra Desai?" I ask teasingly.

"Yes, I'm a still a virgin, sunflower, and I'm not ashamed of it." Rudra grins. "My ex and I—we did other things, but it wasn't much. It never went there."

It's not fair, but the mere thought of him kissing someone, let alone getting to second or third base, makes me shrivel up inside with envy for that girl. It's so unlike me. Or maybe it isn't. Maybe I'm just that possessive, to be envious of someone's past I was barely a part of.

A past I *chose* to not be a part of.

"Look," Rudra says. "You might not think you've done anything fun, but you did get drunk—at a *house party*, no less. You won a food contest, went out on a midnight trek and lied to your mom about it—"

"Eavesdropper," I accuse.

"Hey, you talk loud," Rudra says before continuing. "You smoothed things over with Priti too. And you're going to be in Goa soon. You're going to . . . do what you came here for." I don't miss the way his lips turn downward when he says the last bit, before he adds, "The *last* thing I would call you is boring—it's the farthest thing from the truth."

I don't say anything to that. I don't say that it's not about Amrit Acharya anymore. I think about Amrit for a second, his easy smile, his charm, the way everything about us just *fit*. But I never felt *this* way with Amrit, the way I do now, with Rudra. Like there are opposite poles of a magnet embedded within us, drawing us to each other. Every time, it feels like the craving inside me to cross this overarching gap and kiss Rudra knocks the breath out of me. And now that I've seen the way my insides seem to catch fire whenever I'm around him, the contrast between those feelings—what I felt for Amrit and what I feel for Rudra—is stark.

With Amrit, it wasn't necessarily because *I* was the problem, or that *Amrit* was the problem. There was *no* problem. Because maybe, like I've already told Rudra, there's no comparison.

"When you put it like that," I say, prying the conversation away from the topic of Amrit. Because this situation is starting to feel a lot more like an ultimatum with every passing second, one I can't afford to reckon with right now. "I *have* been quite adventurous these past few days."

"You're a daredevil, Krishna Kumar." He reaches out and ruffles my hair, and I fling a second pillow at him.

I guess I *am* kind of a daredevil.

25

MY DUTY AS A PASSENGER PRINCESS IS TO PROMPTLY FALL ASLEEP FOR THE WHOLE RIDE

Goa, Monday

When Priti returns, a dance to her step, we head downstairs to where the car's parked, packed and ready to leave.

"You look way too chipper for someone who just got back from an all-night trek," I comment, grimacing.

"I don't know what you're talking about," Priti says, practically skipping to us.

Charu, Digha, Varun, and Jalaj have come downstairs to see us off, and as I load my stuff into the trunk of Rudra's BMW, I feel a wave of melancholy wash over me.

Although my interaction with Priti's cousins has been brief and I'm no stranger to uprooting myself from a place entirely and leaving everything behind—I did it when I was ten—I still feel sad. The chances of meeting them again are slim. Their lives are headed in such wildly different directions than mine.

I shake hands with Jalaj and Varun and hug Digha and Charu, giggling when our heads knock together. Priti joins in, and we stay there, bundled together as if we're players huddling before a game. We exchange numbers, promising to keep in touch.

I walk to the front of the car and open the passenger-side door.

Priti gapes. "Wait, you're serious? You're going to let me have the back seat?"

"You fetched the car, so this is, like, the least you deserve," I say, wrinkling my nose. "I'll navigate."

Priti blows me a kiss, and my suspicions about her being extra happy because she's meeting Mansi tomorrow are confirmed. It doesn't stop me from being taken aback, even though things are better between us now. I'm *not* used to Priti Gaikwad blowing me kisses.

Once our last goodbyes have been said, we buckle ourselves in and wave until the four of them have disappeared around the gate, and then we're off.

The rest of the trip to Goa is so much longer than I thought it would be. I navigate for a couple of hours, but as the sun slowly sinks into the horizon, my eyes start shuttering closed, try as I might to keep them open.

I doze off and only come to when Priti shakes me awake. We're parked on the side of the road, hazard lights turned on.

"Come to the back seat. We can't have you navigating like this," Priti says, but the rest of her words are blearing together in my head, and I'm slowly falling asleep again.

Minutes later, I'm being unbuckled from my seat. Even through my sleepy haze, I get a whiff of Rudra's scent, my cheek smushed against his chest as he lifts me into his arms like a baby. His muscles are taut under my knees and head, and he's holding me firmly like he's never going to let go. But he sets me down in the back seat too soon, much to my dismay.

I mumble something garbled to him—even *I* fail to fully comprehend what I'm saying—and he ducks toward me, trying to make sense of it, so very close, but Priti says, "She's just sleep talking," and he starts to move away.

I grab the front of his T-shirt, eyes closed, knowing he's there just by the warmth radiating from his body. "Don't go," I whisper, and I don't know whether he hears me and chooses to ignore it or whether he can't hear me at all, but he pulls away, gently prying my fingers from his T-shirt.

"What was that?" Priti asks.

"Nothing, she just grabbed my shirt. Her grip's strong even in her sleep."

The back seat door slams shut, and the rest of their conversation fades away. I don't know if this is all a dream, but it feels too real to be one. Rudra's form against mine felt too real.

The next time my eyes open, a dim porch floodlight is shining down on me, and I can hear voices again.

I groan, placing my arm over my head to block out the light. But the voices keep talking, and I'm so parched my throat hurts. I drop my arm and prop myself up on my elbows, squinting out the window through the light.

It's dark outside, the night sky bordered by trees, and it takes me a second to register that those are palm leaves and that . . .

We're in Goa.

The floodlight settles in my vision and I spot Rudra and Priti talking to a plump middle-aged lady—probably Mummy's age or older—by the gate of a multistory building. They're laughing, and the lady hands Priti something. Keys, I think, as metal glints in the light.

I check my phone. It's half past twelve—we made it in the nick of time. I reach for the bottle in the cup holder between the passenger and driver seats and am relieved to find it nearly full. I down the contents in one go and set the empty bottle down before opening the car door.

At the sound, all three of them turn to look at me, and Priti says, "There's our devil." But her tone's not condescending. It's almost . . . affectionate.

"Hello, sweetheart," the lady says, smiling cheerily down at me.

She's got Anglo-Indian looks, as most Goan people with Portuguese descent do; fair skin that's not white, light-brown eyes, hair a mousy shade and threaded with silver. She's wearing a soft cotton maxi nightdress that's pastel blue, like the sky during the trek today, with pink and yellow flowers bordering the hem. She has a slight accent, not too distinct unless you listen closely.

"Hello," I say, smiling back as I walk up to stand between Rudra and Priti. "I'm sorry—it's been a long day."

"Yes. These two were just telling me. It's a wonder you made it here at all."

"Yeah, like we mentioned, it was a family emergency," Priti says, not missing a beat. "Thank you so much for letting us check in so late, Ms. Fernandes. We really appreciate it."

"No worries at all, sweetheart."

She guides us inside the building. It's quite cozy-looking, with a glass staircase and wooden banister leading to the upper floors and an elevator right opposite it. There's no lobby, since this isn't a hotel but rather a beach house they rent rooms out of.

Priti booked this place because it was safe, owned by a lovely couple, and in a quieter part of Calangute, North Goa. There's a dining room and bar up ahead, with exquisite oakwood furniture and polished glasses and bottles arranged in rows along the counter.

A sardar ji is lounging on the leather couch inside, snoring softly. Ms. Fernandes giggles as she presses the button to call the elevator. "That's my husband. Don't mind him. He wanted to stay up to ensure you kids were okay and safe, but he's had a busy day and more than one glass of wine to drink."

The elevator arrives, and we pile all our luggage inside until there's no space left. Rudra presses the button for the second floor and shuts the lift door, and we start climbing the stairs. Golden chandeliers have been hung intermittently on the ceiling of the stairway, and the glass panes looking to the outside of the building reflect the light, throwing our mirror images back at us. There's an ache building in my calves, an aftermath of the trekking, but it's a relief to move again after being cramped in the car for more than eight hours.

Ms. Fernandes quickly shows us around our rooms. They're pretty spacious. There's a living room with a black faux-leather pullout couch, a glass coffee table, and a television. Swiggy's available if we're hungry and want to order something (she recommends ordering from this Punjabi restaurant a couple of miles away that's open twenty-four/seven).

There's a bedroom farther inside with a double bed, one lamp on either side, huge wardrobes, and a bathroom that's so clean it sparkles. I step in and am pleasantly surprised to find there's a tub within with jet sprays, a shower curtain partitioning it from the toilet.

I can't wait to take a nice long bath in it tomorrow before going to the wedding and pulling off our chaotic plan to sabotage it. But the thought of Mansi's fiancé and what he might go through tomorrow if Mansi calls off the wedding fills me with guilt. Now I'm thinking maybe I don't deserve to even have a decent bath.

"There are three bathrobes and three sets of towels for your face, body, and hair inside the wardrobe," Ms. Fernandes says, opening the huge oakwood doors.

"You're supposed to use three different towels for each?" Rudra asks, but I can tell he's joking.

I burst into laughter and Priti nudges him. "Idiot."

"It's up to you if you want to use all three, though it would be the more hygienic option." Ms. Fernandes chuckles. "There's also a locker in here," she continues, showing us how to reset the passcode. "Aadyant and I will be in our room on the ground floor, so if you need anything at all, just dial zero on the landline and I'll send one of my helpers up."

"Thank you so much, Ms. Fernandes," Priti says, smiling up at her. She looks so pretty and radiant when she smiles, with her straight, pearly teeth. "You've been wonderful and such a huge help."

"And thank you for staying up and waiting for us," I add.

"Oh, you lovelies." Ms. Fernandes reaches over and clasps our faces in between her palms, one after the other, and I giggle when she pecks Rudra on his cheek. His eyes widen, but he manages an awkward smile as he pulls away, cheeks filling with color. His reaction is so freakin' cute . . . I *can't.*

Ms. Fernandes says good night and leaves the room. Priti immediately turns to us, an excited glint in her eyes. "So where do you guys want to go?"

"What?" I say blankly. "Why would we go anywhere?"

"Duh, because it's *Goa*? And we're literally in the heart of it?"

"Priti," Rudra says, running a hand through his hair. He looks so tired; I can see it in the creases that have formed under his eyes. "We just got here. We need rest."

"Ruds, how many times are we going to come to Goa together?" Priti grips his shoulders with both her hands.

"I know that, but—"

"No buts! I've come here with my family, and you've been here with your friends multiple times, but we've never been here together!"

"Priti, he's been driving this whole time, and we spent all night out on that trek," I say. "Look at him! He looks like he's about to collapse to the floor right now."

"Dude, come on." Priti lets go of Rudra's shoulders and grabs mine. Oops. That means she is about to work her wiles on me now. "*Listen*. You're going back to Portland this *Wednesday*. These kind of impromptu Goa trips *don't* happen. You know what they say. Goa trips are always planned, but they never pan out. You remember how the cousins were thinking of coming here for Divija didi's birthday, but it never happened? This is a *miracle*. Us three, here."

I'm tempted to remind her that *she* was the first one to back out, saying she had a college event, and that she never really cared if I was even there or not. But there's a sort of earnestness in her eyes that I haven't seen in a long, long time. It doesn't feel put on, or fake, like she's giving me the puppy eyes just to get me to agree, the way she did with Nani. She's genuinely trying to make an effort to heal things between us. The way I am.

And I can't crush that. That's not me. I don't do that. Any tiny chance I see of things getting better or working, I try my level best to see it through.

"But we're heading out tomorrow anyway," I add. To be honest, I'm not against the idea of going out for a bit. I got my well-needed sleep in the car. It's Rudra I'm worried about. "We can see Goa then.

Right now, we should really get some rest."

"Krishna, you can never see Goa enough." Priti leans closer to me, her dark eyes boring into mine, making it impossible to look away. If she's trying to hypnotize me into saying yes, it's already working. "How about this? We'll just head out to Baga Beach—it's only ten minutes from here by car—grab a couple drinks, eat some good food, and get back in an hour." She flips toward Rudra. "What do you think? We'll only go if you want to." She pauses, shoots him a wicked grin, and shrugs. "Just reminding you that the drinks here are unmatched."

Rudra sighs, and I see his resolve crumbling. "All right. One hour can't hurt."

Priti turns to me, clapping her hands together like a little kid. How did I even consider bursting her bubble for a minute there?

"Okay," I say. "I'll come."

"Prepare to have the best hour of your lives!" Priti says as she does a little dance, before rushing over to her duffel bag, throwing it open, and pulling clothes out fervently.

Rudra and I exchange a small smile. And I know what he's wishing—that this moment of elation and happiness she's having doesn't get crushed forever tomorrow.

26

THE EMOTIONAL WHIPLASH OF CRYING ONE MOMENT AND BEING HORNY THE NEXT

Goa, Monday

Getting ready is a whole ritual on its own. Priti pulls a sexy black bodycon dress from her duffel that I just know is going to have her looking *snatched*. Most of her clothes are black, or at least outfits with one piece of clothing that's black, and it suits her vibe. And I'm sure the girlies dig it.

It's both funny and sad that someone as attractive as Priti, who could literally get any girl she's ever wanted, is desperately in love with someone who's getting married tomorrow. For that, she seems pretty sane right about now. I'd be genuinely losing my mind.

Rudra's getting ready in the living room (Priti not-very-politely shooed him away and he stepped out immediately, his bag and guitar case in tow), and the door between us is locked shut, giving us our privacy.

I open my suitcase, surveying my clothes, as if I'm going to find a gorgeous new outfit miraculously tucked into it by some magical fairy godmother. I have two outfits left—the lehenga choli in the saree bag I'm planning to wear to the wedding tomorrow and a half-sleeved sky-blue kurti.

Everything else has been worn and needs washing, or at least ironing and perfuming. All I have is some spare underwear because I live by the policy that one can never pack too much underwear for a trip.

I sigh, taking out the kurti and holding it up in front of me. Not very Goa-like, but it'll look cute with my jean shorts. It'll have to do.

"You can't wear that!" Priti exclaims. "We're in Goa, Krishna, not Varanasi."

"First off, this is a very cute kurti and it's a stereotype that you can't rock Indian-wear in a club. Second, I don't have anything else to wear. Only the lehenga choli for tomorrow."

"Okay, sorry," Priti says, and I gape at her, surprised to hear that forbidden word come out of her mouth of its own accord. "It *is* very cute, but you need something that's sexy. Not cute."

"Well, all I have left is clean underwear."

"How about . . . this?" Priti digs around in her duffel and takes out a black halter-neck bralette and a short black denim skirt with silver chains hanging from it.

"No way." I stare at the outfit as she lays it on the bed. "Nope."

"Why not?" Priti demands, hands on her hips. "It's hot."

"I'm not saying it's not hot. It's just—no. I'll wear my kurti, thanks."

"I'm not giving you a choice." She walks over to me, looking at the outfit from where I'm standing, as if trying to see what I'm seeing. "What's the problem, really?"

"It's—" I start, flushing. "It's going to show my whole stomach. And my underarms aren't shaved. Like, I shaved them four days ago."

"No one gives a fuck if your underarms are shaved or not. And no, it's not going to show your whole stomach, because this skirt is high-waisted. Besides, what's wrong with showing your stomach? You've got a great stomach."

"Says the one with the washboard abs." I grab my paunch, pointing to it. "I have a tummy. It'll stick out. I'm extremely soft around my stomach and hips."

"Listen. Just try them on. If you don't like them, you can wear your kurti."

Priti picks up the clothes and shoves them toward me. I hastily grab them, holding them against my chest. Then I grumble something about the utter lack of right to choose and head into the bathroom to change. I don't have a problem with wearing short stuff, but I'm not confident enough to pull off Priti's style.

Inside, I strip in front of the mirror and stare at the halter-neck top.

Oh shit, wait.

I open the door, poking my head out. "Priti, could you hand me my nipple covers? They're in my suitcase, to the right."

"You don't need them. It's a padded bralette."

I shut the door and pick the flimsy thing up. She's right. There are pads sheathed inside the front lining. Luckily, the bralette can be tied around my neck and back, so I don't have to worry about it not fitting. Once I put it on, adjusting the knots, I find that it's steady on my boobs. If I don't raise my hands too much, the baby hair on my underarms will go unnoticed, as will the ones on my stomach and back. And it'll be dark, so there's that.

I slip on the skirt next, and like Priti said, it's high-waisted, so it covers up my tummy entirely, the denim material bunching around my waist. It flares at the bottom, ending mid-thigh, chains clinking as I rotate, looking at myself in the mirror.

Fuck.

I look hot.

The first thought that comes to my mind is Rudra seeing me in this, and it makes my mouth go dry. But I dismiss the thought just as quickly.

I step out of the bathroom, and the AC makes goose bumps prickle up along my arms. I rub at them furiously, walking over to Priti. She's dressed as well, and she looks mind-blowing.

The dress fits her like a glove, hugging her sharp, slim curves and baring her brown shoulders and legs. She's putting on fresh coats of thick kajal, eyeliner, and lipstick. She steps away from the mirror once she's done, to check and see if her makeup's good.

"You look unfairly hot," I say. "As always."

She turns to me, looking me up and down, and her eyes widen. "Shut up."

"Um. Okay?"

"Shut. The. Fuck. Up." Priti walks over to me, and her strong perfume wafts to my nose. She grabs my shoulders roughly, making me crane my neck to look at her. "Krish. You look like a total baddie." She marches me over to the mirror, standing behind me and shaking me vigorously. "Do you see it? Do you see yourself?"

"I—I do," I stammer through the shaking, but I can't help but smile. It feels good being complimented by Priti.

Priti grins. "See? Nothing wrong with taking my fashion advice once in a while." She sits me down on the ottoman in front of the dressing mirror. "Now let me do your makeup. We need to complete the look."

Priti spends the next five minutes patiently working on my face. She does a smoky eye for me with winged eyeliner and kajal and proceeds to pull a packet of tiny silver sequins from her makeup case. She sticks one to the inner corner of my eye, and three in a line along the outer curve, starting from the point where the wing of the eyeliner ends. Then she puts some brown lipstick on my lips, the same shade she's wearing.

We both sing along to the music playing through her phone set on the bed, and she passes comments and compliments about how *this smoky eye looks so good on you* and how *the sequins really make your eyes pop* and how *you should dress like this way more often.*

In return, I tell her how *I could never be as hot as you* and how *not many people have the balls to revamp their wardrobes the way you have.*

I can't help but enjoy every second of the whole process, not just because Priti's giving me a glow up, but also because this is different. This is the most sisterly thing we've done in eight years. Last I remember spending time with her, we clipped Nani's towels to our heads to mimic wigs and dashed around from room to room, playing house on fire, pretending to be part of a Barbie firefighter squad responsible for rescuing everyone in the house.

Now we're both here in Goa on a road trip after lying to our parents about our whereabouts, getting ready together to go out partying. We're sharing clothes, doing our makeup, blasting music, and singing along. It's the best time we've had together in eight years, and I just never ever want this moment to pass.

A smile sprouts along my face as Priti sets my hair with her fingers, giving it an artfully messy look.

"Why are you smiling?" she asks.

My smile grows more solemn. "I'm just thinking about how I love this."

"Love what?"

"*This.* Us. Right now."

Priti pauses for a moment, stepping away, and I think she's just checking out my final look, but she smiles too. "Yeah." She reaches out and affectionately brushes her fingers through my hair. "It's been a while since we did something without fighting, huh?"

The thought of it makes tears spring to my eyes, and Priti stares at me in horror, immediately scrambling for some tissues. "Eye makeup, Krishna! Eye makeup!"

"I'm sorry, I just—" I grab the tissue and hold it under my eye, soaking up the teardrop before it has the chance to spill out, careful to not ruin my makeup. "I've just missed you so much."

Priti's gaze softens, and she sits back on the dressing table in front of me. "I know. I've missed you too."

"But you hated me." I wave my hands furiously in front of my face, tipping my face toward the ceiling in the hopes of defying gravity.

"I didn't hate you." Priti sighs. "I know I've made you feel that way, but I never hated you."

"I wish we hadn't lost out on all those years." My voice cracks, but at least I've got the tears under control. Barely.

"I guess—I guess there's no point regretting all this, you know? This whole wild trip happened for a reason. And maybe the reason was for us to get over our childishness for once."

"I didn't make you out to be the sort of person who believes things happen for a reason."

"Honestly, a lot has changed in the past year."

I squash the tissue in my hand, tension building in my palm. I want to ask her if she'll come see me in the US, wondering if she'll ever tell me about FIT. But we're finally on good terms, and I know this is just the start. It'll be a slow buildup.

She will tell me. I know she will.

Overcome by the sudden surge of emotions, I lean forward and wrap my arms around Priti. She protests, "I'm not a hugger! No, no, Krishna," and that only makes me laugh and hug her tighter, until I'm probably crushing and suffocating her.

When I pull away, she's scowling at me, readjusting her hair. I snort. "There's the Priti I'm familiar with."

She opens her mouth to throw me a retort, but a knock on the door interrupts us, followed by Rudra's voice. "Hey, are you girls done yet?"

"Almost!" Priti calls out, turning to me and mouthing, *Such a gentleman*, making us both burst into giggles again.

And right then, another broken part of me slowly starts to heal.

After we've had some minutes to get ourselves together and touch up our makeup, we step out fully dressed and ready. Rudra is waiting for us on the couch, playing something mutedly on his guitar.

He sets it aside and gets to his feet when we walk out, his eyes widening. He's coincidentally wearing all black like us—black tee, black leather jacket, and baggy black jeans, a silver chain looped around his neck and his hair down and waving around his face. His feet are snug in black loafers and there are oxidized rings on his fingers, one even shaped like a guitar. Now, *that* outfit? Definitely branded and expensive. Stuff that's bought in three-floored luxury stores in air-conditioned malls.

It's the sexiest I've ever seen him look, and that's saying something.

"Look at us all, matching in black," Priti comments, walking over to him and ruffling his hair. "Society would be a hundred percent more evolved if everyone wore black all the time. It shows."

"Okay, but could you stop messing with my hair?"

Priti feigns a hurt look. "Can't even show my bestie some affection these days without being rudely rejected."

Rudra sighs, and I feel slightly sorry for him because he has to put up with Priti's dramatics. But I'm relieved to see he's not looking as tired anymore.

Priti shuts off the lights in the living room. "Baga Beach, here we come!"

It's a quick drive to the beach, just like Priti said, and Rudra navigates the difficult roads of Goa with expertise (nothing short of what I expected of him). I sit in the front this time, map open on my phone, knowing I owe Priti for having slept the whole journey from Pune to Goa.

What I love about Goa is that it doesn't look like any other city in India. Most of the roads snake through thick forests with greenery all around, palm leaves scraping a moonlit sky. There's a sprinkling of wine shops, thatched huts, and a variety of markets. There are so many tourists walking the roads here it doesn't feel like India.

Calangute has an active nightlife, even past one a.m. Every few meters, there are clubs and pubs and restaurants blasting music, both DJ and karaoke, letting out waves of smoke and featuring crowds of people in shimmering outfits, jubilation painted over their faces.

Everyone's wearing such short clothes that no one really stands out. In India, I'm used to people turning around to leer when I wear anything that shows a little more skin than I normally would. This is *new.* I don't feel out of place in my halter-neck and skirt anymore. Instead, I feel quite the opposite. I feel like I fit right in. Safe.

The excitement pools into every corner of me, making my veins buzz. I look out the window the entire time, soaking up the glorious sights, itching to get to our destination.

When we get there, Rudra stops in front of the path leading to the beach. "Priti, why don't you book us a table while Krishna and I find a parking spot?"

Priti's too revved up to make a comment about why he's specifically asking me to stay or why I can't accompany her instead. She nods, opens the car door, and jumps out, yelling, "We're here, baby!" before sprinting down the path.

And then it's just Rudra and me inside the car. We're restlessly quiet while he looks for a parking spot. I don't dare turn to him, my mind racing with a hundred different possibilities of why he might've asked me to stay, ninety-nine of them being that he's going to confront me about whatever's going on between us.

So I focus on looking for a vacant spot instead. I find one a minute later, tucked away into a dark corner of the lot. This time, I can't help but shamelessly watch as he does that hot steering-the-wheel thing again, with just one hand, his palm pressing into the curve of the wheel and directing it to the right. The BMW smoothly slips into the parking space, perfectly parallel to the cars on either side of us.

I gulp as the car hums to a stop. Rudra's face is dark, barely lit by the green and blue lights from the digits on the dashboard. The only streetlight is five parking spaces away, and it silhouettes him, casting most of his face in shadow. I grab the door handle, pulling, needing to get away—

"Wait."

Rudra unbuckles himself from the seat and leans toward me, his hand touching my shoulder. A tiny current zips out from the point where the skin of his palm and my skin come in contact, and I shiver, loving and loathing how his hand feels on my bare skin.

"What?" I whisper, turning to look at him. He's so close our shaky breaths cloud together in the space between our faces.

"I didn't get a chance to tell you," Rudra says, his voice so hoarse it's like he's struggling to dislodge it from his throat. His calloused fingers brush my shoulder, just briefly, and a million unholy thoughts fog my head.

"Chance to tell me what?" Now it feels like *my* voice is stuck in my throat. I can barely speak. I tilt my head, moving my shoulder up, nudging him, begging him to do it again, to brush his fingers against my skin.

Granted the permission, he skims his knuckles up to my ear, that same spot he touched last night, when we were standing under a hundred fireflies. My eyes flutter shut, and I can't breathe, can't think, can't move. It's like he read my mind. It's like he knows exactly what makes my knees weak and my veins catch fire.

He brushes a lock of my hair behind my ear, and I can feel him looking at me with that dark gaze of his, and god, if I look at him again, I'll disintegrate to dust. There'll be nothing left but the essence of me. And just the essence of me isn't enough to become a doctor, so something must be done about it.

He draws closer, his inexplicably feverish form oozing warmth into my side, and his lips touch my ear, grazing it so lightly I don't even feel his lips on my skin, just on the tiny hair now standing to attention all over my body. The part of me that shouts *This is wrong* is overpowered, conquered by the part of me that's on my knees, longing for him to kiss me.

"Just that you look really fucking hot right now," he finally responds, right into my ear. His voice is deep and rough, and the blood pulsing in my throat turns to steam. His fingers knot into my hair from the back, tilting my head up, and his lips move from my ears to my cheekbone, my cheekbone to the corner of my lips. I give in, mouth parting to kiss him—

And he pulls away.

I nearly scream as he draws his hand back to grab the door handle and wrenches it open. My eyes snap open and stare at him, flushed and hot and embarrassed, my body an absolute mess of nerves. I can't believe he had the audacity to come that close, to almost kiss me, and then . . . and then *pull away*.

"Why would you do that?" I gasp, wanting to bring my hands up to my cheeks to siphon some of the heat from them but finding myself unable to move. My lips are tingling, and I can't wrap my head around the fact that he almost kissed me.

Almost.

"Because I want you to make up your mind about what you want, Krishna," he says. The distant chaos of the outside leaks in through the open door. "And as much as I want nothing more than to kiss you so hard you see stars right now"—he locks gazes with me one more time before stepping out onto the pavement, and the fierceness of the desire I see in his eyes nearly bowls me over—"it's just going to have to wait."

27

SERIOUSLY, IN PUBLIC?

Goa, Monday

We're inside one of the bars in Baga Beach, seated on a sofa, sipping our drinks and eating fried, oily starters. Most of the items on the menu were seafood and nonvegetarian; the only options on the veg menu were fried baby corn, aloo, and paneer.

I'm too preoccupied to be able to digest anything, so I nibble at my toothpick once I'm done eating one serving of the starter, feet nervously tapping the floor. We're on the outer edge of the bar, facing the beach directly, and the view is so breathtaking I can barely get myself to look away.

The crests of the waves shimmer as some hawkers by the beach shine laser lights on the water, sending green streaks of lightning arcing over the undulating surface. The night air is cool, tinted with sweat, perfume, alcohol, hookah smoke, and the heat of forms pressed close together. The waves are tipped in white from the moonlight, and the midnight-black sea seems to stretch out forever, to no end.

On the beach, people walk on the sand, feet dipping in and out of the water, past tables set up for couples and small groups, covered at the top like tents, pretty lamps and fairy lights frolicking in the wind. Deeper inside the bar, a band plays, and the purple and pink lights illuminating them throw hued light all the way out to the deck where we're seated.

Rudra is sipping Hoegaarden from a can—I notice that despite being excited about the alcohol in Goa, he's holding off on getting sloshed because he has to drive us both back. Priti's clutching a whiskey sour, while I'm having a Jamaican passion Breezer because it's the least alcoholic drink on the menu and I'm not sure I want a repeat of what happened the night of the house party.

While it's impossible to get drunk on something with 4.8 percent alcohol content, I still feel dizzy. Because I can't stop thinking about Rudra and what happened in the car earlier—or rather, as is always a pattern with me, what *didn't* happen in the car earlier.

We're all three huddling for warmth and leaning close to have our words heard over the mayhem (even though it's mostly Priti engaging both of us in a conversation because Rudra and I don't look at or speak a word to each other).

I don't know why he would think I haven't made up my mind. He must have been talking about Amrit, because what else could it be?

Even though *I* was the one to misdirect him, make him believe I'm still in this for Amrit—can't he see it, see the way I react to him whenever he's close? Can't he see I was lying, that I've made up my mind already? Why do I have to tell him that outright?

But deep inside, I know that his confusion and frustration are justified. I did this to him—to us.

The more I think about it, the more my head aches. I set aside my drink after a bit, staring out at the ocean, mind swimming. I feel faint. I need air.

Just when I'm contemplating excusing myself from Priti and Rudra and taking a breather by the side of the beach, an emcee announces that some world-famous DJ Sujin is in the house and that she's ready to bring the roof down and wants everyone on the dance floor. I was so lost in my thoughts I didn't hear the band stop playing, step off, and leave the stage.

A deafening cheer erupts around us, and Priti looks between Rudra and me eagerly. "Ohmygod, let's go!" She leaps to her feet, both hands outstretched.

At first, the two of us protest, but then she takes our hands and drags us to our feet, her grip astoundingly strong. I did want a breather, didn't I? And dancing is a good way of letting loose. It's not like Rudra and I are going to find ourselves in compromising positions together with Priti around.

"Fine!" I say, and Priti cheers, clearly a little inebriated from the alcohol. She did say the whiskey sour was a mild drink, though, so it could also be her exhilaration paired with the atmosphere of the place. She kisses both my cheeks as I stand, and the two of us turn to Rudra, who, at my surrender, has no choice but to oblige.

We follow the shuffling crowd to the dance floor within, the energy radiating from Sujin almost palpable as she screams, "What's up, Goa?"

The clamor that follows is so loud I have to clamp my hands over my ears. As we draw closer, I can see why Sujin commands the crowd the way she does: she's pretty, with curling dark hair and a winning smile, and plays a sick beat that builds to a crescendo as we gather around her.

Priti's still clasping my hand as we come to a stop in the middle of the surging throng. The three of us form a triangle, and it puts Rudra and me directly opposite each other. Our eyes can't help but meet as the music builds, the energy crackling like electricity around us.

The beat drops, and everyone goes absolutely wild.

Including Priti, who cups her hands around her mouth and crows. I burst into laughter at that, and Rudra splits a grin. The music oscillates over my skin, and my body moves of its own accord. The crowd insistently pushes the three of us close, and I find myself nearly face-to-face with Rudra in the little vacuum left.

His hand comes up, and I stare at him in quiet shock as he places it on the small of my back, thinking he's going to pull me close and kiss me in front of Priti, right here . . . but he guides me to his side instead.

Seconds later, a throng of guys drunkenly crash into the spot where I was standing. *Oh.* I look up at Rudra, his hand fraught against my back as he shoots them a menacing glare.

"Hey!" he snaps sharply, making me start. "Watch where you're going!"

My breath catches in my throat, and I think a fight might erupt between them, but then one of the men just raises his hands in apology, smiling sheepishly before herding his friends elsewhere. I'm staring up at Rudra, stunned, as the group stumbles off. His hand relaxes, then drops, and he tilts his head down toward me, eyes warm again.

"Are you hurt?"

No, I mouth, my voice stuck in my throat. They hardly had the chance to crash into me, he knows it, and yet . . .

"Are you okay?" Priti asks, stepping toward me, her eyes blooming with concern. "You'll always find a pack of drunken guys like that in clubs."

"I'm good," I finally say.

The assault of emotions I feel right now nearly makes me burst into tears. Here's Rudra, on one hand, whom I'm beginning to care for, who makes me want so much more with him, and then there's Priti, my beloved cousin, my once best friend I'm so close to having in my life again. My mind duels, swords clashing endlessly, because no matter *what* I choose, I'll end up suffering a loss.

I step away from Rudra and let the music wash over me again, shutting my eyes. I dance like I've never danced before, feeling my body turn damp with sweat, craving the distraction from the conflict roaring in my head. I don't know how long I dance, but at some point, Priti pats my shoulder, and I open my eyes after what feels like forever.

"I'm headed to the washroom. Be back in two."

"Do you want me to come along?" I ask.

"No, you stay. Dance. You look like you're really enjoying yourself." She smiles. I *did* lose myself in the music there. It dragged me from my thoughts, which I've been needing for a while. "Just pay attention to your phone. I'll text if I have trouble finding you two again."

Priti disappears into the dancing throng, leaving Rudra and me alone again.

Rudra stares down at me, his breath quickening. It's such a contrast to how he was in the car, or with the group of boys. My heart jolts with how he looks at me, as if he can see all my thoughts. And I wonder . . . will anyone else ever make me feel the way he does? Will I ever again be capable of attraction, of romance like this? Why is it that every time, something gets in the way?

Priti didn't want me with Rudra because she didn't believe I could think with my head when it came to romance, but now that things are better between us, I could make her see it, couldn't I? That I'm changing, and deserving of someone like Rudra Desai, *if* he wants more to do with me?

I step closer to him and wrap my arms around his neck. His Adam's apple bobs in his throat and his eyes widen when I raise myself onto my tiptoes, speaking directly into his ear so my voice can only be heard by him. The music is softer, aiding me.

"I've been thinking about what you said," I say. "And you're right. I needed to make up my mind, and—"

Rudra plants his hands on the curve of my waist, pulling away, his eyes pained. I think it might be the gravity of my emotions, but he looks scared. Scared of what I'm about to say, of what I've made up my mind about.

"What?" I ask, my stomach in my throat.

"Not here." He lets his hands fall from my waist, takes my hand, and guides me through the crowd. The throng fills the space we previously occupied, the swarm of people parting ahead of us as we make our way back to our table. The music isn't as loud out here, and the sea breeze replaces the smoke inside. My body instantly cools, and I take in a deep breath as Rudra sits.

I sit next to him, shifting closer, and turn my body to face him entirely so that my knees brush the side of his thigh. He glances down at the point of contact and then up at me, his pupils dilating.

"And?" he asks, unmoving but not tentative, not like he was on the dance floor a minute ago.

I pick up right where I left off. "And whenever I try to think about anything at all, all I can do is go back to thoughts of you. And thoughts of kissing you." I pause, hyperaware of our proximity, my heart picking up speed inside my chest. I know I'm going to regret this later, but the way he's looking at me right now, like he would crush his mouth against mine if I just let him, makes a fire ignite in my gut. "I want to kiss you, Rudra."

Rudra says nothing, and I wonder if I've dreamt the past few days, whether I've confessed to wanting to kiss a boy who has zero interest in me.

The pace at which I second-guess scenarios needs to be studied.

When he finally speaks, I want to burrow a hole through the wood and the sand below. "Anything else?"

Excuse me?

I grit my teeth. "What else do you want me to say?"

Rudra smirks, and the sudden motion pulls my attention to his lips, so full I can't help but look at them, admire their shape. "I don't want you to say anything else, Krishna." He leans closer, and I automatically mimic the motion, until we're a hairbreadth away from each other.

My eyes are half closed. I'm fully ready to give in. Rudra brings his hand up and knots his fingers in my hair, bunching it up at the nape of my neck. He could pull away or pull me in at this point. "I just want you to kiss me," he whispers, his warm breath tickling my mouth.

Our lips brush, gently. And then he does it.

He tightens his grip on my hair and draws me toward him, seizing my lips fully. The fire spreads from my stomach to my chest and then it's in my head, my lips, touching his.

Kissing his.

At first, my lips barely move because I have no clue what to do. This is my first kiss, ever, and it's with someone I never imagined I would be kissing until a few days ago. My brain practically erupts at the thought that this is happening, utterly failing to comprehend it.

But Rudra moves his mouth, and his lips are so soft I nearly melt into his arms, and it all starts to feel real. Too real to be true, if that even makes sense. His fingers splay against my neck, and he tilts his head sideways, my lips parting fully underneath his.

His movements aren't rough but slow and gentle, so it doesn't feel like he's being pushy or too demanding. He gives me the space to breathe, to figure out how our lips fit together.

And not for the first time this summer, my conscience is sent packing on a vacation—I start kissing him back. Tugging at his lips the way he does mine, bringing my hands up to his shoulders, his neck, and his cheeks, so I'm clasping his face between my palms. His cheeks and chin are lined with the slightest of stubble, and it scrapes my face as he kisses me, eliciting a sound from the back of my throat that could almost be a moan but is much rougher.

I don't know who breaks the kiss first, but my body is so hot I think I might be running a fever. I'm incapable of thinking of anything but *him*, the stark lines and angles of his face accentuated by the flashing purple and pink lights from inside the bar. He looks so good, I want to kiss him again.

I haven't had enough. I don't think I could ever have enough with him.

Rudra gazes back at me with unwavering intensity, and before my embarrassment has the chance to come creeping back, his hands catch my waist. In one quick motion, he whisks me onto his lap.

I gasp, legs flailing around him and sandals hooking into the material of his jeans. My skirt slides farther up, baring my legs, and his ravenous eyes drop to them. He drags his hands from my waist down to my thighs, his movements unbearably slow, and digs his fingers into my flesh, pulling me even closer. That sends a heady flutter pirouetting up my body.

It wracks me, *wrecks* me.

Rudra tilts his head up, captures my lips with his, and kisses me again.

While our previous kisses were dry and slow, this one's rough. Our mouths are open and we're making out with such aggression that it numbs my mind. He tastes like beer, and for a moment it feels like I'm getting drunk on it, drunk on *him*. Whatever preconceived notion I had about French kissing, I was wrong. Done like this, eased into, it feels intense, in a good way.

My hands are around his neck, fingers weaving into his silken hair I've been longing to touch. I'm wrapped around him like a koala bear, and my hold on him is the anchor that's grounding me, keeping me in this reality, which feels like it's fracturing like a kaleidoscope, pieces breaking away chip by chip.

There's a friction in my lower body because my legs are pried apart, pressed against his sides, and he has a solid grip on my thighs that he uses to direct my body to move on him. My breaths are harsh, ragged, and quick, and this is *wild*, because we're in public, visible for everyone to see. But then, it's Goa, and this probably is the least scandalous thing to happen here.

Rudra's breathing hastens, and he breaks our kiss to bury his face in the crook of my neck, eyes shut tightly. I'm here, on his lap, holding on to him for dear life, but I'm also three feet above, separate from my body. Staring down at us. At what's happening.

"Krishna," Rudra whispers into my neck, his hands settling against my lower back, fingers spreading and flat on my spine. "You don't know how long—"

"What the actual fuck?"

Rudra and I tear apart as if we've been burnt. I jump off his lap and scramble away from him, landing butt-first on the sofa. The sudden movement disorients me so much I have to prop my hand against the back of the couch to steady myself. My thoughts zip through my head at lightning speed, a dizzying mess.

Priti stands in front of the glass table, staring down at us, absolute, unbidden rage on her face.

Rudra straightens his hair, his outfit, and grabs a pillow from the couch and places it on his lap. It takes me a second to realize why, and when I do, my eyes widen. After that, I *can't* look at him. My lips are swollen with the kiss, and blood pulses through my body so loudly I'm sure everyone in Calangute can hear it.

Priti doesn't say anything for ten whole seconds, just stares and seethes. Then she spins on her heel and walks out of the bar.

28

I'M ASSUMING BOYS WHO HAVE A BONER CAN'T RUN WITH SAID BONER

Goa, Monday

"I'm going after her," I say, leaping to my feet and nearly falling back down because I'm so dazed. "You . . . you stay . . ."

Because of your situation.

I don't say it, but Rudra understands, his face flushing with color. A sequin has come off the corner of my eye and gotten stuck to his cheek, and the sight of it would be *precious* if things weren't going to shit right now.

Rudra doesn't notice, too preoccupied with his embarrassment, and instead stammers, "Y-yeah."

There are tremors erupting all over my body as I dash after Priti, who is speed-walking down the slope to the beach. I cut through the deck, taking the wooden slope to the fluffy sand below. My sandals filled up with sand on the way here, so I bend down and yank them off, letting them swing from my fingers as I dash barefoot the rest of the way to Priti.

"Priti!" I call. "Priti, wait!"

"No, Krishna," she snaps back at me, her long legs carrying her forward at a speed I can't match. Given the cardio workout she does every week, I know if she decides to take off into a sprint, I will not be able to catch up to her. But she does come to a stop at the edge of the rolling waves then, fists clenched by her sides. I reach her, panting.

"Priti," I say, gulping, because I dread explaining this turn of events to her, how I might've just had the hottest first kiss with Rudra Desai. The thought makes my stomach flip, and images from a few minutes ago come back to me with startling fervor.

No.

Now is *not* the time to be thinking about any of it. Especially not about how good a kisser Rudra is, or how soft his lips are, or how his hands were all over me, or how he—

Shut up, Krishna.

"What you saw . . . that was . . ." I start, shaking my head. "You weren't supposed to see that."

Fuck.

Wrong thing to say.

Priti turns to look down at me, her eyes a furious black. "Seriously?"

"No, I mean—"

"What *did* you mean, then? That you didn't expect me to come back to find you and Rudra all over each other?" She covers her face with her hands, looking so frustrated and pained it stings. "Ohmygod. You and Rudra. Fuck. This can't be happening. *Fuuuck.*"

I don't know why, but tears spring to my eyes at her words. I'm still rattled by all that's happened.

I'm so done. With everything. With this trip, with constantly having to strain to mend broken relationships, with living up to others' expectations of me all the time.

I need a break.

"Would it be so bad?" I whisper, a tear slipping down my cheek. I wipe at it hastily, folding my arms over my chest because I suddenly feel cold. "If Rudra and I got together? Do you think I'm not good enough for him?"

Priti snaps her head up, her hands dropping. "This is not about you, Krishna! Everything is not about you all the time!"

Her words hurt. She could've slapped me and it would've hurt less.

"This is about compromise!" Her voice is sharp, harsher than before. "I was honest with you about how I felt, and you promised me there was nothing going on between the two of you. You told me you liked Amrit!"

"Because you were finally giving me a chance! You were talking to me, and I didn't want to lose that. I know I said I didn't feel anything for Rudra, but I did like him." I swallow the lump in my throat, determined to not let any more tears slip out. "I *do* like him. A lot. And I think he likes me. Why is that so bad?"

"Because—" Priti exclaims, her voice getting high-pitched and squeaky. "Rudra is *not* that kind of guy."

Frustration morphs into anger so fast my head spins. I can't believe, after all we've been through, after our conversations during the trek and in the Airbnb, we're back to square one.

Because I couldn't keep a grip on my emotions. Because I ruined it. Because I hoped Priti would understand. Because, after everything, I hoped she would think I'm worthy of dating her best friend.

But I guess I never will be enough for her. Nothing I do will ever be enough.

"Are you saying I'm that kind of girl?" I choke out.

"He's not the kind of person to say one thing and mean another!" Priti says. "I trusted you enough to come out to you. And you lied to me! I was only ever honest with you, and you lied to me."

That's it.

"Like you haven't been lying to me this whole time?" I spit.

"What the hell are you talking about?"

"About applying to US colleges," I say, finally laying out what I've been keeping to myself these past couple of days. I've gone from preparing to use it as a trump card because I was indifferent to Priti after years of being let down to holding it close because of our reconciliation, hoping she'd one day trust me enough to tell me about it herself, to this . . . "About cutting me off from your life."

Priti's face turns white. "Rudra told you?" She looks so betrayed it sends a rush of glee through me. But the sensation is immediately smothered by guilt when I think about how Rudra might feel if he learns that I threw him under the bus. How Priti might feel to believe her best friend betrayed her.

I can't do that to either of them.

"He didn't tell me," I say, my teeth clenched, once again left feeling like I'm always the one trying to fix things, to set things right. "At least, not intentionally. But that doesn't matter. The truth is, you applied to American colleges, got into FIT, and didn't even bother to tell me." My eyes are growing cloudy again, pooling with tears. "You said you had been giving entrance exams. You said you might go to

NIFT. And this whole time, you were applying to the US instead!"

Why do I *cry* when I'm angry?

Priti groans in frustration. "I *did* give entrances. I *did* apply to NIFT. But I decided on the US just last year, when Rudra started working on his applications."

What a bucketload of bullshit.

"Don't you see how that's worse? You had a whole year to say something—anything. How do you lie so effortlessly, and then blame me for doing the same?" I say, amazed more than hurt at this point. "You know how much planning moving abroad takes. Were you ever going to tell me? Or were you just planning on avoiding me there?"

"I *was* going to tell you."

"When? After moving? Through a post that'll just pop up on my feed, with no call, no message from you? You're so fake, Priti! So two-faced!"

Priti's eyes are pools of lava. "You know what? I take it back. You *are* that kind of girl. The kind who uses people only when they serve some purpose, who doesn't hesitate a second before abandoning one shiny thing for another. You led Amrit on all summer, only to fling yourself at Rudra the moment he started being nice to you."

The blood drains from my face at her words, her *horrible* words, and I think I'm about to faint or collapse or break down because I'm so tired and devastated and overwhelmed.

The optimist in me used to believe what people say about how bonds once broken, while forever changed, are reparable. But with Priti's words, I've come to realize that our relationship has been severed too many times to be redeemed.

As long as we have secrets, even if we do keep patching things up, we'll end up hurting one another and undoing all that work eventually, only to come back less trusting. It's a vicious, never-ending cycle.

"You don't deserve him," Priti says, her final, skewering remark only cementing my realization. Priti and I—we're never meant to be best friends again.

"Fuck you," I say, a near whisper at first. Then louder, so loud I'm yelling, my voice carrying over the waves. "FUCK YOU!"

I turn on my heel, tears running hot and fast down my cheeks. Everything burns, everything hurts, and I just want to wake up from this horrid dream to realize none of this happened, that I didn't spend the wildest days of my summer . . . no, my *life*, with her and Rudra.

But I don't wake up. This is not a dream. This is real life, and what Priti said?

It's true.

All of it.

29

THERE'S ONLY ONE BED (OR SOFA BED, IN THIS CASE)

Goa, Monday

When we get back to our room after a long, harrowing, quiet drive, Priti shoves past us both, stomps straight to the bedroom, slams the door shut, and *locks* it. I let out a sound that's halfway between a gasp and a scoff. Then I march up to the door and rap the wood sharply. "Priti, open the door!"

No answer.

"Stop being so childish!"

Still no answer.

I bang my fists on the door, letting out a groan of frustration. "Priti, for god's sake, I need to *sleep*! Open the fucking door!"

When I'm met with radio silence, I press my ear to the wood. I hear shuffling inside, followed by the creak of the bed.

Priti's getting into bed. The goddamn audacity—

"ARGH!" I try the knob furiously, ramming my shoulder into the door.

She's locked me out for good.

I turn to Rudra, slumped on the couch, looking so exhausted I feel sorry for him. His spine curves with how much he slouches, just sinking into himself. He was weary even before Priti convinced—no, *coerced*—us to head out, and now that it's past three a.m., I have no idea how he managed to drive us back here after the terrible night we've had.

That's when it occurs to me that I am left with no choice but to sleep *next to him*. On the creaky, tiny sofa bed. What is wrong with Priti? First she wants me to avoid Rudra, and then she locks me out with him, leaving only one bed?

I don't think Rudra fully registers the gravity of the situation, because his voice is lacking any hesitation at all when he says, "You can sleep out here."

"I don't think I have a choice," I say, pushing my hair off my face. I'm so sapped, and so fed up with Priti. I just want to go home.

If anything, Rudra looks more worn out than I do.

"You should get sleep," I say softly. "You've been up the whole day."

Rudra turns to look at me, and his eyes are flitting closed. His movements are so slow it's like he's glitching. "Yeah."

I hesitate for a second, then walk over to him. "Rudra."

"Hmm?"

"You need to sleep."

"Hmm."

I stare at him, sleeping with his eyes half open, and inhale deeply. My anger just seems to dissipate entirely around him, because I feel nothing but concern as I reach forward and help him out of his leather jacket. He mumbles something about how the bed needs to be pulled out and I shush him.

I might as well get us settled in so I can sleep my anger and disappointment off. I would've rather done it after removing my makeup and brushing my teeth, but the bathroom is inside the bedroom, and, well, Priti's claimed the space now.

God, she's just so irritatingly immature sometimes!

Once Rudra's jacket is discarded to the side, I reach down and pull his feet out of his boots. I place one hand on his shoulder and one on his arm, slowly helping him up. He protests and collapses against my side, but I hold him up, guiding him to the corner.

I make him stand there, leaning against the wall for support, and walk back to the sofa to pull out the bed. It takes a bit of effort, and the metal frame squeaks and groans in protest, but the bed springs out. When I'm beside Rudra again, he's drifting in and out of slumber.

I gently guide him back to the bed and lay him down, adjusting his head on the pillow, his hair silken under my touch. There's a blanket on a shelf below the glass table, so I grab that and spread it out on top of him, tucking the edges under his body so he's snug inside.

He stirs, looking up at me through half-lidded eyes, and I look away, knowing if I look too long, I'll probably end up doing something I will regret later.

I start to pull away, ready to walk to the other side and sleep as close to the corner as possible. But Rudra grasps my wrist, and a tiny current shoots through my arm and along my body.

"Krishna," he whispers, stroking the inside of my wrist, eyes still half closed. "Could you . . . Would it be too much to ask you to lie down with me?"

I stare at him, confused, his lean form curled up under the blanket, exuding warmth. "I *am* going to lie down with—" My voice trails off when I realize he isn't suggesting what I was already about to do. He's suggesting I lie down *close* to him.

"It's okay if you don't want to," he says, his words tripping over one another. "You don't have to."

"Maybe for a bit," I find myself saying, even though I shouldn't, I shouldn't, I shouldn't . . .

I pull up the edge of the blanket and gingerly get in bed next to him. The springs creak under my weight and I drag some of the blanket up over myself. I turn my back to him, facing the glass windows staring out at the indigo night sky and sea. He's so warm I automatically snuggle closer.

My back presses against his front, a kaleidoscope of butterflies thrashing around within my stomach. He lets out a gravelly sound, right into my ear, and my body trembles with how cozy and mellow he feels.

His arms hesitate behind me, and I grab them, hooking them around me, inching closer to him. My stomach is practically assaulted by sensation. A moan involuntarily rips from my throat, and Rudra reacts by brushing his lips against the nape of my neck, his breath sweeping over my skin.

I have never ever felt this way in my life. So out of control with my own body, incapable of establishing a connection between my brain and my limbs. Some *other*, fervent attraction, drawing me to him, is at force.

"I keep thinking about our kiss," Rudra whispers, trailing kisses along the back of my neck to the spot behind my ear.

"You need to sleep," I whisper back, eyes shutting with pleasure.

"I can't. Not with you so close to me." His hand trails down my stomach, and I feel self-conscious, worried about my tummy and whether he hates it. But the thought doesn't even seem to occur to him. He just wants to hold me. His fingers spread and rest right on top of it, the spot where the butterflies are going gaga.

My neck arches, giving him more space, and he kisses the curve of it. I readjust myself under him just slightly so his lips are now against my jaw, his kisses like the gentlest whispers of the wind. I shouldn't be doing this, shouldn't be letting myself do this. But I can't think beyond how well our bodies fit together under the blanket, legs tangling. I could spend *weeks* like this.

"How are you not already asleep?" I ask him as his lips pause under the curve of my cheekbone, both of us trying to catch a breath.

"Honestly, I don't know," he says throatily. "Perhaps this wasn't the best of ideas." But there's not an ounce of regret in his voice.

I adjust myself again, this time rolling over entirely so we're lying facing each other. My arms slide around his waist to his back, and the muscles there flex under my touch. His lips brush my forehead and mine skim his neck. I tilt my head up to find him looking at me, eyes dark in the dim gold lights of the room.

"Rudra."

"Krishna."

"I should move away."

"Why?"

"Because Priti will flip if she finds us sleeping together. She's already pissed with us."

His wandering hands come to a stop at the base of my spine. "That *will* be a problem."

"Which is why—" I start.

"One of us should probably move," he says.

Next thing I know, we're kissing again.

I didn't know every kiss with him could feel so different from the last. This one is not soft, but not rough either. It's somewhere in between, and so unhurried it drags on for what feels like hours. His lips achingly tug on mine, and my head swims with disequilibrium. I kiss him back, drawing closer to him, if that's even possible.

His fingers trail my spine, hitching on the bare skin revealed by the halter-neck top. As we kiss, they lazily stroke my back, up and down my vertebrae, and then they're in my hair again, tugging at my scalp.

"Rudra," I gasp in between lagging, sultry kisses. "You need to sleep."

He nibbles at my ear. "I've never been more awake."

I lose myself in him, wrapped around him, his mouth ravaging mine like he can't get enough of me. And for a second, as his leg thrusts up between my thighs, I think I might be able to get away with it. Because Priti is asleep, and there's no way she's going to come out here and see us right now, is there?

But all the terrible thoughts, all the things Priti said, which momentarily left me, replaced and quashed by desire, come back. All at once. They rain down on me like a hundred tiny stones.

I'm doing *exactly* what she said I would. I'm treating this as a one-off thing, unsure whether I might ever be with Rudra after this. I do want more than that. So much more.

But if I keep going, whatever little chance there is of Priti forgiving me, that will be gone too. And despite everything she said to me tonight, I still want a relationship with her. I want her to accept us and this. I don't want to be the cause of a rift between them.

I rip away from him, gasping for breath.

Rudra's lips are parted, swollen from all the kissing, and he stares at me, eyes widening in question. Tears overcome me again, prickling my eyes, and I get off the bed, away from him, away from the irresistible heat of his body.

"Krishna?" he says, sitting up, his hair tousled in a manner that makes me want to leap back into his arms and resume what we were doing . . . put his thigh back in between my legs and move against it until I lose myself in bliss.

But I'll only be hurting myself in the process, because now I know what it's like to have Rudra. I would've rather never known any of this, because I now must live with the pain of *knowing* and the possibility of never being with him again.

"We can't," I say, brushing away the tears with the backs of my hands.

"We don't have to," Rudra says, shaking his head. "We don't have to do anything. I'm sorry if I made you feel like you had to, or that I wanted—"

My heart lodges in my throat, making it difficult for me to breathe. "You didn't want to?"

"*No,* I didn't mean it that way. I do want to. I've wanted to for so long—but we don't *have* to do anything."

"I know," I croak. "I'm sorry."

Rudra takes my hand, stroking it. "Don't apologize."

"I'm going to move away, okay?"

"Okay."

This time, I don't let the attractively boyish, utterly kissable sight of him faze me. I crawl into bed, sticking to the corner, even though it feels like there's a hook embedded in my skin attached to him that snags as I move away, sending pain shooting through me.

There are kajal-stained tears and snot running down my face, but I clamp my hands over my mouth, swallow my silent tears, and will myself to sleep.

30

BETTER TO CRASH A WEDDING LATE THAN NEVER

Goa, Monday

Thud.

When my eyes open the next morning, the sun is blindingly bright, streaming in through the glass. I turn onto my side, away from the dratted sun, rubbing my hand over my eyes and face. My fingers come away smeared with kajal, and my mouth is drier than a desert.

Oh god, my head hurts.

I sit up, groaning as I massage my temples. Priti's skirt and bralette are pasted to my skin, forming red marks, and I need to brush my teeth and wash up so bad. What was that noise that woke me up? What time is it?

I get off the bed with effort and grab my phone from the table, glancing at Rudra. He's asleep, in his fitted black tee and baggy jeans, lying on his stomach with his face pressed into the pillow. Oh, and he's drooling.

I can't help but smile. How cute is that?

Memories of last night trickle in. Of curling up beside him, latched on to his form, kissing him . . .

But my eyes find my phone screen right then, and I let out a gasp.

Rudra stirs, eyes cracking open. "Krishna?" he mumbles.

I'm leaping to my feet. I frantically rush to the bedroom door, which is still shut, and bang my fists on the wood, hard. "Open the door, Priti! It's four o'clock, ohmygod!"

We were asleep for *twelve fucking hours.*

When there's no response, I press my mouth to the door, hoping my voice will carry through better and louder. "Priti, open up, *please*! We're late!"

Rudra's up fully now, pushing his hair away from his face. He gets off the bed—it grates and creaks loudly, and I don't even want to think of how loud the bed might've been last night when we were making out—and joins me by the door.

"Let me try," he says, gently motioning me back so he can take my place. "Priti! It's four p.m. and we're late! Open up!"

When there's no response even after Rudra's attempt, my heart speeds up inside my chest. Something's gone horribly wrong. What if Priti drowned in the bathtub, what if she choked on her toothbrush, what if she knocked her head into the nightstand and fainted, what if—

Rudra turns the handle, as if on instinct, and the door swings open.

Wait.

What?

He pushes through the door into the room, and I hurry after him, my heart beating so loud I can hear it pumping in my ears.

The room's empty.

The bedsheets are rumpled, the pillows are out of place, and there's no sign of Priti.

"Krishna, check the washroom," Rudra says, walking over to the bed. I rush to the bathroom and find the door open. Steam coats the mirrors, the floor is wet, and Priti's hair dryer is lying on the basin by the power port, plugged in, as if . . . as if she took a bath.

When I walk back out, shaking my head, I find Rudra holding an empty plastic saree bag. It's the same one that previously held Priti's black lehenga. Understanding rams into the both of us at the same time.

"She left for the wedding," I say, the blood draining from my body, making me feel faint. "She left without us."

The thud that woke me—that was the main door shutting behind Priti.

"She took the car," Rudra says, cursing under his breath. "I didn't see the keys on the table." He slaps his forehead. "Jesus fucking Christ, Priti, why do you always do this?"

Everything is going horribly wrong. Even after Priti and I fought, I never once considered how it might affect Rudra's and my plan. I thought I would have a chance to help her reunite with Mansi regardless.

But now she's gone. She's gone on her own, and oh god, what if she chickens out? Or worse, what if it all goes horribly wrong and Mansi doesn't feel the same?

What if she needs us and we're not there?

My head is consumed in a white-hot panic, the sort I haven't felt in a long while. This is like the panic I felt the day before my SATs, when I had this horrible pain in my gut and I desperately wanted to fall sick so I wouldn't have to attend my exams the next day.

I thought I'd left that sort of feeling behind forever when things worked out exactly how I'd planned.

But I was wrong.

My chest is moving up and down rapidly and my head is spinning. I'm seconds from bursting into tears again.

Rudra closes the space between us with one stride and clasps my cheeks, a worried look creasing his face. "Krishna—"

"The plan," I gasp.

"It's okay." He strokes my hair, my cheeks, my shoulders. "It's not the end of the world."

"It is! It is to *me*, Rudra. We need to get to the wedding *now*."

Rudra scans my face helplessly before realization dawns on him and something fissures behind his eyes. "You still want to go ahead with your original plan." He says it not like a question but a statement. Hurt laces his voice.

"Of course!" I cry out. "Why wouldn't I?"

Rudra steps away from me, his hands dropping to his sides, looking crushed beyond measure. My body instantly misses his warmth.

"Okay, then," he says, and his voice is completely devoid of emotion. His face hardens.

I stare at him, bewildered. My head is aching from anxiety. Why the hell is he reacting like this? Does he not want to do this for Priti anymore?

"Get ready," he says, his shoulders stiff. "We'll leave in fifteen minutes." He walks out of the room, shutting the door behind him. Hard.

I want to go after him, ask him what's going on, what's changed since last night, but I need to be there for Priti. Helping her is my priority right now. I don't think I could bear to see her come out the other side of all this even more heartbroken and tormented.

We take thirty minutes more than I thought we would. Which means we're forty-five minutes late.

I brush my teeth, wash my face, rinse my arms, underarms, and legs, and let Rudra freshen up and get dressed in the bathroom while I get ready outside.

He's being cold with me, and it stings because I don't understand *why*.

Horrible thoughts peal through my mind as I chew over why he might be acting this way. Does he regret our kiss? Does he not see a possibility of *us* anymore? Or was it not truly serious for him? Has he ascertained I'm getting attached to him and is finding ways to break away? Because why would someone like him fall for me in such a short span of time?

Trembling through the motions and shoving those god-awful thoughts into a mental box, I get into my choli. It's half-sleeved with a sweetheart neckline and shows a hint of my stomach, while the lehenga falls to my ankles, swirling and rising perfectly when I spin around, just the way I like it. I know this because I've worn it once before, at a shaadi, not because I'm twirling right now. I'm neither in the mood nor have the time to twirl.

The chunni goes around my neck, two pallus draping down my back. The whole set is the loveliest shade of beige, patterned with tiny swirls and flowers all over in muted gold. It's one of my favorites, though I'm always terrified of spilling daal on it. Luckily, it's easy to hook, even at the back, so it takes me less than two minutes to get into it.

I can still hear water splashing inside the bathroom when I reach for my makeup bag. I don't do a full makeup look because that would take way too long. Instead, I just put on tinted sunscreen. I top it off with eyeliner, kajal, lipstick, and a crystal bindi.

I'm clasping on my jewelry—necklace, earrings, and a maang tikka set—when Rudra steps out. This is the fastest I've ever gotten ready in my life. It's a miracle I haven't screwed up my makeup. The crystals of my jewelry throw flecks of light around the room as Rudra walks out of the bathroom, steam curling around him like he's in a movie. My mouth nearly drops to the floor.

Because he's wearing a freakin' *black kurta*. And . . . his sleeves are rolled up to his elbows.

Fuck me.

No. Fuck #desitiktok, actually. *Thanks for the corruption, y'all.*

Half of his hair is in a man bun again, wisping softly in the mist. Our eyes meet across the room. Then his trail my body, from top to bottom, and I can almost feel invisible hands caressing my form.

When he looks back up at me, I find myself wishing he would just stride up to me, slam me into the dressing mirror, and—

He breaks eye contact. Clears his throat.

"You ready?" he asks, adjusting his sleeves.

"Y-yeah, just a sec." I pick up my gold highlighter and dab the inner corners of my eyes, needing something to do. "Okay, done."

He doesn't say anything, just walks right out. I stare after him, dismayed. But there's no point. If he wants nothing to do with me, then all right. Priti's more important right now, anyway. Squaring my jaw, I gather my skirts and follow him.

"How are we planning to get to the wedding now that the car's gone?" I slip on my high-heeled sandals as he takes the room key from the holder. "Uber? Ola?"

"There are no Ubers or Olas in Goa," Rudra says.

I stop short. "What? How are we going to go, then?"

Rudra opens the door and steps out, holding it for me. I hurry out. He closes the door, and it automatically locks. "There was a motorbike parked outside. I saw it last night," he says, not looking at me as he calls the elevator. "I think it belongs to one of Ms. Fernandes's helpers. We could borrow it."

"You know how to ride a bike?" I ask, eyes wide. We step into the elevator.

"Yes." Rudra presses the button for the ground floor, and the doors shut, leaving us in this closed space. During the ride down, we're both quiet and standoffish, refusing to meet each other's eyes. Internally, I'm fuming.

Downstairs, we find the sardar ji instead of Ms. Fernandes this time, and he confirms that the bike does indeed belong to one of the helpers. Luckily, the helper himself is easy to convince, and within minutes, we're both rushing out into the parking lot, armed with the keys. The bike is parked next to where Rudra's car was. It's sleek and black, with *Hero* scrawled across the engine.

Rudra props open the compartment beneath the seat and takes out two helmets. He hands me one and puts on the other, strapping it under his chin. This is totally going to ruin my hair, and possibly my makeup, but I have no choice. Safety comes first. I scurry to the side as he mounts the bike and kicks up the stand. He twists the key in the ignition, and the bike roars to life.

"Get on," he says, resting his foot on the kick-starter. He doesn't even turn to look at me when he says it. I mentally jam a toilet plunger down my throat to unclog the hurt wedged in there, eyeing the kernel of space left on the bike behind Rudra. There's no way both my lehenga and I are going to fit there. Not unless I sit sideways, the way I've seen Indian women in sarees sit behind their husbands.

And the seat—it's so high. How on earth am I going to get on?

"Is it okay if I—" I can't even get the full sentence out because I'm practically talking to the back of his helmet at this point.

"If you what?" Rudra asks.

"If I hold on to you? While I'm climbing?"

"Sure."

His response is so aloof it sends a shudder through me. I ignore it and place my hand on his shoulder. Under the kurta, his muscle contracts, as if he can't bear the thought of me touching him right now. I grab the rear handle and hoist myself up. But the satiny material of the lehenga slips, and I drop back down to the ground, a sharp pain shooting through my ankles.

I try again. Fail again.

The late-afternoon sun is beating down on me and I'm sweating in my heavy lehenga and under the helmet. I'm embarrassed and angry and anxious and I want to cry.

"Wait," Rudra says, sighing when I attempt to pull myself up a third time.

"What?"

"Step away."

I obey as Rudra kicks the stand back down and gets off the bike, pushing the visor of his helmet up. My mouth goes dry when he steps closer to me, his eyes shadowed and challenging under the helmet. I let out a squeak as his hands sharply clamp onto my waist. And right then, I forget the name of every single one of the eight bones in my wrist even though I've prided myself in knowing them forever.

My spine presses into the seat, and he's touching bare skin, fingers digging into my waist. I stare up at him as his body brushes against mine, and my head is fuzzy, starting to spin. I love how he isn't too tall, just taller than me, because it feels like we fit together even better. He doesn't feel far, far away. If it weren't for the helmets, or his reticence, I would probably kiss him right now.

Frankly, though, it's the damned helmet on him making things hot.

He scoops me up so easily it's almost as if I weigh nothing. My butt plonks on the seat, and I grip his shoulder with one hand and the rear handle with the other, steadying myself.

Of course that's what *that* was about: helping me onto my seat.

Rudra steps away, his fingers scraping slow, agonizing lines along my waist before falling to the side. Right about now, my stomach resembles one of those firecrackers we used to burst during Diwali.

Rudra's hands are shaking as he pushes the visor back down and mounts the bike again.

The ride is torturous.

I'm navigating, so I have to wrap an arm around Rudra's stomach to prevent myself from flying off and have my lehenga turn into a parachute. It doesn't help that time is trickling away faster than water from a sieve, and the sun is dipping lower and lower in the sky.

When we get to Baga Beach Resort, it's evident there's a wedding going on. The place is in a state of pure chaos.

Rudra rides through the main gate. The security guards let us in immediately because of our grand Indian attire—the easiest hack to crashing a wedding. There's a short drive leading up to the entrance of the resort, the road forking to curve around a gorgeous blue fountain that sparkles in the sunset light. The road is lined with palm trees, and the garden is covered in patches of colorful flowers. The streetlights speckling the sides of the road start buzzing to life, indicating that dusk is setting in.

As we're looking for a space to park, I spot the familiar blue of Rudra's BMW. My heart lurches in my chest.

"Hey, that's your car!"

"Where?"

"We just passed it." I shake my head. "Priti's already here."

I can't even imagine how she must be doing right now. Did she get a chance to speak with Mansi? Or did she bow out and is sitting somewhere alone, helpless, and shattered?

We find a space after a few minutes of scouring. Getting off the bike is a lot easier than getting on, and I don't need Rudra's help this time, but my mind's not on him anyway. My stomach sinks, and a heavy weight settles in the bottom of my gut, making it difficult for me to stand upright. The heels are not helping.

The BMW is parked on the opposite side of the lot, beyond the fountain, and my eyes go to it as I wait for Rudra to put our helmets in the trunk. The glass isn't tinted, and I can vaguely make out the familiar interior.

"Let's go," Rudra says, shutting the helmet compartment closed.

"Rudra," I say, grabbing his wrist just as he's about to start walking away. He glances down at my hand, wrapped around his, then at me, and I notice how delightfully mussed his hair looks. His thick eyebrows are raised in question, and he makes no move to take my hand. He's limp in my hold.

Something in my mind snags on his car.

I drag my gaze away from him and back to the car. And there it is. A flash of movement. A shadow of a person.

I start speed-walking toward the car, dragging Rudra after me.

"Krishna, where are you—"

"Just follow me."

We cross the patch of grass around the fountain and cut across the road on the other side. I bring a finger to my lips, gesturing for him to be quiet, and duck behind the car next to the BMW, a black SUV. Rudra follows suit.

This close, I can hear "Supermassive Black Hole" by Muse playing on Rudra's speakers. I turn to Rudra, and his eyes are wide.

"I'll count to three, and we'll go over to the front, okay?" I whisper.

Rudra nods.

"One." I'm still holding his hand. I drop it like a bag of hot coals. "Two." Rudra flushes, and I have to turn away. "Three."

We dart out from behind the SUV, approaching the BMW from either side. I'm at the front in a flash. I grab the handle of the driver door, find it unlocked, and yank the door open. Rudra has the front passenger door open in seconds.

"Gotcha!" I exclaim, eyeing our culprit.

Priti.

31

IF YOU'RE A HEARTBROKEN GOTH LESBIAN, MUSE IS TAILOR-MADE FOR YOU

Goa, Monday

Priti lets out a shriek so loud Rudra and I have to clamp our hands over our ears.

"*Jeez,* Priti!" I cry.

"Guys, what the actual fuck?" Priti places a hand over her heart and turns off the music she's been blasting. She's wearing her all-black lehenga choli, the same *FUCK YOU* fit she wore to one of our relatives' weddings.

The choli is a tube-style, fitted bodice blouse; the skirt flares out, glittering with hundreds of black sequins; and a shimmery gossamer chunni is thrown over her left shoulder. The choli is about the length of a bra and the lehenga is low waisted, so it shows off almost her whole torso.

"You're so pathetic," I say, and if our horrible fight had happened before this trip, I might not have been able to even look at her. But right now, my relief outweighs my anger. Because we made it, and although the likelihood of convincing Priti to take the plunge in the nick of time seems implausible, I'm willing to try. Because even though we've hurt each other beyond repair, I want to see her happy again. Last night I got a glimpse of a version of her that I haven't seen in eight years, and I want that Priti back.

"Gee, thank you, Krishna," Priti says, shooting daggers at me with her gaze. She flips to Rudra. "Why the hell are you both even here?"

I place my hands on my hips. "Considering *I'm* the reason we're on this road trip, in Goa, in the first place, the answer should be pretty obvious, shouldn't it?" I'm looking at Priti, but from the corner of my eye, I can't help but notice Rudra's features twist with hurt. A flicker and then gone.

Priti's eyes flash with anger. "So you're still going after Acharya, are you?"

I can't believe she's turning this on me! *Again!*

"That's not—" I groan in frustration. "Stop diverting the conversation, Priti."

"I'm not diverting anything. Last I checked, you and Rudra were screwing."

"We weren't screwing!" Rudra and I protest in unison. Our eyes meet, and both of us flush.

Priti sees it, the red all over our faces, and barks with laughter. "And you were calling *me* pathetic."

"Cut the crap, Priti," Rudra finally says. Thank god—I was getting jittery waiting for him to say something. "I'm sick of your tantrums, and I'm sick of your lying." Rudra glances at me, and we both realize, at the same time, that it's now or never.

We need to tell Priti that we know about Mansi, tell her what we've been planning. It's not sunset just yet. We don't have long, but it's enough to turn things around for Priti. It's enough to sabotage this wedding.

I let out a heavy breath. Then I take her hand. She startles, like an antelope caught in headlights. It would be funny if the situation weren't so serious.

"Tell her, Rudra," I say.

"We know you're here because of your girlfriend," he says. "Mansi Joshi. The one you dated in Powai and broke up with a while ago. We were supposed to help you stop her wedding, but you hightailed it here without us—in my car, mind you—so we came here on a borrowed bike to find you. We discussed the possibility of you chickening out, which is why we're here to tell you to get your shit together."

"Guys—"

"No, we're not going to listen to any more of your crappy excuses," I interrupt. "There's still time, and we can find a way for you to catch Mansi before she ends up making the biggest mistake of her life by marrying this Soumyaroop dude. But we don't really have a plan either, so we're just going to have to wing it. We initially wanted you to have a talk with Mansi before the wedding, at noon, but, well . . . all of us overslept."

"Krishna, what are you—"

"I was thinking we could empty the buffet table so you could get on it and profess your love for Mansi just before—"

"Krishna," Priti says, clamping her right palm over my mouth, cutting off the rest of my words. There's shock written all over her face. "Rudra. You idiots. Stop for a minute."

I mumble into her hand in protest. Priti holds up her other hand, shaking her head, and we give in. She shuts her eyes, furrows her brow, and clucks her tongue.

"Okay," she says after a minute. Her eyes open, and she drops her left hand, sucking in a long breath. "First, I don't know how the two of you figured out I was here to meet my ex-girlfriend, but good detective work, I guess. Maybe I wasn't nearly as slick as I thought I was."

Rudra and I roll our eyes in unison.

"Nuh-uh," I mutter through her hand.

"Shh. I'm not done." Priti scoffs. "I didn't come all the way here to *ruin* this stupid wedding. I don't even care about it. The only reason I'm here in the first place is because Krishna happened to propose her wild-as-fuck plan to me and I knew my ex-girlfriend would be here, *and* I was free, so it just sort of . . . fit?"

"Nah-nah-nuh?" I ask. *Can I talk?*

Priti sighs, letting her hand fall.

I gulp, eyes wide. "But why wouldn't you care about the wedding when your ex is the one getting married?"

"Because, dufus," Priti says, slapping my head lightly, "Mansi Joshi isn't my ex-girlfriend. Nikita Joshi, her younger sister, is."

32

OHHHHHHH

Goa, Monday

There are a few seconds of silence before Rudra and I collectively go, "*Ohhhhhhh.*"

Just when I thought we couldn't be closer to the truth, we find out that this whole time, it wasn't the bride at all.

It was the bride's *sister.*

Priti hesitates for a moment before speaking. "I met Nikita in Powai when I was doing my internship. She was staying with Amrit's family during that period because she's, well, his cousin. We broke up because I'd *just* started applying to FIT with you, Ruds, and there was no way we would've been able to sustain a long-distance relationship. Not when her life is here, in India." She smiles sadly at me, shrugging. "And as you already know, I'm not exactly an expert when it comes to long-distance relationships."

I shake my head, bewildered. "But, Priti, you *loved* her. You still do. You came all the way to Goa just so you could see her again. It was different with us. We were kids. Young. I moved when I wasn't fully *me* yet. Things are always changing when we're growing up. They don't stick. And they're rarely constant. But you and Nikita are adults. Why would you break up over the fear of a long-distance relationship?"

"Because you leaving affected me more than you know, Krish," Priti says, and her eyes glitter with tears. "If there's one thing I'm terrified of, it's change. I'm not good at adjusting. Applying to American colleges was the most daunting decision I've ever made in my life. I couldn't imagine going so far away from home at eighteen. I still don't think I can."

"I get why you didn't tell me about Nikita when you were *in* a relationship with her. You didn't want to set things in stone before you were sure about her. At least you told me you were dating someone." Rudra's voice quavers. "But why wouldn't you let me be there for you when you were dealing with a heartbreak? We're best friends."

Priti's face saddens. "Trust me, Ruds, I wanted to. I felt so alone that whole time, because I was going through a horrible heartbreak, but if I'd told you *why* Nikita and I broke up, you would've said I could manage long-distance—and I *should*, for her—and that would've had me second-guessing everything.

"I didn't want anything or anyone to affect my decision about going to FIT. I needed to see the applications through. It wasn't about you at all. It was about me. I needed to keep some things to myself. I'm sorry if I hurt you in the process."

Rudra's shoulders seem to loosen, as if a tense cord holding them taut snaps. "Don't apologize. I get it."

"I'll tell you this, though," I say, and squeeze Priti's hand. "Just because *one* long-distance relationship didn't work out for you doesn't automatically mean *all* long-distance relationships are doomed."

"But what if we get back together and it doesn't end up working out?" Priti says, staring down at our linked hands, her voice cracking. "It'll break my heart, and I can't go through that again, Krish. I *can't*."

"But would you rather spend the rest of your life regretting not having at least given it a try?" I say, tipping her chin up with my other hand and fiercely meeting her gaze. "You're in love with her. You haven't moved on, and it's been almost a year. If you don't take this chance right now, you could end up regretting it forever. There's a reason you came on this trip with me. Because a part of you knows—"

"That I want to try," Priti whispers, ducking her head, and a tear slips down her cheek. I'm not used to the sight of her crying, but I know she needs to let it out. This road trip has been way too overwhelming for all of us. It's sapped our energy and brought out the absolute worst in us.

"Exactly."

"I want to," she says, her voice small. "But I'm so scared she won't want me anymore."

"Trust me, we know."

Priti looks up at me, then Rudra, her eyes shining. She's so earnest; my heart goes out to her. "Do you really think I should go find Nikita and talk to her right now?"

"Yes!" I say.

"One hundred percent," Rudra says firmly.

Priti swipes at the tear, a small laugh breaking out of her. "I can't believe you guys were actually going to wreck this wedding for me."

"Trust me, we were legit this close to seeing it through." I raise my hand and bring my pointer finger and thumb really close together, not letting them touch. "I don't know about Rudra, but I was *scared*."

Priti crows with laughter again, and it's full of life, swelling with happiness. "You mean you would've actually emptied that buffet table and let me climb on top to profess my love?"

"We would've carried you on our shoulders and paraded you around so you could tell everyone how much you love the bride and how this wedding needs to end," Rudra says, grinning.

"Like in the movies," I say. "ये शादी नहीं हो सकती!"[1]

"And you would've braved the fury of five hundred guests?" Priti says. "Aunties and uncles? The security at the hotel?"

"Yes, yes, and yes." Rudra gets into the passenger seat and wraps an arm around Priti. I watch, heart pinching in my chest as she sinks into his hold and he pecks her on the forehead. And that hankering, that utter, gutting longing for what they have, the sort of friendship and care Priti and I had once, nearly knocks the breath out of me. I step away, feeling like I'm privy to something I shouldn't be . . .

When Priti tightens her grip on my hand and pulls me into a side hug. The three of us huddle close, giggling, arms wrapped around each other. I can't put into words how at *home* I feel with them. I've never ever felt more like I've belonged.

"I thought you weren't a hugger," I tease, one arm around Priti and the other around Rudra. It's a mess of limbs, what with the steering wheel and the seat restricting our movements.

"I'm not, but you guys are the biggest, most idiotic pair of dorks, and I love you both to death." Priti pulls us in even tighter, and we stay like that for a long while, just soaking up the comfort. "And I'm sorry," Priti says suddenly, focusing on me. "I'm sorry for being an absolute bitch to you, Krish. I know we've made up and fought too many times now for you to believe my apologies mean anything, but I am. I truly am sorry."

---

1 *Language*: Hindi; *Translation*: This wedding cannot happen!

"I'm sorry too," I say, and my eyes are burning with tears again. "For not trying to mend whatever went wrong between us from the start."

When Priti looks up, she's crying. "You more than made up for it."

My next words are a blubber, and oh boy, I'm crying too. "Will you come see me in Baltimore? Can we not make this our last interaction?"

"Yes. *Yes.*" Priti hugs me tight. "We're going to make up for all the years we lost."

I hug her back even tighter. "Yes, we will."

In this moment, it's like the tension that has been building up in me for years and years suddenly dissolves, moving down my skin like rivulets of water and seeping into the ground. It makes me feel so calm, so *free* inside that I nearly crumple over.

When we break apart, crying and giggling, Priti dabs at her eyes even though our makeup is already running down our faces.

"Okay, I hate to ruin the moment, but now we should *really* go in," Rudra says, even though he's grinning ear to ear.

Once both Priti and I have adjusted our lehengas and salvaged our makeup, the three of us head toward the entrance. For a moment I feel like we're part of a Bollywood movie montage, Priti in the middle and Rudra and I on either side of her. It's just the universe's way of proclaiming to me that I was never meant to be the main character.

And I'm okay with that.

It's glittering chaos inside. There are hundreds of people loitering about the gorgeous reception, intermittently pausing by a banner that reads *Mansi Weds Soumyaroop* in cursive letters. Everyone is dressed in traditional Indian finery—women in exuberant sarees, stylish lehenga cholis, and sweeping anarkalis, and men in sharp sherwanis, kurta pajamas, and lungis.

We fit right in; nobody throws us a second glance. Priti eyes our surroundings nervously, doubt crawling over her face again, and I take her hand, squeezing. She looks down at me gratefully, and a small smile appears on her face. Her mouth sets with determination.

Loud wedding music thrums through the floor and the soles of my feet. Most of the guests seem to be heading down a corridor decked in bright, flower-packed lights. The floor is lined with a red carpet, and the three of us push through the throng hand in hand, the air in the tunnel thick with perfume and suffocating warmth. Lights hang from every corner of the space possible.

We step out into a gallery by the beach. The carpet slashes to the sand, down between rows and rows of velvet-covered chairs facing the sparkling sea. The sun is slowly sinking into the horizon, filling the sky with startling colors of gold and pink, sporadically daubed with midnight blue.

A grand mandap has been constructed on the beach, a few meters short of the waves licking the sand, inching ever closer as the furious night tides start to take over. It's so beautiful I have to force my mouth shut to not gape at it.

It's a pavilion with four pillars standing atop a platform that's three steps high. Billowing sheaves of cloth twine around and up the pillars, wreathed with leaves, flowers, and more lights like the ones in the corridor, and a swinging chandelier throws flickering light on the darkening sand around it.

Mummy once told me the four pillars of the mandap symbolize many elements from Hindu myth: the four Vedas, the four stages of life, the four directions, and most of all, balance, with the pillars signifying the stability required to hold a relationship together.

At the center of the altar is the stone pedestal for the sacral fire, and right behind it, at the edge of the mandap overlooking the sea, are two chairs set side by side, for the soon-to-be married couple. The bride and groom themselves are having a photo shoot on the beach, interrupted by the occasional guest offering their congratulations. I can't help but stifle a hysteric giggle at the thought of how Rudra and I might've ruined the wedding of two innocent, very-much-in-love people if we hadn't spoken to Priti first.

The three of us pause at the edge of the wedding scene, staring at the beautiful sight, the guests laughing and chattering, the happiness and excitement of the moment coasting in waves along the beach.

Indian weddings are so beautiful. They remain unmatched.

"So—" Priti says, and gulps hard. "I'm doing this."

"Yes, you are," Rudra says, smiling tenderly down at her.

I let go of Priti's hand. "Shoo, now. Go find Nikita."

Priti's eyes sparkle, and she starts walking backward, blowing us kisses, before she turns and briskly heads in the direction of the guests. Rudra and I watch her go, and I just feel so emotional I think I'm about to sob.

But most of all, I feel happy for Priti. For my cousin, my sister.

My best friend.

When Priti disappears into the crowd, I turn to Rudra. He stares after Priti for a bit. Then, sensing my gaze on him, he meets my eyes. The part of his hair not gathered in a man bun swells in the sea breeze, brushing the edges of his sharp face. The sun has fully sunk into the sea now, and it's dark, but the whole place is aglow with a thousand lights. It reminds me of the sight of him standing a step below me, under all those fireflies.

The music is soft and sweet, flutes playing in the background, signaling that the bride and groom are soon going to step onto the altar. I can see the reflection of all the mandap's lights in Rudra's dark eyes.

My throat tightens. There are so many things I want to say. It's all brimming to the surface now that I've had a chance to help Priti find happiness again. I need to tell him how I—

"Krishna?"

My heart lurches so hard in my chest I nearly gasp in shock while Rudra's eyes darken. I turn to the source of the voice, the oh-so-familiar voice I swooned over all summer.

Standing a few feet from me is Amrit Acharya.

33

THE UNIVERSE SURE DOES LOVE TO SEND ME SIGNS

Goa, Monday

"Krishna?" Amrit says again, staring at me as if I've just been ejected from a swirling portal in front of him. I might as well have been, because this situation is making me delirious. My head feels all funny.

"Hey, Amrit," I say, waving awkwardly. Two days ago, I was flirting with him, sending him texts, telling him I liked him. Three days ago, I was embarking on a fucking road trip to *kiss* the guy. And now, *everything* has changed.

I think I'm going to throw up.

"I can't believe my eyes," Amrit gushes. "Like, you're here. You're actually here!" He's wearing a sea-green kurta and a matching pair of mochi shoes, contrasting well with his stark white pajamas. He's clean shaven, as always, and his wavy hair is pushed away from his face, making his features stand out. He looks good. He always has, always does.

And yet, I feel nothing for him.

Zero, zilch, nada.

Because the guy I feel *everything* for is standing right beside me.

Or he *was* standing right beside me. Because when I turn to look for Rudra, all I see is him walking away from me. And I have no idea what to make of it.

My words nearly bubble out. Why is he leaving? Why has he been acting so distant all day?

"What are you doing here?" Amrit says, and when I turn to him, gulping heavily, his eyes are practically alight with happiness.

Amrit thinks I'm here for him. I was, but not anymore. And as much as I want to run after Rudra, I know I need to clear things up with Amrit first.

I can sense a thin layer of his uncertainty floating on top of his skin, like malai on milk, the longer I don't respond. I hate to do this to the first boy who ever felt anything at all for me, but I need to curdle the milk.

"I know, it's kind of wild, honestly," I say.

"But your flight? You didn't go back to the US?" All these questions, hope replacing uncertainty bit by bit.

"No, no, I didn't. There's—" I say, and laugh suddenly, the perception of everything that's changed completely in a matter of *days* hitting me like a wall of bricks. "There's so much that's happened. I don't even know where to begin."

He smiles. "Why do I get the feeling it's a hell of a story?"

"You're not wrong. Are you okay to talk? Like, right now?" I wave my hand, motioning to the festivities unfolding around us.

"Yeah, of course," Amrit says. "Do you want to sit?"

"Please."

Once we're seated on two of the white chairs at the very back, facing the mandap, I tell him everything.

It doesn't take too long, because I leave out the unimportant details—about Priti, especially—and, well, it's a few days' worth of adventures (although it feels like a lot more). I see a motley of emotions pass across his face.

When I'm finished, I feel like I've emerged from a vacuum, because the sounds and sights around me are suddenly thrice as dazzling. The number of people has also tripled, and the seats around us are starting to fill up.

Amrit leans back, stunned, gazing out at the dark sea. I let him regroup, knowing that's the least he deserves after everything I've done.

"So . . ." Amrit finally says, turning to me. "You and Rudra, huh?"

I smile mirthlessly. "I don't think there's going to be a me and Rudra. He vanished just as you appeared, probably to avoid me."

"No, that's not it. You didn't see his face." Amrit breathes heavily out his nose. "I didn't realize it then, but after everything you've told me, it's obvious he looked heartbroken."

"Heartbroken? Why?"

"Because of *you*, Krishna," Amrit says. "Because he thought you were going to get together with *me*."

My mind takes me back to the moment with Rudra in the room earlier, when he asked me if I wanted to go ahead with my original plan, and I told him yes, *Why wouldn't I?*

Oh *fuck*.

When Rudra said *original plan*, he meant my plan to kiss Amrit. The reason why we were on this road trip in the first place. He thought . . . He *thinks* I still want to kiss Amrit. After everything that happened between us last night.

He still thinks I'm in this for Amrit!

He thinks I'm getting together with Amrit *right now.*

I'm so shocked that I let out a choked laugh. I want to go after Rudra and tell him that Amrit has literally been the last thing on my mind since the night of the trek. I want to ask Rudra how he could even think that after I had my first kiss with *him*.

"Fuck me," I say, incredulous. "I'm such an idiot."

To think, this whole time, I let that boy believe I was . . .

"I don't think you realize it, but you're pretty easy to fall for," Amrit says, laughing. "Take it from me."

I shake my head. "Why are you being so sweet to me? I haven't treated you right."

"Look." Amrit leans toward me. I expect my pulse to flutter, or my heart to race, or that adorable smile of his to make my stomach do cartwheels, but all I feel is warmth. Genuine warmth. "I know we've been kind of into each other since you arrived, and that we texted, but I knew that this, *us*, was only for the summer. And I don't think I'm wrong to assume you thought the same?"

"No, you're right," I admit. "But after we kept texting, I was worried I led you on."

"Hey, you can't blame me for wanting to keep up with some casual texts with a girl I like. But you're going to be in the US, and I have no idea how things are going to pan out for me over the course of the next year. Sometimes people are in your life forever and sometimes just for a moment. And I enjoyed our moment. Can't say it wasn't fun."

I stare at him in disbelief and amazement. "You're really setting a new standard for summer crushes everywhere, Amrit."

How did I find not one but two emotionally mature eighteen-year-old boys in a row? If anything, it seems I have impeccable taste.

"Well, I will gladly take that compliment. Feel free to spread it around," Amrit says cheekily. "Now, after being surrounded by aunties the past few days, I can't be held accountable for the meddling I'm about to commit. But Rudra Desai's going to Juilliard, you said?"

I bite my lip. "Yeah, he is."

"Good." Amrit nudges me teasingly. "See? It works. You're going to be hours from each other. And, Krishna, if I'm being honest, it looks like Rudra might be a lot more into you than you think. I don't think this is new for him."

My heart stutters. "What do you mean?"

"I think he's been into you for a while. I've caught him looking at you over the summer. You didn't notice. But I did. I just never pointed it out."

His words make me heady with déjà vu because that's the same thing Rudra told me about Amrit in the bookstore. *I've seen the way he looks at you.*

Then I'm reminded of what Priti has been telling me this whole while.

Rudra is not that kind of guy.

He's not the sort of person to hook up or mess around.

More memories trickle in, things Rudra said that I didn't fully register because I was so caught up in the moment.

Krishna, you don't know how long—

I do want to. I've wanted to for so long.

I can't breathe.

Have I—have I been utterly blind to Rudra's emotions all this while? How long has he had feelings for me?

"Are you okay?" Amrit asks, and his voice drags me out of my thoughts. "You look dazed."

"I need to find Rudra," I say, suddenly getting to my feet. My mind is running a mile a minute, but before I can get up, I glimpse

Priti, walking next to a very pretty girl in a pink lehenga.

They're smiling and holding hands. To anyone else, it might seem like they're best friends, but I know better. It makes me feel so giddy and *special* to know the truth.

But then Priti spies Amrit and me and her smile instantly tenses. She whispers to the girl, who heads off in the direction of the bride, while Priti weaves through the crowd toward me.

"Was Priti with Nikita?" Amrit says, frowning. "She's the bride's sister."

"Yeah," I say, smiling. Even though I'm terrified of what Priti thinks is happening between Amrit and me, my heart feels so full after seeing them like that. "They're friends," I say, because I can't out Priti to him. "Priti did an internship in Powai last year."

Amrit's furrow clears. "Oh. I didn't know that."

"You should probably save yourself," I say, rolling my shoulders back. "I'm pretty sure Priti is coming to murder me because she thinks I've betrayed Rudra with you."

"That would be my cue to go, then." He laughs, a little tight around the edges before softening once more. "And don't apologize again. Seriously, I'm not heartbroken. In fact, I see some bridesmaids there in need of drinks."

"Can we stay friends?" I ask him hesitantly.

"We *are* friends, Krishna."

That's when I do it. Priti be damned.

I lean over and kiss him on the cheek.

When I pull back, Amrit's red as a tomato and there's a goofy look on his face.

"I *did* set out on the road trip to kiss you," I say, grinning. A week ago, I would've probably combusted at the thought of kissing Amrit on his cheek. But now, it feels like the most natural thing ever.

Maybe this is what our connection always meant. Maybe this is what we were always meant to be. *Friends.* For once, the word doesn't bother me.

I truly have changed.

Amrit chuckles, stepping away from me. "See you soon, Krishna."

I don't say *It's a date* back to him, the way I did when he left for Goa. Instead, I just raise my hand and wave.

And when he's gone, I whisper, "See you soon, Amrit."

Thankfully, Amrit has made his escape by the time Priti reaches me. As she draws closer, I ask, "So you two made up?" in a bid to distract her.

It's a testament to how blissfully happy Priti is that it kind of works, because she doesn't roll her eyes or brush off what I'm asking. In fact, she doesn't seem to want to bite my head off at all.

"Yes, we did," Priti says, smiling briefly before her face changes once more. "You're with Amrit." I can tell she's trying to swallow her disappointment.

If anything, I think Priti is . . . concerned? Not just for Rudra, but for me. Wow, she really is a different person when she's in love. Or perhaps this is the real her and I finally get to see it, see *her*.

"No," I say, shaking my head. "I just spoke to Amrit and cleared things up with him. There was no chance of anything happening between us in the first place. The kiss would've been a one-off thing, but—"

Priti's face clears. "Rudra happened."

I nod. "Rudra happened." I finally ask what's been gnawing at me ever since Amrit pointed it out. "Priti, Rudra has feelings for me, doesn't he? And he's—he's had these feelings for a while, hasn't he?"

"Do *you* have feelings for him?" Priti hasn't answered either of my questions. I don't blame her. She won't tell me about her best friend's feelings unless she's assured I'm not going to break his heart.

"I do," I say, and saying it makes me feel so at peace, like I've finally admitted to myself what I've been avoiding. "I do have feelings for Rudra."

Priti scans my face for a few seconds. She sees the honesty in my eyes; I know she sees it. But I also know I can offer her a lot more.

"I know that the reason you got pissed with me is because you didn't want me to break his heart. I don't know how I didn't see it before, but I do now. All the hints you've been dropping are finally falling into place in my head. And that's why I'm not angry anymore about the things you said to me yesterday. You didn't mean them. You just wanted to put me off because you thought I hadn't made up my mind about him. But I have, Priti. I really, really like Rudra. I want more with him. I want to be with him. And there's a possibility. You know there is."

Priti sighs. My heart sinks with disappointment. The ideal situation would've been to have Priti say it's okay for me to be with Rudra, because I *want* her to be okay with it. I don't want anything to come in the way of what we've struggled so much to build. And I don't want to start anything with Rudra if I don't fully have Priti's support. Because no matter what, I'm the third person here. I can't be the wedge between them.

Priti pushes her hair behind her ear. "So you're asking me for my blessing? Is that what this is?"

"You make it sound so dramatic."

"If my blessing is what you want, Krish, you have it."

I can't believe my ears. "Wait, what?"

"I'm not saying it again," Priti says, but she's smiling.

My world is tipping. "Does that mean he—does that mean he's—"

“I think it’ll be better if you hear it from him,” Priti says, cutting me off. She takes both my hands, and her eyes are twinkling. “Go. Be with him.”

I spin on my heel, grab my skirts, and run.

34

IF HE CALLS ME SUNFLOWER ONE MORE TIME, I'M GOING TO KISS HIM

Goa, Monday

I find Rudra in the parking lot, sitting in his car, which seems to have become a haven for heartbroken individuals. I really should've known to check here first.

I'm out of breath when I skid to a stop on the tarmac, panting. I nearly gave up and sobbed multiple times as I scoured the resort to look for him, and now that I see him . . . now that I *finally* see him, my heart is accelerating faster than particles at CERN.

I go over to the passenger side and knock on the glass.

Rudra looks up from where he's slumped over the wheel. His eyes are red, as if he's been crying. I want to kick myself. *I'm* the reason this beautiful boy has been crying.

I'm going to make it up to him if it's the last thing I do.

Rudra's eyes widen when he sees me outside the window, and it takes him a few seconds to gather his wits. When he finally does, his shaking hands get the door unlocked. I open the door and get into the car.

It's quiet at first, both of us just staring at each other in this small space. The same space where we almost kissed.

"What are you doing here?" Rudra says, and his voice is a croak. His second question is quiet, unsaid: *Why aren't you with Amrit?*

All my emotions for him bubble to the surface again.

"I don't want him," I blurt.

Rudra looks so bewildered it's almost as if he has no idea what I'm talking about. "What?"

I shift closer to him, smiling so wide it's a surprise the corners of my mouth aren't touching my ears. "You heard me."

Rudra stares down at me, a million emotions tiding through his eyes, like the waves on the ocean. He looks stupefied.

"What I felt for Amrit was a silly crush and it's over—*been* over." I clasp Rudra's cheeks. His pulse is racing; I can feel his blood pounding against my fingertips. I love that I can make him feel like this. "Because I like *you*, Rudra Desai."

He opens his mouth to say something, but nothing comes out, and he shuts it. I smile; let him be the blubbering mess for once.

"But you said . . . in the room . . . that you . . ."

"I said I wanted the plan to work out. Not my plan, *our* plan. I wanted to make sure Priti was able to reunite with Nikita." I drop my gaze to his lips, and my breath hitches. So does his. "I get why you might have believed it until our kiss, but even after that? How did you still think I had feelings for Amrit after everything that happened between us?"

Rudra brings his hand up and touches my cheek. This is nothing like his other touches. It's so delicate it's as if he's afraid he'll crack my skin if he applies even the slightest amount of pressure.

"Because I didn't think you could ever feel the same way about me that I do about you."

I hold his gaze with my unwavering one. "And how do you feel about me?"

"I'm in love with you, sunflower."

I can't breathe.

"I've been in love with you since we were kids," Rudra whispers. "Since I've known Priti. It's always been you. I never had the guts to say it because you're leagues beyond me. You're like—the sun. Untouchable. Blinding to look at. I've craved your warmth, for so long, and I knew that craving was all I could ever have. You would never notice me, never look in my direction, and I was okay with that. These past few days—they've felt like a dream." He brings his other hand up so he's cupping my face, just like I'm cupping his. Tears streak my cheeks, *again*, and he wipes them away as they fall. "I can't believe I finally got to talk with you, be around you, touch you, *kiss* you. It felt surreal."

"Why?" I say through my tears, my throat, mouth, and nose clogging with emotion. "What's so special about me?" The question feels silly, and the moment it leaves my mouth I wish I hadn't spoken at all, because it feels like I'm fishing.

"What's so special about you?" Rudra repeats, as if he's stunned I could ever ask him that question. "You're kind, smart, beautiful, talented, and a little unhinged, but I love that about you. Every summer that I saw you, you were somehow always better than my memory of the year before, and I didn't even know that could be possible."

I burst into laughter and tears all at once, feeling like I'm floating in a dream. But his hands, while delicate, are so solid, and so firm, and so *real*, and the clues and hints from my life are suddenly all there, and it doesn't feel so unbelievable anymore. Especially not with the way he's looking at me right now.

Priti was right.

It's a hundred—no, a *thousand* times better hearing it from him.

"Then why didn't you say something?" My whole body is trembling, and I'm so out of control I feel like my bones will disintegrate with how shaky I feel. "Why didn't you ask me, *once*, how I felt about you?"

"Because it would've broken my heart to get so close to you, to be with you, only to have you choose Amrit. I wouldn't have gotten in your way. Because I only want to see you happy. I never want"—he drops his hands, his voice breaking—"to be the one who takes your light away from you."

I grab his hands, gripping them tight. My heart is full, blown up like a balloon. I could float away into the sky and never come back. But he grounds me, yet again, with just his presence, and what I want has never been clearer to me.

He gazes down at me, hope sprouting in his eyes like tiny wings. He's halfway between giving in and letting go.

"Rudra," I say, looking straight up at him. "The only one I care about . . ." I lean into him until his nose is brushing mine, until the heat of his breath is on my skin, searing, until physically being away from him feels like it will kill me. ". . . is you."

I kiss him.

I kiss him like he's going to vanish off the face of the earth if I don't, like he's going to turn to dust if I don't, like he's going to melt into the leather, into the tarmac, into the sea far below the ground, and become one with it if I don't. I kiss him without a shred of hesitation. I kiss him until my head spins and my knees are weak.

Rudra's lips hiccup on mine as I pull away to catch my breath, body numb and mind wheeling, and his eyes are half lidded with pleasure. I'm floating two feet in the air.

Rudra's eyes open, and as we gaze at each other, his face breaks into the most beautiful smile. Which makes me kiss him again, and again, and again, until I'm a wobbly mess. And he kisses me back with the same intensity, the same longing, his hands catching my waist, my hips . . .

Something buzzes in Rudra's pocket.

We break our kiss in shock, and Rudra's lips are swollen red from making out. I watch him, watch those lips, as he fumbles for his phone and frowns at the screen.

It's Priti.

"Answer it," I say breathlessly.

He does.

"If y'all are done fucking, do you want to grab some food?" Priti's voice is loud and booming.

"We're not fucking," Rudra and I say in unison, but we're both smiling.

"Whatever. The ceremony is over"—wait, already?—"and the buffet's on, and, well, it's free food."

Rudra looks at me. "What do you want to do?"

"I'm actually quite hungry, to be honest," I say, clutching my stomach—my very empty stomach, I suddenly register. No wonder I've been feeling so faint. "We haven't had lunch or breakfast."

"All right, then," Rudra says. "We'll be there."

"Cool. Nik and I are waiting by the buffet tables."

The line clicks, and Rudra and I sit still for a moment, soaking up everything that's happened the past week. I would love to make out more with him, but I don't want to pass out halfway with hunger.

Rudra probably senses it too, because he doesn't initiate kissing me again. Instead, he gives me one last peck on the nose in a manner that makes me want to squeal like a little girl. He's looking at me with so much adoration and . . . *love* in his eyes I can't believe I was stupid enough to have missed it these past few days.

No, *all this time.*

When we're inside the resort again, holding hands, I catch sight of Priti and Nikita by the buffet tables, as she said they'd be. They're far away, but even from here, I can see Priti's face, radiant with the sort of happiness and energy that can't be manufactured or feigned. I hope I get to see her this happy for a very long time, and given that both she and Rudra are going to be joining me in the States soon, I think I will.

That's when it suddenly hits me that I'm no longer going to be the sole bearer of Srishti's One and Only American Cousin title. Not with Priti there.

But I'm not too disappointed, because after everything, I've earned some pretty good and brand-new alternatives. For starters—I'm the Cool American Cousin, the one with exciting, wild stories to remember and ones yet to be told. Or the *Best* American Cousin, who helped Priti reunite with the love of her life.

And frankly? I can't think of a better ending to this summer.

ACKNOWLEDGMENTS

I'd like to begin by thanking you, dear reader, for picking up this whirlwind, silly, fluffy rom-com of my heart and reading it to the very end. Krishna, Rudra, and Priti have resided in my head since I was just a college student with dwindling dreams in my heart and fading stars in my eyes. So I cannot believe that after an arduously long but enriching journey here, everything I've ever dreamed of is finally coming true and you're getting to read this project that is three years in the making!

My showstopping editor, Carolina Mancheno Ortiz, thank you for believing in me and *Krishna Kumar*. Without you, this book wouldn't be where it is today, and I'm truly so honored I got to work on my debut novel with you. You were always my dream editor! Your edits and vision have shaped this book into what it is today—a project I'm ridiculously proud to call my firstborn child.

Thank you to my agent, Rebecca Podos, for being the first person in the publishing industry to take the plunge with me and my projects. Your faith in my writing has never diminished, and I'm blessed to have you championing me in this turbulent industry that will never *not* be painful to navigate. With you by my side, it gets a little bit easier each time.

The entire team at HarperCollins and Epic Reads, thank you for all the hours of effort you've put into pushing this project out to readers and packaging it into the most stunning book-shaped thing ever. Ivee Pendo, I couldn't have asked for a better artist to work on my cover—you brought Krishna, Rudra, and the city of Mumbai to life and gave me the cover of my dreams! As generative AI models continue to steal from artists, you keep demonstrating why AI could never replicate the human touch. Thank you also to Chris Kwon, who designed the cover, as well as Mikayla Lawrence, Colleen Fellingham, and Lana Barnes, who helped smooth out the rough edges of this book during edits.

To all my favorite people—friends and family—who've made a cameo in this book, I remain ever so grateful to all of you for molding me into the writer and person I am today.

Padam, Manas, and Varija, thank you for being the first listeners of my stories and my biggest cheerleaders. Manas and Padam, you ground me, tease me, and stand by me in a manner no one else has, and it is the biggest gift of my life to be your elder sister. Now that you're both so far away from me, I miss the days when we used to be together all the time, and I wait for the next occasion when I might get to see you. Varija, I fell in love with writing because of you, your reactions to my stories, the glorious artwork you bless my inbox with, and our brainstorming sessions. Rajeev and Divija, the steady rocks you are, the calm in the eye of a storm, thank you for always taking care of me. Neeraja, thank you for sharing my love of writing. I'm blessed to be one among the seven Rajgopal cousins.

Srishti, thank you for our decade-long friendship and our shared obsession with books and all the hours of fandom discussions and rants. Digha, Varun, Charu, Jalaj, Soumyaroop, and Aadyant, my fellow bandmates and dearest friends, you were part of my best memories from college. Mansi, thank you for being the first person to read *Better Catch Up, Krishna Kumar*, ever. Nikita, thank you for the unlimited perfect conversations.

Endless thank-yous to all the authors who graciously took the time to read my book and blurb it: Meg Cabot, Charlene Thomas, Sujin Witherspoon, Nisha Sharma, Aamna Qureshi, Farah Naz Rishi, Ananya Devarajan, Talia Tucker, Stefany Valentine, and Clare Osongco. As an author who's taking her baby steps in publishing, I hope to be able to match your prolificacy and resilience one day.

Sujin, your sheer talent and wit have inspired me more than any writer I've known, and I am honored to call you my alpha reader and "writing wife." I couldn't have finalized my chapter titles (or written a rom-com, for that matter) without your chaotic comments and critique. I hope fans of yours smile when they read your cameo, because I loved writing you into this book (as I adored being cameoed in *Bingsu for Two*). Sarang Cho and Krishna Kumar are canonically roommates for life at JHU!

Birukti Tsige, thank you for being the best person the writing community could have given me—you made my Cambridge years the most magical two years of my life, and there is never any dilemma (publishing-related or otherwise) you don't help me navigate. Swati Hegde, you are who I look up to and aspire to be: my bi-disaster writing sister and the most hardworking person I know—thank you for always being there for me. Cynthia Timoti, I thank SmoochPit every day for bringing us together—your writing shone light on my darkest days.

Isha Raya, I'm so thrilled our queer, brown books share the same release month, and it was super fun exchanging early drafts with each other! Aymen Ali, thank you for reading nearly half the book as I was writing.

All the bloggers, readers, and librarians who have been supporting me in the days leading up to the release, thank you for helping push my book in a time when stories that are unapologetically Indian and queer like mine are being systemically erased. My street team, your gorgeous posts are the highlights of my days.

Pratyush, I dedicated this book to you, but no matter how much I say, no matter how much I attempt to put into words what you mean to me, it'll never be enough, and this is a small gesture compared to everything you've done for me. We've been together for more than six years, since before I even began querying, and you've stuck like glue by my side through my worst and best moments. Without you, I don't think I would have half the strength I do now to cope with the ups and downs of publishing (and life). Thank you for believing in me even when I don't believe in myself, and for the endless sweet treats, video calls, and healing hugs.

And finally, thank you to my parents: Mummy and Daddy, my twin pillars of support. I remain standing here today, happy and healthy, because of you. No amount of thank-yous will ever suffice, because you provided me a springboard to leap toward my wild writerly dreams. Still, thank you for never denying me my ever-growing library of books, for keeping my belly full, and for understanding and supporting me even when I left engineering to take the "unconventional" route.

Mummy, you're the reason why I read *Malory Towers*, the reason why I started writing brown characters, the reason why I fell in love with romance books. You read every fiddling thing I write, listen to every idea I have, and console me through every rejection. Daddy, your excellent vocabulary has helped me build mine, your laptop was the first to store my stories, and you worked your hardest all those years just so I could have a comfortable life.

Everything I have done, everything I do, has only been to make you both proud—that is all I could ever want.